LUNA LAKE · BOOK TWO

Illicit

Cathy Clamp

TOR

A TOM DOHERTY ASSOCIATES BOOK

NEW YORK

ILLICIT

Copyright © 2016 by Cathy Clamp

A Tor Book
Published by Tom Doherty Associates
175 Fifth Avenue
New York, NY 10010

www.tor-forge.com

Tor® is a registered trademark of Macmillan Publishing Group, LLC.

The Library of Congress Cataloging-in-Publication Data
is available upon request.

ISBN 978-0-7653-8831-5 (hardcover)
ISBN 978-0-7653-7722-7 (trade paperback)
ISBN 978-1-4668-5461-1 (e-book)

Our books may be purchased in bulk for promotional, educational, or business use. Please contact your local bookseller or the Macmillan Corporate and Premium Sales Department at 1-800-221-7945, extension 5442, or by e-mail at MacmillanSpecialMarkets@macmillan.com.

First Edition: November 2016

Printed in the United States of America

0 9 8 7 6 5 4 3 2 1

ACKNOWLEDGMENTS

As always, I want to thank my wonderful husband, Don, for his amazing capacity to take on the weight of our world while I write. For thirty years of laundry, dinners, pet exercising, and cleaning while I slaved over a keyboard, this book, and my heart, are dedicated to him. I would also like to thank my terrific editor, Melissa Ann Singer, and my agent, Merrilee Heifetz, for their continued help and faith in my worlds. You guys rock!

ILLICIT

CHAPTER 1

Moonlight struggled to shine through clouds heavy and swollen with rain. The breeze, once light enough to be held back by the towering spruces, became a steady wind that swayed the trees and turned the mist coming off the Drina River into icy daggers. Dalvin instinctively tried to fluff his feathers to warm himself, but he was in the wrong form for that, so he flipped up the collar of his leather jacket instead.

He wished the collar went high enough to cover his ears and mute the jackhammer snoring of the delegates sleeping in the cabin nearby. Maybe earbuds would be better. But he wasn't certain even the loudest rap could drown out the reverberating bass thrum.

Babysitting bears on the ground. Hell of a waste of a Wolven agent who can fly. I should have been the one they put on aerial patrol.

Branches cracked in the distance, and his senses went on high alert. The peace talks were contentious, objected to by both sides and by who knows how many other packs. He had to check out the sound. Dalvin slipped through the trees, keeping his footsteps light on the carpet of needles. After a few hundred yards, he blinked, concentrating, forcing the pupils of his eyes to completely dilate. The trees took on an almost surreal texture as fragments of light turned the darkness into a million shades of gray. It was easy to make this change in owl form, but it always earned him a splitting headache when in human form. Still, being able to see better usually helped him ferret out thugs pretty quick, which made the pain worth it. He forced himself to slow his breathing, to listen and sniff.

The scent of fruity perfume intensifying an underlying musk of sweet raspberries revealed the intruder moments before her pale face popped out from behind a tree. Another false alarm— just one of the delegates. "Hello, Dalvin. I thought you might be out here." As usual, her low, sultry voice seemed to make his pulse pound.

Tonight she was wrapped in a fluffy lamb coat dyed dark brown, nearly the color of her fur in bear form and her hair in human.

He didn't move closer, though he wanted to. Really, *really* wanted to. "You need to go back to the lodge, Larissa. I'm on duty. I have to get back to the cabins."

Lips that would put Naomi Campbell's to shame dropped into a pout. "But it's so cold out here. We could stay warm . . . together." Larissa opened the front of her jacket to reveal next to nothing underneath. As the chilled mist touched her skin, she gasped and let out a little moan, somewhere between pain and pleasure. Her body swayed under the thick fur, but she didn't close the coat.

He bit at his bottom lip, almost unconsciously. Tempting. So very tempting. In the distance, the snoring continued, loud even this far away. It would keep going until dawn, just like the six previous nights. Plus, the framework of the agreement was already done. The negotiators were working on the last fine details.

When Larissa started to walk forward, her open coat revealed a long line of light brown skin that led down to a tiny yellow thong that didn't cover much. Wide black eyes beneath lids coated with golden shadow transfixed him. It was wrong to get involved with one of the delegates. Dalvin knew that. But Larissa was hard to resist, and she had been flirting with him for days. Rubbing up against him, blowing in his ear, running painted nails along his arm when nobody was looking. It had been driving him mad.

I need to stop this. This is wrong. But he didn't step back, didn't stop her when she glided barefoot along the forest floor and wrapped those fur-covered arms around his neck. Her mouth found his, and he couldn't help but kiss her back. When she pushed him against the tree and pressed her hips against his, his hands lifted and glided over her chilled breasts, and he felt his arousal grow.

Their kiss deepened and her hands began to roam over his body. When she started to unzip his pants, he realized he was losing the battle.

A pair of cries of alarm, in rapid succession, made Dalvin's head turn back toward the cabins. He tried to pull away, but Larissa wouldn't let go. She wrapped herself around him and started using raw magic to keep him steady, trying to pull his erection out of his pants.

It wasn't the time for fun. He had to get back, was already kicking himself for getting distracted. "Larissa, stop it!" He pulled her hand away, pushed her back, then headed toward the cabins as shouting in several languages filled the air. He hopped a few steps, trying to get his trousers zipped up and realized her scent covered nearly every inch of his clothing. The only way to keep people from knowing what he'd been doing was to change forms.

Dalvin jumped high into the air, summoning enough raw power from the full moon hidden by the clouds to burst through his clothes. Now in his preferred form as an eagle owl, he spread his wings wide, caught the wind from the leading edge of the storm, and rose quickly above the tree line.

The same airflow that lifted him tried to tumble him end over end. He fought against the quickly shifting wind as rain started to rocket out of the clouds like icy daggers. Before the rain got any worse, he opened his eyes fully and tried to take in the situation. People were moving around the cabins and the lodge, running with purpose. The bad weather kept him from making out faces, but could see at least one stretcher being carried toward the cabins. He let the wind take him higher to see who was trying to *leave* the scene. His first circle around the area didn't reveal anything during the brief flashes of lightning, so he made another loop.

Wait—there! Something running away from camp! Whatever it was, it was too big to be a rabbit or a deer, so perhaps a person? Narrowing his wings and tipping into a sharp dive, Dalvin spun and danced through branches being whipped by the storm.

Soon he was close enough to see that he was chasing a man who was dressed all in black, including a stocking cap and gloves. Somehow, the runner realized he was being pursued and turned to face Dalvin, revealing that a black face shield covered his features. The man pulled something from his pocket—all Dalvin could tell was that it wasn't a gun or crossbow—and made a sharp movement of one elbow.

The owl shifter heard no sound over the howling wind and thunder, but pain erupted in his wing and he let out a screech, twisting in the air. A second missile from the weapon barely missed Dalvin's ear; he could hear a sizzling sound as it passed. Suddenly things added up: the man was using a slingshot!

The attacker was good with it . . . really good. As Dalvin tried to get behind him, his enemy turned and fired again, striking him on one clawed foot and sending a bolt of pain up into his chest. *Getting clumsy. Stay focused.* He dove quickly and tried to grab the man's face mask with his good leg.

Maybe if he was closer in, the slingshot wouldn't be as effective. When he tried to swoop nearer, the man produced a knife the size of a machete and slashed at him, only narrowly missing.

Another dive, another flash of the blade across his path.

When Dalvin tried to gain altitude again, he realized the second slash *hadn't* missed—the blade had cut a hunk out of several feathers on his right wing. Tufts of white, like cotton candy, soared across the forest on the wind.

Tightening his wing to limit the disruption, he went around again. The man wasn't holding the knife anymore—had he dropped it, or did he have some other plan?

Better play it safe.

Diving, at the last second Dalvin twisted sideways, reaching for an arm. It wouldn't be easy to lift the man in black with a bad wing, but maybe Dalvin could get him high enough that being dropped would stun him.

Once again, his opponent was ready. With speed that marked him as a Sazi of high alpha level, he grabbed Dalvin's leg and used the owl shifter's own momentum to spin them both around. When he let go, Dalvin shot across an open space in the woods, completely unable to control his flight. A massive tree rushed toward him. Twisting, he just barely managed to avoid knocking into the trunk skull first, but his body took the full force of the impact. Gasping for breath, in pain everywhere, he dug his talons deep into the wood, clinging desperately to the tree.

He scanned the nearby forest without success. The attacker had escaped. *Damn it!*

Letting go of the tree and flapping for all he was worth despite the bad wing, Dalvin tried to rise above the tree line and find the man's trail. But it was no good. With his wing clipped, he couldn't get enough altitude. Frankly, he was lucky he was still airborne at all. Breathing was a struggle. Every inhale felt like fire burning him from the inside.

The icy rain became a heavy, drenching downpour. It was hard to see; even closing his inner lids didn't help. He knew his only option was to return to base. When he finally got back to the camp, his wings were completely numb and he was exhausted. He could still barely breathe. The entire episode had been humiliating.

When Dalvin fluttered to the ground, fellow agent Tamir Marovik, a Russian black bear, raced to greet him. Tamir's hands and sleeves were stained with blood.

"Where the hell have you been, Adway? We've got a dead negotiator on our hands. Drugged, then stabbed. Each sloth is blaming the other. Who the hell managed to get past you? I thought you were on perimeter duty."

Dalvin honestly intended to tell the truth and apologize, but when he opened his beak, to his own surprise, a half-truth came out. Displaying his wounded wing, he said, "I heard an intruder and gave chase. He damned near cut my wing off and I lost him when I tumbled. I thought you had the inside covered."

Tamir stared at him for long moments, eyes narrowed, sniffing the breeze, scenting for falsehood. What Dalvin had said wasn't a lie, not completely—it just wasn't as expansive an answer as it could have been. Tamir's reputation wasn't good: it was well known that he handed out harsh punishments, including death, to Wolven agents who fell down on the job. Dalvin had no desire to die over a moment's inattention.

The owl shifter tried not to breathe or move as Tamir stepped forward.

CHAPTER 2

*R*achel pulled the orange-patterned kerchief from her head and used it to wipe her sweaty brow. The cloth came away dark with dirt—unsurprising, since she'd been clearing out closets and cleaning up for the move. She turned off the blaring Pointer Sisters' "Neutron Dance," leaving a sudden quiet that was almost dizzying. "Well, I think that's about it."

The pile of trash bags full of garbage towered over the small stack of boxes containing things she planned to keep. So many memories were tied up inside those black plastic bags . . . horrible memories that soon would fester and rot in a landfill somewhere, out of her life at last. Rachel kicked the closest bag hard enough to make the whole stack vibrate.

"Man, I'm really going to miss you." She turned at the sound of the medium tenor voice behind her and saw her best friend, Scott Clayton, collapse onto the couch. He'd been helping her pack. "Do you have to leave right now? It's barely light."

Rachel snorted harshly. Inhaling, she was surprised to smell that Scott really was wistful. The thick, wet scent of his sorrow made her respond with less sarcasm than she might have otherwise. "I wish I could have left a week ago. I can't believe you're going to stay. I've only got a reprieve until Claire's term as town Omega ends." Just the thought of the Ascension made her stomach sick. Maybe it started out as a good idea—Sazi testing their skills in competition instead of fighting each other—but it had turned out to be just another way to keep the lesser shifters "in their place." Under the boot heels of those at the top.

"Claire's an alpha," Rachel continued. "You know that if the next challenge is between me and you, you'll win—you're just flat out a better flyer than I am. So if I don't leave town now, I'll be the Omega again. I'll never be free.

"This owl wants to spread her wings. Every corner I turn in town, every person I see, makes me . . . damn, I just want to beat their faces in with a shovel." She couldn't help that there was real vitriol in her speech.

Scott shook his head; his blond hair, with its one long streak of white, fell into his face. Even though he was sweating and had been working hard, his skin was so pale that it nearly matched the streak.

"I'm staying because I want to believe Mayor Monk was the one behind everything we had to deal with," he said. "Hell, *we* were mind-controlled, Rach. Why can't you believe other people were too? He's dead now. People should get back to normal."

Rachel shrugged. As far as she was concerned, there was no use trying to fix what was broken in Luna Lake. "After a decade, this *is* normal, Scott. People who have never actually been the Omega don't know what goes on and wouldn't believe us if we told them.

"Hell, our own family didn't believe how bad the abuse was, and the rest of the townspeople will lie through their teeth, deny that there were any problems." That was the worst part . . . the lying, the hiding, the pretending.

"I still think you should go with me and Dani to Spokane. Dani wouldn't mind you sleeping on the floor until you could get your own place, and frankly, the expenses would be easier with three. No more free ride from the town; we're going to have to hit the street to find jobs so we can pay tuition."

Scott leaned back and sighed. "It's not that easy for me. I know what I want to do with my life. I want to open an herb shop, and most of what I want to sell grows in the woods around here. If I don't live in town, I doubt the Council will let me harvest herbs. I can't take plants from state or federal land, and I sure as hell can't afford to buy them, even at wholesale prices. Not yet, anyway. I'll just tough it out for a year or so, while I get my business started.

"At least those two bastards are dead," he said with a grin that was more like a show of bared teeth.

Rachel still couldn't believe that Mayor Monk and Chief Gabriel were gone. After the years of abuse the two men had put her and Scott through, being free of them seemed like a dream, one she kept fearing she'd wake up from.

"Maybe sane people will take over. I wouldn't mind if one of the Kragans became mayor. They're cool." A smile came unbidden as she thought about the old white Cajun woman who ruled their owl parliament. Hell, black, white, or even green, Rachel had never had a real pack leader before and was thrilled that Aunt Bitty was encouraging her to find her own way.

By habit, she reached up to run her fingers through her hair and flinched when the curls fell through her grasp in just an instant. She still wasn't accustomed to the loss of her formerly long, luxurious, straight hair. Now her hair was barely shoulder length and completely unprocessed and without product.

As always, Scott noticed. "For what it's worth, I like the new do. Sort of predisco '70s. You look good with shorter hair. Shows off that long, dark neck of yours. You'll drive the guys in Spokane crazy."

She grimaced. "I hate it. But the store-bought straightener I was using ruined the ends. I never should have stopped making my gramma's special conditioner. When my hair started tearing off in chunks in the shower, I knew it was a lost cause." She shrugged. "Since I'm making a big change in my life, I might as well have a big change in my looks to go with it."

Scott smiled. "College. So cool. What are you thinking of studying?"

Sitting in the chair across from the couch, she curled her legs up under her. "I don't know. I like to do a lot of things . . . Dani suggested not declaring a major right away. Maybe I'll just take basic classes and try a few electives my first year and see what grabs me."

"You're going to sign up for a full load?"

She didn't even have to think about it. "Oh, yeah. I'm planning on at least fifteen credit hours, more if I can do it. I want to finish in four years or less. I'm already the same age as people who are graduating, and I'm just starting school. Competition for a job in the real world will be stiff. But even college and work combined won't be as bad as being the Omega in this hellhole."

Scott nodded with a snort. "No doubt. When you're used to breaking your ass for eighteen hours a day, twelve will feel like a vacation."

The phone rang as Rachel was nodding agreement. She jumped up to retrieve her cell from to the other side of the room.

"That must be Dani. She was looking for a truck big enough to hold my bed." Seeing Scott's puzzled expression, she explained. "Dani's place has only one bed—hers. It's easier—and cheaper—to take mine from here instead of buying one there."

Dani Williams was what Rachel had always imagined a sister would be like, though they didn't look all that much alike. Dani was curvy, with a dancer's grace. Rachel felt like she was a twelve-year-old in comparison, all skin and bones, without enough butt to hold up a decent pair of jeans. But she and Dani had been close from the first, trading gossip, books, and tips on hair and makeup.

Even so, Dani wasn't her sibling, not really. A pang of regret swept through Rachel as she thought about her brothers, wondering what had become of them in the decade since she'd last seen them, the day she'd been kidnapped. Sometimes she really missed her family. Scott and Dani were supportive, but it just wasn't the same.

She was surprised to see that the phone's screen wasn't displaying Dani's name but Alek Siska's. Perplexed, she asked Scott, "Can Alek talk yet? This call's from his number."

Alek had been attacked and seriously injured by the former town leaders just a few weeks earlier. Saving him, Scott had been one of the heroes of that night. Rachel was so proud of him—to go from being an omega to protecting his brother from the toughest alpha in town, wow. It gave her hope that maybe something better was out there for her too.

"Yeah, for a few days now." Scott smiled.

Rachel nodded and accepted the call. "Hey, Alek. How's the newest Wolven agent?" New job, new love. Good things to good people.

"Hey, Rachel." Alek's voice was lower than it used to be, and hoarse, but being able to talk at all after having his throat nearly torn out was very awesome. "Better every day."

"Scott and I just finished packing. Will I see you and Claire before Dani and I leave? I didn't realize you were out of the hospital yet." For Alek to find Claire, another awesome. Claire was Rachel's sorority sister in captivity. Both had been attack victims of the snakes and both had come out of that dungeon, made it through. A lot of other kids hadn't.

He paused long enough that she prompted, "Alek?"

"Yeah . . . about leaving." His voice was hedging, making her nervous.

"Don't mess with me, Alek. Dani and I are leaving today. I got approval from Wolven."

"Which . . . just got overridden by the Council. I'm really sorry, Rachel, but something has come up."

Her expression must have been thunderous. Scott got to his feet and came toward her, his face full of concern. No doubt he could hear what was being said. One of the good things about supernatural ears. Panic made her start to pace.

"Something came up? If Dani can't leave, that's fine. I'll go anyway. I'll do anything I have to, to get out of here. Seriously, I have to be gone by Saturday."

Claire's voice came on the line. "Rachel, I'm really sorry about this, but it's only for a couple of weeks."

"Claire, you can't let them do this to me! I have a chance to escape. *Please* don't let them screw me over. I'll wind up the Omega again, back in the cave."

"No, you won't," Claire said confidently. She lowered her voice. "I shouldn't be telling you this, but it's not just you. It's everyone. All trips canceled, all competitions postponed. You can't be the Omega if there's no Ascension challenge. The whole town is getting locked down. For *peace talks*, if you can believe it."

Rachel took the phone away from her ear and stared at it. Scott looked as confused as Rachel felt. Putting the phone back to her ear, she asked, "Peace between who and who?"

"Bears, from somewhere in Europe. Warring tribes."

From the distance, Rachel heard Alek say, "Sloths. A group of shifter bears is a sloth."

"Okay, sloths then. The Council's been trying to broker a deal for a while; the last time, their location in Serbia was compromised and the mediator was killed."

"And there's nowhere closer to go than Luna Lake, Washington?" She knew she sounded incredulous, but her mind was spinning. "Is this a joke?"

"Nope." Alek had taken the phone back. "Apparently they couldn't find anyplace else where people weren't already taking sides. The only bears in our town are American ones, and as far as the Council can tell, none of them are related to anyone in either sloth.

"I'm getting the impression that this is a really big political deal, not just for the Sazi but also in terms of human politics."

In the background, Claire said, "Tell her that I'll take the Omega slot for another month, until she can leave. I owe it to her."

Eyebrows raised, Rachel asked Scott, "Could that work? Can someone volunteer for the post?"

Scott shrugged. "I have no idea. Nobody's ever chosen to be the Omega before. I mean, really . . . who *would*? It sucks."

"Thanks for the heads-up, Alek," Rachel said into the phone. "I really mean it." She forced a smile onto her face, which she hoped translated to her voice.

"I'm really glad you're taking this so well, Rachel. I appreciate it."

Hanging up, she looked at her boxes and sighed. "Okay, so that's it, I guess."

Scott's voice sounded sad, but she couldn't figure out why. "Sorry, Rach. I'll help you start unpacking. Maybe just do the important stuff, like dishes and clothes."

Rachel shrugged, picking up her purse and heading for the door. "Your choice. I won't be here."

He stopped moving, giving off a concerned scent that was edged with fear. "Why? Where are you going?"

"Spokane, of course."

She opened the door and the fresh, clean air of the hallway blew away her doubts. This was the right choice. Scott put a hand on her shoulder, and she flinched.

"You're not thinking this through," he said. "This is a *Council* decision. Don't mess with them, Rachel. It's not worth it."

The snort came out as bitter sounding as she felt. His hand started massaging her shoulder. She didn't turn to look at him . . . couldn't bear to see if his expression matched the scent of sorrow that filled her nose. "Of course it's worth it, Scott. Freedom is *always* worth it. I'd forgotten that. But I never will again."

The hand paused, then let go. Did she hear a snuffle from him? *No, don't look.* Her eyes started to burn and her breath had developed a hitch.

"Good luck, girlfriend," he said. "Fly free."

A hint of his clove-tinged pride buoyed her as she walked out into the apartment building's hallway. The door shut behind her with a soft click. Every step away she took from her apartment, the gilded cage of her Omega status, the better she felt. The rusty shit-brown Pontiac next to the building looked like the sleekest Porsche in the world to her at that moment. As she opened the door and slid behind the steering wheel, she heard the *thup-thup* of helicopters overhead. It wasn't light enough to see them yet, but there wasn't much time. The clock was ticking.

The moment she started the engine, she pressed Play on the CD player. The whirring while the disks shuffled lasted only a few seconds and then the all-knowing '80s car picked one of her Patti LaBelle favorites—"New Attitude." That was exactly right. She cranked up the volume and started to sing.

Nearing the edge of town, she felt the first brush of an aversion spell. A strong one. No surprise they would try to lock down the town, keep the locals in and make humans want to avoid the area, overcoming any natural curiosity about multiple helicopters landing.

"Okay, I can do this. Just gotta keep my foot on the gas." She pressed down on the accelerator and felt the powerful old engine drive the car forward. She opened the window, hoping the fresh air would give her courage, but instead full-blown fear hit her, as if a tiger were charging right toward her. Fighting the paralyzing panic, Rachel jammed her foot down on the gas pedal. If she could just get through the spell's area of influence . . .

Her skin began to crawl, the hairs standing on end and seeming to try to pull out of her skin. It felt like tiny, unseen ants were biting and stabbing her. She gasped for breath.

Bad, bad, bad. Something bad is coming. Fly! Fly home! Hide!

Her heart was beating so fast her head was throbbing and there were flashes in her vision. Rachel gripped the steering wheel for all she was worth, struggling to resist the urge to turn the car around, determined to ride it out. Surely the spell couldn't cover more than a mile. Could it?

The road flew under her, but the panic didn't ease. In fact, it got worse, until it was all she could do not to pass out. When the car started to slow, she was almost relieved, until a new fear hit her. Why was she slowing down? Her gaze dropped to the speedometer: the needle was dropping, from 70 to 60, 55, 45, 30 . . .

She checked the gas gauge. *Plenty of gas. WTF?*

The engine stopped. All the lights on the dash turned red.

The car rolled to a stop, the music silenced.

Shifting into Park, Rachel tried the key again and again. No response, not even a sound from the engine. The car was dead.

Her overwhelming fear faded to a level that was powerfully unnerving but not deadly. Rachel drew a deep breath, then nearly shrieked when a mass of feathers fluttered outside her window.

"Going somewhere?" The golden-feathered owl that had landed next to her car was the biggest she'd ever seen, and she wasn't entirely positive which species it was. She could tell it was an alpha, though, for it spoke in a rich baritone and gave off such strong magic that she felt like she was standing next to a blast furnace—which she remembered doing once, years earlier, when her Girl Scout troop toured a foundry.

She tried to keep her voice calm, but it was hard to get words out. "Spo . . . Spokane. Just . . . heading . . . *home*. But the car died."

The golden eyes blinked and the owl shook his head. "Not today, you're not. No unnecessary travel. That's why I killed the spark. Don't tell me you didn't get the message, because we had confirmation that everyone was called."

She tried to respond. She honestly did. But his power, combined with the aversion spell, was simply too much. It was all she could do to breathe.

He noticed. "Oh. Yeah, shielding would probably help. My bad." The owl shifted forms, turning into a tall, handsome dark-skinned man whose close-cropped hair looked as soft as down. To Rachel's surprise, he looked like he was wearing clothes—blue jeans and a flannel shirt. Only the most powerful Sazi could create such illusions. Rachel had never known anyone other than Asylin Williams, her guardian, who had that ability. In the same instant, his magic was sucked back inside him and the immense weight on her chest lessened. "Is that better?"

She nodded. "Much. Who *are* you?"

"I'm with Wolven. That's all you need to know." He opened the driver's door. "Scoot over. We're heading back to town."

Her fingers tightened on the steering wheel and she didn't budge. "Maybe you are. I'm going to Spokane."

He glared down at her, his scent not angry but stern. "Look, we're not here to tromp on your rights, but you know I can freeze or discipline you, right? You don't get to say no to a Wolven agent."

Rachel's mouth set in a tight line, and she glared what she hoped were daggers at him. She knew she would regret what she was about to say, but she couldn't stop herself. Tensing her muscles, preparing for the pain that was sure to come, she said, "No."

There was no agony. She wiggled her pinkie. Not frozen

either. She risked a sniff of the air, and the scent made her look at his face, where she saw bemusement mixed with frustration. He crossed his arms over his chest and raised his brows. Something seemed familiar about his expression, but she couldn't place it.

"You're going to be a pain in my butt the whole time we're in town, aren't you?"

"Probably." It was the truth. "I need to leave this place, and unless you kill me, I'm going to keep trying."

He shook his head and sighed. "Go," he said, waving a hand in dismissal. "I'll lose a strip of hide for letting you leave, but better another one now than the dozen you're likely to cause me later." He turned and started to walk back toward town.

Before he could change his mind, Rachel turned the key and . . . miracle! The car started right up. Had the Wolven agent really killed the engine from a distance? She had never heard of anyone doing that. But that was a question for another day. Shifting into Drive, she hit the gas, hearing the tires spin for purchase as the music started to blare again. Free! Her heart soared.

Seconds later, she braked hard and pressed the Off button on the CD player. "Do they really take an actual strip of hide?" She'd heard the phrase so many times: *Ooo! Better be careful. You'll lose a strip of hide for that.* The rat bastards that ran the town had never actually done it, but something in the owl shifter's voice told her it was no mere figure of speech.

The Wolven agent stopped walking and turned to stare at her. He took a deep breath and approached the car. As he neared the back bumper, the illusion of his shirt disappeared. Like most birds she knew, his chest was wide and muscular. He lifted his right arm and she winced at the sight of a wound, raw and red, under his arm, along his rib cage. The shape and size of a playing card, the injury was just starting to heal. If that was illusion too, it was a good one.

"Yes. They do. It'll take until the next moon to heal, and it hurts like hell to fly. It's usually done with a silver knife, but this was made with silver-tipped claws. Go. Better me than you. I can tell you're not alphic, and a wound like this could really mess you up, especially if it got infected."

"Crap! What did you do to get that?" Unable to help herself, she reached out to touch it. He stepped back, out of reach.

He shrugged, smelling hot and bitter, like he was ashamed of whatever he'd done. "Something stupid. I deserved it. Sort of like now. Last chance . . . *go*. Before—"

The engine died again. Damn it! A new voice, a deep, growling baritone, filled the car. "Before what, agent? Before *I* show up?" Something heavy thumped onto the roof, and Rachel ducked instinctively.

The light in the car changed. Rachel turned toward the passenger window to find it covered with thick, coarse black fur.

The man on her left spoke to what she presumed was a bear shifter, if the hideous, rancid musk smell was any indication, over the top of her car. It had to be a damned big bear, judging by the fact that she couldn't see its head. "No . . . *sir*. Before the delegates arrive. This woman is an omega, and an owl. She's no threat to anyone. If she leaves before anyone arrives, there's no reason to think the peace talks would be in any danger."

There was a pause, then a sarcastic response with a thick accent from the carpet of fur to her right. "Oh, then I suppose you've run a comprehensive background check in the few minutes since we landed? You know for positive this woman has no bear family members and hasn't been bribed or coerced into spying or setting a bomb before getting away from the fallout? Omegas are known to do that."

What? Rachel's mouth dropped open. "Hello? Rude much?" she said, turning toward the mass of fur. "I'm right here. I'm not some sort of whack-job terrorist. And, by the way, who the hell are you to question my background or *ethics*?"

The fur moved. As it did, the driver's door was yanked open and the owl shifter pulled her out of the car. The very real fear that was bleeding from the owl's every pore and the fury coming off the bear shifter in waves were nearly overwhelming.

Getting her feet under her, Rachel looked at the Wolven agent currently leaning on her car. She'd never seen the high school principal—the only bear in Luna Lake—in his animal form and had never been this close to a natural bear. Still, she was sure that this bear was far too large to be normal.

Snarling, it towered over her car. Paws the size of hubcaps flexed, driving claws the size of carving knives through the steel roof of the Pontiac, which bent and protested with a screeching sound before giving way. The bear had put its claws through her car without even breaking a sweat, if bears sweated! *Holy baby Jesus!*

The owl shoved Rachel behind his back and she stayed there, frozen in terror, heart pounding as tension flooded the air, the scent strong enough to make her sneeze.

"Tamir, don't," her protector said. "This is between us. It has nothing to do with her."

"This has *everything* to do with her, because it has to do with your judgment. You're supposed to be protecting the delegates. You know *I* would never have picked you for this assignment. People have died where you were assigned."

"I'm pretty sure you were on that same assignment. In fact, I think your body count is higher than mine. Maybe we need to ask the delegates who are still alive which one is the better protector."

Whoa. Peeking around the owl agent, Rachel said, "For what it's worth, I feel a lot safer around the one who pulled me out of my car rather than the one who just destroyed it."

The owl shifter turned his head sharply. "Quiet. Be grateful it's just your car."

Though she could see his shirt, only skin brushed her hand

when he moved. With a jolt, she recalled that despite what her eyes saw, she was pressed up against a stranger's very naked backside. She took a step back, nearly blushing.

The bear—Tamir—reared back and pulled his claws out of her roof. "Return her to town. The councilman will decide who should be punished . . . and *how.*" With that, the bear turned and loped off into the trees, shrinking before her eyes until he was the size of the wild bears she'd sometimes spotted from a distance in the forest, near the lake.

The owl was just short of livid, and Rachel didn't know if he was angrier with her or the bear. He opened the driver's side door.

"You should have gone when you had the chance," he said flatly. "Get in."

Rachel wanted to stand firm, wanted to appear as tough as the two Wolven agents, but knew she wasn't. She was *all bluff and bluster,* as her gramma used to say. Plus, this man had risked his neck for her. She got in the car and slid over into the passenger seat, ducking to avoid the sharp slivers of metal hanging down around the puncture holes in the roof.

Without another word, he seated himself behind the wheel. When he slammed the door, the whole car shook. He started the engine, threw the car into gear, and soon had them turned around and heading for Luna Lake. After a long silence, broken only by the sound of his fingers thrumming on the steering wheel, Rachel sighed and said, "Sorry."

He grunted in acknowledgment but didn't respond, which annoyed her, and the smell of his anger continued unabated. She crossed her arms over her chest and stared out the side window. *Jerk.*

She reached over and turned the music back on. She didn't sing, though—with a pissed-off Wolven agent in the car, that seemed somehow . . . inappropriate. But she kept the mantra in her head. New Attitude. *I am in control.* She noticed that his fingers began to tap in time with the beat of the music.

As they drove into town, Rachel spotted a half dozen or more strangers wandering along the street next to the police station. The Wolven agent parked near the station and took her keys, then hopped out of the car. Rachel was reaching for the passenger door handle when he opened it from outside. She wasn't sure whether he acted out of courtesy or suspicion that she might bolt, but she thanked him as she got out and stood up.

The area was full of animal smells she didn't recognize— exotic cats and birds and even a *snake.* That made her head turn, searching—she knew the scent of snakes all too well. The odor pulled an old fear from deep inside her, something she thought she'd overcome. She eyed the newcomers with suspicion but couldn't figure out who smelled of reptile.

Her foster father, John Williams, separated from the crowd and half ran toward the car. He pulled her into an abrupt, powerful hug. It surprised her, since he wasn't much of a hugger. His thick green cable sweater was warm against her face. "For God's sake, Rachel! You could have been *killed.* What were you thinking?"

What could she say? He put a dark, cool hand on the side of her head, pressing her cheek against his fluffy sweater. His smell, warm feathers and cologne, made her feel safe. She whispered, "There's a *snake* in town, Dad."

He hugged her even closer as warm concern flooded her nose. "Is that why you ran? He's a councilman, just here to check security. He's leaving. A cat will be taking his place for the meetings."

She decided to let John believe the snake was why she'd tried to escape. "As long as he's leaving."

She felt his head turn as he addressed the owl shifter who had captured her. "Thank you for bringing her back. She still has PTSD from her time with the snakes. But she's not a spy or a threat. Please don't let them hurt her, Agent Adway."

Adway. Wow. That was a surname she hadn't heard in a long time . . . in a lifetime. The owl agent let out a long sigh. "It's not up to me. I'm not in charge of this operation. But I'll try to get them to understand. What's her name, so I can pull her file?"

Sliding out of John's hug, she faced the other man, holding out her arms in frustration. "Again . . . right here in front of you. What is it with you guys?" Not really expecting an answer, she continued. "I'm Rachel Washington."

The owl's jaw dropped and his eyes narrowed. He stared at her for a long moment, pointing at her with one finger. All that came out of his mouth was, "You—" Abruptly he spun on his heels and sprinted toward a black SUV a dozen feet away.

Her dad put his hands on his hips, raising his shoulders and lowering his head just a bit, like he would in owl form when annoyed. "Well, that was rude. What's his problem?"

She shook her head, staring after the agent and feeling a weird mixture of gratitude and frustration. "Pfft. They were both like that."

"Both?"

How to explain? "Another Wolven agent, I'm guessing this guy's boss, stopped us on the road. He's a big black bear and he was a total jerk. Look what he did to the top of my car!"

John blinked at the sight of the roof, where four messy punctures cut through to the headliner inside. "Okay, that is not acceptable. Someone needs to fix this." He glanced around, then nodded and touched her shoulder. "Wait here."

Rachel had no intention of waiting. She wanted to hear more about what was happening in town, so she followed her dad over to the trio of vehicles parked near the diner. He called, "Excuse me, Mrs. Monier?"

A short, slender woman with reddish-blond hair, dressed in a fluffy tan jacket with a fur ruff that matched the trim on her boots, turned away from a small group of strangers. Amber Monier had been hanging around town since Monk and Gabriel had died, and Rachel assumed the bobcat shifter was part of Wolven. The woman had never taken the time to introduce herself around, which Rachel thought was bad manners. Bitty seemed to know her quite well, based on things the older woman had said.

"Actually, it's Wingate. Monier was my maiden name, but old friends like our *esteemed* snake councilman tend to still call me that."

A few steps behind her father, Rachel crossed into scent range just as the woman said "snake." The reptile's scent made the young owl stumble to a stop and gasp for breath. Her father must have been trying to protect her from this when he told her to stay away.

She saw the snake now, right in front of her. He was tall and Middle Eastern in appearance, with a clean-shaven, narrow face . . . a viper's face. He wore a headdress similar to the keffiyehs she'd seen back home when she was growing up, but the cloth flowed like silk and was embroidered with golden thread that glowed in the rising sun. From the side, he looked just like the man her captors had spoken about in hushed voices, the man she'd seen only once: Sargon, who had inspired emotions far beyond terror.

Like Sargon, this man absolutely reeked of power, which was cast out around him in a halo of pain. Maybe it wasn't the sun that made his headdress glow. Her skin burned, her hair felt ready to ignite into flame. She couldn't go any closer. He was just *standing* there, with people fawning over him. Even her dad had slowed and bowed his head.

Owls do not bow to snakes! She had to master her fears.

"How dare you show your face among owls! How *dare* you!" She spat the words, shouting across the distance that her body couldn't tread.

All conversation stopped, all faces turned toward Rachel. The snake's gaze met hers. He narrowed his eyes and started to walk toward her. Though Rachel's instincts screamed *fly!* her feet were frozen, as though set in cement. Her dad tried to step between them, but the snake's hand made a slight movement, tossing John aside as easily as if he were brushing off a mosquito.

The owl agent walked up to the snake without hesitation and put a hand on the taller man's shoulder. The snake again tossed his hand lightly and seemed surprised when the owl was able to grab him, momentarily arresting his motion. His brows raised in an almost elegant way, but his scent was thick and oily, as angry as a pan burning on the stove. The agent dipped his head, staring at the snake's neck, but his voice was calm and steady when he said, "Your eminence, please. She was one of those rescued from *the cave*."

The snake looked at Rachel again. He nodded once. The woman who smelled of cat touched his other arm. Power burned between them, hot enough to scorch as the cat tried to hold back the snake. Rather than fight her, he turned his head slightly and said quietly, "Release me, Amber. You know this must happen."

Something unspoken passed between them, Rachel could tell. When the cat dipped her head and stepped back, so did the owl.

They were going to let him kill her!

Rachel knew she was going to die. Nobody in town could stand up to someone of this power. Even the guards in the cave, as sadistic as they were, feared Sargon's level of evil. Like him, this snake had no soul.

Maybe this was best. Perhaps the only way she could escape her past was to end her present. She let all the hate she felt bleed into her words. "Go ahead. Kill me. Because if you don't, you'll never catch me and you'll never make me fear you again."

A few drops of spittle landed on the snake's face. Both Wolven agents twitched.

The snake regarded her with narrowed eyes. Oddly, his scent had lost the fire it had held when Amber Wingate had touched him. The tone of his voice matched the surprisingly soft expression in his dark eyes.

"I believe you." Something shifted in his face; he had come to a decision. "I will not be leaving today. Place this woman in custody. Hold her until after the delegates arrive." Rachel felt magic wrap around her, freezing her.

Amber sputtered a little. "Ahmad, what are you doing?"

Ahmad. Rachel burned the name into her memory as he turned and walked away, leaving her locked in place.

"I have calls to make," he said. Looking sharply at the owl agent, he ordered, "Do your job, Adway. I presume there is a holding facility here?"

The Wolven agent nodded. "There's a jail. But isn't that a little . . ." He tried to come up with a word.

The snake fixed glowing eyes on the owl. "Extreme? Hardly." He enunciated each word as though speaking to a child. "Do. Your. Job. Or I will feed you to my staff. They enjoy bird meat." He flicked a glance at the cat and smiled thinly. "Don't they, Amber?"

Though he kept walking away, the pressure that kept Rachel's limbs immobile didn't waver. She was a statue. "Put some clothes on, Agent. You look like an idiot."

The owl shifter blushed, his dark skin turning ruddy, but he made no move to cover anything. Rachel still saw the jeans and plaid shirt—apparently the snake could see through the illusion.

Amber shook her head, exasperated, then tossed up her hands. "Do it, I suppose. Tamir did say she tried to leave town even though leaves were revoked. But make sure she's treated well. I'll talk to Ahmad, see what bug crawled up his butt."

Ahmad stalked toward a high-priced SUV with blacked-out windows, his white robe moving in a breeze that didn't match the movement of the tree branches overhead. A pale-skinned man with straight jet-black hair met him at the door and opened it. Ahmad whispered something to him as he got into the car, and the other nodded. Once he'd shut the vehicle's door behind the snake, the black-haired man walked toward Rachel and the Wolven agent, a smug half smile on his face. The owl agent swore under his breath.

Crap. It's that bear agent. It has to be.

When he drew near, his scent confirmed her supposition. The moment he took hold of her arm, and not lightly, the magical hold released, so abruptly that her legs gave way. Tamir's grip held her up painfully, and she made an involuntary movement that was part discomfort and part anger. Getting her feet under her, Rachel tried to pull away, but it was no use.

The owl agent reached for her other arm. "Hey, hey. Ahmad said to take her into custody, not treat her like a war criminal."

"You're going to put me in *jail*? Really?" She still couldn't believe how bad this day was going.

Tamir tightened his fingers, digging into her biceps, as they began to march her the hundred or so yards to the police station. "I will be quite pleased to do so. Feel free to struggle. It will excite the snakes. They like their food to wiggle."

Rachel's eyes flicked to the SUV, which was surrounded by men she assumed were Ahmad's fellow snakes. They did seem to be watching her closely. *Crap.*

As they neared the police station, Rachel's nose filled with the lingering smell of gunpowder from when Claude Kragan had blown a hole right through the floor of the building's main room. She could tell Adway and Tamir could smell it by the way each of them paused for a second, nostrils flared. Rachel loved the scent, because it reminded her that Monk and Gabriel were gone.

Luna Lake's former police chief had kept Rachel captive in that basement for a good portion of the past decade, for days at a time. The former mayor had tortured her friend Claire in a secret room under the stairs that even Rachel hadn't known existed. It had taken the better part of the last month for the staircase to be replaced and the lower level of the building cleared of the ex-rulers' little den of iniquity, but now the jail was back in commission.

Even with the town's low crime rate, they had to have a jail. Otherwise the county would require that prisoners be sent to the county seat in Republic. That would never work—any Sazi in a human prison when the moon was full would be exposed as a monster and probably killed, and the entire Luna Lake community could be endangered. Still, Rachel had had her fill of the building and wasn't happy to be dragged into it once more.

Ray Vasquez, the acting police chief, was sitting at his desk when she and the two Wolven agents entered. Marilyn Bearbird, his lieutenant and the town's medic, was at another desk. Both looked curiously at the newcomers.

Everything smelled of the fresh pine that had been used to repair the floor and walls, but it wasn't enough to overcome the scent of old blood and pain that still hung in the air. And angry cat. Lots of angry cat. Like Monk, Ray was a cat, in his case a Belizean panther. When he'd taken charge, one of the first things he did was apologize to all the victims. Not that what happened to them was his fault, but it impressed Rachel that he'd owned his own failure.

"I should have noticed it, Rachel. Damn it! I should have stopped it. There aren't enough words for me to apologize enough." Rachel had liked him ever since.

The police chief walked toward the front counter, his expression serious. His hand hovered near his sidearm, and suspicion rode the breeze from the spinning overhead fan to Rachel's nose.

"What can I do for you gentlemen? You okay, Rachel?"

Tamir pushed her forward, pulling her out of Adway's grip. "Councilman al-Narmer wants this one locked up until the delegates arrive."

"*This one* has a name, you know," Rachel said sharply, pulling away from him and pushing through the swinging gate. "Put me in a cell, Ray. I'm sick of dealing with these assholes."

Ray put a hand on her shoulder and guided her to the chair beside Marilyn's station. The medic looked her up and down, automatically checking to see if she was okay.

"Sit here for a second, Rachel," Ray said. He looked at the Wolven agents. "What's the charge?"

Adway let out a snort. "None I know of. Just the whim of a councilman."

Facing Adway, Tamir crossed his arms over his chest. "You make it sound like there needs to be more of a reason."

With a barking laugh, Adway said, "Oh, I know there usually isn't. But there should be."

Ray let out a loud sigh. "I can hold her for a few hours, but after that, someone is going to have to give me a good reason to keep her. I'll talk to the councilman myself if I have to—this is *my* jurisdiction, after all. You two can leave now."

The Wolven owl shifter shook his head.

"I'll be guarding the door, Chief," he said, his tone firm. "The councilman she pissed off was the snake. I think his decision was bullshit, but I can't change it. I can give an early warning if he comes back in a bad mood."

Getting to her feet, Marilyn said, "Oh, the smell will be warning enough, Agent. I picked up the scent of viper the second they arrived. It gets any stronger . . . I'll know."

She led Rachel to the back of the room, where the door to the cells was. The young owl was glad the cells weren't in the basement anymore—at least now a prisoner could see daylight and stars, since there were windows to the outside. Rachel had even helped paint the walls pale peach. But the moment she passed through the door into the little hall, the thick cinderblock closed in around her, pressed against her senses. She'd been held prisoner far too long, too often. And if the snake wanted her, bars weren't going to keep him out.

Her heart pounded. "Marilyn, I don't know if I can do this," she said in a choking whisper. The cells were so small—like the ones in the cave—and the lighting was indirect enough that the enclosures seemed shadowed despite the sun shining outside. It had been so long that she didn't think those images still haunted her, but something about seeing and smelling the snake had brought it all back.

"Rachel? Is that you?" Denis called from down the hall, shattering the illusion. He was serving a ten-day sentence for vandalism. Rachel's muscles relaxed. At least she wasn't going to be completely alone.

"Yeah, it's me, Denis," she called back, then asked Marilyn, "Would it be okay if I said hi?"

The golden eagle shifter nodded. "Sure. You're not a prisoner, and he's barely one." They walked down the narrow hallway, their footfalls echoing.

The sixteen-year-old stood at the front of his cell, hands clutching the bars almost desperately. His ash blond hair fell long across one eye and was short above the ears and had gone stringy with dirt and sweat. His skin was so pale he nearly matched Scott. "Man, am I glad to see you! I'm going nuts in here. No TV, no Internet, not even an iPod."

Marilyn gave him a long-suffering look. "It's not a hotel, Denis. It's *jail*. Punishment. Hopefully, the quiet time has given you a chance to think about your life and where you want it to go."

He let out a harsh laugh. "Oh, I'm pretty sure I know where I want it to go. Anywhere but Luna Lake. This town sucks rocks."

Rachel couldn't help but agree. But she wasn't going to talk about leaving with Marilyn standing right there.

"Marilyn?" Ray called.

"Be right there." She opened the door to the cell next to Denis's. They wouldn't be able to see each other because of the concrete wall separating the cells, but they could talk. It took a surprising amount of courage to step into the little room, and Rachel's whole body flinched when the door clanked shut behind her.

"I'll call Mary," Marilyn said, referring to the wife of the postmaster, who provided meals for the town's prisoners. "She'll make you up a nice lunch and dinner. I'm sure this will all be worked out by morning, Rachel. Just relax. If you start feeling anxious, give a shout and I'll come keep you company. And I'll make sure nobody bothers you.

After Marilyn left and closed the outer door, a strange stillness settled over the space. Rachel heard nothing but her own breathing—and Denis's. No sounds from outside the building or even from the main room. Being an omega, she really didn't know much about the magical side of shifting, but it sure felt like a spell to her.

"Hey, Rachel," Denis said, "what's happening in town? Nobody's come to visit."

Oh. Should she tell Denis that Ray had told everyone not to visit, so Denis would get a taste of being really alone? The new chief felt that the teenager had gotten too accustomed to people stepping in to save his butt when he got in trouble. Alek, his older brother, had still been healing and not around, but Rachel knew it had been driving the rest of the family nuts to let Denis stew in jail.

She agreed that he needed some tough love, so she'd stayed away, but she didn't imagine Denis had found it easy to be so isolated.

"Well, you've been doing a fine job of pissing everyone off. What did you expect?"

There was a long pause—was he sulking? Finally he answered, his voice small and quiet. The scent that barely rose above the fresh paint and new varnish was the dusty smell of shame.

"Yeah, I know. I don't know what's wrong with me lately. I'm just angry at everything. Does everyone totally hate me?"

"Bro, nobody *hates* you. But the fact that you did something as stupid as going back to tag the bathrooms after you'd just gotten tapped for doing the same thing by the sheriff . . . well, a lot of people have been trying to keep you out of trouble. They're just really disappointed you don't seem to even care."

She could smell shame mingling with anger now.

"Even now, you're all *nobody's visiting me* instead of asking how *other* people are. You haven't even asked if Alek is getting well, if Kristy and Darrell are recovering from being kidnapped, or whether Tammy came out of her coma. Hell, you haven't even asked about *me*, and I'm right here. You're just asking about you. Why would anyone come see you when they know you don't care about them?

His voice was sullen. "You don't know what it's like to be human in this stupid town."

Rachel let out a bark of a laugh. Wow! Was he really that clueless? "Denis, have you forgotten who you're talking to? I've been the Omega for the last five years. I'd give nearly anything to be part of the protected class of humans. Hell, they threw me in here because I'm so desperate to leave before the next full moon that I tried to sneak out before Wolven could catch me."

"Yeah, but at least you shift. I'm the defective one in the family."

Sitting down on the surprisingly comfortable bunk, Rachel stared at the tiny metal sink and toilet attached to the opposite wall. He considered being human *defective*? No way she could fix that, though she should try to remember to tell someone about Denis's attitude when she got out . . . if she lived long enough to talk to anyone, that is. She sighed and very deliberately changed the subject, hoping he would follow her lead.

"What do you want to do when you graduate high school? It's just next summer, right?"

Denis snorted. "What is there to do? It's not like I can leave town until I'm twenty-one. Alek will be gone probably in a year. So will Dani and most everyone else my age, headed to college. I suppose I'll just hang out at the house and get stoned a lot."

So much for a change of subject. She wanted to beat her head against the wall. "Denis, *really*? What could that possibly do but get you in more trouble? The whole world is open to humans. You could buckle down and study, maybe get a scholarship for college."

"You can't possibly understand how hard it is here." He really did sound defeated.

She wanted so much to tell him just how hard life as the Omega was. But she and Scott had agreed not to tell the younger kids what asses their parents were. Because maybe Scott was right. Hopefully, it was just the mayor and the chief who were in on it.

Maybe. But she doubted it.

Outside the police station, Dalvin slid his satellite phone into his pants pocket. He'd gotten the phone and clothes out of a bag in his car, dressed quickly, and taken a position near the station's front door. Then he'd called home, but no one answered, so he left a message for his folks.

He always tried to let them know when he was back in the States. Wolven had him traveling so much that they worried.

Spotting the police chief walking down the street toward him, Dalvin realized his outfit—black pants and a thick chamois shirt—nearly matched the chief's uniform, except for the insignias of Ray Vasquez's office.

"Hey, Chief, do you have a few minutes?"

The man paused, took off his trooper-style hat, and ran his fingers through his dark hair. He put the hat back on, then hitched up his utility belt, which looked well worn and fit him like a custom job. Dalvin realized he was watching a performance, that Ray's gestures, like his apparently easy stance, were a carefully constructed lie. The chief's weight was centered; if he had to, he could move easily in any direction. It was the way Dalvin himself was standing.

"Not really," Ray said. "But if you want to walk with me to the town hall, you're welcome to and we can talk." Dalvin nodded and fell into step beside the other man. "You're Adway, right? Wolven? And—" The chief took a quick sniff. "An owl?"

"Right on all counts, Chief Vasquez. And you're a jungle cat, but I don't recognize the variety. Doesn't smell very snow-friendly, though." The snow hadn't started here yet, but it wouldn't be long before the tall pine trees that ringed the town would be dusted with white. The town was nestled in the valley between several mountains, so when the snow came, it would likely be deep.

"Panther. My grandparents were from Belize, and no . . . snow isn't my happy place. You're not a species I know either," he added.

"Eagle owls, originally from Mali, long time ago. Tell me a little about the town, since I just got here. How many residents? Who are the dangerous shifters we need to watch for? Who are the alphas in command?"

Vasquez let out a sharp laugh. "The alphas in command *were* the dangerous shifters to watch out for. Van Monk was our mayor and Lenny Gabriel was the police chief. They're dead now. I wish I could say I helped kick 'em out, but I was unknowingly part of the problem.

"Monk and Gabriel did an illegal binding on most of the townspeople. We had no idea our thoughts were being influenced. It's embarrassing as hell, and I'm feeling lucky that I didn't get put down when it all came out. We're damned lucky the Council got suspicious.

"It was your fellow agent, Claire Evans, who uncovered the whole scandal. One of our own, Alek Siska, helped. You probably haven't met them yet." Ray gave a rueful laugh. "Once the news came out, a lot of people just up and left. Went back to where they lived before the cure or moved somewhere completely new. Only about three hundred souls left in Luna Lake now."

A gust of chilled wind hit Dalvin in the face and he coughed. *There were three hundred people in the town? Where was everyone?* He hadn't seen more than a handful. Were they all hiding from the invaders—from Dalvin and the others who had come in for the peace talks? Was that why the place looked so deserted, with no one on the streets?

"So you got promoted to Second? Who is the new Alpha?"

Vasquez picked up a discarded soda can, as if that was a routine part of his job. He dumped the remaining cola on the ground before tossing the can, underhand, into an open-top fifty-gallon recycling barrel at the end of the block. His scent was both annoyed and embarrassed.

"Damned kids have no regard for the environment. We don't have an Alpha right now. Or, at least, we haven't picked a formal one yet."

Dalvin couldn't help but chuckle. "I wasn't aware you got to *pick*. Usually, the next alpha just sort of walks in and takes over."

"Actually, we do pick," Vasquez replied. There was no deception in his smell, just clean cat fur. "The pack Alpha is whoever is elected mayor. Before Monk took over, the alphas of various species took turns leading the town. Right now, because of all the drama, nobody's really interested." He put a hand in his pocket and started to jingle some change.

"Well, that's not quite right. Some of those who are interested, the rest of us don't really want in charge. Sort of like national elections after a scandal. People are suspicious of anyone who wants the job."

Okay, that was useful. "Which alphas want the job? Maybe Wolven can do a little vetting of the possible problems for you."

That made Vasquez stop and purse his lips. "A Wolven vetting? Well, that would be useful. I don't really have the technology, or the records, to do that. When the town was founded, Luna Lake took in whoever showed up on the buses. There were almost a thousand people living here then." Dalvin whistled at the number, and Ray grinned. "Times have sure changed," he said.

"Lenny and Van probably had everyone's history memorized. That's my guess, because other than school and arrest records, there sure weren't any files I could find after they died. So I don't know what Van and Lenny knew, even though I worked with both of them."

"How are the human authorities in the area taking the deaths?" That could be a problem; they didn't need a lot of county-or state-level non-Sazi authorities watching while a variety of obvious non-Americans traipsed around town.

His question caused a small chuckle from Vasquez "The truth is always easiest. The report says several wild animals chewed on them, including at least one cougar and a couple of wolves. The tricky part was that they were both apparently naked in the snow when they were attacked."

Dalvin struggled not to laugh.

"Lot of raised eyebrows from the first responders," Ray went on. "I had no choice but to call it in. Like you say, public officials can't just disappear off the face of the earth. I decided not to even try to explain the lack of clothes. Don't ask, don't tell, y'know? I didn't have to pretend I was a little shocky after the day's events. There was so damned much blood out there, it looked like the set of a slasher film."

The chief looked Dalvin square in the face. "You've probably noticed no one's exactly rushing to welcome you. My people are nervous and scared. Lots of Wolven and Council people around lately, more than most of us have ever seen. I told folks to stay out of the way, out of sight if possible, until the meeting tomorrow night. But you've got to know the whole town is damned curious about this *peace talk* thing. Could you really find no place better for it than Luna Lake? Haven't we been through enough?"

"I wasn't part of the decision-making process," Dalvin said—which was the truth, though he'd heard much of the discussion. "I can tell you there were other towns in the running. My opinion is Luna Lake wouldn't have been chosen except for the thing with your alphas. The Council wanted some extra eyes checking out the area."

A sour expression darkened the other man's face. "I suspected as much. Not a surprise, but it's an annoyance. It's tough to try to get life back to normal with all this crap going on." He took notice of something behind Dalvin and clapped him on the shoulder. "Hey, there's the snake representative. I need to go bend his ear. Let me know when you want to look at the town records. I could use some help getting some backstories on a few people."

"I'll see what I can do, Chief." Dalvin watched Vasquez trot diagonally across the street to the town hall. Ahmad was just exiting the SUV, now dressed in a suit instead of his formal robes. Still out of place for the small-town setting, but not nearly as noticeable if a human happened along. The aversion spell should keep everyone but thrill seekers away, but there were always a few people who ignored the tickle at the back of their neck and leaped into danger.

Maybe he should do a flyover before the delegates arrived. The air was so clean and thin up here that it was a pleasure to fly.

Deciding to check in first, Dalvin was swiping his finger across the screen of his satellite phone when he smelled Tamir behind him. The senior agent grabbed Dalvin's hand, looked at the phone, and let out a disgusted noise.

"Four digits? You have a *four-digit* passcode on a Wolven secure phone? What is wrong with you, Adway? Do you not care about security at all, or are you just stupid?"

Dalvin's teeth ground together in reflex. *Don't rise to the bait.* Instead of yelling or yanking his hand away, he said calmly, "Wolven phones rotate frequencies every eight minutes, Tamir. They use a dedicated satellite. And I'm pretty sure Luna Lake, Washington, isn't a hotbed of terrorist activity."

On top of which, the four "digits" weren't digits at all. They were characters from four different languages—and you had to double-tap the space bar when the keyboard popped up to get the other languages to load. Even if someone figured out that the four characters spelled out his family's surname from before they immigrated to America, they still had to know what languages he was using and in what order. Dalvin wasn't worried about his phone being hacked, though he wasn't going to say any of that to Tamir.

"None of that helps if they get hold of your phone, Adway," the bear shifter said. "Download the biometric software from the Council site. Today." He growled the last word.

Was it worth it to argue? Part of Dalvin wanted to, but he

knew this wasn't the time. He let out a slow breath, closed his eyes, and said, as agreeably as possible, "Fine. I'll do that."

Before Tamir could vent whatever other complaints he had—and he always had things to complain about—the sound of helicopters filled the air. So much for a flyover. It was time to get back to work.

CHAPTER 3

"Okay, what do you want to hear next?" Rachel called.

Marilyn had propped open the door to the row of cells so she could hear Rachel sing without having to leave her post. It had been a good way to pass the time last night, once they were finished bitching about the former mayor and making predictions about the next one.

Sleeping in the cell hadn't been too bad—the mattress was reasonably comfortable and Rachel had woken up screaming only once, when she'd accidentally bumped into the bars of the cell. Denis had woken her then, just like he used to at the Williams house, by rapping a rhythm on the wall, like a happy drumbeat, and repeating her name as if it were a child's song.

This morning had been tough, though. She was starting to get twitchy about being in captivity. Breakfast had been late and Mary had been distracted and nervous, unwilling to stay and chat. The jail's phones had been ringing nearly nonstop since a second set of helicopters had arrived, carrying more delegates.

"Just a sec," Marilyn said as the emergency line rang—it had a more piercing ring than the regular line, Rachel had learned the previous evening, and Marilyn or Ray jumped to answer it. "Nine one one, what's your emergency?"

Last night, Fred the postmaster had called that number to

say his wife hadn't made it home from delivering meals to the jail and he was worried, with all the strangers in town. Ray had gone out to look for Mary and found her at the diner. She'd stopped in to visit and had forgotten to call home.

"Marvin," Marilyn said after listening for a bit, "this is an emergency number. You can't tie up the line asking about the delegates. There'll be a meeting tonight." A pause. "No, Marvin, seeing a snake in town isn't an emergency either. He's a councilman and he's been here for days. Nobody's died yet." Another pause. "Yes, the snakes get a seat on the Council too." Finally, she sounded fed up. "Marvin, stop. Just stop. Wolven is here to protect the delegates. They're not here to snoop around your house. Unless . . . you don't have anything to hide, do you?"

The sound of the receiver being set down was accompanied by Marilyn's throaty chuckle. "That did it. He'll start digging holes behind his house to bury his *Penthouse* collection pretty soon."

The image made Rachel chuckle too.

Denis snorted and said, "Idiot."

Somehow overhearing Marilyn's conversation had put Rachel in a better mood. "Pick a song. Either of you."

A clanging came from Denis's cell. It sounded like he was kicking at the bars, maybe tapping them while lying on the bed. "How about that old one about people keeping their noses out of your business?"

"Oh, yeah! 'Tain't Nobody's Business.' I like that one. Do you know Bessie Smith sang that nearly a hundred years ago?" It did sort of fit the present situation too. Rachel took a second to get the tune in her head, then started to sing.

Her mother had always told her she sounded like Bessie. Rachel didn't agree, except on this song. "'There ain't nothing I can do or nothing I can say, that folks don't criticize me. But I'm goin' to do just as I want to anyway.'"

She let her frustration flow into the notes, sinking so deeply into the song that she didn't hear the door to the station open. Didn't hear the beginning of the conversation that followed. Didn't tune in until she heard Marilyn's tone change, becoming both firmer and more upset.

"I'm sorry. I know you're a councilman, but you can't just barge in and . . . hey, stop!"

The wave of power that preceded the councilman's appearance was immediately recognizable. Rachel backed up until she was in a corner of the cell, as far from the bars as possible. It was like she was ten years old again, locked in a feces-laden cave, waiting to be raked open by sharp talons. She did her best to own her bird form, but becoming Sazi would never be something she wouldn't blame on the snakes.

Ahmad was dressed in an impeccable gray suit that had a sort of sheen. His hair, no longer covered by the keffiyeh, was cropped close to his head and was the same coal black as his brows. She supposed some people would consider him handsome, but to her, he was still a snake. He pulled in his power as he got closer to the bars; it was as though he was full human. But his magic was still there, still powerful. At a gesture from him, Rachel felt herself rise to her feet. She tried to hold still, not let him move her like a puppet, but it was like trying to hold off the pull of the moon. Her motion was barely jerky as he forced her to walk to the front of the cell and thrust her arm out between the bars. Though she was nearly kissing the bars, she managed to clench her fist and tighten her arm muscles, fighting his attempt to make her raise her hand.

Rachel's arm shook with the effort of trying to keep still. The snake stopped in front of her, so close she could smell his musty reptilian scent mixed with an exotic spiced cologne. Her body started to tremble so hard that his power was the only thing keeping her upright.

She didn't want to be afraid, but her body wanted to curl into a fetal position. Her shaking hand had risen almost to her waist, but the snake still had to bend to reach it. He put one hand under her fist, steadying it, then lowered his head and lightly touched his lips to her hand.

Memories of Roberto, Sargon's right hand, filled Rachel's mind. He used to kiss hands through the bars too. People didn't live long after that happened. Touching meant painful, torturous death with snakes.

But here and now, all she felt was the pressure of Ahmad's cool, dry lips. No bite. No venom. When the man rose to his full height, she saw that his eyes were warm and sad. His voice held something close to pain when he spoke, so quietly that even the best ears might not hear his words.

"I am not who you believe I am, young owl. I am Ahmad, the son of Sargon, the man you hate. I apologize for keeping you here against your will, but I had to be sure you were truly one of those in the caves before I shared this secret with you." She felt a wall of magic drop over the two of them. Whether there were a dozen people in the next room or a thousand, she was certain they wouldn't hear a word he said. Not even Denis, right next door, would hear. "Little owl, I share your hatred of my father and of Nasil.

"What you endured at the hands of my father and his people, I have also endured. I have more scars on my body than you can probably imagine. I wish I could end your pain as much as I would my own, but I can only offer my sincere apologies and the knowledge that I killed Sargon, using every ounce of hate and desire for revenge that you feel right now. You are one of only a very few who know that I murdered him—and that I *enjoyed* it."

She could read his hatred and revulsion on his face, knew that his feelings were as strong as hers. His grim expression was wiped away by a small, dark smile that told of the satisfaction of doing what she would not have been able to. Something inside her dissolved, a pain she didn't even realize she still had.

The wall of silence lifted. The magic that held her in place eased. Ahmad turned to several robed men standing near the door. "This place and these people are protected. Let it be known." They bowed low, their long robes flowing as they moved. The councilman nodded to Rachel and stepped away; her cell door popped open as though he'd used a key.

"You may leave this building, but I regret we cannot allow you to leave town. If you try, you will be brought back here. The reasons for this I cannot share with you. But I hope you no longer feel such an urgent need to run."

He strode quickly out of the cell block, Rachel several steps behind. He must not have stopped to talk to anyone in the outer room, because by the time she got there, the jail's door was closing behind him.

There was a little crowd in the main room, their scents radiating confusion: her father; Marilyn; the cat woman—Mrs. Wingate—who was wearing a gold sweater dress that made her red-gold hair pop; the big bear, Tamir; and the owl shifter who was a Wolven agent, Adway.

Her dad came close and put a hand on her arm. "What just happened? What did he say to you, Rachel?"

She shook her head. If the councilman had wanted everyone to hear, he wouldn't have used magic to block his voice. "Just that he wasn't who I thought he was." She could tell the others wanted to ask more questions—which she didn't want to answer. "I need to go home now. Please."

It wasn't an excuse. Home really was where she wanted to go. Ahmad was right. Her desire to run had lessened. But she wanted a shower and clean clothes. She knew the jail was clean; she was probably only the second person to be held there since it had been rebuilt. But she itched.

The owl agent stepped forward, almost too quickly. "I'll take her."

The cat shook her head. "Not yet. There are some things we need to discuss first."

Ooo . . . that didn't sound good. That rat bastard of a bear must have thrown them under the bus. Rachel raised her hands in what she hoped was a placating gesture, knowing she was probably oozing guilt along with the remnants of her fear. "Look, that whole thing on the road . . . that was sort of my fault. Agent Adway has already had a strip of hide taken. Please don't beat him up again." Mrs. Wingate raised her brows and put one hand on her hip, and Rachel added, trying not to sound like she was pleading, "Or me."

"I have no idea what you're talking about, but you've piqued my curiosity. Officer, could you please clear the building?"

Rachel's heart sank, Her father cast a worried look over his shoulder as he left. Marilyn ducked into the cell block and returned with Denis, in handcuffs. Rachel wondered fleetingly where he was going to wind up as Marilyn escorted him out of the jail.

Dalvin stood at parade rest in what was now a makeshift Council chamber while one of the Monier siblings stared at him. That she now called herself Wingate made no difference. He'd never encountered any of the Moniers before, though of course he'd heard the rumors of a family plagued by power so strong it could lead to madness. Tamir was right beside him, reeking of annoyance and grumbling under his breath, clearly pissed that Dalvin was here. Or maybe it was the fact that he was exhausted, just like Dalvin was. All night in the forest searching for threats to the delegates, crawling around in the dirt and shining flashlights tied to his wings up into trees. Later, they'd gone knocking on doors, interviewing the locals.

And then they'd had to chase Rachel. Dalvin didn't know about Tamir, but his muscles felt like lead, and he suspected, from the way they itched, that his eyes rivaled Rudolph's nose. Tamir probably felt the same.

It was the snake councilman's fault. He'd ridden them like hobbyhorses since they'd arrived. Every one of them came back from an assignment praying that it was time to find a bed to crawl into, and he'd sent them out again on a new inspection. The man rose to a new level of ass.

Rachel had moved as far away from the three of them as she could without leaving the room.

Amber Wingate's power stung Dalvin's skin as she inspected the wound on his side. "So you had a strip of hide taken, and fairly recently from the look of it." She asked Tamir, "Care to explain?"

Tamir's all-black outfit paired well with the darkness in his the voice and the Russian accent that came and went with his mood. Black boots, jeans, and shirt, a dark gray tie to match his stormy eyes. Dalvin thought, not for the first time, that Tamir really liked playing the villain of Wolven.

"He deserted his post," the bear shifter said in a near growl. "The mediator died and it nearly started a war between the sloths. He's lucky *all* I did was take a strip of hide.

Amber pursed her lips and turned to face Dalvin. "And your version?"

Dalvin wasn't sure what she wanted to hear, but the truth was probably best. Like he should have done the first time. "The same." That earned him a look of astonishment. "Except I was lured away—I didn't intentionally desert my post. But Tamir felt that deserved a strip of hide. I couldn't disagree that it didn't really matter why I left. The result was the same."

The jail's front door opened, and a blast of power hit Dalvin so hard he wondered if his feathers would come in singed next time he shifted. He was starting to wish he was wearing Kevlar instead of a pullover and slacks. The man who entered was Middle Eastern, like the snake councilman, though he didn't move like a snake. He was dressed in a well-fitting dark blue suit with no collar. A gold-and-white cloth covered his hair, similar to the one Ahmad had worn yesterday, but with different patterns. The cloth blew in a breeze generated by his magic as he stalked around the Wolven agents, arms behind his back. He smelled of no particular animal and no emotion except curiosity. Dalvin didn't recognize him, but from the way Dr. Wingate backed up in deference, he must be a Council member.

The man stopped in front of him and stared. He was the same height as Dalvin and stood so close their noses almost touched. His eyes were glowing golden. "Did you arrest her?"

He blinked at the man's very American accent. "Uh . . . did I arrest . . . *who*?"

"The woman who lured you away." His breath smelled of spearmint.

His gaze was so intent, so focused, it was hard not to twitch under it. "Why do you think it was a woman?"

"Your file is thicker than I expected given your time in service, Agent Adway. I keep hearing the word 'troublemaker' when people talk about you, but I don't think that's completely true. I don't think you go looking for trouble; I think you have help getting into it. Nearly every page of your file includes a woman's name. I would frankly be surprised if there *wasn't* a woman involved when you screw up."

The swallow was involuntary. He'd never thought of himself as a troublemaker or someone who had a thick file. But women? It was hard to dispute there had been a lot of women in his life. "No. I didn't arrest her. She's . . . one of the delegates."

A low growl rumbled up from Tamir's chest. Dalvin risked a glance sideways and saw the bear shifter's hands clenched into fists and his jaw clamped tight enough to show ropes of muscles in his neck.

"Ah," was all the councilman said. He turned to the redhead. "What do you suppose we should do with these two, Doctor?"

"Three. Mustn't forget the woman du jour." The physician made a Vanna White gesture toward Rachel.

He could look at her now, since everyone else was too. Could she *really* be his childhood friend? Rachel Washington had been kidnapped so long ago . . . but this woman sure as hell smelled like Rachel—cherry snow cones, hot cement, and daisies. Summer scents from the inner city. She even had a tiny scar at the corner of her eye where a pop bottle rocket had glanced off her head and nearly set her hair on fire. Yet she didn't seem to recognize him.

Admittedly, he'd changed a lot. He hadn't shed his baby fat until he was a senior in high school, long after she'd disappeared. To him, she looked much the same, only with smooth curves and shoulder-length natural curls replacing the skinny kid with braids down to her butt. He'd never really thought about what she might look like grown up. She was stunning.

Yesterday, he hadn't had a chance to ask if she was the Rachel he'd known all those years ago, not with everything else that was happening. And if it was her, why was she in a tiny town in Washington? Her family had been mourning her loss for a decade . . .

His attention was dragged back, eyes front, when the councilman asked tersely, "Were you in the Navy, Agent Adway? You seem to have a girl in every port. Or are you just a player who doesn't give a shit about the women he screws?"

His face was burning and he struggled to make his words sound civil. "No, *sir.* Neither one."

"Excuse me? Do I get to talk here?" Rachel said from her corner. Dalvin saw the little girl he'd once known in the woman, eyes flashing, jaw jutting out defiantly, staring down any threat or punishment for speaking out. Didn't matter if it was her mama, the minister at church, her second-grade teacher, or Wolven and the Council. He struggled not to smile.

The councilman turned all his intensity on her. "Speak."

She paled, going from chocolate to coffee with two creams, realizing that she'd just stuck her foot in it. Then she plowed forward, determination in her voice. "I'm not 'his girl.' I just got caught in the middle trying to get the hell out of town . . . which, by the way, I had permission to do from the Wolven agent in charge yesterday. Can I get your guys' names and ranks? I don't even know for sure that anyone in this room is more in charge than he was. Can anyone I know vouch for any of you? Are you even Wolven? Or Council?"

The councilman disappeared. Flat *disappeared*. He didn't just move quickly, he blinked out. Dalvin, Tamir, and Rachel looked around the room, trying to figure out where he'd gone. Amber raised one red-gold eyebrow and kept staring at Rachel.

A voice filled the room from the far corner. Rachel spun around and backed away from the phantom sound. "A pathetic Sazi *dares* to question the power of the sahip of the Hayalet Kabile?" A big cat roar made the hairs on the back of Dalvin's neck stand and twitch, and Rachel let out a high-pitched screech that was worthy of the owl she smelled like. Except she smelled more of great horned than screech.

Silence settled over the room, and the tang of fear and adrenaline rose to overpowering. Dalvin felt his muscles prepare to fight. Tamir caught his eye and nodded, saying without a word that despite their argument, he had his fellow agent's back. Knowing Rachel was the most likely target, Dalvin moved toward her, placing himself between her and the rest of the room, so she could keep the wall at her back.

After long, tense moments, Dr. Wingate burst out laughing. "Oh, for God's sake, Rabi, quit scaring the kids."

A chuckle sounded near the table, and everyone spun to look as the man in the suit reappeared. He was now seated in a chair with his crossed feet propped on the table, rubbing a freaking apple on his shirt. His suit jacket was off and his sleeves were rolled up . . . and he was *smiling*. WTF?

"Okay, okay," he said, then laughed again. "Man, you should have seen yourselves jump. Why isn't there a Sazi version of *Punked?*"

Wingate shook her head, then walked over and attempted to swat him on the side of the head in a friendly way. He ducked, still grinning, and she missed.

Amber looked at Rachel and let out an exasperated sigh. "I'm Amber Monier Wingate. You can ask your friends Claire or Alek to identify me if you'd like. If you have the nerve, you could also ask Ahmad, before he leaves. I'm the senior physician for Wolven and the Council. The chief justice of the Council, Charles Wingate, is my husband. This joker, I'm sorry to say, is my brother-in-law. Rabi Kuric really is the sahip of the ghost tiger tribe from Turkey, and he really is a Council member. His sister is married to my brother, who is also a Council member. And before you ask, yes, he was invisible. That's his most annoying talent."

The tiger shifter took a bite of the shiny red apple in his hand and shrugged. Talking through the mouthful of fruit, he corrected, "Technically, I'm the liaison to the Council for my tribe. We don't acknowledge being Sazi. That's why I'm at this mess of a meeting. I don't have any stake in who wins. And I speak the language enough to be sure nobody is translating wrong." He looked at his sister-in-law, with twinkling eyes. "You're just annoyed with my ghosting because I caught you turning up the thermostat when you swore to Charles it wasn't you."

She sniffed and shifted the subject. "You've been spending way too much time with Ahmad, Rabi. You've gotten sneaky about the wrong things."

"Gotta give the guy chops for instilling fear in his enemies, Amber. Even Antoine is learning a few things. And it's for a good cause. The three of us have become a force to be reckoned with in the Middle East. It's really calmed down the tension among the different species of shifters there. If we can extend that peace to the Serbian and Bosnian bears, most of Europe will calm down too." He took another bite and gestured with the apple. "Speaking of Antoine, he sends his regards. He's been trying to e-mail you for a week. Tahira's pregnant again and wants to schedule a physical."

Amber smiled. "Another kitten? That's wonderful! I'm sure Antoine is hoping for a boy after two girls."

Rachel finally found her voice again, with the talk turning to mundane things. "What is *wrong* with you assholes? You scared us half to death! Disappearing, reappearing, growling out of thin air. You lock me in a cage for no reason and then pull this shit."

Councilman Kuric turned serious suddenly and pointed the apple at her. "Be careful, Ms. Washington. Just because I'm a little more laid-back than most, I *am* still on the Council and don't like being insulted. And if you think carefully, you'll notice that something very significant happened just now." He paused and swallowed. "All of you stopped being mad at each other and got scared. Then you got mad at *me*. In many places in the world, that's how peace happens. If that makes me an asshole, so be it."

Rachel looked taken aback and sat down, nodding.

"And," Amber added, "we answered your question of who we are and why we get to make the decisions. Including you spending a night behind bars."

"Yeah," Councilman Kuric said, "don't let that tiny bobcat frame fool you. If her brother wasn't the cat leader, Amber would be. She does enforcement even better than him. He gets too emotional."

Tamir spoke up. "I always thought Fiona was the member of the Monier family most likely to be on the Council. She's utterly ruthless."

"That's why she ran Wolven," Amber replied. "She was too ruthless for diplomacy. Enforcement was better for her. And, hopefully, will be again someday."

"I thought she went rogue." Dalvin didn't realize he'd said that out loud until everyone turned his way. Tamir and Councilman Kuric winced at Dalvin's faux pas—nobody ever mentioned the former Wolven chief, who had been taken out by an early batch of the plague drug—but Amber responded.

"Not rogue. She's still in her right mind. But she has . . . episodes where you don't want to be around her. It's better for everyone if she stays off the grid. Safer."

A roar of pain from outside nearly made Councilman Kuric fall off his chair. Everyone except Rachel raced for the door. Rachel went to the window instead, shaking her head as the others opened the door to look out.

"Some people," she said loudly, obviously intending to be overheard. "Running straight into a fight before they know who's fighting or why."

That made sense to Dalvin, who joined her at the glass. A pair of massive bears, one brown and one black, were rolling on the ground, clawing at each other and roaring loud enough to send people racing for cover. "Oh, Gawddamn it! It's Suljo and Bojan. They've been the only two *sensible* ones up to now."

Rachel shrugged and turned away from the scene. Her scent wasn't concerned, wasn't even interested anymore. "Eh, they're just playing. They're probably tired and bored."

The tiger councilman looked at her from the doorway, his head cocked with interest. "Really . . . Why do you think that?"

"You can't see their gums, so they're not baring teeth, and when they grab, they're not shaking their prey to kill."

Thanks to Rachel, Dalvin saw it too—the bears were like dogs roughhousing; one would fall over while the other mock mauled him. But there was no effort, no real fire to the struggle. "Huh. I think you're right."

"Yep," Amber agreed, "they're blowing off steam. I see it all the time with Charles's family."

Another loud roar rattled a framed photograph on the wall. Rachel looked out again, then let out a small raspberry. "They're not even using their claws. I saw what bear claws can do without much effort on my car roof." She looked pointedly at Tamir. "Thanks a lot for that, by the way. I'm going to have a soaked front seat next time it rains."

Sinking into a red-cushioned chair, she began pushing back her cuticles with purple-tinted nails. "I don't blame the bears. This town is so boring it makes people want to fight just to keep themselves sane. That's why I still want to leave. Just say the word and I'm out of here."

The door opened and Larissa burst into the room. A fluffy white scarf wrapped around her neck over a long brown top and her white leggings showed off her long legs even better than her high-heeled black boots. Spotting Dalvin, she raced over and wrapped herself around him.

"Agent, come quickly. They are fighting. They will kill each other. You must stop them."

A sarcastic snort came from two spots in the room simultaneously—Amber and Rachel.

He untangled Larissa's arms; it felt strange to have her holding him just then, but he wasn't sure why. "I was watching, Larissa, and I really don't think they're trying to hurt each other."

"Yes, yes," she insisted. "They are tearing at each other! It will end the peace talks and there will be war."

"Oh, there'll be war all right—especially if Agent Adway charges out there and forces them to stop playing." Hands on hips, Amber was glowering at the Bosnian bear shifter, who turned a face full of innocence to her.

"Oh! Madam Doctor," Larissa said, "I didn't see you there. But please, you must believe me. There is no *playing* between our sloths. If both were part of my family, then yes. But not this."

"Uh-huh," Rachel commented not so quietly from the corner. "There's playing going on, all right. Playa getting played right in front of me."

The young bear's eyes narrowed as she focused on Rachel for the first time. She raised her nose and sniffed delicately, her nose wrinkling in an expression of disdain. "I do not know you. You are barely Sazi and smell of servitude. Why do you believe you may even *speak* in my presence?"

Dalvin saw the volcano forming. Rachel stood in a rush. "Excuse me? I smell of *servitude*?" For someone with barely any magic of her own, she could move fast. He raced forward, grabbing Rachel by the shoulders just before she reached Larissa.

CHAPTER 4

She was going to rip the brown hair right off that bear. Servitude? *Servitude?* Yeah, she might have been the omega, but she was nobody's *servant.* "You're going to miss the peace talks, lady, because I'm going to smack you into next week."

The owl agent grabbed her before she could reach the startled bear. "Chill out, chello pop!"

His words stopped her cold. She turned to him, studying his face for long moments, putting together what he'd said with his last name, searching for familiar features. The eyelashes. She remembered those eyelashes, so very long for a boy. A flash of memory: the two of them sitting on her parents' stoop, him growling at her for wanting to brush mascara into those lashes, wanting to see how long they could get. But this face, this body, were so very different from the ones she remembered. *"Dalvin?"* The word was a whisper, simultaneously horrified and amazed.

He nodded. "Yeah. It's me. Been a long time, Chelle."

Everyone was staring at them. Rachel couldn't get her voice to function, but *escape* was screaming through her mind. She yanked away and ran out the door, passing too close to the tussling bears and catching claws across one arm. The pain was intense enough to bring tears to her eyes but not to stop her.

She felt, rather than heard, someone chasing her. Glancing back, she saw both bears loping after her. They didn't look like they were playing anymore. She ran straight out of town, ran until her legs felt like butter, until she knew she couldn't last much longer. Her mind finally loosened up and something occurred to her. *These were alpha Sazi, not rogues. There are brains in those furred heads. They damned well know better than to chase birds.*

She darted into the brush as she rounded a bend. They skidded to a stop on the road, looking for her. Stepping back out onto the pavement, she screamed at the top of her lungs, "Stop it! I'm not food!"

Both bears reared back, stunned. Even if they didn't understand English, they should understand *pissed off* by her scent. Taking advantage of their disorientation, Rachel jogged into the woods and put some distance between herself and the road before sitting down next to a tree to catch her breath. She was in shape, but Jeez!

She heard the bears moving off, heading back toward town. Good. She closed her eyes for a moment and tried to get her heart to stop pounding. The soothing scent of pine needles and warm wood decay made her feel safe, like inside a hollow tree. Moments later, she heard soft footsteps.

"Rachel?" The voice was soft, kind and, most important, both female and familiar. Claire—someone who had seen Rachel at her worst and her best. "You're bleeding pretty bad, hon. We need to get something on those wounds."

Rachel looked at her injured arm. Her adrenaline was so high, she was only beginning to really feel the pain, but the gashes were ragged and ugly. Looking at it made it hurt worse; her arm began to throb. Blood was dripping onto the leaves in a nearly steady stream. Claire tore off one of the sleeves of her T-shirt and started sopping up the blood. The throbbing turned to stinging and then pain enough to make Rachel utter the kinds of swears that would have gotten her mouth washed out as a child.

"What happened back there?" her friend finally asked. "I got there just in time to see a really good-looking guy start to chase you and the bears. Amber made him stop, so I came after you instead."

Rachel blew out a breath and shook her head. "Believe it or not, I grew up with that guy, back in Detroit, before I was kidnapped. I didn't recognize him until just then."

Claire's eyes went wide. "That's *great!*" Rachel glared at her. "I mean . . . isn't it?"

Rachel shook her head again, wincing as the movement jiggled her wounded arm. "No. It isn't. He knows *everyone*, Claire. Everyone I grew up with, my mom and dad—the whole extended family, people at church. He'll tell them where I am . . . *what* I am."

The Texas red wolf shifter sat back on her heels. The front of her pants were covered with mud, but one of the nice things about Claire was that she didn't care if she was messy. "Ohhh." She let out a sad chuckle. "You and me, we're both attack victims. We can't ever go back. Our families and friends—they'd never understand. Those damned snakes." Rachel felt her chin quivering. She didn't dare try to talk, or she'd start bawling.

Claire reached out in solidarity, and Rachel took her hand, squeezing tight as she blinked back tears. "Tell me what you need," Claire said.

"Same thing I've always needed. To leave. Start over somewhere else." But the more she thought about it, the more she realized she was doomed. "Fuck. Now I can't even do that. Ahmad said I can't leave, and if I tried, Dalvin would track me down. He's always been a bloodhound, even when we were kids. I have no idea how he got turned, but he's with Wolven and he's always been really close to my family."

Claire's shoulders dropped as she realized what that meant.

"So, even if he lets you go, he'll drop a hint without meaning to, and they'll start looking too." She closed her eyes and squeezed Rachel's hand tighter. "I'm so sorry."

A new voice contradicted her. "No. You must trust your family. Femily is everything."

Rachel and Claire looked up simultaneously. A young woman was standing in the shadows of the nearby trees. She was a stranger to Rachel.

"You're Anica, right?" Claire said a little stiffly. "From the Serbian sloth? I'm sorry, but this is a private conversation." She pointed back the way they'd come. "If you're lost, the town is that way."

"I am not lost. I never am lost," Anica said, stepping into the light. Her large eyes seemed too big for her pale-skinned face— like one of those creepy photos of little kids—and her black hair had been tousled by the wind. "I am sent to find you. The mediator has arrived and has called a meeting. All Sazi are to come home."

Claire let out a slow breath. "Okay. You head back and we'll follow in a few minutes."

The other woman nodded and turned away, then shook her head. "No, I think they be angry if I come back alone. You come now? Please?"

Anica was surprisingly small—Rachel had assumed that all the bears would be large and muscular, like the two she'd seen outside the police station—and her pleasant manner was a nice contrast to that witch, Larissa. *Tell me I smell like a servant, will she? Make that "witch" with a "b."* But if the Council had asked her to find them . . .

Rachel let go of Claire's hand and used the Wolven agent's shoulder as a brace to get back to her feet. "We might as well go now. If we don't, they'll send more people after us."

With a sigh, Claire stood easily. "I suppose you're right."

The three women started toward Luna Lake, Anica following

fairly close behind Claire and Rachel. Though she wasn't quite guarding or herding them, it seemed clear she'd been given explicit instructions to ensure their return.

"I am sorry I . . . what is word, *interrupt* your talk."

Rachel shrugged, saying, "It's okay. But you don't know where I'm coming from, so please don't judge me."

The other woman sighed. "But I do. Not . . . I say it bad, but I know, because I am like you. I was human once."

Rachel stumbled to a stop and turned to look at the Serbian woman. "Wait. Maybe you don't understand what we mean by *attack victim*. Your whole family is Sazi. Ours aren't. They're still human. They don't know what happened to us and we can't tell them. They don't know shifters exist."

Anica nodded vigorously. "I *do* know. I am very like you. I was taken by bad men who are viper snakes, chained in cage, nearly killed by bears. I *know!*"

Whoa. "Were you taken here in America, or were there other places in the world where kids were taken and turned?"

Anica's arms crossed across her chest and her brow lowered angrily. "Many more places in world. Not just here. *Many* more. Many children."

No shit! She'd never heard that before. It made sense, but nobody had ever said a word about other kidnap locations.

"I'm so sorry," Rachel said automatically, and Claire nodded. "At least you got turned into the same kind of animal as your family. That's something."

Anica let out a burst of laughter. "After! You don't see, even now. My femily came *after*. Is why I tell you to trust your femily. If you let them, they will join you, help you. Femilies are stronger than one little bear."

"Wait," Claire said, holding up one hand. "You're telling us the snakes took you and turned you into a bear, and that you went home to your *human* family and they agreed to become Sazi? So what, they just let you attack them and turn them too?"

Anica grinned. "Yes! Now you understand. Our sloth is strong because our femily is strong. Is why we must win the talks. Our femily will grow and we will need land to hunt."

The shock of what Rachel was hearing was so great that she couldn't completely wrap her head around it. She looked at Claire, whose mouth also was hanging open, whose eyes were as wide as Rachel's own. She couldn't even begin to think of what to say in response, so she kept walking, her thoughts racing. Claire and Anica were silent as well.

How was Anica still alive? She attacked her family and turned them! It's like the number one rule of the Sazi. A death sentence crime.

Anica led them to the Community Center. The doors were open and the meeting had already started. A woman was calling out names, none of them familiar. Alek, holding the door open, noticed the blood-soaked, makeshift bandage around Rachel's arm, and winced.

"You okay?" he asked.

She shrugged, causing a fresh burst of pain in her biceps.

"Been better, but I'll live."

"If you can hold out until the end of the meeting, Amber can probably take care of it. She's an amazing healer. If you can't wait, I'll go in and find Marilyn."

Claire chimed in. "It's pretty bad, Alek. Claw rips that will probably need stitches. I know the meeting is important, but if it it's going to last more than a half hour or so, we should probably interrupt."

He nodded. Pointing to the far side of the room, he said, "Rachel, Bitty saved you a seat. Claude's there too, and he can probably do some minor healing, enough to get you through the meeting. If you start to feel even a little woozy, let Bitty know and we'll get Amber.

"Anica, please join your sloth on stage. Claire, you're here with me." As Claire stepped to one side and the other two women entered the building, Alek called to the woman at the podium, someone else Rachel had never seen before. "That's everyone. All residents accounted for, Miss Sutton."

Everyone in the room seemed to be watching Rachel and Anika make their way to their assigned spaces. Rachel slunk to the empty seat beside Bitty, trying not to make more of a spectacle of herself than she already was. Almost involuntarily, she scanned the crowd until she spotted Dalvin, guarding the family opposite Anica's on the stage.

The moment she sat, Claude Kragan, Bitty's brother and the Second in Rachel's parliament, frowned, his sharp, intelligent gaze focused on the bloody wrapping on her arm. He started running his clawlike, age-spotted hands over the injured area. Warmth penetrated the sharp pain, which soon subsided enough that her head was no longer pounding; it felt sort of like the moment aspirin kicked in.

Bitty, a snowy owl shifter, smiled at Claude and patted Rachel's knee, letting her know she knew everything. That was the thing Rachel loved most about her new parliament. Because of their psychic connection, they knew when another owl was upset but didn't intrude—and whenever Rachel was ready to talk, Bitty would be happy to listen.

The woman on the stage took a sip of water and tapped her finger on the microphone, drawing everyone's attention. The vivid pink, fitted dress suit she was wearing worked well with her chestnut hair, which was held in a loose bun at the back of her neck. Rachel wondered if she was a little too young to be in charge—she looked like she was maybe in her late twenties—but she definitely had an air of authority.

"Okay, our stragglers have arrived. Since we were only a few minutes in, I'll start over for their benefit and I thank everyone for their patience. My name is Elizabeth Sutton-Kendall, but you can call me Liz or Miss Sutton."

Liz. That was a nice name. Long ago, Rachel had had a babysitter named Liz and she had had that same sort of calm, sincere voice. There were so many scents in the room that Rachel didn't have a clue what kind of animal this Liz was, but she radiated energy that felt like Council magic, though without the sting.

"Those of you over the century mark have likely have heard of my grandfather, Nigel Sutton. I've spent the past ten years at his side, learning the craft of Sazi mediation. Those who have already worked with me"—she nodded at the doctor, Amber, and Dalvin—"can tell you that I'm fair but tough, and I will *not* brook any sabotage." Her voice dropped an octave and took on a dark edge. "Those who attempt it will *die*. No appeals."

"A-yup," muttered Claude Kragan with a nearly silent chuckle. "She's Nigel's get, all right." He reached out and touched Rachel's arm again and the pain lessened a little more. He'd noticed the throbbing was distracting her from the speech. She really did like the old hoot owl.

Bitty leaned over to whisper in her ear. "Nigel was one of the greatest negotiators of all the Sazi. I hope she's as good."

"Without going into specifics," Liz continued, "I can tell you that this is basically a territory dispute. In Europe, border disputes among the human governments of the continent's tightly packed small countries can drastically impact Sazi hunting grounds. Such is the problem here. The Bosnian/Serbian war twenty years ago changed the division of territory between these two sloths."

Rachel furrowed her brow. Twenty years? How was that possible, when Anica said her sloth had existed since only she was turned? The bear didn't seem much older than Rachel or Claire.

This random thought made Bitty cock her head questioningly. Rachel shook her head, dismissing the subject. There was no use speculating until she'd heard everything the speakers had to say. Bitty had the tact to not push farther into her mind and instead tapped Rachel's hand, their signal that they would talk later.

"Bears have the *reputation*"—Liz paused and met the gaze of each of the older men in the sloths—"of being unreasonable, hardheaded, and quick to anger."

With her pain fading into the background, Rachel was able to take in the arrangements on the stage in more detail. The bear sloths, made up of men and women of varying ages, were arranged on opposite sides of Liz Sutton. The two alpha males were easy to spot—they were older, sat bolt upright, and were frowning at each other. Anica and the bear bitch Larissa stood behind them, whispering to them quietly and unobtrusively. Rachel presumed they were translators.

Both alpha males chuckled at the mediator's comment, but the audience was not amused; people were murmuring to each other. Noticing that, one of the men whispered something to his translator, Anica, who nodded and spoke loudly enough to be heard by everyone in the room.

"I would like to think that Sazi consist not only of their animal half, but the human half as well. And humans *can* negotiate, can be reasonable and thoughtful, can step above their anger for the good of their people."

"With that," said Liz, "let me introduce the *humans* on stage with me today. To my left is the Kasun family, from the Bosnian side of the border. Mustafa Kasun is the head of the family; next to him is his wife, Iva." The Kasuns looked like they'd stepped off the red carpet at some exotic European resort. Iva's high-heeled, ivory-colored suede boots matched her furred hat and jacket. The outfit was lovely but wouldn't withstand a single snowstorm and would probably be ruined the moment she stepped in damp grass. She was a tall woman, taller than her husband when seated. Mustafa Kasun was wide and stout with thick black hair and piercing eyes. His suit was a shiny serge fabric that even a snowflake would stain. Based on nothing more than their clothing, Rachel immediately distrusted them, though she chastised herself for making assumptions.

"Their twins, Suljo and Zara, are next to them. Larissa Grebo, standing behind the alphas, is a family friend and will be acting as translator for the family."

Well, see there? Anyone who is friends with the "servant" bitch . . . Bitty turned her head and let out a little snort.

Suljo was the only Kasun who was watching the audience instead of the rival sloth, his eyes moving from face to face with apparent interest. He took after his mother, tall and slender, while his sister, Zara, had the same broad face as her father. She looked bored.

"None of the Kasuns speak English," Liz added. "If they approach you to ask questions, or if you need to speak to them, please find one of the Council members"—she waved toward the chairs edging the stage on right and left—"or either of the Wolven agents presently guarding the doors, to find a translator."

"To my right is the Petrovic family from Serbia. Zarko Petrovic is head of the family, and his wife, Draga, is next to him." Zarko and Draga were both medium height and weight and looked like blue-collar workers, though both were neatly, if not elegantly, dressed. Draga didn't wear much makeup. To Rachel, she seemed sure of herself, and her expression indicated intelligence, possibly more than her husband, whose gaze lacked Draga's intensity.

"With them are their two eldest sons, Bojan and Samit, as well as a younger daughter, Anica."

Bojan was a looker. He had a soft face, wide eyes like Anica, long fingers, and a curl of hair on his forehead that probably made girls swoon. They had their mother's features, while Samit resembled his father—wide face, smaller eyes, and a permanent frown. Did she only imagine that Samit was staring at her, the corner of his mouth curled in a satisfied smile? Boy, she sure hoped it was her imagination. It wasn't a very friendly look.

"Again," Liz went on, "most of the family does not speak English. Anica and Bojan can translate."

Liz took another sip of water. Somehow her movement and the pause in the flow of speech had a calming effect, which Rachel found interesting. Most people would cause tension by going slow; Liz managed to make it seem natural. Very cool.

"I do not speak either language, but am fortunate that our esteemed Council liaison, Rabi Kuric, does. He will translate for me." She inclined her head to the tiger councilman, who was looking very stoic in his folding chair at one side of the stage—a total change from the smiling cutup in the police station. He gave a brief nod in reply.

The mediator turned her back to the audience to address the sloths directly. "Please know that he will translate *everything*, even private conversations. He is a ghost shifter. You will never know when he is listening, so watch your tongues. Again, I will not tolerate any attempts at sabotage. So long as everyone acts in good faith, we'll get through this with everyone alive and satisfied with the result." Larissa and Anica started whispering frantically in their Alphas' ears, expressions of alarm on their faces.

The Kasun family Alpha raised his hand, and Liz motioned to him. He spoke harshly, in a language that seemed to have too many letters in each word. Rabi frowned but didn't respond, waiting for the translation. Larissa blushed and hesitated. The Kasun Alpha poked her with a beefy finger and she finally spoke.

"My Alpha wishes to ask the esteemed negotiator how the Sazi Council dares to presume they may listen to personal conversations between a man and his wife, or a father and his children. He refuses this requirement."

Bet that won't go over well.

Rabi Kuric stood and pulled down on his jacket in a way that reminded Rachel of Captain Picard on *Star Trek: The Next Generation.* Then he disappeared, just like he had in the police station. Gasps went up around the room. He reappeared behind the Kasun Alpha, holding a long, curved knife to the bear's throat. The room went utterly silent, but the scents of fear, amazement, and adrenaline were so strong that about half of the audience started sneezing. A stinging wash of power swept out from the stage, freezing the delegates in place and making Rachel's skin try to crawl off her bones again. She flinched and scratched at her itchy neck as quietly as possible, not wanting to draw anyone's attention.

Kuric pulled back the bear's head by his hair, exposing his bare throat. Despite his West Coast accent, Kuric's words were venomous. "You smiled before your translator finished speaking, Alpha, and you commented on something that was not translated. You understand English. Now you seek to make demands on the *gift* of negotiation that is offered by the Council?"

A hissing sound pulled Rachel's attention away from the pair. Liz Sutton-Kendall had shifted forms. She was a badger, and at least the size of a Great Dane, or maybe a small pony. Long claws clicked on the polished wood of the stage and she hissed again, revealing a row of sharp teeth.

Rabi spoke loudly enough for everyone to hear. "The terms of the negotiations are not subject to your consent or approval. Perhaps I should turn you over to Miss Sutton's tender mercies right now. Negotiation is not the only skill she learned from her legendary grandfather. It would be far simpler and less time-consuming to dispose of your whole family and let the Petrovics take the land."

The whites of the eyes of the bears said everything. The tiger shifter disappeared. His magic released the delegates so

abruptly that they nearly fell out of their chairs. Rachel's skin
stopped itching and she noticed that her arm hurt even less.
Cool. Nothing like random magic for healing.

Kasun rubbed at his throat, probably making sure no blood
had been drawn. Back in human form, Liz adjusted the pink
suit jacket she must have hurriedly put back on and stepped
again to the microphone. "Let me repeat, we will *not* tolerate
sabotage of any kind. Deception is sabotage. Councilman Kuric
just gave the only warning you will get. Does everyone understand the rules?"

Interesting. Though their translators remained silent, the alphas nodded. Both of the bastards could understand English!

Liz noticed and her eyes narrowed just a bit. "Good." Her
voice then took on a sarcastic edge. "And how handy that translators aren't required anymore. It makes things so much easier.
Ladies, could you please sit down?" Dalvin and Tamir placed
an additional chair on either side of the podium and the young
women sat.

"Next on the agenda is housing. Since there are no Sazi-
owned motels nearby and an arctic front is headed this way,
we are asking for volunteers to house the two sloths and our
Wolven and Council partners."

She paused, but no hands were raised. A pinecone could fall
in the forest and everyone would have heard it.

Fred, the postmaster, called out, "They can stay at the
mayor's and police chief's houses. They're empty."

Rachel heard a few comments, like "good idea" and "perfect,"
from the townspeople, but Liz shook her head.

"Unfortunately, that isn't possible. Both homes are still
considered crime scenes." Her tone lightened as she continued,
"Of course, you will be compensated, since the Council had
intended to spend money on room rental. How about five
thousand dollars for each resident who houses a visitor? That's
pretty good money for a week of your time."

Five thousand dollars! With that kind of nest egg, Rachel would be set for months in Spokane. Okay, that would make it worth it to stay for an extra week, as long as she didn't get paired with Larissa. She raised her hand, as did nearly a dozen other people in the Community Center. *Good ol' cash money. Greasing the wheels since God was a baby.*

"Those of you who have volunteered, please stay after the meeting. Last, we need some people who can cook for large groups."

At the door, Claire raised her hand, and Liz tipped her head in acknowledgment. One of the younger Petrovic males said, in accented English, "I am a trained chef. I would offer my skills."

Mustafa Kasun stood in a rush, speaking first in his native language before switching to barely understandable English, "*Ne! Neću dopustit!* I will not allow this!" He pointed a thick finger toward the other sloth. "They have reason to harm us. He could poison us. He likely was the one who drugged and killed the negotiator, Melo."

The Petrovics responded in outrage.

"I would not!"

"*Your* sloth are the killers!"

"How dare you!"

Rachel was not surprised that everyone was speaking English.

Bear shifters jumped from their seats, shouting and spitting at their enemies.

The negotiator raised her hands and her voice: "Everybody calm down!"

Liz and other Council members threw out bursts of magic to hold the visitors in place, but the alphas could be surprised only once. They threw back their own magic, strong enough that they and their families were able to stand up and start across the stage at each other. The inhabitants of Luna Lake, crammed into the single room, were becoming agitated by the scents of aggression being blasted at them on the waves of powerful magic.

Rachel was almost too distracted by her stinging skin to feel Bitty's tap on her hand. But she dragged her attention to her Alpha.

"Use your voice, dear," Bitty said softly. "Tell them to stop."

Shaking her head, Rachel said, "This isn't my fight and I can't imagine they would listen to me, Aunt Bitty. I don't think they'd appreciate me getting involved."

"We all do what we must, when we're needed. Remember?"

An exasperated sound burst out of Rachel's throat. She hated it when Aunt Bitty used her mama's words against her, pulled from her own memories.

Nobody noticed when she stood up. She took a deep breath and let out a screech that rattled the walls.

"Shut up!"

Everyone—*everyone*—froze in place, hands over their ears. In the stillness, Rachel continued quietly: "Could everyone please stop fighting? It's really painful to all of us who aren't alphic." She sat down, but then half stood and added, "Thank you."

The bears on the stage glared and growled, but those few moments had given the Council members the opportunity to burst through the bears' magic. She couldn't tell for sure whether the anger that roiled off the stage was directed at her or at the Council members, who magically forced the delegates back to their chairs.

"Very nice, dear," Bitty said, while a smattering of applause made Rachel's face burn. She looked around to see who was clapping. Her foster parents, Asylin and John Williams, and their daughter Dani. Scott, of course, and S.Q., the falcon

who ran the ice cream shop. Even after her family and friends
sat down, someone was still applauding.

Dalvin.

He was smiling, with just one corner of his mouth curled
up. Her mind flashed back to the park near the house where
she grew up. The boy in her memory wore that same smile,
mingling admiration with sarcasm. She used to punch him in
the arm when he gave her that look.

Liz cleared her throat noisily into the microphone. Dalvin
stopped clapping and turned to the stage, as did the rest of the
audience.

"Not quite what I would have done," the badger shifter
said, "but effective. Thank you . . ."

Rachel didn't want to give her name, but that didn't matter,
not with her alpha right beside her. Bitty said, "Rachel. Rachel
Washington. She's got an amazing voice. Quite the songbird for
an owl."

The cat councilman, Rabi Kuric, nodded and smiled. He was
pretty cute when he smiled. "She is indeed."

Looking straight at Rachel, Liz said, "I'd like to see you after
the meeting, please." Then she addressed the room again.
"Okay, that's it for now. Treat the two families as though they
are guests of your family, but don't discuss the dispute or take
sides. Let us do our jobs. We'll do our best to stay out of your
way. Thank you."

The sound of conversation rose in the hall as people began
making for the door or just milling around.

Bitty said, "Go talk to young Elizabeth, Rachel. I'll see
about having Amber fix that arm for you."

The townspeople who had offered to board the visitors
seemed to be gathering around Tamir; Rachel spotted Scott and
her adoptive dad in the group. "I need to check in over there,"
she told Bitty, pointing. "Do you think the negotiator will mind

if I get a roommate sorted out first? I could really use that money."

Getting to her feet, Bitty said, "I told you . . . I'm happy to give you money until you find work in Spokane. Even enough to live on until you finish college."

Her alpha's offer was very tempting, but work—and what it meant—was important to Rachel. "I know, and I appreciate that. But I'm tired of being bought and paid for. I want to make it on my own."

The old woman sighed and shook her head, smiling. "You go see Miss Elizabeth. I'll find you a housemate. Is there anyone you'd particularly like to have?"

"The translator for the black bears, Anica, seemed nice enough. Weird, but nice."

Bitty nodded and walked toward Tamir while Rachel headed for the stage. When Miss Sutton spotted her, she immediately excused herself from a conversation and came over. The mediator offered her hand for a shake, then drew it back when she realized Rachel was wounded. If she noticed the scent of blood, she was tactful enough not to mention it. She smiled warmly and touched the owl shifter lightly on the shoulder of the uninjured arm.

"That was very impressive . . . Rachel, is it?"

"Yes, ma'am, and thank you. I'm a singer, so I can project well."

"Project?" Liz seemed taken aback. "I see. You don't realize what you just did."

Something more than just screaming loudly? "Um, I guess not."

Brow furrowed, Liz called, "Amber? Rabi? Could you join us?"

The cat councilman nodded, then said something to the Wolven agents around him before following Amber. The agents spread out to surround the two bear sloths, keeping the groups separate and engaged in conversation. Nice divide and conquer!

A minute later, the mediator, the two Council members, and Rachel left the Community Center through the back door. A couple of the black SUVs were parked nearby.

"Amber, if you would be so kind?" Liz said.

A sudden, overwhelming sensation of some kind made Rachel feel like her feathers were being sucked out from inside her. It was similar to what Ahmad had done, but more like a pulling sensation. She staggered but kept moving.

"What's happening? I feel like I can't breathe."

Liz opened the back door of one of the vehicles. "It'll be better once we're inside."

The seat covering was butter-soft black leather, and polished wood panels decorated the armrests. The seats faced each other, like in a limousine. The weird sensation lessened, then passed, as Liz had promised, once Rachel was inside.

"Wow. Nice car."

Amber scooted in beside her. "Let's get a look at that arm while we're talking."

Rachel hissed in pain as the doctor began to unwrap Claire's hasty bandaging job. Most of the blood had dried and the cloth was stuck to her skin.

"Have you ever screeched like that before? I mean, to stop a fight?" Liz's tone indicated that something important had happened, but Rachel had no idea what. The badger shifter's hazel eyes were serious, but not in an angry way. There were no scents in the car, not even of their own animals. It was sort of creepy that Rachel could smell the leather seats and her own pain but nothing else.

She thought about it. "Not like that, no. I mean, well . . . once. Back a few years ago, we had a rogue. One of the wolves went insane and attacked the Williams house. I was living there then, and I screamed when she broke down the barred steel front door. She stopped. Just stopped. Everyone said my screech had startled her long enough for the others to tackle her.

"I'd told Aunt Bitty about that once, when I was the Omega. She liked us to chat while I worked. She isn't really my aunt, you know, but she's sort of an honorary one, and now she's my parliament leader so—" She knew she was rambling, but the others didn't seem to mind. She took a breath and finished: "Anyway, I guess she thought it might work here."

Liz shook her head. "Not startled. Paralyzed. Momentarily paralyzed. At least me." Rachel felt air on her tongue, as her jaw dropped open and she gasped. She'd *paralyzed* everyone?

"Paralyzed," the tiger shifter confirmed.

A tingling sensation in her arm caught Rachel's attention. Amber's hand was hovering over the rips in her flesh, and before her eyes, the muscle began to knit together. She could feel the nerves reconnecting—tiny bursts of pain created flashes of white light in her vision. It made her a little dizzy, but didn't last long. "Whoa. That's freaky."

Amber smiled. "You get used to it. But yeah, it's freaky. As for your screech, it didn't affect me the same way. I just felt a little stiff for a few seconds, but I'm also a healer. The symptoms were likely more acute in those without healing abilities." She pulled her hand away from Rachel's arm. "There you go. The wound was pretty bad, so you'll still feel the nerves reconnecting for a few days and you might have some weakness in that arm for a week or more. But it should be as good as new soon."

Other than dark red, ragged scars, it was as though she'd never been hurt. Rachel moved her arm around, flexing the muscles. She felt a single sharp twinge and that was it other than a low ache, much like the way she'd felt the previous day, after a morning spent packing. "Wow. No wonder everyone sings your praises."

"Speaking of singing, what do you prefer to sing?" Amber asked.

Rachel shrugged. "R and B mostly. Older stuff. I like a lot of '80s stuff, and some of the blues singers from the '20s and '30s are awesome. Crippen, Smith, Waters, Rainey, that sort of thing."

Rabi's fingers were thrumming on his knee. "I get where you're going, Amber. Rachel, have you ever noticed that when you sing, people's moods change?"

"They're called the blues for a reason." She shrugged. "Yeah, I suppose people get more mellow or sad or happy when I sing. That's sort of the point. People are supposed to feel things." She was getting nervous. "Wait. Are you saying I did something wrong? If so, it wasn't intentional. I swear."

Liz waved her hands. "No, no. Just the opposite, in fact. I think you might be a projecting empath—that you can make people feel your mood, change their mood."

She laughed. She couldn't help it. The idea was so ridiculous that it was barely worth disputing. But they didn't live here, probably hadn't even read the reports. "I highly doubt that. If I could have projected my pain and humiliation and anger on the people who inflicted it on me just by singing, everyone in this town would be curled in a fetal ball or throwing a rope over the nearest tree to hang themselves, and I wouldn't wake up screaming most nights."

To say the others in the SUV were taken aback was an understatement. "Wait," Liz said after a few attempts to decide what to say. "Explain what you mean."

Lord, she didn't want to relive it all again. The thought of it made her exhausted and depressed. "Read the reports that the Wolven agent, um, Barry Holden, wrote. He left just as you arrived. Then let me know whether you think I can project shit. If so, I'll help you. But I haven't even been able to help myself. That's why I need to leave Luna Lake."

She looked out the darkened window and spotted Dalvin headed their way. She opened the opposite door. "Look, I'm sorry. I'd like to help, but I really want to go home now. Would that be okay?"

The three of them looked at each other but apparently couldn't think of a reason to keep her there. "Sure, I guess," Liz said. "We'll look over the reports and get back to you. Is your phone number in the file?"

"Yeah, but phones are spotty here. Just come by the apartments. I'm in Apartment 202." Dalvin had nearly reached the SUV, then stopped, probably held at bay by the aversion magic that felt like a vacuum. He cupped his hands to his eyes, like he couldn't see clearly, then turned away and headed back into the Community Center. *Whew.*

Rachel closed the vehicle's door. "If you give me a ride over there now," she said, "then you'll know where to find me if you want me." Anything to get away from Dalvin as fast as possible.

"Sure," Amber said. "I'll drive."

"It's the two-story building over on Third Street. Just two blocks down on the right."

Amber got out of the passenger area and got back into the car, behind the wheel. The source of Rachel's sudden anxiety must have been apparent to the others because Liz asked quietly, "Is there a reason you're avoiding Agent Adway?"

The two powerful predators were watching her in a way that said they would get the truth out of her one way or the other. Was this something worth hiding? She sighed as the car began to move.

"Yes. I grew up with him in Detroit, back when I was human. Everyone there thinks I'm dead, and really, I might as well be. I was an attack victim; my family doesn't know anything about the Sazi, and a bunch of them would think I was evil or possessed if they knew.

"I don't think I could stand my mama having to choose between me and her family. I think she'd pick me. I pray she would. But it's a lot to ask." Tears filled her eyes. "I wish I could undo him seeing me here."

Rabi seemed to relax slightly; Liz sighed and leaned back in her seat.

"Been there," she said. "My family is also human. The Sazi gene skipped a bunch of generations. The man I always thought was my grandfather is actually my great-great-great-grandfather. He's powerful and very long-lived.

"When no shifters were born in several generations, people sort of forgot, except for scary stories told around the campfire. The first time I shifted was during a bad storm. I got caught outside with a tornado coming. I panicked and shifted . . . didn't even remember doing it. I tore apart a bunch of buildings, collapsed the water tower right onto the school!

"Thankfully, Wolven and the Council came and made everyone think the tornado did the damage. Only my parents knew why I really went to live with my grandfather—the rest of the family thought I got a scholarship to graduate school in England." She paused and shook her head, then shrugged.

"All these years later, I still haven't told them. I just can't."

"Me too," Rabi said, nodding. "Even though my family are shifters, they're American. The Iranian part of the family is much more in touch with their 'inner tiger.'" Rachel could almost see the quotes around the phrase.

"It's a whole different world, one that I can't bring home to California. My family are absolute left coast liberals. People killing each other over how a deer was split . . . ? Totally beyond their comprehension. That my sister was an outcast and might be put to death in my grandparents' village because she has a stripe of orange hair when she's in human form? They'd be appalled on Rodeo Drive.

"We'll keep you two apart and figure something out. You should be able to live your life how you want."

Having them be so receptive to her worries lifted a huge

weight off her chest. She thanked them earnestly. The conversation about attack victims had brought something else to mind, so she said, "Miss Sutton?"

The mediator smiled. "Call me Liz. Miss Sutton is my aunt. It makes me feel weird."

"Thanks," Rachel said, then went on. "You said that the war twenty years ago was the cause of the dispute."

Liz nodded.

"Well . . . Anica told me out in the woods that her family had only been shifters for a decade."

"Hmm." Liz's brow dropped and her head tilted. Still no scent, which was unnerving. Liz should have smelled of rich, warm soil—like the community garden when Rachel was growing up—and the inside of a candy store. "Nooo, I don't think so. The Council did a lot of investigation before deciding to become involved. Maybe Anica just meant that *she'd* only been a shifter for a decade."

"Maybe." Rachel wasn't convinced.

The darkened window between the front and rear seats started to roll down and Amber said, "We're coming up on the apartments. Seems like there's some sort of commotion ahead."

CHAPTER 5

How could Rachel have disappeared so quickly? Everyone he'd asked had said she'd left the building with the mediator, but when he went to look for them, they were nowhere to be found. When he'd gone toward the road, he'd felt the effects of an aversion spell near the SUVs. Rachel might have been shielded by that. Whoever had set the spell was damned good; Dalvin hadn't been able to see or hear anything beyond it, couldn't even get close to the vehicle.

"Dalvin!" Alek Siska called from behind him. The new agent was a bit of an odd wolf, Dalvin thought. Very gung-ho, very law and order, but completely untrained. He'd said he was eager to learn, but Dalvin could already tell that he didn't always listen to what he was told.

Maybe Claire would be able to straighten him out. Rumor had it she'd been trained by the Wolven chief himself. If that was true, she ought to be able to bring Siska to heel. The rumor also said he was mated to her, which meant he would probably listen to her.

"What's up?" he said, turning toward the other man.

"Found a room for you." He introduced the tall, pale, slender man beside him, who smelled of owl. "This is Scott Clayton.

He's got two beds and will put you up. Grab your gear and we'll head over."

"Are the delegates settled? How are we setting up guard posts?"

"The Kasun alphas will be staying at my old family home," Alek explained. "It's literally a fort, easy to defend, and when it's locked down, it can keep out just about anything. The Petrovic alphas will be staying across town at the principal's quarters, which is also one of the town's original forts. Both are heavy-duty log structures with steel reinforcements.

"The younger bears are staying with individual townspeople, all in the same apartment complex. I live there and know every entrance and exit and every quirk of the place. It'll be secure by the time we're done."

Impressed by both the content of the report and Alek's delivery, Dalvin nodded. "Great." Trying to sound casual, he asked, "Do you guys know a local girl named Rachel Washington?"

Alek and Scott looked at each other. After a beat, Scott answered hesitantly, "Yeah. Why?"

He shrugged. "She looks like someone I used to know." *Was that offhand enough?*

Apparently not. Alek responded with a touch too much force, and the two men's scents were as suspicious and protective as if they were related to Rachel. "We've known her since grade school, and since this is the first time you've been here, I'm thinking you're mistaken."

So much for that approach. They were lying to protect her. He tried to wave it off. "Yeah, you're probably right." Dalvin smiled, doing his best to look satisfied. After a few moments of slightly awkward silence, he said, "Let me grab my duffel. After we drop it off at Scott's place, we can locate Tamir and find out what our watch schedule is."

Once again, the two locals looked at each other before commenting, making him wonder if they were part of a bound pack that mind-spoke. Alek finally responded, "Sure. Let's do that."

The aversion spell was gone from the area around the SUVs and so was one of the vehicles. Dalvin retrieved his duffel, weapons cases, camera case, and a stack of documents about the delegates from the SUV closest to the Community Center. Neither the Wolven agent nor Dalvin's new host offered to help; they watched with amusement in their eyes and citrus in their scent as he juggled everything. When he had the load as balanced as possible, the other two set a blistering pace toward the apartments. Determined not to let their attitude bother him, Dalvin followed as best as he could.

In less than a minute he'd nearly tripped over the camera case half a dozen times. Alek and Scott burst out laughing and stopped walking, then strolled back and relieved him of some of his baggage, leaving him with just the duffel and his paperwork. Dalvin laughed too, and held up his fist. Alek bumped it.

"I thought I was supposed to razz you as the newbie," Dalvin said.

"Oh, I'm sure that's still coming," Alek replied with a chuckle. "I had to get my licks in while I could."

Their amusement was short-lived as screams and growls erupted from the buildings not far ahead—one of which, Dalvin assumed, was their destination.

All three men dropped what they were holding and ran toward the commotion until a crowd of people blocked the way. Dalvin pushed through the mass of bodies, anticipating the worst. He discovered Larissa locked in a hair-pulling match with the younger Petrovic daughter, Anica. Clumps of thick brown hair littered the ground and mud splattered Larissa's white leggings. Some of the splotches were shoe shaped—Anica had apparently been kicking her.

"Let go of me, you Milošević lap pet!" Larissa roared. People covered their ears and birds scattered from trees into the darkening sky. The cold north wind carried the scents of anger and fear, but it was hard to sort out who was feeling what.

Anica threw the taller woman to the ground and pounced on her, slamming her head into the dirt. "Unwashed raja! How *dare* you spread lies about me!"

Taller and with more mass, Larissa rolled the Serbian bear onto her back and started to pound *her* head against the ground.

Dalvin fought not to sneeze from the emotional turmoil bombarding his nose. He grabbed Larissa and pulled her off Anica. "Ladies! Stop fighting!"

Anica jumped to her feet with the ease of a trained gymnast. Launching herself at the now restrained Bosnian, she got her hands around Larissa's slender throat and started to choke her. Dalvin twisted his prisoner away, but not before Anica spat on the taller woman and snarled, "Where is the nearest willow tree? This stable girl needs to be put in her place."

Larissa let out a roar of rage; the raspberries and honey of her natural scent took on a sickly-sweet, burned odor. The sound shook the trees, sending even more birds into flight, and made Dalvin's head hurt and his arms vibrate.

Anica dove in again, landing a solid punch to Larissa's ribs. Larissa responded by kicking out sideways, catching her opponent in the stomach and sending her flying backward. Anica landed hard, then sprang to her feet and came after Larissa again.

Trying to protect Larissa, Dalvin kept twisting and turning her away from Anica's assault, which meant that every other punch or kick hit him instead.

Where were Alek and the rest of the Wolven agents? Why was nobody helping him?

Someone finally pushed through the crowd and grabbed Anica by the shoulders, and somehow Dalvin was not surprised that his rescuer was Rachel.

"Anica, knock it off!" she hissed. "This isn't going to help you or your family."

She pulled the black bear away, easily holding Anica in place. Dalvin realized that though Rachel was slight, the muscles of her shoulders and arms were solid as tree limbs. Someone must have healed her arm, because he saw brand-new, shiny scar tissue all down one biceps.

Once the women were several feet apart and no longer actively trying to attack each other, Dalvin took a moment to catch his breath, more tired than he'd expected.

"What is *wrong* with you two?" he said angrily. "Who started this?"

He wasn't surprised when the women responded simultaneously, "She did!"

The strong odor of bear musk hit his nose like a wall as the two alpha males and their mates burst through the crowd.

"What is happening here?" Zarko Petrovic put his hands on his wide hips and glowered at the young women. Neither seemed impressed. "Anica, answer me!"

The dark-haired Serbian took a deep breath and let it out slowly. Dalvin saw her muscles relax slightly in Rachel's grip, but Rachel didn't relax, and he was glad. Realizing she wasn't going to be freed, Anica settled for raising her chin proudly.

"The Bosnian delegate said even if we somehow managed to bribe the mediator into giving us a meter or two of land, the ground would be forever barren from the blood of all the innocents we killed. Then she called us lap pets of General Milošević."

He'd heard the last part but not the rest. Ouch.

Petrovic let out a slow, rumbling growl that made the nearby townspeople back up slowly. He stared hard at Larissa, then turned to the head of the Kasun family. "How do you plan to discipline your omega for this insult?"

The elder Kasun was chuckling lightly, though his scent said he was furious. Who was he angry at? Dalvin wondered. "It was a good curse. Clever and inspired. What did your omega say in return?"

Larissa tried to lunge forward, but Dalvin held her firmly. "She called me a blackhead! I am *not*! I am purebred no matter the color of my skin! Nor am I an unwashed raja from some small village. I live in a city! If you can find a willow tree in this forest, lead me to it. We'll see who is hanging from it in the morning!"

Petrovic stifled an amused snort. "It seems that our omegas do not care for each other."

Dalvin was trying to figure out what he was missing in the conversation—what was making the alphas smile? Larissa said something that froze the expressions on the faces of both males. "*Krvne osvete!*"

Too many scents burst into the air to sort out: rage, hate, fear, joy. Joy concerned him, and he tried to trace its source. Someone was happy that the others were angry, and that might signal a problem. But he couldn't figure out who it was. The townspeople all looked worried, and the bears were trying to show no emotion, as if they were sitting at a table at the World Poker Tournament.

Councilman Kuric stepped out of the crowd, his hands in the air. "Stop. Before anyone says another word, just *stop*."

The doctor and the mediator were right behind him. Liz nodded to Dalvin and Rachel, and they released the two omegas. Amber began to skillfully separate the families, using both words and magic. Rabi went to talk to Mustafa's sloth, edging them toward one of the black SUVs now parked nearby. They hadn't been there a moment ago, Dalvin realized. Maybe that's why there had been a delay in helping him—no one was around.

Liz addressed the watching crowd. "I would appreciate it if you could return to your business. I know this is fascinating, but these families need to be alone right now." She lightly shooed people away with her hands.

Despite a little grumbling, the spectators—about twenty residents of Luna Lake—slowly began to disperse. Dalvin noticed Scott walking away with his bags and headed after him, but Tamir grabbed his arm. Where the hell had the supervising Wolven agent been when the fight had broken out?

The older bear hissed in his ear. "Where do you think you're going? Didn't you hear Delegate Grebo? She just declared a blood feud!"

"Sorry. I don't speak Bosnian. Besides, what does that even mean? Aren't they already in a blood feud?"

Councilman Kuric answered Dalvin's question. "It's true that the sloths are in a political dispute, but a blood feud is personal in their culture—a battle between two people. Normally, a fight between omegas is to first blood on the full moon. But—"

It was easy for Dalvin to finish the thought. "But since the sloths are already practically at war, what's to stop one of the Alphas from adding a little oomph to their omega when they help her shift?"

Tamir nodded. "So first blood becomes a mortal wound. If one of the bears dies, there will never be peace. S'blood. So what do we do about it?"

Claire trotted over to report. "The sloths are in separate cars, headed to different houses. We've checked both buildings, and there's nothing more dangerous than a feather duster in either one, so unless they want to pillow-fight to the death, they should be fine for a few minutes.

"But we have to change our plans. No way we can spread them out among the townspeople—we'd have to secure too many places in light of this new threat. The Kasuns will all stay together, at the Williams house. All the Petrovics except Anica can stay with the principal. Turns out Alpha Petrovic has a problem with Principal Burrows being unmarried, even with the rest of the family on-site. Liz is looking for a suitable location for her.

"We'll have to bring in cooked food, since we took all the dishes, glassware, utensils, and cookware. Amber will stay full time with one group and Alek with the other. What happens next?"

Stinking of angry cat, Rabi let out a harsh breath. "Both sloths are insisting on blood combat and saying the peace talks have to be postponed until after the full moon. Between now and then, the sloths will prepare their omegas for battle. They want ceremonies and banquets, and meetings to set out the rules, just like in their home villages. It's a nightmare."

Liz Sutton-Kendall walked up to the group, with Rachel at her side. Dalvin couldn't help staring at Rachel until she finally glanced his way, but then her gaze immediately dropped to the ground. Why? Was she angry with him?

"I might have a solution," Liz said. "Tell them what you told me, Rachel."

Rachel shrugged and tucked her fingers into her pants pockets, looking nervous at the sudden attention. "I suggested they have Larissa and Anica do an Ascension challenge. It's how we settle disputes in Luna Lake."

The cloying scent of curiosity filled the air. Kuric asked the obvious question: "Ascension? What's that?"

The owl shifter let out a sigh. She smelled both angry and sad—such an odd combination that Dalvin wondered what, exactly, this challenge was. "It's sort of a long story. Can we maybe go to the town hall? I think it will be easier to explain if I can show you the maps and the rule book. And it would be helpful to have Alek there. He's the local expert on the rules, since the police chief's dead."

Councilman Kuric said, "Agent Adway, please ask Alek Siska to join us at the town hall."

Dalvin nodded. "Sure, but I don't know the town layout well yet. Where is the house where he's staying?"

Claire interjected. "I know where he is. I'll get him."

Tamir nodded. "I'll go with you and we'll both take his place with the sloth. Claire, I want you to show me how your empathic talent works. Dalvin, you guard the councilman and the mediator. I don't want anyone important walking around alone right now."

With an exchange of nods, the group broke up, Claire and Tamir heading for the Petrovics while the others made their way to the town hall, Rachel in the lead. Dalvin trailed the others so he could keep an eye on everyone and their surroundings. He couldn't imagine who would want to attack the peace conference, but he'd thought that last time too. He just hoped the killer of the last mediator was an outside threat and not someone they'd brought with them.

It was a short walk to the town hall. The door wasn't locked, which made Dalvin extra cautious. He kept the others back while he used ears and magic to be certain there were no threats inside. Once he was certain all was clear, he waved them in, then stood guard at the door. No way was he going to let Tamir find any more fault in his performance and no way was he going to allow Rachel to get hurt. Not when he'd just found her.

Rachel seemed to notice that something about Dalvin had changed. She stared at him as she slowly walked past. He couldn't tell what she was thinking by her expression or scent, which were primarily puzzled. He dipped his chin slightly and lightly put a hand on her shoulder . She jumped like his touch had burned—though that wasn't how he would describe the sensation. Tingled was closer, like touching a live wire.

He stared at his hand for a second, then focused on his work. Rachel pushed open a swinging wooden gate perched between two heavy wooden tables. The room's layout sort of reminded

Dalvin of an old-fashioned courtroom, where the attorneys sat on one side of the gate and the gallery sat on the other.

Pointing to the large map hanging on the far wall, Rachel said, "This is a topo map of the whole forest around Luna Lake . . . well, at least the part that's state land. Some of the land is owned by the Colville Confederated Native American tribes or by private companies. We hunt on our own land, but the racecourse covers territory we don't own. Since we race in animal form, nobody notices, or if they do, they don't care."

Liz traced a finger along several colored lines on the paper. "What do you mean, racecourse?"

"I was just a kid when the town was settled," Rachel said, taking a fat binder from under the counter. "It began as one of the refugee camps after the snake attacks. Everyone was scared, and I guess there were a lot of fights among the different species. They tended to keep the kids out of them, so I don't know the details."

Dalvin locked the door—Alek could knock when he arrived—and started walking the perimeter of the room, checking for listening devices or boobytraps.

"Of course," Councilman Kuric said with a nod. "The whole idea of the camps was to protect the children. Everyone was really careful to keep them safe."

The scents of anger and sadness filled the air. Dalvin glanced over in time to see Rachel's eyes narrow briefly.

"Yeah, sure," she said. He heard disbelief in her voice and wondered if the others noticed. "So, the wolves fought with the cats, and the cats fought with the birds, and the bears, except for the principal of the school, just left town because they couldn't deal. The early fights were apparently pretty bloody, so the town Council got the bright idea of using the Ascension course to relieve stress. It's like a track and field competition, held every full moon, and focusing on Sazi abilities. At least it started out that way."

"Oh?" the mediator asked. "So it evolved?"

Rachel dropped the binder on the table with a heavy thud, which made everyone look at her. "You could say that. But more *devolved*. It became a way to pick the Omega of the town. All the individual packs or prides or parliaments had their own Omega, but who was the lowest of the low? Which of the competitors would be the ones to ascend"—she added air quotes to highlight the word—"to become respected citizens, versus being the town custodian. That's a lovely word, 'custodian' . . . unless it's shorthand for slave and pariah, someone to be looked down on and kicked."

Her eyes flashed, angry and hurt. Dalvin had seen that look before, more than once. He remembered when they were eight and Rachel had partnered with another classmate for the science fair. They'd won, but there was only *one* blue ribbon, and it went to the pretty redheaded girl, the one who had just sat on Rachel's bed and watched the work being done. Her mother had offered to go down to the school and ream the principal a new one, because funnily enough, there were two ribbons each for second and third place. But Rachel had just shaken her head and given her mom that same look.

A thought made him suddenly sick to his stomach.

"You were *the* Omega," he said softly, somehow standing beside her though he didn't remember crossing the distance. As his words sank in with the others, their shoulders drooped and the scents of sorrow and anger filled the small room.

Both Sutton and Kuric opened their mouths, then closed them without saying anything. There really was nothing to say.

Rachel's smile was bitter. "That's me. On and off for the last five years. So I know how the process works to the nth degree. Trust me when I say I wouldn't normally recommend it to anyone. But it is a good test of skills, and because Anica and Larissa are the same species, you could use one course and really make them work for a win. The cat course—that's the green line—

should work. There are climbing and jumping challenges combined with tracking and food-hunting events that a bear would be good at. Plus, everything is timed, so they're racing the clock as much as their opponent."

Councilman Kuric pointed to the map. "So the other colored lines . . . the yellow, white, and blue, are for different species?"

Rachel nodded and crossed her arms over her bosom. Odd that Dalvin hadn't really noticed that part of her body until this moment. But . . . wow. "Yellow for birds, blue for wolves, green for cats, and the white for mixed species."

Brow furrowed, Liz tipped her head and stared at the map like it was going to talk. "How could you possibly put a wolf and a raptor on the same course and have it be fair? The bird has a straight shot. The wolf could never win."

A snort was the answer. "Sure it can. There's an elevation restriction. Birds can only fly at a certain height—right where all the branches are. A tracking unit is attached to a talon and you get a little shock when you fly too high. You get three freebies because of updrafts you might not be able to control, just like the wolves and cats get a couple of freebies for jumping unknown obstacles, like dead trees that fell after the final practice. But the whole goal is to test your skill, so three strikes and you lose."

Rachel patted the top of the binder. "Everything is in here. Three hundred pages of rules on course design, how to train, and penalties for every possible cheat. The whole shebang." She pushed the book toward the two Council members. "Two of the original town founders were lawyers. There are releases to sign and binding blood oaths for the alphas to swear to that the Council could enforce."

Rabi Kuric opened the binder and quickly flipped through the pages. "And you've had to race under these rules before? They seem pretty complicated."

Rachel nodded. "Every month for the past five years, since I turned seventeen, and occasionally before that. Even teens can understand the rules. They're not that hard. Up until five years ago, Scott Clayton was the Omega. Then he got bigger and faster than me, and I've been on the bottom ever since. Until last month."

The mediator leaned back against the counter. "What happened last month? Did someone new turn?"

"Sort of," Rachel acknowledged. "That's when Claire Evans arrived. How she lost the race is a long story, but right now, she's the Omega. I probably would be stuck with it again if I planned to stay around, but I'm not. I'm going to move as soon as this 'peace conference' of yours is over. Like I said, I'm starting college in Spokane."

Dalvin smiled—that sounded like the Rachel he remembered too—but stopped when the doorknob rattled. He sprinted through the gate and sniffed carefully near the door jamb before asking, "Alek?"

"Yeah." His voice was low. "I'm clear."

Dalvin opened the door and let him in, then locked it again.

"What's up? Claire said you needed me over here, something about a rule book?" He walked through the gate and Dalvin followed.

"I suggested that Anica and the bitch be—" Rachel blushed and amended with a cough. "I mean Larissa, compete on the Ascension course instead of duking it out in the street."

Alek looked shocked, then surprised, then started grinning. "That's *brilliant*. That would solve so many problems."

Rabi Kuric shook his head. "I just don't see how the alphas would be able to read and agree to all these rules before tomorrow."

The young wolf shifter walked over to the table, shaking his head. "No, no. It's not that bad. Each rule is on a separate page and some are only a few lines long. We did it that way so if a rule changed, we'd only need to reprint and replace a single page instead of having to reformat and print the whole thing."

Alek shifted the binder so the others could see. Dalvin found himself once again standing right next to Rachel. She didn't move and didn't seem freaked out, so he stayed put. "See? There are revision dates at the bottom of each sheet. Sometimes a rule would be challenged for fairness and would get changed out."

"Fairness . . . pfft." Rachel's mutter was tight and angry.

Alek noticed. "Rach, give people a chance now that their heads aren't being messed up by the mayor. They might be just as appalled as I was when I found out. I just didn't know."

She let out a slow sigh. "That would be nice," she said, then shook her head. "Let's get the bear peace or war or whatever over with, and then we'll see."

Dalvin realized that Councilman Kuric had slipped away. Almost panicked, he looked around the room and breathed a sigh of relief when he spotted him seated at a computer in the corner. That ghosting thing was going to make him crazy.

Alek tapped his finger against his chin, staring at the race-course on the wall. "Someone is going to have to work with the competitors, walk them through the course. They're omegas, so we don't know how much of their conscious minds they'll retain after they turn; that's always hit or miss.

"It might be a good idea to have their alphas turn them today so we can figure that out. In bear form, they might not be multilingual, which means Tamir might have to show them the course because he speaks their native tongue. We had a falcon here a long time ago who only spoke German when he shifted.

"That means I'll have to walk Tamir through the course first."

Dalvin was impressed by Alek's logical thinking. Maybe the wolf would work out after all. "I'd be happy to take Larissa through the course."

Rachel and Alek laughed simultaneously, sounding both amused and sarcastic. "I'll just bet you would," Alek said, "but there are plenty of bunnies in the woods already."

Liz stifled a snort. Alek let out a whoop and gave Rachel a high five.

Crossing his arms over his chest was automatic. "Just what is *that* supposed to mean?"

The cat councilman called out from the corner. "It means your attraction to the Bosnian delegate is so obvious that even strangers have noticed, Agent Adway. Your judgment may be a little compromised." He leaned back in his chair and stared at the group for a long moment. "No, I think Rachel is going to show you the course and then you will show Anica."

The mediator frowned. "Rabi, we just got done talking about who would work with who."

He held up a hand. "Yes, I know. But there's something you need to see." He waved her over. She bent to look at the monitor while he clicked the mouse. "Read that."

She stared at the screen, then stood up abruptly. "Oh! I see. Right, well, that changes everything." She pulled her phone from her pocket and tapped the screen, then said, "Rachel, review the rules with Anica tonight. She and Claire will both be staying with you. Tomorrow, you'll train Dalvin on the course."

Rachel's eyes widened. "What the hell?! I just got done telling you I can't still be here when the moon is full."

"Please, Rachel. Trust us on this. It'll be fine. Then, if you want, you can leave town as you planned and the Council will cover your schooling . . . as reparations. You have my word and Rabi's, and the Council has agreed to back our decisions here, so nobody can interfere."

Her shoulders dropped and her mouth opened, face slack with astonishment. Her eyes were incredibly bright, golden and brown and a dozen other shades that made Dalvin want to never look away. Her voice and scent were almost suspicious when she said, "You'll pay my tuition? A full ride, with books and everything?"

The mediator nodded, and Kuric said, "Yes, if that's still your choice. You might have other opportunities to consider once this is over."

Dalvin wondered mightily what they had been looking at on screen and what Rachel had already discussed with them. Four years of school was a lot of reparation for being the Omega here for a few years. No, there was something else going on, and he was determined to find out what.

He turned to Rachel, and his heart dropped when she seemed to steel herself for their conversation. He spoke as pleasantly as possible. "Okay, then, when do you want to meet to go over the course?"

She shrugged. "In the morning, I guess".

Alek picked up the binder. "I'll make a few copies of this. We can deliver it to the sloth alphas to read overnight." He looked at the Council members, who were still at the computer. "Are we asking them if they to do this, or telling them they have to?"

Rabi stood up and tugged his shirt down again. "Telling them. This is a good solution. It'll delay the talks by a day, but only a day. And nobody gets hurt."

Rachel let out a small noise, somewhere between a hoot and a raspberry. "I wouldn't count those particular chickens just yet. The eggs are barely in the basket."

CHAPTER 6

He was staring at her again. It was unnerving as hell. She should just walk out and go lock herself in her apartment. But no. It was time to be a grown-up.

A full ride. Four years of college were hers if she could just get through the next few days. But could Liz and Rabi be trusted to keep their promise? She hadn't had good luck with authority figures, but Alek had heard their promise too. The one thing about him that nobody could dispute: Alek was honest. Annoyingly honest. Just to be safe, she turned to him. "You got my back on this, right, bro?"

He nodded and touched her arm. "Always." He checked his watch. "You better get moving. You have to get Anica settled in, and Mom is expecting you at the house to help with Darrell and Kristy tonight."

"Oh, shoot. I forgot all about that!" She really had. What would her adoptive mother have done if she'd made it out of town this morning? Sure, at some point they were going to have to get used to her not being here, and Darrell and Kristy were doing a ton better now that the mayor was dead. But they weren't completely well yet, and Tammy also was still recovering from her brief time as a rogue.

Rachel had been spending every other night at the Williams house so Asylin could get some sleep. The kids would wake up from nightmares, needing someone to crawl into bed with them and hold them until they fell back to sleep. She wasn't going to be able to do that tonight, not if she had to explain Ascension to Anica, but she should explain in person and see if she could help in some other way.

"Thanks for the reminder. Mom would have had my head."

Speaking of heads, Dalvin was suddenly looking at her like she'd grown a second one. The confused anger in his eyes made her uncomfortable.

"I'll go with you," Alek said. "I need to check on the house-guests there anyway and make sure everybody is going to be civil to the family, since the Williamses are still living there." He turned to Dalvin. "Why don't you come with us to the apartments? Scott took your bags over to his place when the fight was broken up, so you can get unpacked. Once I check in with Amber, I'll let you know how the schedule is going to work."

Scott's place? Goddamn it! Dalvin was going to be right down the hall from her! Well, he had to sleep somewhere, and there weren't many options. Most of the residents lived farther out, at the fringes of the land the pack owned, and obviously, as a Wolven agent, Dalvin had to stay in town.

Hoping for a little alone time, she smiled broadly. "Nah, you two go on ahead. I'll walk over and help Mom with the kids. Alek, could you see if Anica's at my place yet and tell her I'll be back soon?" Without waiting for a reply, she headed for the door, then hesitated. She looked at the two Council members. "Is it okay to go? I've got family stuff."

Liz nodded. "Sure. Be back here at eight tomorrow morning and we'll go over what we've decided."

The blue sky had never looked so good. There was a bite in the air that was as crisp as apples. She walked fast, hoping nobody would be able to follow her.

"Running away again?" Dalvin said behind her. "Aren't you tired of that yet?"

Rachel stopped. The rebuke, the sadness and anger, filled the air like a toxic cloud, filled her lungs, suffocating her. Running wasn't her usual style, and yet, with Dalvin, she kept doing it. No more, she decided.

She turned and faced him, staying poised on the balls of her feet, ready for whatever came next. "I don't run. Never have, never will." He looked taken aback, unsure of what to say. That was probably best. Go on offense. "You have something to say to me, boy? Say it."

He reared back like she'd hit him. "Baby, I ain't your boy. Not after all this time."

She shrugged one shoulder. "Well, I ain't your baby either."

He bared teeth while his fingers thrummed, staccato, on his pants. Oh, he was pissed now.

"That's it," he said, his voice rising. "I've held my tongue since yesterday, trying to figure out why you're living here. I wondered if you forgot where you came from or were too traumatized. But y'know what? I don't give a shit anymore. I don't care *why* you're here. All I want to know is this: How *dare* you call another woman your mama? How fucking *dare* you!

"Ten years, your mother's been waiting back in Detroit, worrying, going gray over your sorry ass. She's put flowers on that same street corner every year on the anniversary of the day you disappeared; she and your pop have spent more than their mortgage on investigators, looking for some clue, *any* clue, to what happened." He threw up both hands, and she was glad she was far enough away that she couldn't smell his emotions.

"And here you are, safe and healthy, fine and dandy, going over to your *mom's* house to *help with the kids.*" He closed the distance between them so fast she didn't even see him move, grown-up, muscled anger now right in her face. "What. The. Fuck, Rachel?"

Her heart was beating like a trip-hammer, but not from fear. "*What the fuck?* You think I'm here because I *want* to be? You think a street kid from Detroit wants to be stuck in the fucking wilderness? Away from my family, my friends, everything I ever loved? Did it occur to you that I might be here to *protect* my family? I'm an owl, Dalvin. Not a big, powerful alpha owl like you—I'm a tiny, unpredictable three-day owl who has no say over when she shifts or what she does when she's shifted. I eat fucking *mice* and *bunnies*, Dalvin.

"Do you ever hunt down little animals because you can't stop yourself? Have you ever woken up a hundred feet up in a tree, on a branch, buck-ass naked, unable to remember how you got there, covered in your own nasty-smelling vomit that's filled with the bones of creatures you apparently ate the night before? Huh? Or do you get to change whenever you want, eat whatever food you want, and remember what human words mean even when you're wearing feathers?

"Is that what you want my mama to know about? To see?" She was screaming at him now, right in his face, tears flowing down her cheeks. "You want her to fear for her life every full moon, when a three-day owl the size of a fucking condor appears in her house? Or to have to worry about me being in the same house as the nieces and nephews I probably have by now, who would all smell to me like *food*?

"You want her to have to keep this all secret from the whole family and lie to Auntie Krystal about why the house smells like a zoo because the stink never comes out, and why all the little dogs in the neighborhood are missing?" The words tumbled over each other, coming out as quick as she could catch her next breath. "Yeah, Mrs. Williams took me in after the attack. And yeah, I was traumatized, all right. Maybe you were too. I don't know how you got changed—but you didn't ask me how I got turned either.

"And yeah, I call Asylin Mom because she's taken care of me

for the better part of a decade and I owe her my sanity. But she will never be Mama, and she knows that. So don't you dare tell me I don't care about my mama, Dalvin Adway. I'd rather she keep looking for the child she lost than find the one those bastard snakes turned me into."

He stared at her in silence for a long moment; she met his gaze steadily. Then, still without a word, he turned and walked away, past the crowd that had gathered. She hadn't even noticed the audience until now. She was surprised to see that more than a few of the bystanders were crying.

Now that her own tears had started, she couldn't seem to make them stop. Unable to move, she just stood there and cried as townspeople slowly closed in around her, hugging her. Mary and Claude, Scott, Bitty, S.Q., and Claire. Even Paula from the diner, who hated Claire because she stole Alek away, stood side by side with the Wolven agent and offered comfort, shutting out the intruder who had made her cry. Hell, maybe they had changed.

Rachel hadn't cried during her time in the caves or in the terrifying moments after the rescue. She'd never shed a tear during the loneliest times after she'd been brought to Luna Lake on a bus filled with other frightened kids. Not even the horrible nights in the basement of the police station, when the police chief abused her, humiliated her, posed her and took pictures, made her cry.

She was strong, but she'd finally had too much. So the tears flowed. She barely noticed the gentle pats on her arm, the offers of tissues from the people around her. She wept until there were no more tears. Until she was empty.

The sun had nearly set by the time she was able to start toward the Williams house. Her eyes hurt and it was hard to breathe through her nose. But she was done crying.

Rachel wasn't surprised that the house was barely in view when the front door opened and Asylin Williams came out to wrap arms around her. News traveled fast in a town this size even on a slow day. A full-fledged meltdown would burn up the phone lines.

And though Rachel thought she was done crying, tears fell again when Asylin said, "I am so proud of you, girl. You're still alive. You still have your soul."

She hugged the dark-skinned woman like she desperately wanted to hug her own mama.

Asylin led her inside, an arm around her shoulder. Even the guests seemed to have heard about her screaming match with Dalvin. Iva Kasun, the alpha female of the family, came out of the living room to pat her on the arm as Asylin and Rachel headed toward the kitchen.

"Poor little owl. Is true what they say, ignorance is peace. Sometimes, those who don't know Sazi exist, they are the lucky ones."

Asylin shooed everyone away once Rachel was seated in the kitchen. The wide room had always reminded her of the one at her Gramma Bertha's place, a big, old, rambling house just a few blocks down from her own, much smaller home in Detroit. Was Gramma Bertha still alive? There were so many things she wanted to ask Dalvin, yet so much she feared knowing.

"Does he really think I don't already feel guilty because my family doesn't know what happened to me?" She didn't expect an answer, but Asylin sat down and took Rachel's hand in hers before responding.

"He's got to be confused. It must have been pretty big shock to see you here. I think you said the right things. He'll get it."

"You know what I told him?" She figured that Asylin would have heard about the fight but not what was specifically said.

She laughed lightly. "Honey, the whole town knows. Every word. You weren't exactly quiet."

Rachel dropped her head onto her folded arms. "God. Why didn't anyone stop me before I made a complete ass of myself?"

Asylin began to gently stroke her hair, which helped a little. At least she didn't feel like crying anymore. Instead, she just wanted to crawl under a rock.

"You didn't make a fool of yourself," her surrogate mother said. "You spoke a great truth. No matter how uncomfortable, it's a truth we all have to live with. Now, your dad and I made sure nobody outside of the general area heard it. We kept the sound from reaching any human passersby, but you've needed to get that out of your system for a long, long time. It's been like a piece of shrapnel embedded in your heart for ten years. You needed to say it and he needed to hear it."

"And now he hates me and will probably go back and tell my family I'm dead."

Asylin sighed. "He might, at that. Is that what you want? For your mama's pain to have closure?"

Closure.

Hearing that her mom still put flowers on the street corner and that they went into debt searching for her . . . that made thinking about her family worse somehow. She'd always thought she was protecting them by not contacting them, but maybe she wasn't.

"You're a mom. What would you want?"

The older woman leaned back in her chair and let out a slow breath. She ran slender fingers through her shoulder-length, straight black hair, tugging at the ends like she always did when she was thinking hard. Her scent was difficult to sort out, sadness blended with determination and the warm cookie spices of caring, which Rachel was thankful for. "Sweetie, I don't really know. I've had a child go missing and I've had a child die.

"They're different pains. I suppose, if I had to pick, it would be knowing the child was dead. I could at least then imagine that he or she was at peace, not in pain anymore. When children are missing, not knowing what they're going through is very, very hard. But the greatest joy I've ever experienced was when Darrell and Kristy were found. I can tell you—" She shook her head, her eyes shut and a beautiful smile on her face. "Mmm, mmm, oh my. I felt like I'd won the mega-millions lottery and the Nobel Prize that night. I wouldn't have cared that they were owls, snakes, or demons from Hades. Not that night."

But that was the problem, right there. Rachel felt her fingers tapping on the table. "But what about in the morning, or a month later? That's what I'm afraid of. That I'll raise her hopes, and my papa's, only to confront them with the reality of living with a demon." There was a pain deep in her chest when she spoke that *great truth* Asylin had referred to.

Asylin leaned forward, her breath smelling of mint over raw squirrel meat . . . which smelled good, while a decade ago it would have horrified her. Another stab in the chest. "That's the question, isn't it? My little babies have always been owls or cats or wolves. And John and I have always been Sazi. It's not a surprise to us. This is our reality. But humans? Well—" She clucked her tongue. "If everyone could accept the Sazi, we wouldn't have to hide.

"But nowadays, race wars are on the front page of every paper, religious battles on the nightly news. Even people who want to love folks of their own gender aren't accepted. *Shape-shifters?* I don't know that I want us competing for space on *Good Morning America* or being talked about in congressional subcommittees."

The owl shifter shook her head again. "This is *your* family we're talking about. You know them far better than I ever could. It's your decision. I wish I could make it for you—I do, because that's a mother's job, to make hard decisions for her children when they don't have the mental or emotional tools. But you're not a youngster anymore. You *have* the tools.

"To me, it sounded very much like you'd made a choice

when you were talking to that young man. Whether he accepts it . . . ?" She held out her hands and shrugged one shoulder. "Well, that we don't know."

"What if he does, Asylin? Tell them, I mean. Even if I don't want him to."

That made the older woman let out a snort and smell of hot metal determination. Again, a decade ago, smelling emotions? Telling her mama that she could smell anger or fear would have gotten her a glare and an admonishment to *stop being foolish, child.*

"Oh, believe you me, he'll be reminded by the Council members that he may not endanger the Sazi, and he'll be reminded that the rights of an attack victim are sacred. I don't know these two particular Council members, but I have no doubt they'll be watching him closely after that little scene and will likely talk to him about his duty as a Wolven agent. I don't think they'll let him tell if you don't want your family to know."

"I have to think about it. I just don't know." Rachel straightened up and deliberately changed the subject. "Until I decide, what do you need help with around here? How are Darrell and Kristy? And Tammy?"

Asylin winked. "Why don't we go see?" She stood up and crooked her finger for Rachel to follow, then put her finger to her lips. Rachel tiptoed behind her down the back hallway that went under the stairwell. She could hear screeching and laughter coming from not far ahead. Asylin opened the door to the great room just a crack, so they could peek in.

The two younger Williams children were seated cross-legged on the couch, each holding a video game controller. An adult cougar shifter, Tammy, her hair now a brilliant Jell-O green, was in a nearby chair, also gripping a controller. All three were intently watching the television screen, where three brightly colored Mario Karts were racing around a track.

"Ooh, no fair, Darrell!" Kristy complained, hitting him with her free hand. "You can't push people into the wall."

"No problem, little sis," Tammy shouted gleefully. "Got your back!" Then it was Darrell who let out a groan as Tammy's car sideswiped him, throwing him into the tires. Kristy cheered as her vehicle passed the spun-out cart.

"Ah, man! I was winning!" Darrell complained in a slight whine.

The smile on Asylin's face as her children played made Rachel smile too. She tapped Asylin on the arm and they retreated before the kids caught them watching. Back in the kitchen, Asylin let out a contented sigh. "They all slept through the night. First time in a month. I pray it happens again. Children are so resilient. I can't thank Claire or you enough for all your help!"

It was enough to make Rachel blush all the way up to her forehead. "Oh, I didn't do anything."

Asylin smelled suddenly of surprise and disbelief. "You did too! All the nights you sang to them, kept them calm? I call that doing something. Sweetie, that beautiful voice of yours tamed the savage beast right out of Tammy and let the others sleep in peace."

Rachel didn't know how to respond to that, so she moved on. "So you think no more nightmares for Darrell or Kristy?" Darrell had been trapped in a waking nightmare for days, silently screaming and trying to run from an attacker that had been in his own head. Kristy had been nearly catatonic when they'd rescued her. To see the three of them, playing games like before anything happened . . . well, it was a blessing.

Asylin shrugged one shoulder. "Oh, there will still be nightmares. Of course there will be. But they'll fade over time. Like yours did, and Claire's. Once the bad guys are dead, they're just memories. I feel more sorry for the kids whose families don't remember them at all. That has to be hard for everyone. I don't know what to do to help."

"I heard about that—the Havens family?"

"Poor boy comes back from captivity to discover his family doesn't think he ever existed. I would like to have skinned Van Monk alive for that. His mental control made them throw away every picture of that child before he wiped Sammy right out of his parents' and siblings' memories . . . just so nobody would know to come looking for the boy. Three yearbook photos are all that's left. Makes me furious every time I think about it!"

"I had no idea Monk was that powerful. It never even occurred to me."

"Well, he wasn't. Not really. But he was stealing magic from everyone. All of us. No wonder we had so many rogues." Asylin walked to the refrigerator and took out a pitcher of orange juice. She poured some into a glass already sitting on the counter, took another glass out of the cabinet, filled it, and handed it to Rachel.

"We never had a clue he was sucking on all of our magic to make himself more powerful." She raised the glass to her lips, then lowered it to say, "And if I hadn't experienced it myself, I wouldn't have believed it."

Rachel nodded and drank, realizing that talking with Asylin had made her feel a little better. She knew the things she shared with the people in this town weren't anything her mama, papa, or brothers would ever truly understand.

"Hey, is Dani here? We should probably decide what we're going to do once the travel ban is lifted."

Asylin motioned with her head toward the door as she put away the juice pitcher. "Up in her room, pouting about that very thing. It might make her feel better to see you."

It might help me too. "Thanks. I'll do that."

She was on her way up the stairs when Larissa came around the bend in the hallway and started down the steps. She gave Rachel a smug smile and said sarcastically, "Poor little owl, so wounded and helpless. Come to Bosnia. We show you what means to be tough."

Excuse me? "You can't be talking to me, because if you were, you'd find out damn fast just how tough an American is. Go ahead. Say 'blood feud' again. First blood will be your nose, hitting the floor from the top of these stairs."

The past and the present were colliding in Dalvin's brain. He wanted to keep being pissed at Rachel, but . . . she was right. Every word she'd said was right. He *did* know her family: her mother, her Aunt Krystal. They wouldn't be able to handle her being Sazi. He himself had never even known a three-day shifter. Everyone in his family was alphic.

"Thanks a lot, asshole," came a furious male voice from behind him. "I just barely got Rachel thinking she was okay." Scott's face was set in tight lines, his nostrils flared.

Feeling contrite, Dalvin kicked the wide concrete steps leading up to the apartment building and shoved his hands deep in the pockets of his pants. "I deserve that. But what would *you* do if you'd watched someone's family suffering for a decade?"

The question took some of the anger out of the other man's face. Scott sat down on the stoop and looked at his hands.

"Well, I'd probably start by asking why, instead of just assuming she was a callous bitch, y'know? She's not. Rachel is the sweetest woman I know."

"I know. I know. And I was trying to get to where I could ask her. It took me the whole first day to convince myself I knew her. But hearing her say 'Mom' so casually, and with obvious affection in her scent . . . that . . . it just got to me." His anger had faded into a dull lump of lead in his gut. He hated that he'd made her cry.

"So how *do* you know her? I wasn't kidding that I've known her since we were in grade school. We've been best friends most of my life. But you obviously know her real family, so I guess that trumps me."

"My family lived down the road from hers in Detroit. We went to school together. I was her best friend too. Well, more than friends, really. She was very special to me."

The rest of the anger left Scott's face and he started looking sad. "Let's go upstairs before we go any farther. You need some background and so do I."

People exiting the building gave Dalvin hateful looks. One older woman opened her mouth, and Scott put up a hand to stop her.

"Don't, Jenny. Please. Let's all just try to get past this."

The woman closed her mouth, but the five-year-old with her didn't hesitate to punch Dalvin on the arm. "You made Rachel cry. You better tell her you're sorry."

He nodded and rubbed the spot, though the kid hadn't hit him hard. "I will. I am sorry."

By the time they made it to Scott's apartment, Dalvin had collected a good number of dirty looks and more than a few mumbled curses from other residents of the building. It seemed a little strange to him. If Rachel was right that she was a slave and pariah, why was everyone protecting her?

Scott pulled two beers from the fridge in his small apartment and offered one to Dalvin.

"Sit. It's not the fanciest couch in town, but it's comfortable. It folds out. That's where you'll be sleeping." Dalvin saw that his bags were piled in the corner of the gold shag carpet. Where in the world had they found harvest gold shag carpet if the town had been here for only a decade?

"If you want a drawer, I'll clean one out," Scott continued, sinking into an ancient threadbare brown recliner, "and there's a little room in the closet if you need it. So, you knew her for the first twelve years and I've known her for the last ten. Give me three words that you'd use to describe Rachel the kid."

Three words? Dalvin sat down on the couch. It was sort of comfy—not too springy and with thick cushions under the plaid '70s green-and-brown upholstery. He thought for a second while he took a pull on the beer. He shouldn't drink on the job. He knew that. But hopefully the hierarchy would make an exception, considering they'd probably all heard the fight.

"Happy. Talented. Determined." He motioned with the bottle to Scott. "You next, for adult Rachel?"

"Traumatized. Angry. Determined." Scott stared at the label on the bottle. "I would like to have known her happy. With the world open to her and a loving family. That would have been cool." He paused, then continued. "I didn't get to see much of her talent, except in school choir. We both just tried to keep our heads down. Singing, especially her kind of singing, attracts attention."

"I guess the trauma was from the snakes?" Dalvin had met a few other kids who had been rescued from the clutches of Nasil and the others. They were pretty messed up. "I tried to find her. We all did. But there were no clues. None."

Scott waved that off. "Yeah, I get that. Even the top people in the Council didn't know what was happening. Rachel was just one of many. Claire was too, if you didn't know. That's how they know each other—from the cave. But that was only part of the trauma."

Dalvin hadn't known about Claire. "Claire seems so . . . well-adjusted."

Scott lifted one foot onto the seat, revealing an elegant, patterned sock under his gray slacks. Everything about him was well put together. Far better than Dalvin's mismatched wardrobe.

"Yeah. That probably comes from a good foster family. Don't get me wrong, I'm not saying the Williamses didn't do their best. They did. They rock. But there were so many of us, and we were all messed up. It was like the lockdown ward in a psych hospital some days. You do the best you can to deal with the crisis du jour."

So part of the trauma came from being here, in this town. "Rachel said the Omega position in town was like being both a slave and a pariah, and that you've done your time too. Was that how you saw it?" Scott hesitated, so he continued. "Because I saw this whole outpouring when she started crying, and I feel like I'm the pariah now."

"Well, yeah." Scott acknowledged the comment with another swig of beer. "But both things are true. I can understand how it looks weird to someone outside our little slice of hell, though. See, there's Luna Lake, B.G and Luna Lake, A.G—that's before Lenny Gabriel and after.

"Lenny Gabriel, our late police chief, was a sadistic, manipulative bastard. He liked to inflict pain and humiliation on Rachel and me, and probably our predecessors, just because he could. I guess it made him feel powerful to beat up the little guy. Maybe it got him off. I don't know. But he and Van Monk, along with all the upstanding citizens you just saw rallying around her, were also our abusers. Both of us have spent the last seven years being the town's whipping boy and girl. We've been pushed, slapped, shoved, beaten, humiliated, and worked until our fingers bled. And half of the time, we weren't sure we'd survive shifting on the moon."

Wow. How could he possibly respond to that? "What do you mean, *survive shifting*? Once you're a shifter, you shift. Right?"

Scott was taking a drink and choked, tumbling forward as beer shot out of his nose. Once he could breathe again, he stared in astonishment. "You're joking, right?"

When Dalvin shook his head, Scott blinked. Several times. "Wow. I would have thought they'd trained Wolven agents on all aspects of shifting. No, bro. That's *not* how it works. Just because an Omega shifts okay one month is no guarantee they'll survive the next. We're barely—and I do mean barely—shifters. Every single month is a crapshoot.

"The Omega before me died while shifting. Every single month it hurts like it did the very first time because you don't have enough magic to get rid of the pain. An alpha has to help us shift, or we might have one wing and one arm, or maybe our feathers won't come in.

We're no longer human, but not quite Sazi. It sucks rocks. The one thing Monk was decent at was making sure we shifted. We could always count on him to do that. He wouldn't really watch us afterward. We might wander off and wake up somewhere weird, but somehow that was okay, probably because we were mind-controlled."

Holy crap. Apparently, he needed to spend some time with Amber and get a better sense of what omegas went through before he made an ass out of himself again. "Sorry." What else could he say?

"Not your fault. But don't pick on Rachel. Okay? Her life has sort of sucked since you knew her." They sipped beer in silence for a few minutes; the emotions swirling around in the room were strong enough that they both sneezed more than once.

Scott took a deep breath and gave a weak smile. "So, tell me about Rachel as a kid. Back when she was happy."

That he could do.

CHAPTER 7

*L*arissa's eyes narrowed and her fingers dug into the bannister. She had just opened her mouth to respond when Rachel heard a heavy thump, like something hitting the floor hard, behind her, attracting the bear's attention. Rachel looked over her shoulder and saw Iva, who had comforted her when she'd first arrived, at the foot of the stairs.

"Larissa!" the woman said sharply. "No more. Win one battle before starting another. Come down here. Alpha would speak with you."

Eyes flashing angrily, Larissa started down the stairs. As she passed Rachel, she fake-stumbled and tried to push Rachel against the railing, but the owl shifter was prepared. The bear shifter hit her unyielding body and wound up nearly spinning around on the stairs. She had to grab at the rail for balance and ended up with her legs at awkward angles on two different stair treads.

Rachel tipped her head, stepped over Larissa's leg, and said, with sweet innocence in her voice, "Oops. You'll have to be more careful. These stairs can be tricky."

Larissa's low, rumbling growl should have bothered her, but frankly, a physical fight with someone she could whup would be almost welcome. Hair pulling and kicking? Really? She'd graduated from that when she was five. She'd love to see how the bear would take a punch straight to the face.

Turning left at the top of the stairs, Rachel walked down the hall to Dani's room and gave an obligatory knock before poking her head in.

"Hey, girlfriend," she said, raising her voice slightly to be heard over the music playing in the background. Rachel sighed without making a sound. She still didn't know what Dani saw in bubble gum pop.

Her foster sister's smile lit up the room. Her teeth could have been feathers, given how white they were. "Rachel! C'mon in. Pull up a beanbag."

The beanbag chairs scattered around the room were a shade of pink that would have made Malibu Barbie's eyes hurt. Another thing Rachel didn't get about her friend. The bags were hard to sit on, hard to get out of, and not all that comfortable. She grabbed the rolling chair from the desk instead.

"So little miss Larissa tried to roller-derby me off the staircase just now. Have you met her?"

Danielle rolled her eyes. Her long, wavy hair was swept off to one side of her heart-shaped face and held with a barrette that was the same pink as the beanbags. Even on her best day when she'd had long hair, Rachel wouldn't have been able to get her hair to do that. Dani always looked like a model ready for a shoot, just waiting for the photographer to call for her. She had no interest in being in front of a camera, though—Dani was focused on science. She planned to be a wildlife biologist, studying owls. Rachel laughed every time she thought about it.

"Oh, yes," Dani said. "Mom introduced the whole family. Suljo, the oldest son, is a hunk and seems sweet, but Zara and Larissa are prime-grade witches. They wanted *my* room instead of the guest rooms. Uh, no." She let out a snort. "And I am so sick of the sinister whispering in French. Hello? You're in America. Just speak English."

"French? Why would they be speaking French? And how do you know that's what it is?"

Dani leaned back on the bed and propped one dark calf up on the footboard. "First term, I had to have a foreign language and French sounded cool. I want to go to Europe someday to study, and French is spoken in a lot of places where English isn't. I got an A-minus in the class and the professor suggested I take the advanced course. She says I'm a natural." She shrugged. "I haven't decided yet. Hey, you should take it too! Then we can sound sinister like them."

Rachel leaned forward, resting her palms on her knees. "What were they talking about?"

"Mostly about this fight Larissa's supposed to have. She keeps telling Zara that she's going to kick Anica's butt. But I accidentally overheard her on the phone, telling someone that she's going to throw the fight."

Whoa. That *was* interesting, but she couldn't tell Dani why. "Who was she talking to?"

Dani shrugged again. "Not a clue. Like I said, it's always in low whispers and I wasn't really listening."

"She's going to be surprised at what comes next," Rachel said with a chuckle.

Dani raised her brows, her dark eyes questioning, and sat up straighter, stuffing a second pillow behind her back. "Details, girl."

"I suggested an Ascension challenge instead of a physical fight," she said as casually as possible. She knew Dani would smell her pride anyway. "The Council people thought it was a pretty good idea."

Her friend let out a loud hoot. "You *didn't*! Oh, you're bad!"

"The cat course, so she can tear up those perfect nails on pine bark." Rachel was giggling.

Dani started laughing. "The full treatment, robes and everything?"

"Alek made two copies of the whole rule book. That hot councilman, Rabi, is going to give them to the two male alphas. But there's a downside."

Another questioning look, and the scent of oily sweet curiosity filled the room. Dani rolled one finger in a circle, urging Rachel to continue.

"I have to show Dalvin the course route so he can train the other girl, Anica."

"Ooo, I heard about that. What's with you and him? How do you know him?" There was a knock on the door. "Yes? Who is it?" Dani called.

From the other side of the door, Scott said, "Just a little owl looking for a place to roost his tired claws."

"C'mon in."

The door cracked open just wide enough for Scott to slide through. He looked even paler than usual in a white pullover sweater and gray pants. "Big powwow downstairs with lots of angry bears. I was a little nervous walking past them. Thought I should warn you that the Council is headed over here and Dalvin will be with them."

"Ah, crap," Rachel said. "Guess I'd better hit the back stairs and scoot."

Dani sat up and threw open her arms. "Wait, what happened? All I heard was that you two had a fight."

Rachel opened her mouth, but Scott held up a hand, saying, "If I may? The über-short version: Dalvin and Rachel were hooked up back in Detroit before Rachel got grabbed by the snakes. He didn't know she was still alive. She didn't know he was Sazi or that he'd joined Wolven. Fast-forward to today and they each discover the other exists. Drama ensues, fighting commences, and here we are."

Rachel blew a raspberry. "We were not *hooked up*. We were twelve. But we were friends, and the rest really was the short-and-sweet version."

Scott tipped his head, causing his waist-length hair to fall over one eye. "Eh, I beg to differ. Boy says hooked up, girl says not. Salt to taste."

That made her fall back against the padded chair back. "Wait. Dalvin said we were *hooked up*?"

He nodded.

Dani let out a low, hooting whistle. "Ooo. Drama ensues. What did you tell Claire when she and Alek fought? 'When people fight like that, lust is in the air.'"

"Is not!" Rachel exclaimed, but an odd feeling made her head swim, and her stomach felt like she'd swallowed a pound of lead.

Scott lifted his head and tapped her on the shoulder. "Go, go. They're nearly here."

Rachel jumped up and headed for the door, then turned around and gave each of her friends a swift hug. "Thanks, guys. I have to do some thinking. Cover for me."

Dani followed her down the back stairs. They had to stop short when two of Anica's family walked by on the ground floor, speaking what Rachel presumed was Serbian. Dani tugged on her sleeve and whispered in her ear, "That's her, Rach!"

She shook her head, not understanding. Dani leaned in again. "On the phone with Larissa. The tall woman is the other person who was speaking French."

"How do you know?" Rachel asked quietly. The "tall woman" was Draga Petrovic. Why would the omega of the Bosnian sloth be speaking French to one of the Serbian alphas?

"The way she says Anica . . . Ah-nee-ka. She puts the emphasis on the middle and drops the last syllable until it's almost an 'o.' The other people here don't. French has really taught me about vowel sounds."

Rachel stared at the crowd in the living room, the whole lot of them stinking of angry bear musk. Too many voices, talking in too many languages.

While she was trying to figure out what to do, the front door opened and Amber and Rabi came in. Rabi shouted, "People, *people*, please quiet down and listen!"

Maybe she should stay and find out what was going on. If it had anything to do with Ascension, they might need her anyway. Looking more closely, she realized Dalvin was nowhere to be seen in the room. *Maybe he's guarding the perimeter. If he is, I'm safe.*

Feeling movement behind her, she glanced back. It was Scott.

"I thought you were leaving," he said quietly.

"Big happenings in the last ten seconds," she replied. All three of them crouched down so they could see into the living room, through the door near the fireplace, without being noticed.

The alpha for the Kasun family spoke from the big chair by the window. "There is nothing to listen to. Footrace is not combat."

A snort from the other side of the room. "Is not footrace. Obstacle course is like Olympics. You do not believe your omega can win, so you refuse. I have pride in my daughter. So much, in fact, that I would let entire dispute be settled this way. Is interesting game, this Ascension."

The whole room turned to him, and Anica gasped.

"Papa?"

Zarko Petrovic smiled, his gaze fixed on Mustafa Kasun. "Your omega is taller, but my little bear is slim and quick. Obstacle course is not for big bulky bears. It is for little sleek bears who are fast and agile. Anica is also excellent climber with a nose that can find a single ripe raspberry in a whole field."

Anica made a small whimpering sound that Rachel had heard often enough coming from her own mouth. It was the what-the-hell-is-he-getting-me-into? sound.

Iva Kasun touched her husband's shoulder as if to calm

him, and spoke to Zarko. "You would give up your claim on our land if Larissa wins?"

The Petrovic Alpha nodded. "But if Anica wins, you remove your fence and put it back to where it is before the war."

Mustafa Kasun let out a low, rumbling growl. His wife nudged him several times without getting a response; finally, she leaned over and whispered to him. He must not have liked what he heard, because he frowned before pushing her away. "They have full day to train on course?"

Petrovic nodded. "Agreed."

Rabi Kuric stepped forward, extending a hand toward each of the alphas. "Let me understand. You are agreeing to have your omegas compete in Luna Lake's Ascension course, not just to settle their personal blood feud but also to decide the entire border dispute?" He sounded incredulous.

"Yes," said Mustafa with a nod. He smashed his fist onto the arm of the chair with a sharp *thwack*.

The head of the Petrovic family waved off his wife and son, who were frantically trying to get his attention. "I decide for this family," he said, looking at them with narrowed eyes. "My word alone. And I say yes."

"Excellent!" said Rabi. "Alphas and omegas, if you please? We'll travel to the town hall to review the maps and discuss the course."

The alpha males stood and herded Larissa and Anica out of the house. Both young women were talking to their leaders. Rachel saw fear in their eyes and posture, smelled it in their scents. The men ignored them and kept moving.

Rachel and Dani each let out a slow breath, settling back on their heels at nearly the same moment.

"Wow. This just went to a whole new level," Rachel said. Dani nodded in agreement, but Scott looked confused. Rachel quietly explained what Dani had overheard earlier in the day.

"Dani, you need to tell someone," he said insistently.

She shook her head. "Uh-uh. You want to tell, go ahead. I'll back you up if I'm asked. But no way am I going to be the one to raise the alarm. What if I'm wrong?"

"Do you think you are?" Rachel asked. Below them, Liz and Amber ushered the Kasun family toward the door.

"No. But I'm still not telling," she said in a determined tone. Rachel knew how stubborn Dani could be; she decided not to push her on this.

Scott shrugged. "I'm at the I-heard-it-from-a-friend-who-heard-it-from-a-friend level. I'm out."

"Fine," Rachel said to her two cowardly friends, "then I will." She slid out of the narrow hallway and sprinted for the front door.

Behind her, she heard Dani say, "Girl's nuts."

Scott replied, with a note of admiration in his voice, "Did you say, 'nuts' or 'guts'? I vote for guts."

She smiled at Scott's assessment, but the smile fell off her face and she nearly skidded to a stop at the sight of Dalvin getting into the front of the SUV with Amber. *Damn it!* She didn't want to deal with him now. But this was important.

"Amber? I really need to talk to you. Like right this second."

"Rachel, I'm sorry, but it'll have to wait. We have to get the sloth back to their cabin."

She tried to telegraph her urgency by scent and expression, but Amber just looked confused, even when Rachel nodded toward the backseat of the car.

Dalvin got it, though. He leaned over and whispered to Amber, "I think it's *about* the sloth."

Rachel hoped mightily that the backseat was vacuum-sealed, like when she had been back there with the Council.

Amber sighed and got out of the SUV. She took Rachel by the elbow and quickly moved her toward the trees, putting a thick trunk between them and the car so nobody could try to read their lips.

"Okay, make it fast. What's the problem?"

"My foster sister, Dani, overheard Larissa on the phone, maybe attempting to sabotage the contest."

Amber frowned and crossed her arms over her chest. The twin scents of suspicion and curiosity warred in Rachel's nose. "And why isn't Dani telling me this?"

"Because Dani doesn't think it's a big deal and I think it is."

The cat shifter tapped her foot on the ground, crunching fallen leaves under her boot. "I think it is too. But I'm going to have to talk to Dani."

"Unfortunately, what she overheard was in French."

Now Amber smiled. "That's my native tongue. I think I can handle it." She leaned out from behind the tree and called to Dalvin, "Go on to the house. I need to finish something here."

His eyes narrowed, but he scooted into the driver's seat as Rachel and Amber started for the house.

CHAPTER 8

*W*hat the hell was so important that the two of them had to hide behind a freaking tree and whisper like *schoolgirls?* Dalvin thought as he drove the Bosnian bears away. He was getting sick of being treated like an errand boy instead of a Wolven agent. Hell, Alek had less than a month on the force and was getting more respect than he was right now.

It took a whopping two minutes to reach the other end of town. That was another thing! The whole place wasn't more than a quarter mile long—why were they driving everywhere? All the townspeople walked, and now he understood why. Granted, the SUVs had bulletproof glass, but what was the likelihood that someone would take a shot at any of the delegates?

Trying for calm, he took a deep breath and let it out slowly before opening the door for the Kasuns. Apparently, he wasn't successful at concealing his feelings, because the alpha female wrinkled her nose, then stepped back like he was a hot flame. And maybe he shut the car door a little too firmly, because the alpha male's brows raised and he muttered something into Tamir's ear when the big bear shifter approached from the other side. The senior Wolven agent flicked his attention sharply to

Dalvin. *Great. Another strip of hide.* Just thinking about it made his side hurt, which made him even more pissed off.

Once the family was inside, Tamir crooked a finger at Dalvin, who stepped forward, his gaze averted. "Are you having a problem today, Agent Adway?"

"No, sir." The words were flat and hollow. Even *he* didn't believe them.

"Look," the word was softer than he expected. Suspicious, he looked at Tamir and was surprised to see sympathy in his eyes. "Claire told me what happened with the local girl. I didn't realize you had history with her. I know you're upset. Why don't you go over to the school and help with the cooking? Might take your mind off problems for a while."

"What?" Tamir had been such an asshole until now. Why the change?

The big bear shrugged one shoulder; he smelled uncomfortable to be talking about anything personal. "My oldest brother ran away when I was ten. Wanted become a big star in Bollywood. He never came home, and my father felt . . . so much pain. For years, all the time I was growing up. I do not know what I would say to him if I found him and he dared to be *happy*. I think I would punch him. Maybe many times." He shrugged again. "You only yelled. I was impressed."

Dalvin nodded. "I was raised not to slug girls." Although he recalled in vivid detail that the reverse wasn't true for Rachel. She'd clobbered him nearly as often as her brothers. "I'll be at the school if you want me," he said with a nod. He wasn't going to ask Tamir anything about his brother—he didn't want to get involved with the bear's personal demons—but he did have a question. "Hey, what do you know about three-day shifters?"

Tamir shrugged. "That they turn every night of the moon. Why?"

So it wasn't just him. "Nothing. Never mind."

He could smell the Russian agent's confusion and frustration as he walked away.

The trip to the school took longer than it should have because Dalvin kept stopping to think. Good thing there was no traffic.

Long-ago memories colliding with today's. A mischievous pixie smile in a mouth that was too wide for her small face; now that face was all grown up but lacked a smile. A skinny kid running beside him in her brother's rolled up pants, constantly tugging them up because she had no hips; now her jeans hugged her hips and stayed taut against the curve of her waist.

He found himself at the school. The chili cooking inside smelled really good, and he suddenly realized he hadn't eaten all day. He was about to open the door when he heard voices behind him and turned to see the two male bear alphas, plus Councilman Kuric, Larissa, and Anica, leaving the town hall. Alek was locking the door behind them.

Larissa was rubbing her shoulder and moving it around like it hurt. Turning to look at her, Mustafa Kasun noticed Dalvin standing at the school entrance and smiled thinly. He spoke to Larissa and pointed at Dalvin. The young woman nodded and began to walk toward the school.

Seeing that she was limping, Dalvin stepped forward to meet her.

"You okay?" he asked."You're looking a little banged up."

She shrugged, then winced. "I should not have turned my back on that woman . . . the one who yelled at you."

Frowning, Dalvin asked, "Why? What did Rachel do?"

"Tried to push me down staircase." She tried to wave it off as though it didn't matter, but her arm was obviously not working well. "She did not succeed, thanks to heavens. But I am sure it was to slow me down in race. Anica has likely bought her loyalty."

Rachel sabotaging the race? While he wouldn't have thought

that possible of the Rachel he'd grown up with, it seemed he didn't know the adult Rachel at all. Who knew what she might be capable of? She had demonstrated that she didn't like Larissa one bit, and she had been the one to suggest the race in the first place. He picked up Larissa's good hand and raised it to his lips.

"I'm reviewing the course tomorrow. I'll make sure Anica doesn't have an unfair advantage."

Larissa smiled and ran the back of her fingernails down his cheek. "You are sweet. The only thing I worry of is that Anica is smaller than me in animal form. I will be able to run, but I worry of crouching or crawling in places where she can slip under. My shoulder, it will be difficult."

He squeezed her hand. "Clearing brush should be no problem at all. You just head back to your quarters and rest. You told your Alphas about this, right?"

She nodded but smelled of deceit. "Of course."

His face dropped into stern lines. "Larissa, I'm not kidding. You can't let something like this go. Tell your Alphas or I will." It wasn't his decision about what to do about sabotage, if there was any being planned. Especially if it was a third party like a town resident.

But it's not just any town resident. It's Rachel. She wouldn't—

He put the thought aside. He couldn't know that. He watched Larissa struggle with her dilemma—he knew her Alphas could be moody, and there were disadvantages to telling a disgruntled leader about problems. Finally, she sighed and her scent shifted to the wet mop of resignation and defeat. "I will tell my Alpha female. This is a womanly matter."

He nodded. If it made her feel better to talk to the female, he was fine with that.

Her head tipped flirtatiously. "Would you walk me home? There could be dangerous things in the woods." She walked two of those red-tipped fingernails up his arm.

Tempting . . .

His chuckle was automatic. It didn't say *no*, just *not now, you little flirt*. "Sorry, but I have duties. Maybe tomorrow we can walk down to the lake." A chilly wind brushed the back of his neck; the hairs there stood up, trying to be feathers.

Her voice lowered and her lips puckered. Sexy. "Mmm . . . cold water on bare skin. Delicious. No need to bring swim shorts, I think."

He gently pulled her hand off his arm and laughed. "I have to go now. Duty calls." Skinny dipping with a woman like Larissa would be something a man would never forget.

What does Rachel look like naked?

The stray thought took him by surprise and made him shake his head, but it was like trying to wipe the image of pink polka-dotted elephant from his mind. Larissa thought she had caused the distraction and smiled broadly.

Suddenly angry, Dalvin turned away, his voice harsh when he said, "Get some rest, Larissa. It's going to be a long few days."

The sudden change of attitude confused her, he could tell, but he didn't turn back. It had been a very strange day and he needed a chance to get his head together.

A chance he apparently wasn't going to get, at least not yet, because Scott was jogging toward him with a concerned look on his face. *Would this day never end?*

"What's up?" Dalvin asked his new roommate.

Scott offered him a phone—the one Dalvin kept in the side pocket of his duffel—and said, "This rang like twenty times. The display says it's your mother. I know you're technically on duty, but when a mom calls that many times—"

Yeah, that was weird. He took the phone and flipped it open. Twenty-two missed calls. While his work phone was state of the art, his personal line was whatever crappy prepaid one he could find, so there was no voice mail. But the prepaid ones seemed to have the best coverage in the middle of nowhere because they piggybacked on whatever wireless carrier was in the area. "Thanks. I appreciate it. I'll give her a call."

Scott got the hint and waved farewell. "No problem. Just thought you'd want to know." Then he snapped his fingers. "Oh, and I found the spare apartment key."

"Great. Do you have it with you?" God only knew when he'd make it back to the apartment complex. It would probably be late.

Scott shook his head, his long mane of hair blowing in the breeze as if he were a cover model in the *Sports Illustrated* swimsuit issue. In fact, several of the women in last year's issue didn't have hair nearly as nice. "Sorry, I should have grabbed it, just didn't think. You'll probably be working weird hours, but don't worry about disturbing me when you get back. I'll probably be up. I'm a night owl."

That made Dalvin chuckle. Scott grinned and trotted off.

Dalvin raised his finger to return his mother's call, then hesitated. Could he handle any more news today? Everyone was healthy when he left, and it would take a lot to hurt either his mother or father. As alphas go, Dalvin's father could still wipe up the floor with him, and his mother was flat-out vicious. Probably everything was fine and she was just returning his call. He pressed the button.

His mother picked up before he heard a second ring. "Dalvin?"

"Hey, Mom. What's up? The guy I'm rooming with said you've been burning up the phone line trying to reach me. Is something wrong?"

Her voice took on the same note as when he was a kid and his room was a pit. "Dalvin Clarence Adway. You promised me you would call as soon as you got back to the States. Here I find out you're on the West Coast already and not a word."

What? "I did call you. I left a message yesterday. And how did you hear I was on the West Coast?"

Now her voice took on an I'm-so-innocent-that-if-I-walk-past-a-lemon-stand-I-sweeten-the-fruit tone. "Oh, here and there. You know how family is."

Except he hadn't told a soul in the family that the peace talks were moving. "Look, Mom. I have to get back to work. Why did you *really* call me?" If he sounded a little short, he didn't care.

And now the pout. "I'm your mother, Dalvin. I get worried."

He heard a click and then his father's voice. "Quit upsetting your mother, Dalvin."

Goddamn it! He wanted to yell, but he kept his voice low so the whole town didn't hear—like they had when he'd argued with Rachel. "Dad, I work for Wolven. You know the drill. I can't talk about stuff. I can't call you every day. You aren't supposed to be tracking my every movement. It's a security breach and I'm going to get fired! Or worse!" Every word was staccato, a tiny verbal dagger. He heard sighs on the phone, one deep and one delicate. He wanted to scream. "Okay?"

His dad spoke first. "The boy's right, Maggie. He's not a teenager anymore. Wolven doesn't play games."

His mother responded, but to her husband, not Dalvin. "Oh, I know he's not a teenager anymore, Robert. But he's still acting like one. The only thing that gets him riled up enough to yell at us is women. You had a fight with your girlfriend, didn't you?"

Now he *did* scream . . . silently. "Okay, yeah, Mom. I had a fight with Ra—" With the word halfway out of his mouth, his whole body froze up. Holy God! What had he nearly said? Part of his brain was stupid and the other part was seriously messed up.

"Rae?" his mother asked. "*Another* one? I swear, Son, you need to slow down a little. Women aren't toys."

He tried to respond, but his jaw wouldn't move. Literally wouldn't. He couldn't move a single inch of his body except his eyes. It was even hard to breathe, and a stinging sensation enveloped him like he was being stung by a thousand bees. He felt the phone being plucked from his hand.

"Robert? Maggie? Hi, it's Amber. Hey, sorry to interrupt, but this really isn't a secure line and we need Dalvin for the next session."

Now his mother's voice sounded tinny and distant through the phone's speaker. "Oh, Amber! Hi! I'm so sorry. You know how I worry. So many nights Robert didn't call when he was on assignment and it made me crazy. You understand, don't you?"

He still couldn't see the councilwoman, but he felt the sting strengthen, becoming knives cutting into every pore. His eyes started watering from the pain. A fly landed on the tip of his nose and crawled around while Amber continued casually chatting with his parents. "Of course I do. The number of nights that Charles forgot to call drove me nuts too. But it's the life of an agent, Maggie, as you well know. Just like the number of nights I didn't come home when I was healing people in crises."

Amber stood in front of Dalvin and stared right into his eyes. The fly buzzed away. "You just forget to call, or you"—fire burned in her gaze as she said the next words, enunciating very carefully—"*can't discuss the situation*, so you don't *dare* talk to anyone."

Oh, he was in for it. The pain he was feeling was nothing, not even a mosquito bite. He knew that now.

His mother relented. "I'm sorry, Amber. I'll try to be more mindful."

"And I'll keep reminding her," his father added. "Whatever Dalvin is doing, if he's with you, Amber, I know he'll be fine. Right, Mags?"

Another sigh, sounding like a bird trill from this far away. "You're right. Of course. Thank you for taking care of him, Amber. Give our best to Charles."

"Good to talk to you and I certainly will. Gotta go. Dalvin and I have things to talk about. Bye now." She pressed the red button on the keypad very carefully and then shut the flip phone. She tucked it into a pants pocket and put her hands on her hips. "You brought a nonsecure phone to a secure facility? Really? Now, what shall I do with *you*?"

CHAPTER 9

*I*s what you heard what you thought you heard?" Rachel sat cross-legged on the bed in the holding cell in the basement, a pillow tucked behind her back. It was the only place in the house where nobody could overhear a conversation. The cage had been specifically constructed to hold captured rogues and was soundproofed so that the household would be able to sleep without hearing the snarls or screams of a shifter gone insane. "Is bear bitch trying to sabotage the race?"

Dani was in a similar pose at the foot of the iron-frame bed, which had been set into the concrete floor. No rearranging furniture in this room. She had to shift her head so the twisted corner post didn't dig into her back. So far, that was the only damage a rogue had managed to do to the room.

Despite the security measures, it was actually a cozy bedroom . . . and a place all the kids had used as a refuge more than once, a chance to get away from the noise and confusion in their large, tumultuous family.

Dani checked that the door at the top of the stairs was shut and the inside lock bolted. "I think so. But neither of us could figure out why. Amber said she's never seen Larissa even look at the other family except to spew insults."

Rachel uncrossed her legs, straightening them before they cramped. "Yeah, it seems weird. Maybe if Larissa was dating one of the other sons or something. But you definitely heard her talking with the Petrovic alpha female?"

Her friend leaned back against the metal frame, couldn't find a comfortable spot, and finally lay down on her side, facing Rachel. "It sure sounded like her. But Amber is going to do a test over at the other house, like we did here."

"A test? What test did you do here?"

Dani let out a little laugh. "We walked through the den, talking in French, and insulted the Kasun alpha female's dress. Amber said it looked like a cheap imitation of a bad set of curtains. Only Zara flicked her eyes to watch us."

"So nobody else speaks French, because if they did, they would have at least looked over at you guys."

"Exactly," she agreed. The ozone scent of realization burst into the air. "Except that Larissa wasn't here," Dani said excitedly, "which might be why she can speak French freely. None of the Kasuns except Zara can understand it."

"So now you just need to wait for Larissa to get home and test her?"

Dani shrugged one shoulder. "I think that's the idea. But Amber decided she'd go to the other house and call her brother. The whole Monier family speaks French. I guess his wife is having a baby, so they can talk about that while Amber watches the people to see if they're paying attention to what's being said."

"Oh, yeah, I remember Rabi mentioning that earlier. He's Amber's brother-in-law. His sister is married to Amber's brother."

"Ooo! He's *Rabi* now, is he?" Dani said with a grin. "He is a hunk."

Rachel felt her face heat up. "It's not like we're on a first-name basis. We've barely even talked. I just feel weird using all these formal titles. In my head, I think of them as regular people." She paused and then smiled. "He is hot, though, and that disappearing trick—scary, but very cool."

Dani wiggled her eyebrows. "Maybe you should show *Rabi* the cat course, instead of Dalvin. Quiet woods, hot guy . . . who knows what might happen?"

The snort wasn't intended. It just came out. "Better than fighting with Dalvin again."

A bump on the sole of her shoe. "Sorry, Sis. That must have sucked. And now you're stuck with walking him through the course? Any chance of appeal?"

"Nobody to appeal *to*. Rabi and Liz looked at something online and decided that's what would happen. And that was after I told them why I can't go back home."

"What do you suppose they saw?" Dani's hair fell forward and covered one eye. She pushed it back and tucked it behind her ear. "Hey, what if we go look? I'll bet they didn't delete the history on the computer."

That might be useful, but . . . "What if we get caught? That wouldn't be pretty."

Dani thrummed her fingertips on the bedspread for a second, then snapped her fingers. "Not all the college portals work well with tablets, and the computer in the town hall really is the only desktop around with Internet access. We could say we're looking at our class schedules. We need to print out the syllabuses and look into buying the books." She paused, then added, "Which we actually do need to do. And soon."

"There's nothing saying we can't have two tabs open in the browser . . ." Rachel said, almost laughing.

Nodding, Dani got to her feet, brushing fur from the last occupant off her pants. "Man, we have got to throw this stuff in the wash. Yellow fur *everywhere*." She tapped Rachel's leg, motioning for her to get off the bed. "Help me get these sheets in the laundry and then we can head over. I know where Dad keeps the spare key to the Community Center."

The two women began to strip the bed. Dani said, "I'm surprised Mom didn't change the bedding once Tammy starting sleeping back in her own room."

"I think she left it as a negative reminder, so Tammy would really work hard to get better. But it's been a week now with no relapses or hints she's going rogue again. Claire's done amazing work with her. And with Darrell." Rachel didn't tell Dani what Asylin said. It still didn't feel like she'd done anything to help.

Dani nodded. "I heard Marilyn say that calls to the suicide hotline have dropped to nothing." She gathered up the sheets, shaking her head at the havoc the dead alphas had wrought. The angry, burned-caramel scent of anger that always reminded her of day-old coffee filled the small, barred room. "Bastards."

Rachel's own anger was still too close to the surface not to agree. "Yeah. Monk was a total bastard. But not nearly as bad as Lenny." She picked up the pillowcases and bedspread and followed Dani up the stairs. "Both of them deserved to die."

"Yeah," Dani agreed. "I don't know who was worse . . . Lenny for the weird bondage games or Van for covering them up and forcing people to forget what happened. We need to buy Claire flowers or something. It would still be going on if she hadn't dug out the truth."

The women walked out of the cage, across the room, and up the stairs. Dani unlocked and opened the door, revealing Asylin on the other side, reaching for the handle. Dani backed up so fast she nearly pushed Rachel right down the stairs.

"Ah, there you two are," Asylin said. "I've been looking for you. We need to go over to the school and help set up for the delegate dinner." She stepped aside so they could get through the doorway, touching each woman on the shoulder as she passed. "Thank you for getting the sheets. I was just about to start a load of laundry. Why don't you give me that stuff and head over to the school? Tell everyone I'll be there in just a bit."

Laundry wasn't Rachel's favorite thing, so she was happy to be rid of the smelly bedding. "Use bleach. Freaked-out cat is tough to get out of cloth."

Asylin took a delicate sniff of the sheets and wrinkled her nose. "Maybe I left them down there a little too long. Cat and musty. Never have been able to get the damp completely out of that basement."

Dani added her items to the pile. They could barely see Asylin's eyes above the towering mound of laundry. "You sure you don't want help?"

Their mom shook her head. "You go on ahead," she said, and added, "Oh, Rachel, I told them you'd sing a couple of songs at the dinner."

"Mom—!"

"Don't *Mom* me, Rachel. You have a beautiful voice and they expect entertainment, like at a banquet in their home country. Scott is going to do some card tricks, and Dani, maybe you could repeat that interpretative dance number you did at the recital last fall?"

Well, there went any hope of getting a chance to dig through the computer! Rachel and Dani looked at each other with resignation. They could refuse, but they'd never hear the end of it. Dani sighed. "Okay, we'll think of something to do. But now we're going to have to dress up and practice."

Asylin eased past them on her way to the laundry room. "Just pick out something pretty and don't worry about the details. I don't think they're expecting a Las Vegas revue." She took a couple of steps, then stopped again. "Definitely not a revue. Come to think of it, everyone is already riled up. Do something that will keep them calm and happy. Dani, stick with ballet, and Rachel, maybe some R and B. Slow beat, but nothing sad or angry."

Rachel threw up her hands and let out a sigh. "Would you like to just pick the song?"

Asylin tapped one foot, like she was thinking. "How about 'Dock of the Bay' to start?"

Actually, that wasn't a bad suggestion. The Otis Redding song was one of her favorites for kicking back. "And maybe 'Georgia on My Mind' to finish?"

Lowering the laundry so she could peek over, Asylin nodded. "Good. You sound just like Ethel Waters when you sing that."

Dani raised one finger, excited. "Oh! I just remembered. I learned a dance from India in my class, set to a song called 'Peace One Day.' I think I have the music for it on my iPod. It's really an ensemble piece, but I could work it up as a solo."

Asylin smiled. "That's the spirit. It would be nice to send these families home with an actual agreement so that they can live side by side, like we do here. So it will help to have them in a peaceful frame of mind."

It wasn't quite what Rachel had had in mind for her evening, but it actually might be sort of fun. Tomorrow was likely to suck, so might as well have a few laughs. Plus, it gave her a great idea. Sanctioned snooping!

"C'mon, Dani. Let's go over to the town hall and download the instrumentals for my songs. We can run them through the iPod to the amps at the school."

Dani's eyes lit up as Asylin nodded in approval. "That's a wonderful idea, Rachel. It's probably locked, though. Dani, the key's in the drawer in the kitchen—it's the one on the blue key ring. Now get moving, you two."

"Okay, Mom. Thanks." Dani ducked around the laundry and gave her mother a kiss on the cheek. "See you later."

Once they were outside and headed down the road, Dani held up her hand for a high five. "You are *brilliant*! I never would have thought of that. Of course, you realize we'll have to actually download the music."

"Fine with me. It sounds sort of like fun, if you and Scott will be there too."

The temperature had dropped to near freezing, but the cold felt amazing to Rachel. She inhaled deeply, letting the frigid air tingle her nostril hairs and lungs. To her, everything had a scent in the cold. Every leaf on the ground, every building and car. Summer muddied the scents, but come winter, the whole world came alive.

They'd just reached the hair salon when Dani grabbed Rachel's arm and pulled her into the doorway. "Ooo, look!" Dani pointed toward the school. Dalvin was standing stock-still while Amber walked around him, talking on a cell phone.

"Crap, he's being *held*. I can feel the magic from here. Man, that stings." Rachel had been frozen by magic enough times in her life that she didn't wish it on anyone.

She turned her head so she could hear better, trying to figure out what was going on. Amber stopped right in front of Dalvin and spoke very carefully into the phone. "But it's the life of an agent, Maggie. Just like the number of nights I didn't come home when I was healing people in crises. You just forget to call, or"— she got inches from Dalvin's face, probably spitting on him as she spoke—"*can't discuss the situation*, so you don't *dare* talk to anyone."

Maggie? As in, Maggie Adway? Holy God, Amber was talking to Dalvin's mother. Amber *knew* Dalvin's mother!

Amber nodded several times, listening to Maggie, but Rachel couldn't hear the voice of the woman who had been like her second mother in Detroit. While her own parents were always working, Dalvin's mother was the lemonade and cookies mom. She was the "in case of emergency" contact for probably a dozen kids in her class. Always the worrier, she kept track of everyone's movements. Knew more about the kids than their own parents did. God, she missed that.

Amber nodded. "Good to talk to you and I certainly will. Gotta go. Dalvin and I have things to talk about. Bye, now." She closed the phone, put it in her pocket, and set her hands on her hips while staring at Dalvin. "You brought a nonsecure phone into a secure facility? Really? Now, what should I do with *you*?"

Dani elbowed Rachel in the ribs and whispered, "C'mon, there's nothing we can do for him. And aren't you mad at him anyway? She's probably going to read him the riot act for yelling at you. Wolven agents aren't supposed to yell at people for no reason. Maybe he'll lose a strip of hide."

Crap, he looked scared. She remembered that feeling, the helplessness of being unable to move while someone *did* things to you. And even though she was still mad at Dalvin, nobody deserved to be held. It was mental torture. No wonder the humans decided they'd had enough and fought back. Before she even realized what she was doing, she shook off Dani's grabbing hand and sprinted toward the healer and her prey.

The street was empty except for them, and Rachel quickly realized why. Amber had put up her own personal aversion spell. The itch she'd felt at the hair salon became ants and then wasps. She closed her eyes and ignored the pain.

"Amber, don't!" she yelled.

Taking a deep breath, Rachel let out a screech that stopped the cat shifter cold. The woman recovered in seconds, but by then Rachel had reached them. Amber had a finger in her ear and was moving it in circles while opening her jaw wide, probably trying to pop her ears. Her scent was definitely anger, with confusion mixed in. Dalvin staggered, nearly falling, so Rachel guessed Amber's magical hold on him had vanished. He started rubbing his arms like she always did after getting the feeling back in the muscles.

"Man, that was loud!" Amber shook her head again. "That is one heck of a screech you have. Best I've heard since Angelique. You don't have strong magic behind it, thank goodness. She could blow out eardrums. Mine only sting a little."

Wow. Angelique Calibria was the Council representative for all the raptors. It was like being compared to Beyoncé or Alicia

Keys. If screaming could be compared to singing, of course. "Sorry! I didn't want you to hurt Dalvin. I guess I panicked a little."

Amber tipped her head to the side. "But you were concerned that he might tell people you were here, and he nearly did just now."

Shaking out the kinks in his legs, Dalvin said, "No, I stopped myself. But you're right. My parents make me nuts sometimes and I blurt out stuff. You were right to take the phone." He looked at Rachel. "Chelle, I'm sorry for yelling at you. You have good reasons for wanting to hide away up here. It was just a shock, y'know? So do whatever you need to do. I'll stay out of your way. And I won't say a word to your folks."

Stunned, Rachel couldn't say a word. Dalvin walked the few feet to the school. Just before he opened the door, he snapped his fingers and looked back at the women. Focusing on Rachel, he said, "Please don't take sides in the race."

Without another word, he stepped into the school building, leaving her and Amber standing there, dumbstruck. Dani came up the hill to join them now that the aversion spell was gone.

Amber raised one eyebrow and asked, "What did he mean by that? Were you planning to do something stupid? Like sabotage?"

Rachel looked at Dani, who shrugged. "No, of course not. I bet Larissa talked to Dalvin and smack-talked me. She tried to push me down the stairs earlier, but I grounded myself and she nearly fell instead. Pissed her off."

Amber shrugged. "Yeah, then she's gunning for you. Watch your back."

A surprised laugh bubbled up out of her chest. "That's it? Watch your back?" She used air quotes to acknowledge the absurdity. "You were about to kick Dalvin's butt, but you're just going to let Larissa throw down on me?"

Amber opened her mouth wide again and shook her head.

"I'm not a Council member. I'm like everyone else in town, a bystander. I'm just here to patch people up if the peace talks go south. I got tapped because I was close by. I don't have any authority to kick butts. And I have to tell you, I'm really looking forward to having this settled by omegas. Lots easier to heal."

That made no sense to Rachel. "Wouldn't alphas be easier to heal? They already have magic. That should make it easier."

The laugh that came out of the woman threw citrus scents into the icy wind. "You'd think that, wouldn't you, but no. Alphas know they can heal, so they keep fighting until they're nearly dead. Omegas know they can't heal for crap, so they're smart enough to stop before the wounds become life-threatening." She laughed again. "As for Larissa attacking you, just screech at her. It'll be a short fight. It'll drop her like a rock."

Oh. That actually hadn't occurred to her.

Dani raised a finger. "If you can't kick butt, what were you doing to Dalvin?"

Amber patted her left ear with her palm again, blinking her eyes repeatedly. Wow, her screech must really pack a punch. She needed to learn more about it. The wind blew the scent of lemon shampoo and cat musk Rachel's way. "Getting his attention. He doesn't listen well."

No joke. "Pfft. He never has listened well. Bet his mother wished she could have held him like that when he was screwing up."

The bobcat shifter laughed. "Where do you think I learned it? I've known Robert and Maggie Adway for years. 'Go stand in the corner' had a whole different meaning in their house."

Rachel blinked and her jaw fell open. "Whoa, whoa. Do you mean to tell me that Dalvin comes from a line of shifters? Uh-uh!"

Amber looked at her quizzically, like she didn't understand why Rachel was confused. "Of course. Robert Adway was a Wolven agent for decades, the bureau chief for the Midwest."

Crossing her arms over her chest, Rachel shook her head. "No way. You must be talking about someone different. Robert Adway worked in advertising. He came home every night. People say Wolven agents are often gone for weeks on end, but he never was."

With a little smirk on her face, Amber said, "Except for his regular Wednesday night poker games and his golfing weekends and the semiannual executive conferences he went to in New York or Chicago . . ."

"You're not shitting me, are you?" Rachel said, as her view of the world tilted and rearranged itself. "He was really with Wolven?"

"Absolutely," Amber replied. "The whole family is alphic. You'd probably never even notice them out hunting. They had enough magic to look like any other owl. Nobody notices owls at night, even in the city. Where there are trees and mice, there are owls. In fact, most Sazi owls live in cities. They can pass for human completely unnoticed."

"So Dalvin was a shifter when I knew him as a kid?" How could she not have noticed? Shouldn't she have spotted *some* sign?

"Nope. He was still absolutely human. All of the Adway kids were a decade ago. Robert and Maggie were absolutely terrified during the snake attack, thinking that their kids couldn't defend themselves." Amber shrugged.

"Being human actually saved them, since the snakes were only taking out Sazi. Robert wasn't as lucky. He got *cured*. He's full human now, which is why he's retired. But Maggie is still okay and all the kids eventually turned. Dalvin didn't shift the first time until he was a senior in high school, so you were a shifter before he was."

Wow. She'd had no idea. None. Now it made sense why Margaret Adway was always watching, always vigilant. "So she really *could* turn her head all the way around! I always swore Dalvin's mom was like the girl in *The Exorcist*. Nobody could ever sneak up on her. But everyone told me I was crazy."

Dani nodded. "Hiding in plain sight. Just like my folks when we lived back in New York. They hunted in Central Park when I was little. I don't really remember it, but Grandma always told me that New York City mice were the plumpest in the world."

"So I could really . . . go *home*."

Amber sighed, and the smell of her sorrow covered Rachel's scent of shock, surprise, and hope. "Maybe. You're not alphic and you can't control your change. The Council would never allow you to be unsupervised. No, your instincts were right to begin with. We put you here for a reason. Someone will always have to help you during the moon. Your family can't."

Crap. Right back where she started. "So, back to plan one. Spokane."

A scent full of regret filled the air. "Actually, I'm sort of surprised the Williamses were letting you go even that far. I don't know that Danielle here is alpha enough to turn you." She looked at Dani. "Can you? Like, right now? I need to see you do it before I can recommend that Rachel go with you."

Dani's mouth opened and shut. "Um, I mean I—"

Holy God! Rachel stared at her friend, her sister, like she'd grown a second head. "You *can't*? What were we going to do on the moon, Dani? We talked about this!"

Suddenly uncomfortable, Dani hedged. "Well . . . on the moon, you're going to turn anyway. I can help you finish the change. I've done that before, like that Saturday after graduation."

Rachel remembered that night well. It had been horrible! They'd snuck out of town a day before the moon. She hadn't felt like she needed to change until they were miles away, in the middle of nowhere. She'd changed in bits and pieces. Her legs first, then one arm became a wing, then a beak appeared on her human face. The pain had been nearly unbearable.

"Jesus. Don't you remember that night? I had a beak and one wing for like twenty minutes!"

Now Dani had tears in her eyes and couldn't look at her. "Rach, I'm sorry. I wasn't even thinking about that when we talked about Spokane. God, we couldn't do that on campus."

Rachel slumped down until she was sitting on her butt in the dirt. It was over. She felt like she wanted to throw up. As much as she hated the mayor, he had shifted her effortlessly. No pain and fully formed. What was she going to do now? "I'm trapped. I can never leave here."

"That's not necessarily true," Amber said, squatting beside her and putting a hand on her shoulder. "If you really want to go, we can find somewhere to take you. The Kragans can easily change you while you're here, and there are other parliaments in other cities where you might be able to go to school. It could take awhile to find the right one, but I can start the wheels in motion once the peace process is over."

So, maybe not trapped forever. Rachel tried to take heart from that, even though it would mean going someplace where she didn't know anyone. "Yes, please. I can't take this place anymore. There are too many bad memories here."

Amber stood and offered her a hand up. "We can sort this out after the competition. Let's just get through the next couple of days." Rising to her feet, Rachel stared into the healer's face, looking for any hint of deception. Amber noticed and let her. "I promise . . . and I don't break my word."

"And I'm a witness," Dani said. She touched Rachel's shoulder, her scent full of sorrow and self-loathing. "I'm so sorry, Rachel. I guess I didn't really think things through. But I promise you that whatever place they find for you, I'll come along. We'll just be roomies in a different city. Okay?"

That made her smile. She knew Dani's oversight hadn't been intentional—and it was a lot better to find out now than a week from now, when she might accidentally change in full view of a bunch of humans. That could be dangerous. Fatal. Plus, if Dani came with her, she'd still have personal backup. "Deal."

Amber looked at her watch. "Shit. I'm late. I've got to escort the Petrovics over." She turned and trotted away.

Watching her go, Rachel realized that the sun was right in her eyes, about to drop behind the mountain. "Oh, man! We need to get dressed."

"What about the computer?" Dani asked.

Damn. That's right. "Okay, but we only have a few minutes."

The computer in the town hall was still on, and after hooking through the insanely slow dial-up, Rachel opened the browser. "Check the history," Dani urged, pushing at her mouse hand.

"No, let's get the music download started first so we can pop back to it if someone comes in."

"Oh, yeah, yeah. Good plan." Dani pulled over a second chair and sat down.

Fortunately, the songs they were going to use were so popular that finding instrumental versions was fairly simple. Once she had the phone synced, the files selected, and the download begun, Rachel opened a second tab. She clicked to open the browser history. The first URL was to an article on her hometown newspaper's Web site. She hesitated. Did she really want to know?

"C'mon, open it." Dani must have noticed her nervousness, because she softened her tone and added, "You need to know. Whether or not you ever go home, you need to know why."

Dani was right, Rachel thought. Closing her eyes, she clicked the link. The headline came first, "A Decade Later." An image began to load, slowly, so she scrolled down and started to read. Beside her, Dani read out loud.

"'For families all over Detroit, this summer has special sig-
nificance. It was ten years ago that their children disappeared.
Florence Washington remembers the day clearly. "Rachel was
supposed to be home by dark. Everyone in the park said she left
right on time. But she never arrived."'"

Rachel said, "The snakes grabbed me just a few blocks from my
house. It happened so fast, but I remember it so clearly. There
was a florist van, with a big bouquet of flowers on the side. It
whipped around a corner and squealed to a stop right next to
me. A man jumped out and grabbed me."

Dani touched her on the shoulder, and she flinched. "Rachel,
I'm so sorry." Dani's apology was for now and for then, Rachel
knew. Her foster sister kept reading aloud, which was a good
thing, because Rachel's eyes had filled with tears.

"'In neighborhoods all over Detroit, the stories are remark-
ably similar. On September seventeenth, ten years ago, a
dozen children went missing. No trace has ever been found of
any of them. No motive has been uncovered, no suspects have
been brought in for questioning. And the families still ask why.
Police officials claim there were no witnesses, no clues, no
evidence.

"'A police spokesman said, "We found no connection among
the victims. They were between the ages of seven and twelve.
Some were Caucasian, others Latino, Black, or Asian. They did
not share a religious faith, didn't go to the same school,
after-school program, or playgrounds. We had nothing to go on."

"'No bodies have ever been discovered and the pattern has
never repeated.'"

"Bullshit!" Rachel shouted, not even trying to lower her
voice. "There were a dozen people on the street when it happened. Nobody came forward? *Nobody?!*"

Dani's voice was soft. "A dozen *humans*, Rachel. If there was
a powerful alpha in the van, nobody would remember even seeing the van."

That had never occurred to her before, even though she knew what Sazi magic could do.

"Yeah. And they could have put up an aversion spell too." She shook her head. "The people in my neighborhood probably never even knew what hit them."

She'd lost interest in the rest of the story. Out of habit, she scrolled back to the top of the page, then stopped. The picture had finally loaded. It transfixed her.

In the center of the image stood her mother, one hand holding a candle, the other raised to heaven, crying. There were lines in her face Rachel didn't remember, and a lot more gray hairs. She looked tired, weary. Standing right next to her, with an arm around her in support, was Dalvin, his expression both heartbroken and furious. There were a dozen other people in the photo, people she didn't recognize, some holding candles and others putting flowers on the street corner. *Her* street corner.

The caption wasn't sufficient to convey the tragedy in those faces. "The families of the victims at a candlelight vigil, still searching for answers and pushing police to reopen these decade-old cold cases."

"That's Dalvin," Dani said.

"And that's my mom," Rachel said, pointing. "No wonder he was so angry. To him, I'm scum."

Dani reached past her to close the Web page. "You're not scum, Rachel. You couldn't possibly have known this was happening."

Rachel shook her head, grimacing. "In my heart, I'd hoped they were still looking. But I was so focused on just about surviving day to day here . . . Now that I've seen this, I can't unsee it, Dani. Now I know that every day that I was growing up in Luna Lake—playing hopscotch or tag or getting dressed up for a dance, or just laughing—my mom was doing *that*.

"Dalvin's right. I *am* scum."

The burning metal of determination and the pepper of

anger, along with Dani's cold tone of voice, made Rachel look at her friend. "While that was happening there, here you were being beaten and humiliated and worked to death. You haven't been living a charmed life, girl. Nobody would envy what you've been through here, and nobody better *dare* fault you for not making it back home yet.

"If your mama was mourning, it's because you were living through the pain she feared you were. That's not your fault. You're just as much a victim now as you were when it happened. Think on that."

The iPhone on the desk let out a chirp to let them know that their music had finished downloading. Dani disconnected her phone from the computer, and the women sat in silence for a long moment.

"What are you going to do next?" Dani asked.

Rachel shrugged. Part of her wanted to cry, and part of her agreed with Dani. She couldn't have changed anything.

"I don't know what to do. While I was in the snake caves, I was locked up in a cage, chained right to the rock. Then I was brought here and was mind-controlled, like the rest of the town. Now I can finally think for myself but can't move away without permission. I don't consider myself a victim, though. Just a survivor."

That got a sad laugh out of her friend. "That's something, I guess. Take it and run with it." Dani paused. "You want to beg off from singing tonight?"

"No. I'm pretty confident I can belt out some really good blues right now. Blues are all about being pushed around by circumstance and living through it anyway." Taking a deep breath and letting it out slow, Rachel pasted on a fake smile. "Let's go get dressed and we'll give them a show to remember."

CHAPTER 10

Dalvin stood in the kitchen of the school, watching the cooks frantically put finishing touches on plates. He could tell which were the chefs and which were just home cooks. He was surprisingly impressed by Bojan Petrovic's skills. He was as good as any chef Dalvin had seen on TV cooking shows. Bojan couldn't be more than twenty, yet he wielded a knife the size of a small machete as if it were a surgeon's scalpel, slicing and dicing vegetables. The care he took to run a clean cloth around the outside of every plate was impressive.

Every plate held exactly the same-size portion, identical garnish and decoration. Dalvin couldn't see a single moment when any sort of poison or foreign substance could be added, so he'd just let people do their thing. Bojan had pronounced the Latin dishes Claire had made ahead of time to be excellent, and Dalvin, who had tasted the chili she had made that day, agreed.

The only difficulty had been when Bojan said that an appetizer, main course, and dessert wouldn't be enough. Everyone had been perplexed. But when the young man explained that fall was when bears gorged, anticipating hibernation, there was a mad scramble to create several more courses.

Two crazy old local owls took a couple of sticks of dynamite out to the lake and came back with a whole bushel basket full of fish, chortling the whole time, near as Dalvin could tell. They were the same birds he'd seen sitting next to Rachel at the town meeting, so he presumed they were part of her parliament.

Suljo, who was wearing a custom chef jacket, had quickly fried up the fish as a second appetizer. Claire and Alek made a big stack of tamales and what looked like a cauldron full of chile relleno as an additional entree. Like Bojan, Suljo knew his way around a knife. Despite their official enmity, the two bears worked seamlessly to create a weird middle course out of the cornbread that Claire had made to go with the chiles, using fresh raspberries and a puree made from cooked carrots. Dalvin had tasted it and thought it was surprisingly good.

He hoped that having a member of each family working in the kitchen would ensure that both sloths would eat.

Since the last negotiator had been drugged, Tamir and Alek would be the only servers. That way, they could be sure no food was touched by anyone else before it reached the diners. None of the chefs knew who would be given which plate, so it would be hard for them to single out someone to poison.

"And that is the end, people! Excellent service," Bojan said as the last of the desserts left the kitchen. He held out both arms and smiled. "My thanks to Suljo and all of you for your help." Boy, if these two ran their sloths, there would probably never have been a land dispute in the first place.

Claire sat down and slugged half a bottle of water before huffing out a breath that blew her sweaty bangs into the air. It was boiling hot in the school kitchen. "That was more work than I expected."

Bojan smiled at her. "You would make an excellent sous chef, Claire, and your crème caramel was flawless."

"We call it *flan* in Texas, but thank you. My alpha would be pleased I've learned well."

Tamir and Alek brought stacks of empty plates around the barrier that had been hastily erected, using rolling dividers from elsewhere in the school, to shield the diners from sight of the frenzied preparations. "Nearly licked clean. Good job, guys. Is there any left for us?"

Suljo nodded. "They will not be as pretty as the guest plates, but there is plenty left." He began to make up servings for the chefs and the kitchen help.

They could hear rustling out in the main room, then Amber's voice came over the PA, echoing off the ceiling.

"First, let me express our thanks to the residents of Luna Lake for their hospitality in hosting us and making this fabulous meal. Sharing a meal is one of the first avenues of peace, and we think you'll agree the food was excellent."

There was a smattering of clapping from the attendees. Dalvin had peeked out during a brief lull; the diners were primarily the European delegates plus most of those he'd identified as alphas among the locals. The Williamses and the crazy owls sat with an old woman and a falcon that he would swear was part parakeet from the way her head bobbed around.

Larissa looked luscious in a skin-tight chocolate silk dress that made her look nearly naked. It was easy to imagine her without those clothes, writhing under him like she had the previous night. She'd kissed the spot where the strip of hide had been taken like it was a boo-boo from the playground and then flat wore him out. She was insatiable.

Liz spoke next. "While we are all digesting our food, several of the town's residents have offered to entertain you. Please join me now in welcoming Danielle Williams, who will dance for us."

Okay, that might be worth watching. The others apparently agreed because everyone in the kitchen shifted around until they could see past the barrier.

He'd only seen Danielle from a distance before. All legs, she was dressed in a simple white tunic with a neckpiece similar to ones he'd seen in Egyptian displays in museums. She walked up the few steps to the small stage and sank into a low bow with her head tucked to her knees. The music sounded like it was from the Middle East; he wondered what kind of dance to expect.

Interpretative—not his favorite. There always seemed to be some sort of message that he was supposed to instinctively "get" but never did. The others seemed to enjoy it, though. Suljo especially seemed to like the performance. Or the dancer. Hard to tell. But when it was over, the Bosnian bear whistled and clapped louder than anyone else in the room. So much so that his parents looked over at him with raised brows. Dani smiled at him as she left the stage.

Amber again took the microphone. "Thank you, Dani, for that beautiful performance. Next we have a very talented singer. Please welcome Rachel Washington."

Dalvin froze with a forkful of fish in the air, next to his mouth. He hadn't heard Rachel sing in what felt like a lifetime. Would she still have the high, clear soprano he remembered? It probably broke protocol, but he grabbed a vacant chair from a nearby table and sat down, resting his plate on his thigh.

She wore a shimmering black-and-gold top with spaghetti straps that made her dark skin glow. It was cut low enough in the front to hint at the curve of her breasts. Slim black velvet pants looked tailor-made and begged to be peeled off. He still missed her long, wavy hair, which she had often worn in beaded braids, but the shorter hair made her neck look longer, more statuesque.

When the first note of music hit the speaker, he smiled— there was no song that reminded him more of her than this one. For ten years, every time he'd heard it on the radio, he'd thought of her.

The voice that rolled out of her was richer, deeper than he remembered, even more perfect for the tune.

He closed his eyes and let himself be transported back to a simpler time, when he and Rachel used to sit on the edge of the city pier where locals went to try to catch dinner. It wasn't exactly a bay, but it was at least a dock. They always went at sunrise on Saturday, just so they could sing this song. The fishermen never seemed to mind, and neither did the fish.

When she got to the next verse, about leaving Georgia, he found his voice and joined in. She faltered for a moment, then her voice rose, clear and strong. He sang counterpoint to her lead, soaring through the verses.

As the last notes of the guitar faded away, Dalvin opened his eyes to see the stunned expressions on the faces of the audience, who had gone completely silent. Rachel was blushing to the roots of her hair. Then the whole room burst into wild applause, with Tamir and Alek both clapping Dalvin on the shoulder. He lost sight of Rachel during the commotion.

"Well, looks like we have a Wolven agent with some hidden skills!" Liz said, reclaiming the microphone. That's going to be a tough act to follow, but Scott Clayton, a skilled magician, will give it a try."

Scott took the stage, dressed in a dark suit and tie. He had real talent with cards and soon involved the alphas in the tricks. There was a lot of laughter, which was the whole point.

There was an awkward, too-long pause after he left the stage, and Dalvin wondered if there was supposed to be another act. Then Liz wished everyone a good night. The few townspeople in attendance left quickly. Tamir and Alek escorted Rabi, Liz, Amber, and both sloths out, except for Bojan and Suljo. Tamir tried to get them to leave, but they insisted on staying to clean up.

"A chef may only leave the kitchen when the kitchen is closed," Suljo said firmly, Bojan nodding beside him.

Once the dining hall was empty, Claire turned on all the lights and surveyed the room, hands on her hips. "Wow. What a mess. And we're out of gloves." Dalvin realized that so many of the plates had come back clean because the diners had apparently dumped any leftover or half-eaten food on the floor.

Suljo and Bojan came around the barrier and let out what he presumed were swear words in their native languages. "Our families," Suljo remarked, "are pigs, not bears."

Bojan shook his head. "No, pigs at least clean their troughs."

Suljo grabbed an empty trash bag and stuck his hands inside, using the bag as protection as he picked up the discarded food, inching his hands back as it filled. The others watched him quickly clean a whole area without getting a speck of gunk on his hands.

"Clever," Bojan said, admiration in his scent. He copied Suljo's actions and tackled another part of the room.

Claire tossed a fresh bag to Dalvin before opening another one with a flourish of her wrist. "I didn't know you were a singer, Dalvin."

"I'm not. Not anymore, anyway. I used to sing with Rachel when we were kids. I didn't even mean to join in. We just used to sing that song all the time. Instinctive, I guess."

"You're good. I mean, really good. Like *American Idol* good."

He didn't think so. "Nah. But even if so, I'm Sazi. No fame or fortune for shifters. No public spotlight or paparazzi following us twenty-four/seven, y'know?"

Bojan nodded, but his scent wasn't happy. "Yes, I am learning that. It is no life for a chef. I hoped to own restaurants, many of them, all across Europe. But now?" He let out a growl from deep in his chest. "No more. I open my restaurant and a bear came to eat. I learn he is a Sazi bear, councilman for all bears. I never hear such a thing. We live in small town—never hear of Sazi for long time. But he is powerful bear. Russian, very strong magic. We cannot resist, so we must obey."

Suljo sighed. "I know this bear. He is not nice. He tell us we not sell raspberries. We have very fine farm, many years old. We have always sold at market but wish to expand, sell overseas. We are told no, we may not unless we work through Sazi. Feel like criminal sometimes, yes?"

Bojan tossed his nearly full bag into the corner with the others. "Yes, and I wish not to fight or to be criminal. Our countries have been at war for so long. So many want peace to live without fear, without armies and checkpoints and fences. Want to eat fine food and dance to music. But our fathers . . ." His sigh matched Suljo's.

It took Suljo a few tries to figure out how to use the drawstring on the trash bag, but once he did, he smiled. "My father is not fighter. He must *show* strength, but wishes peace. My sister, though . . . she wants war. For money. Much money in weapons and drugs and scarce food. I would leave but for my father. He is good man."

Claire picked up all the bags at once. "I'll toss these. Who wants to do the dishes? The dishwasher is broken, so it'll be by hand."

Dalvin grudgingly raised his hand. He was no stranger to working the closing shift in a restaurant. "I'm game if someone shows me where the supplies are."

Suljo tried to take the bags away from Claire, but she waved off the chivalrous gesture with citrus-scented good humor. "They're not heavy. I do this every day. Plus, I know where the Dumpsters are and you don't. But I'm sick of dishes after a month of cleaning up after schoolkids while waiting for dishwasher parts."

Dalvin pushed her toward the door. "Go ahead. I've got this. If you make it to the apartments, tell Scott I'll be late." Turning, he got a good look at the kitchen and realized the full scope of "the dishes." "Tell him I'll be *very* late."

CHAPTER 11

A light snow had fallen overnight, so delicate that even stepping on it made it disappear. Rachel could see her own footprints, like small dinosaur tracks across the white landscape, crossing the smaller prints of a trio of deer and some even smaller mammals . . . rabbits and squirrels. The clouds overhead threatened more snow and the sun's light barely filtered through. What she wouldn't give to fly across the landscape at this time of day, to see all the animals below instead of just smell them.

The air burned when she inhaled deeply, and every sense had come alive in the cold. But she hadn't worn heavy enough clothes to be comfortable standing still for long, and Dalvin was already an hour late. She'd asked Scott to give Dalvin directions to the start of the racecourse, but maybe she should have knocked on Scott's door, made sure he was awake. God only knows how long everyone partied after she left the school.

Part of her was sorry she'd bailed on her second song, but she'd been so pissed off at the bear bitch that she was afraid she was going to jump off the stage and get into it with her. That Zara was no better, laughing at the racist comment Larissa had made during the first song.

She'd also been freaked out by Dalvin. When he'd begun to

sing, she'd gotten angry—how dare he interrupt! Then she
realized he wasn't trying to steal attention from her. He'd just
joined in at the same place he always had back home.

"Home." It sounded strange out loud. But in a flash she
knew—Luna Lake had never really been home. It had always
been, in her mind, a way station from somewhere to somewhere
else. Nothing more.

"What about home?" Dalvin's voice, from behind her, made
her gasp. The snow cover had made his approach utterly
silent.

"I miss it," she admitted. "I didn't realize that until you got
here. But I miss Detroit."

He shook his head. "It's not the same as you remember.
Whole place has changed. The bank collapse wasn't kind."

She remembered glimpsing stories in the news, but she had
deliberately not paid attention, knowing she could never go
back. "Is the fountain still there, next to the park?"

He smiled and the expression lit up his whole face. "Yeah,
that's still there. There's not always water in it, but when there
is, it's the same." He paused. "Sorry about last night. I didn't
mean to cut in. It was your moment, not mine."

She shrugged. "It wasn't really a *moment* moment. Mo . . .
Asylin asked me to sing, so I did." She tucked her hands in her
pockets, feeling unsure of herself. "Hey, did you tell Scott we
were hooked up before I got taken?"

He looked away, smelling of embarrassment and humor.
And something . . . else. "Not in so many words. We were just
talking, you know, while I was unpacking. He asked what you
used to look like. I told him pigtails and too-big jeans, except
that one time."

She furrowed her brow, trying to think back. It was so hard
to remember the time before the snakes. It's like her whole life
until the van was a book she'd read long ago. It didn't seem
real. "What time?"

He smiled again and leaned against the trunk of a pine. "Your cousin Sydney's wedding, when you were twelve."

Sydney. Oh, yeah. Skinny, too-tall Sydney, who was no good at basketball for someone his height and too tall for the chairs in the chess club room. He always looked like a giant at a kids' tea party. "He married Taffy Prince. Yeah, I remember. They still together?"

Dalvin nodded. "Two kids. He's an engineer for General Electric now. Makes good money."

Again she tried to peer back through the haze of time. Nothing. "I don't remember what I wore."

His face changed, as if he was seeing her in his memories. His look was heated and raw, and made her suddenly uncomfortable. "It was a satin dress the color of a caramel apple. Your mama had done your hair up special in ringlets that framed your face, and your gramma had given you a real cameo necklace to wear."

In a flash, she remembered. The whole day unfolded as though she was there again. Most important, she remembered why she'd worn that particular dress. "I was trying to impress you."

"You wanted me to think of you as a *girl*. I'd insulted you at school—I'm not even sure how—but you were right. I didn't. I mean, I knew you were a girl, but you were a buddy, like Melvin or Shawn. But that day—" He shook his head, slow. "You were a girl that day. More than a girl, really. You were *my* girl."

She felt suddenly overheated despite the cold wind. "I didn't know that."

It was his turn to shrug and smell uncomfortable. "I was a stupid kid. I tried to play tough, not let it show. So how would you know? And then you were gone."

"Sorry." And she was. Sorry she hadn't pushed him to say something. Sorry she hadn't asked him to walk her home that day. "I was a stupid kid too."

She felt like one again, a stupid kid who didn't know how to think or act around a man. And really, she didn't. She didn't date. Nobody wanted to date the Omega, and the police chief would have killed anyone who touched her. She was his playtoy, nobody else's. Yet while there was abuse, and it was sort of sexual, there had been no actual sex. Apparently, even Gabriel had limits.

She tried to get past that memory to a better one. "I saw your picture in the paper. With Mama. Thank you for being there for her."

He looked at the ground for a long moment before meeting her gaze again. He gave a little bow of acknowledgment.

"I'm sorry I was so late this morning. I was up all night. First I washed the dishes after last night's dinner and then I stayed up talking with Scott. He's like your best friend, huh?"

She nodded. "But there's nothing between us."

Dalvin snorted, the citrus of his laughter making the day feel sunnier than it was. "I imagine not. I'm probably more his type. If I swung that way."

A small part of her already knew that Scott was gay, but she'd never said it out loud and they never talked about dating. That Dalvin thought the same thing confirmed her opinion and was both a relief and a cause for sadness. There was no hope of Scott finding someone his type in Luna Lake. She wondered about how to talk to him about it . . .

"Anyway, he told me about your life, at least as much as he knew." He struggled with what to say. "Saying 'I'm sorry' isn't anywhere near enough. I had no idea. I can't even wrap my mind around what happened here."

She didn't want to talk about that. Maybe someday, but not today. "Can you shift me?"

His brows shot up. "Excuse me?"

She looked at the trees and the lightly falling snow that was landing on her nose and eyelashes.

"I've never flown in the daylight, and it's easier to see the course from above the trees." She shrugged. "If you can't, it's okay. We can walk the route."

Dalvin nodded. "I can change you. Did you bring extra clothes?"

Extra . . . "Oh!" She was going to have to undress. She hadn't brought anything to change into if her clothes were destroyed by shifting. Since she usually only shifted on the moon, she hadn't thought about that. "Um, no. I didn't. Just a second."

She felt weird about getting undressed around other people. She knew being naked wasn't personal, wasn't sexual in a Sazi society. But she'd been undressed by force so many times . . .

"Turn around. Don't look."

He gave her a wicked smile—both amused and aroused—that made things inside her turn to liquid.

"I mean it. No peeking." She twirled her finger in a circle until he turned his back. She found a bush to hide her clothes under so they wouldn't get wet and ruined. It didn't take long to strip and fold her things. When she was down to just her panties, she felt magic pour over her. The sensation pulled a gasp from her throat. She turned to find him inches away, staring at her with a weight in his eyes that made her knees weak.

"No fair," she managed to pant. "You peeked."

His chest was bare and his jeans looked too tight. He didn't say a word, just pulled her into his arms and closed his mouth over hers. Her heart was racing so fast she was sure it was going to burst out of her chest. The feel of her skin on his, her nipples tightening as they rubbed against his hard muscles—it was electrifying, maddening. He ran his hands over her body, so lightly. Almost reverent.

Her traitorous hands began to explore him too, feeling the play of his broad back, the smooth texture of his skin. His hair felt like the softest feather down. His tongue tasted of fresh mint, coffee, and cinnamon, and the sensation as he wound it around hers made a moan slide out of her throat. He reached down and cupped her bottom, pulling her against an impressive erection while he ate at her mouth. Sensations swirled inside her, making her putty in his hands. She was hungry for something that she couldn't name.

The feeling panicked her. She pulled out of the kiss in a rush. "Dalvin, we can't. I've never—" She shook her head. "Not with anyone."

He looked dumbstruck. "Oh. Oh. Of course." He swallowed hard, let go of her, took a couple of steps back, then shifted with fluid ease. His jeans shredded and whatever erection he might have had was suddenly hidden under feathers. Magic flowed over her again, taking her breath away. She felt feathers spill out over her skin in a sensual, tingling rush that felt erotic. Nothing like the way she'd felt when the mayor had shifted her, never mind the little Dani had managed.

She spread her wings tentatively. Everything felt perfect. No pain at all. "Oh my God! Is that what it feels like every time for you?"

He bobbed his head, opened his wide yellow beak, and blinked his golden eyes. "Sure. Not for you?"

She let out a sharp sound that wasn't quite a screech. "Hardly. It usually feels like falling down stairs. Most moons, it's just one flight and I feel a little banged up but can walk. Some months, it's like three flights and I bounce the whole way."

Another wash of magic made her feel energized, lighter than air. "I promise you. No stairs today. Only roller coasters. We ride where the wind takes us."

Dalvin rose into the air, wings spread wide to catch the highest lift. Although he was not looking at her, he could feel the moment Rachel left the earth. Like a plane towing a glider, he had a constant sense of her presence. The effort necessary to keep her in owl form was surprising. He'd shifted people before, but usually once he did, they could stay that way. Not Rachel. Her owl form wasn't dominant, so the pressure on him to hold it would be taxing if he had to do it for long.

A virgin. That never would have occurred to him. After talking with Scott and Claire, he'd assumed that sexual abuse was part of what she'd suffered. He was glad to know that it wasn't, but now he wasn't sure what to do next. The desire he'd felt from just that one short kiss was stronger than any other he could remember, than anything he had with Larissa. He would have taken her right then, without a second of hesitation. Now, though? The first time with a woman wasn't something you did lightly. From everything he'd heard, from both men and women, it was too easy to mess up.

But how the hell was he going to be around her without wanting to be inside her?

He kept his wing beats intentionally slow, gliding when he reached above the treetops, so she could catch up and fly beside him.

"Oh. My. God!" Her voice held a level of happiness and excitement that he'd experienced only once—the day of his first flight. He couldn't smell her emotion because the wind pulled it away before it reached him, but he could feel it through the magic tether, like riding on a bubble that was expanded to the breaking point. Even now, with them both in owl form, he wanted her. Crap. She tipped up her head and rode a current of air into the clouds, dragging him along. "How can you stand not doing it every day?"

He let out a few low hoots of laughter at her unintentional double entendre. Flying. They were talking about flying now. "You'd be surprised. The novelty wears off pretty quick."

"Oh, this isn't novelty," she said as she flew a circle around him. "This is pure *joy*! My bird half has brought me nothing but pain until now. To not hurt, to fly where I can see the sky and animals and trees as something other than lurking shadows? Dalvin, thank you!" She finally looked down and let out a gasp. "You can see *everything* from up here. I could keep flying all day."

Ambitious, but—"All day might be pushing it a little. My magic isn't unlimited."

Her elation diminished a bit and she slowed her wing beats. "Oh! Is it hard to keep me in this form? We can land now if you need to."

He dropped a wing and bumped her, like he used to shoulder-bump her when they were walking down the sidewalk together. "Nah, I'm good for a little longer. But maybe you should show me where the course is."

She looked around, and confusion and disorientation came through the magic. "Wow. I've never looked for it in the daylight before. Let's fly back over town so I can get my bearings."

She noticed the buildings in the distance and shot forward, then narrowed her wings into a dive. As dives went, it needed some work. In fact, the more he watched her, the more he realized she'd never been trained to fly. If she shifted only once a month, just to hunt, probably nobody had ever bothered.

He struggled with what to do. He could critique her, but he'd be leaving in a few days. It would be almost cruel to tell her about the faults in her flying and then disappear without helping her fix them.

Why the hell had he kissed her? And why had it been so amazing? He knew what his mother would say. *Son, you spent so many years looking and hoping. You created the perfect reunion in your head. It was bound to be amazing.*

Except this wasn't at all what he'd imagined. *She* wasn't at all what he'd expected. Beautiful, selfless, proud. The more he'd talked with Scott last night, the more he realized he'd been a world-class ass. Yelling at her for protecting her family from the reality of shifters? That was unconscionable. He couldn't take it back, couldn't rewind time and make it unhappen. Yes, he'd been furious, but now he knew that anger was misplaced . . . and that the people he was really angry at were dead. Railing at the dead, his dad always said, is only heard by the living . . . and doesn't make you feel any better.

She waggled her wings. "Okay, I've got it now. Follow me." She darted off, and he hurriedly beat his wings to keep up with her. It would be a disaster to let her get out of range of his magic. She would never stay shifted. After a few moments, she swooped down, brushing the soft pine candles with her belly. "Here's the beginning of the cat course. See the yellow plastic circles attached to the trees below us? They occasionally blink. Not often enough that planes overhead will spot them, but enough that if someone gets lost, they can get back on track pretty quickly."

He dove down into the trees and landed on a wide branch next to a yellow circle. She followed.

"Suljo told me last night that they can see color in animal form, so that should work," Dalvin commented. He hopped farther down the branch and saw the rough path that had been carved out of the undergrowth. "There's a lot of overbrush in some places. I'll clear some of that so Larissa doesn't have to duck under things so much. Anica is shorter." He could feel Rachel's disapproval beat at him and could smell the hot iron scent that was out of place among the trees. "What?"

She blinked those big golden eyes and her feathers fluffed around her neck. "The course isn't meant to favor one competitor over another, Dalvin. This spot might be hard for Larissa, but other spots will be hard for Anica. Are you also going to remove the things she'll have to climb over, that Larissa can just step over? If so, let's just have them run around the football field at the school."

He did his best to keep his cool. "Look, her shoulder is hurting her."

A quick flap of wings and a cold response. "Oh, I'll bet it is. Good."

He felt like releasing his magic and leaving her sitting naked on a branch. "So you admit pushing her down the stairs?"

Hooting laughter wasn't what he expected. "I knew she'd smack-talk me! I didn't push her down the stairs, and I can't believe you'd think I would!" He didn't blink, waiting. After a long pause, she let out a light screech and continued. "Look, I was going up, she was coming down. She insulted me and I offered to throw down with her if that's what she wanted. Her alpha told her to knock it off and get downstairs. I saw her sidestep as she came down and knew she was going to try to shove me over the railing. I planted myself and braced. I didn't move one single muscle toward her—she did all the work.

"I'll bet her shoulder hurts, 'cause she slammed into me hard. The worst *I* did was not offer to help her up. But her alpha didn't run to help either. Bitch got what she deserved."

He smelled the air. She wasn't powerful enough to hide her scent. Damned if she wasn't telling the truth. "Her alpha saw this happen?"

Rachel's head bobbed vigorously. "Sure did. And I'll bet Larissa was getting you to do her dirty work and get me punished because her alpha wouldn't. Racist bitch."

"Whoa, whoa," he said, flapping his wings so he could turn around to face her. "Racist?"

She dug her talons into the bark. "It's something she said last night, while we were singing. I nearly dove off the stage and bashed her face in."

"What'd she say?"

Rachel shook her head. "I'm not going to repeat it. But trust me when I say it was intentionally racist. No accident or 'just kidding' about it."

"You going to turn her in?"

She shrugged. "What for? Everyone at her table heard it, and nobody said a thing." She kicked out with one taloned foot. "Eh. They're racist or they're not. I don't really care. You're the one sleeping with her, not me." Her tone was casual, but her words stung and he realized they concealed her own hurt.

Gesturing toward the east with one wing, Rachel said, "Over that way is the hunting challenge. Hmm, that actually might be too much with a screwed-up shoulder. Just to prove I'm staying neutral, let me show you something." She pushed off from the tree and he followed. When she soared under a branch, he noticed she didn't tuck in her corner feathers. They scraped against the bark, causing her to dip and then flap to right herself.

"Hey, wait," he yelled to her. She rose higher in the air, flapping to hold position. "Mind if I show you a trick I've learned for flying under brush?"

Her eyes blinked in surprise. "Sure. I suck at flying. It's why I keep losing the Ascension."

He patted the branch next to him with one wing. "Sit here and watch."

Once she was secure on the branch, he flew under the same branch where she'd bobbled. "This is how you're flying under." He left his wings wide and caught the very same brush on his wings, causing the same flaps to stay straight. "Right?"

She bobbed her head. "Yeah. So what am I doing wrong?"

Dalvin swung around and then flew back under, slow, being careful to tuck in his feathers on one side and lift the opposite shoulder. "See that? You keep the same balance but don't have to flap." He fluttered to a landing beside her. "Now you try it."

"That was *cool*. Okay, here goes!" She swooped down and narrowed her wing but didn't lift the opposite side. She veered off and nearly creamed into the trunk. "What happened? I lifted my other wing."

"Not the tip of the wing," he called out. "Right at the shoulder. Try it again."

It took four tries for her to get it, but once she did, she sliced through the brush like a hot knife through butter. They'd been out long enough that he was getting tired holding her in form.

"Let's head back. I'm burned out, Chelle."

Though she tried to hide it, she was obviously disappointed. "Sure. I understand. But I should show you the hunting challenge first."

He flared his wings. "You can show me on foot. Let's get back before I can't hold you anymore."

He might have imagined it as he rose into the sky, but he could have sworn he heard her mutter, "Oh, you'll be holding me again. Count on it."

They were nearly back to the spot where they'd left their clothes when a distant scream caught his ears. "What was that?"

Rachel rose higher on the air currents and motioned. "Over there! A bear is chasing some hikers. I don't think they're locals. I'll bet they're heading to the top of the mountain to base-jump. There's a ledge that's sort of infamous near the top. Damned adrenaline junkies."

Goddamn it. Just what he didn't need right now. The pressure of keeping Rachel in owl form was testing his endurance. He thought about setting her down, but he might need her help.

As they got closer, he realized the bear was Sazi! It was a massive brown bear, so one of the Bosnians. And he was most definitely chasing the man and woman, who were dressed in jeans, flannel shirts, and bright-colored down vests. Their oversize backpacks bounced on their backs with every frantic step. Given the size and lightness of the loads, it seemed likely to Dalvin that Rachel was right and the humans were carrying parachutes.

Dalvin let out a battle scream and headed down in a dive. Rachel followed him, matching his pose. At the last second, he reared back and exposed his talons, right in the path of the bear, who stared at them, recognition and intelligence in his eyes. Rachel flapped her wings in the bear's face while the humans scrambled to find shelter among the rocks. Dalvin threw what little magic he had left at turning the Bosnian away. He hadn't seen all of the family in animal form, so he didn't know which one he was facing, and he couldn't ask, not with the humans right here.

The bear kept swiping at them and trying to dodge around them as they swooped at him. Dalvin was trying to avoid hurting the Bosnian and didn't want to draw blood, but that became a challenge in the face of the bear's persistence. He definitely wanted to attack those people for some reason.

Rachel broke the standoff, letting out that insanely powerful screech. Tethered to her magically, Dalvin noticed it didn't affect him as it had before—good thing too, since he might have fallen right out of the sky if she'd paralyzed him. The bear froze stock-still for several seconds, then ran into the woods, bawling and shaking his head.

Circling to gain altitude and make certain the bear had left, Dalvin he heard the man say, "Whoa. That was coolest thing I've ever seen. Did you get it on video?"

"Oh, you know I did!" the woman replied. "I've never seen an owl that big! And two different species cooperating to attack a bear? This'll go viral before we even get home!"

Holy shit! That could *not* happen. Before Dalvin could think what to do next, Rachel said, "I'm on it. Change me back. Hurry!"

She landed behind a tree. He didn't know what she was planning to do but decided to trust her. Releasing the magic that bound them, he felt a sudden surge of energy and circled higher, keeping an eye on Rachel and the humans as well as the Bosnian bear, who was heading into the deep woods. Dalvin wasn't looking forward to trying to figure out the identity of the bear and what the heck was going on.

Rachel screeched again, even louder this time. Without the magic linking them, Dalvin's muscles froze and he began to fall. Twisting in a flat tailspin, he watched in shock as Rachel raced out of the brush, stark naked, and grabbed the cell phones out of the hands of the paralyzed humans. She darted back into the woods, her lean-muscled legs putting impressive distance between her and her victims, just as the hikers realized what had happened.

"Hey! What the hell!" the man shouted, and they began to chase her.

Rachel was holding the phones in her mouth, tight between her teeth. Looking up at him, she started flapping her arms. Hell! He'd never done anything like it before, but he threw down his last reserve of magic. Pain sliced through him as Rachel shifted forms. She took flight just before the hikers caught sight of her. The two owls rose high into the clouds so the humans wouldn't be able to see which way they flew.

Wind and ice crystals that weren't quite reaching the ground slashed at Dalvin's face. His heart was beating so fast that he was afraid he was going to have a stroke. The two owls dove, fast and hard, as he tried to get them close to the ground before his magic failed. He pushed the last bit of his power at Rachel, but her wings turned into arms just before she hit the ground. She rolled over in the wet grass and came up spitting mud right next to where they'd left their clothes.

He lost his own battle to keep his form and fell at least ten feet, landing in a painful heap.

"Dalvin!" Rachel raced over to him. "Are you okay?"

"I'll live." He chuckled even as he scraped mud from his deeply painful shoulder. He'd probably have a whopper of a bruise there by evening. "What a story they'll have to tell! Attacked by a bear, saved by owls . . . and then a crazy bush lady stole the proof!"

She laughed, turned around, and scooped up both phones.

"That's me, 'crazy bush lady.' Thankfully it will only be a story, and hard to believe."

"Well, I believe it." He smiled at her, and her gaze dropped shyly. Then she tilted her face up again and leaned forward, planting her mouth on his. She pushed him back to the ground, and he went willingly, his body exhausted yet hungry. He started playing with her breasts, and she responded by snaking her hand down between his legs. She began to stroke him, and he moaned, moving his mouth away from hers to kiss his way down her neck. "God, I want you, Chelle."

She whispered in his ear, her voice trembling a little, "I'm not quite ready for that, Dalvin. But I'm not a complete stranger to a man's body. I'm ready for this." Her wet hand started pumping up and down on his cock, smoothing away the abrasive mud, making him hard. Her fingers were cold, and the sensation against his overheated skin was delicious. She kissed him again, moving her tongue in and out of his mouth in rhythm with the motion of her hand. Fast, then slow, making him crazy. She didn't stop him from exploring her body, though she was sitting in such a way that he couldn't reach between her legs. But those luscious breasts, oh, he explored them, all right. Felt the weight of them in his hands, played with their tight brown nipples.

It didn't take long to get him past the point where he could turn back, past where he cared about the past . . . or the future. She noticed when he was ready to go and tightened her hand, pulsing it like he was inside her. He thrust against that hand until he felt himself go. He clutched at her head with one hand, tightened his fingers on her back with the other, and pulled her mouth to his in a hard kiss. He sucked on her tongue and felt her heart race against his chest, feeling their magic mingle in a way that was so intense he could barely stand it.

She shivered then and gasped into his mouth. Her whole body stiffened and her hips squirmed on the grass. He realized she had gone over too, even though he hadn't touched that part of her. That excited him more than anything. If sex was this good using just their mouths and hands . . . what would it feel like to actually be inside her?

His head fell back, and he tried to catch his breath. She loosened her grip on his cock, lightly resting her hand on top of it as it shifted with the tiny after-twitches of his orgasm.

"Baby, that was something else," Dalvin said.

Rachel gave him a Mona Lisa smile. "I'm not your baby." She pushed off of him and stood, walking toward the bush where her clothes were, intentionally swinging her bare hips. "Not yet, anyway."

CHAPTER 12

*T*he whole town was looking for Samit Petrovic by the time they got back to Luna Lake. People had heard screams coming from up on one mountain and nobody could find him. Alpha shifter search parties had already begun combing the woods. Rachel spotted Asylin and John Williams winging through the sky above her—going the wrong way.

At least now they knew who was missing. Rachel and Dalvin ran to the town hall, where they presumed the Council members would be working out a strategy. Liz and Amber were there; Liz was talking on a radio. "You need to stop him before he gets to the next town, Rabi. Dead humans would be really bad."

Liz paused, probably listening to Rabi's reply, then said, "If he's gone rogue, he could have gone any which way. All we can do is keep our eyes open. Hopefully, the birds will be of some help."

"These birds can definitely help," Rachel said. "We can tell you where he is, or at least where he was half an hour or so ago."

"Rabi, hold on. I think we have some intel." Liz held out the radio, the button still pushed down.

Dalvin walked closer, so Rabi would be able to hear him. When he drew in front of Rachel, she wished she didn't notice his cute butt right then, but she couldn't seem to get his body out of her mind.

"He's not rogue," Dalvin said. "When he saw us, he knew exactly who we were. He was chasing a pair of base jumpers, trying to kill them. He was in total bloodlust but completely sane."

"Did you get that, Rabi?" Liz spoke into the radio, then let go of the button so they could hear Rabi's reply.

"Yeah." The councilman's voice was tinny and distant through the speaker. "How do you know he wasn't rogue? His family swore he'd gone rogue; they're blaming the Kasuns for poisoning him somehow."

Rachel shook her head. "No, I've seen plenty of rogues—they're a dime a dozen in Luna Lake. The magic they give off has an odd feel, like a vortex. Chaotic. Samit's magic was just fine. He might wind up killing someone, but it's not because he's gone rogue."

"Hello? Did you hear me?" Rabi said. Rachel realized Liz had forgotten to push the Talk button while Rachel was speaking.

Liz rolled her eyes at her own behavior and pushed the button. "Sorry, Rabi. We heard you. Rachel and Dalvin say Samit isn't rogue."

When she let go of the Call button, at first there was a long pause filled with waves of static. "I think we still have to treat this with caution. We have only the word of two people who don't know him, versus his own famil—"

Rachel reached in her pocket and held up one of the phones she'd taken from the human hikers. She'd decided not to destroy them. Instead, she'd turned off the location services and removed the SIM cards, making them invisible. "Oh, we have more than our word. We have video."

Liz said, "Call you right back, Rabi. We need to see this."

"Don't bother," he replied. "I'm nearly to you. Let's watch it together."

Amber, who had been silent up to that moment, asked, "Why were you guys out there this morning?"

Fighting not to blush, Rachel hoped that the quick dip she and Dalvin had taken in the lake before rushing back to town had eliminated the scent of what they had been up to. Her voice was pure innocence when she replied, "I was showing the cat course to Dalvin, like you asked."

The Wolven agent nodded, adding, "Rachel pointed out that the hunting challenge might be difficult with Larissa's injured shoulder. We decided to come back here to chart out an alternate to that portion. That's when we saw Samit."

"Where's this video?" Rabi asked as he stalked into the room, looking both worried and angry.

Rachel handed one phone to Dalvin and began navigating to the camera roll on the other, trying not to smile at the councilman's appearance. He'd definitely "gone local"—other than his olive skin, he looked like any other town resident in a heavy red flannel shirt and weathered jeans. "I'm not sure which phone belonged to the person taking the video, so we should check both."

Liz moved closer to Rachel, brushing her arm with a velvety soft red-patterned chenille top. *Man, I have got to go shopping one of these days. They are wearing some sick stuff.* "These are the hikers' phones? Good job getting them. We can't let any photos be seen."

Dalvin laughed. "We were flying at the time, but she didn't want to risk catching them with a talon so she had me shift her. She screeched and then ran past them, stark naked, and snatched the phones right out of their hands."

Amber had just taken a sip of soda, which she now spewed all over the desk. Fortunately, the cola would blend in with her dark brown sweater vest and not stain it. "Oh, I like you. That pretty well ensures nobody will believe their story." She leaned forward and said, with sparkling eyes, "And then, kids, the crazy naked lady ran out of the trees, screamed at us, and stole our phones!"

Rachel could hear laughter in Liz's voice as she added, "No, really, she was naked! Right out there in the snow."

Rabi raised his eyebrows and asked, mock sternly, "How much have you had to drink today? Could you please empty your backpacks and show me your ID?"

That was it; Rachel cracked up. It sounded completely ridiculous in retrospect, but her actions had seemed perfectly sane at the time. Looking at the phone, she saw the video she was looking for. She held the phone so the others could see the screen and pushed Play.

Everyone crowded around. It was strange for Rachel to see herself in owl form. Her wings were fluffier than they felt on the inside. She hadn't remembered the snow falling so hard when she'd been fighting, but it was really pretty on the video. Dalvin's flying and fighting were magnificent—no wonder he was in Wolven. If she didn't insist he teach her more flying, she was an idiot. And she finally got a chance to see the effect of her screech! It really was a paralysis. Everyone froze as though the video had stopped. Except the trees kept moving in the wind and the snow continued to fall. The video ended with Samit running off.

"Wait. Replay that part right at the end," Rabi said. "I heard something."

With the sound at its loudest, the audio was still just barely audible. Even so, the bear's anger was chillingly clear. "You will *pay* for this, owls."

"He's not a rogue," Rabi said with heat in his voice. He took the phones from Rachel and Dalvin. "Who are these people? Was it personal? Were they Sazi or family?"

Rachel shrugged. She set the SIM cards she'd removed on the desk. "I don't know. But we have the phones. We can probably check out the people. I pulled the cards out in case the location services were on or they had tracking programs installed."

Rabi nodded. "Thank you both for bringing this to us. Now please leave while we discuss it."

"Can I just say that—"

The councilman raised a hand. "I wish I had time. Truly. But I need to set up an emergency video chat with the Council. These peace talks are about to self-destruct and we need firm agreement on how to go forward."

Amber put a hand on his arm. "I think it would be wise to keep them here in case the rest of the Council has any questions about their encounter."

Liz chimed in. "I agree. We need to make this quick, and I don't want to have to track them down."

Cool. She looked over at Dalvin, who was wearing a frown. Not angry; worried.

Rabi produced a laptop from a briefcase, turned it on, then connected it to a strange gizmo that had a dozen flashing lights. He clicked on the touchpad, and a dozen small boxes appeared on the screen. The word "Waiting" was quickly replaced by "Connecting" in each square, and then "Paging."

A man's face appeared in the upper left screen. He appeared to be Native American, with long black hair. The second screen flashed to life, showing Angelique! The falcon shifter looked elegant, even blinking and bleary-eyed and obviously just out of bed. The next to connect was Sargon's son Ahmad, the snake councilman. Even now, the resemblance freaked Rachel out and made her step back. Dalvin noticed, put a hand on top of hers, and squeezed lightly. It helped, just that little touch.

The fourth screen stayed blank. Amber tipped her head toward Rabi. "You won't reach Charles. No connection in the Yukon. Not even satellite where he is."

The fifth screen lit with the image of a handsome blond man who also was just barely awake. He was the first to speak, with a slight French accent. "Really, Rabi? It's three in the morning and I just got to sleep. This had better be important." Amber leaned over and waved.

"Congratulations, Antoine. I just heard the news. Give Tahira my best and tell her I'll drop by the estate as soon as we finish up here."

Oh! He must be the councilman for the cats. Rachel had heard of him. He did an animal show with one of the big circuses. Great cover for when he had to shift into a cat himself!

The man in the top corner spoke. "I think we are all you're going to get, Rabi. Nikoli is off hunting with his pack. I'll fill in as representative for the wolves."

Rabi let out a little growl. "I'd really hoped Zolan could be here. This is about the bears."

Ahmad, rolled his eyes. "We have a majority. We can make decisions without his input if necessary. Many years went by without the Council even having a bear representative, and the world survived. What is your concern?"

"Fine," Rabi said, throwing up his hands in frustration. He quickly but succinctly explained recent events, starting with everyone's arrival in town. "Now we're faced with a situation where one of the delegates has gone off the reservation. Do we continue with the race or should I call this location a bust too, and move the discussions somewhere else?"

Antoine raised a finger. "But both alphas are willing to let this Ascension challenge decide the matter? Did you sense any deception?"

Rabi shook his head. "No, not from the alphas."

"The alpha males anyway," Rachel said under her breath, forgetting that all the people around her were alphic. Amber and Liz both turned to look at her, and Rabi stiffened, his back straightening even more.

The snake councilman pointed right at her. "You there. Come forward. I would like to hear what you have to say."

Antoine was the one to roll his eyes this time. "Ahmad, we don't have time for a Q and A session."

The whole group started to argue: Yes, she should talk, no she shouldn't. Finally, Ahmad slammed his fist down on something that shattered under the blow. The noise silenced the others. When Ahmad spoke, his voice was calm, without even an edge of anger.

"My esteemed fellow Council members, please look closely at this woman. I met her yesterday. She survived one of my father's 'training' camps. She was at the camp personally overseen by Nasil. Please give her a moment of attention, out of respect."

The councilman named Antoine underwent a complete transformation, his expression shifting from annoyed and frustrated to complete admiration in less than a second. It was a little unnerving.

Amber poked her head into view of the camera. "Angelique, this is the woman I spoke to you about this morning."

"Ah." The sharp, slender face peered out from the screen. She spoke in a high-pitched voice with a thick accent that sounded sort of French, but wasn't the same as the cat councilman's. "You are zat one. Very well. Screech for me."

"Excuse me?"

Rabi let out a high-pitched snarl and smelled of angry cat, the nasty scent of ammonia. Angelique made an impatient gesture in her little box while he hissed and said, "We don't have time for this!"

She dismissed him with a wave. "The cat, he ees restless. Someone give him yarn. Screech and then speak, young bird."

Amber turned completely around so the people on the screen couldn't see her and then whispered in Rachel's ear, so softly that she could barely hear, "Give it your best or she won't let you talk."

Rachel took a deep breath. Just as she was about to let loose, something stabbed her in the side, sharp and painful. The resulting screech was equal to the one she'd used on the bear. In the enclosed space of the town hall, the storm of sound froze everyone except Amber in their tracks.

"Nice," the bobcat healer said.

Still recovering from being jabbed, Rachel spun toward Dalvin. His mouth was stuck open, his eyes momentarily vacant. She looked down and saw what he'd stuck her with, still clasped tightly in his paralyzed hand: a metal letter opener. Pain and surprise had enlarged Rachel's screech; she bet she was bleeding under her shirt.

She turned back to the communicator. On the screen, the three men were rubbing their ears. Angelique was clapping her hands gleefully and smiling.

"Oh, zat was very good! Very pretty. Yes, yes, I will work with you. Now speak."

Work with me? Having no idea what that meant, she pushed on. "Um, I just wanted to say that I think I have a way to solve the problem of the bears. There needs to be a third option, 'cause you know the moment someone wins the challenge, the loser will accuse them of cheating. Both sides have already tried to sabotage the challenge, and I'll bet they each know what's gone on and are just waiting for the right time to bring it up."

Now Rabi looked interested. The ammonia scent was sucked into the vents as the heater kicked on. "A third option? Such as?"

"Me."

She waited while everyone thought it over. Dalvin nudged her but she ignored him, her gaze fixed on the Council members on-screen. Liz smiled and nodded.

"You're the local Omega," the mediator said. "The town's Omega."

Rachel nodded. "I've lost every race I've ever run. They can check the records until they're blue in the face, that's all they'll see." *Because it's true.* "The Council puts me in the race as the American Omega. If I win, the Council picks where the fence goes. Nobody loses, nobody wins, and both sides wind up being ticked off. But not with each other."

"The enemy of mine enemy theory. But if you have lost every race—" Ahmad didn't have to finish. She knew what the rest of the question was.

"Until a month ago, this town was under the mental control of an insane alpha." Everyone nodded, so she assumed they'd read the reports. "I was the favorite whipping bird. I believe the mayor and police chief made sure I would never win."

"Or," Rabi said, "you were never impeded and simply never won."

She looked squarely at him. "I don't choose to consider that a possibility."

Angelique reached forward and pressed something. Her screen turned green. "She has fire, zis little bird. Oui."

Ahmad didn't speak, but his screen went green.

The cat councilman, Antoine, became bathed in red. "Nothing against you, but I don't think this would change the result. There will still be accusations of cheating. It just muddies the water further."

The man in the upper corner lit his screen to green. "It does muddy the waters more, Antoine. That's the very point. Who will the saboteurs sabotage? It splits their attention and makes it easier to ferret them out. Rabi, since the majority says yes, it will be up to you to make this a nonnegotiable point.

"Be angry about the sabotage you've already discovered. Tell them you *know* the attack on the hikers was a ruse, an attempt to have the other family put down for killing humans. Heap blame on both sides and throw your muscle around. They'll both object to the Council being heavy-handed and imposing its will. Channel Ahmad's most obnoxious moments when you reply. Heavy-handed imposing is his best thing."

Ahmad tipped his head. "Thank you, Lucas."

Catching on, Rachel said, "Then I need to hate the idea. I need to object and bitch about it."

Liz agreed with a grin. "Absolutely. If we're imposing on them, we have to be imposing on you too."

Amber touched her arm, smelling slightly of worry. "Are you sure you're up to this? Not only do you have to win, on your own, without our help, but people will be trying to knock you out of the race."

Dalvin stepped forward. "I'll make sure nobody gets close."

That was nice to hear, but Rachel had to shake her head. "Can't. You're supposed to be guarding the Bosnians. If that changes, they'll know something is up." She turned and looked into his golden-brown eyes, surprised and pleased to see concern there.

"I'm the girl who yelled at you and humiliated you. You're dating Larissa. We probably shouldn't even talk, except to insult each other." That was going to hurt. But after this was over, he would be leaving and she couldn't. Might as well get used to not talking now.

The man in the upper corner—Lucus?—spoke up. "I agree. So we have a clear path forward? Rabi?"

Rabi dipped his head in acknowledgment. "I agree, with one amendment. Dalvin is the best flyer in Wolven. If the others can be trained for the competition, then so can she, and he is the logical person to do it. That will give her at least one day of protection. I don't want anyone killed on my watch, especially an omega who can't defend herself."

Antoine let loose a hearty laugh. "Were you not just in the room when she screeched? I saw you frozen solid. She can defend herself just fine, Rabi. At least long enough to get to safety. But I'm fine with a trainer. If the others have one, it only makes sense. Otherwise, everyone will know something is up. And if the sloths believe both of them find the match offensive, more the better."

Offensive.

Just a day ago, it wouldn't have been difficult at all to imagine he would find it offensive to be forced to spend time with Rachel. Now he found it offensive to suggest he not. But it was a good plan and he could see it working. He cleared his throat. "Then I should be leaving, probably by the back door. I'll head over to the Petrovics' quarters to see how the search is going. We really do have to find Samit. He may not be satisfied to simply attack one couple. He might keep trying until he kills someone."

The door burst open. Rabi slammed the laptop closed, cutting off the video meeting as Tamir bolted into the room, announcing, "We found him. He's on the back road, headed for the next town."

Amber shifted forms in a flash, shredded clothing falling to the floor, except for one black pant leg, which she kicked off. "I'm on it. Send a car that way. I can put him out, but I won't be able to carry him back." She was out the door in a flash, moving so quickly that she was just a blur of spotted fur.

Rabi looked at Dalvin and managed to come up with an impressive amount of angry scent on short notice. "You have your assignment, Agent. I'm done arguing. You will keep your mouth shut and do your job!"

Dalvin nodded, crisp and professional. It wasn't hard to look angry—but it was a struggle not to look at Rachel as he left, his hands clenched into fists.

In the distance, he heard Rachel shout, "You can't do that to me! I want to talk to my alpha!" He smiled. *Attagirl.* Then he had to regain his anger, so he thought about Larissa, trying to trick him into framing Rachel. Which made him furious. Except he couldn't afford to be mad at her. He was supposed to be snuggling with her. Wow, that was going to be a test of his undercover skills.

Reaching under his shirt, he ran his fingernails along the healing scab where Tamir had marked him. Oh, yeah. That would do nicely. By the time Tamir reached him, he was good and pissed.

"Arguing with a councilman, Adway?" the big bear said. "That is a short path to a grave." He glowered at Dalvin.

"Yeah, well, I don't freaking care. Rachel has her own parliament. Why should I have to train her for the race?"

Tamir's face and scent reflected confusion. "Why would you have to train the owl? What race?"

Dalvin blew a raspberry and yanked open the back door of the nearest SUV, searching around on the floor as though he'd lost something. "Oh, that's the Council's latest bright idea. They're going to have a third competitor in the blood feud challenge. Rachel complained about Larissa to the Council. Told some bogus story about her making racist comments.

"I've never heard Larissa say a single bad word about black-, brown-, or green-skinned people as long as I've known her. Since I'm same race as Rachel, I think I'd notice, y'know? And now I have to *train* Rachel? Bullshit. I swear, I should just up and quit this job."

Tamir shook his head, buying the story completely. His scent was mostly neutral, with a slight edge of dark glee at Dalvin's situation. "The Council, it does what it does. We have to live with their judgments, no matter how ridiculous. When are you expected to do this? Don't you already have a guard shift?"

"Yeah! And that's the other thing. When am I supposed to sleep and eat? Huh? Pisses me off!" Actually, he really hadn't thought about that part. It was going to be a tough couple of days. At least he thought about what he should be looking for in the car. "Have you seen my flip phone? Someone must have jacked it out of my bag. It's my private phone, the one I use for family." Actually, it was the one taken by Amber, and he really didn't know where it was, so it was a semitruthful explanation.

The bear agent shook his head. "No. I haven't seen it. Check with your roommate. You never know the character of people *assigned* to sleep with you."

"Yeah. True. Well, it's not here, so I'll check there tonight. Keep an eye out for it." He got in the driver's seat and started the engine while continuing to mutter about people walking off with his stuff.

Normally, he might have left the car behind, but the problem was, he didn't know when Rabi would come by or whether the Council member would insist everyone come to him, making the car necessary. Detroit's alpha always made people fly in, in horrible weather, for meetings. In fact, Dalvin was pretty sure Frank waited to summon everyone until conditions were truly terrible, so people would be too cold and wet to bitch about how things were being run.

He parked outside the Williams house and took a deep breath, then sprinted up the wide steps and into the log cabin. The alphas and Larissa were in the living room. He wasn't sure where Bojan and Zara were. He tried to decide how much he should know and how much he could tell them.

Middle management, he decided. *I know some stuff, but it might be wrong.* That was frequently the case. It was rare that he knew as much as he now did about any assignment.

He touched Larissa as he walked by. Just like always. She looked up and smiled. There was an unpleasant edge to her smile, one he'd never noticed before. Mustafa and Iva were in twin recliners, their feet up. She was knitting, a constant, never-ending hobby, and he was reading the paper. Well, looking at the paper, anyway—Dalvin had learned that the big man could not read. He listened to Internet radio and managed to bull his way through current events. But reading looked "smart," so he did it.

Iva looked at Dalvin, her scent all curiosity. "Is there any news of the missing bear?" It still seemed strange to have her asking questions of him directly, without Larissa translating. They'd hidden their language skills well; he'd lived with them for weeks without realizing they both spoke and understood English.

The female alpha's eyes sparkled with the hope that he brought bad news.

"Someone spotted him. I just came from a meeting. A couple of the Council members are on their way to the location. He'll probably be put down as a rogue."

Mustafa tried to look sad and failed miserably. "So sad. Some families do not have good genes." Iva nodded agreement.

Dalvin sat down in the chair next to Larissa and leaned toward her, running his hand along her upper arm. "I'm sure someone from the Council will be in touch." She turned and smiled, her expression more genuine this time.

"I went through the course today," Dalvin told her. "We should talk about it before we start training tomorrow morning."

Mustafa clapped a hand down on his knee and Dalvin looked his way, keeping his gaze carefully on the sloth leader's neck, as was proper. "You tell us both. Is good course?"

He nodded. "It's challenging, but yes, it's a good course. There were some spots where Larissa would have to dive too low under the brush. I fixed those so she doesn't hurt her shoulder more."

Her smile widened; it made Dalvin's stomach turn. "You are sweet."

"And since it was a cat course, there was a climbing test to show hunting prowess. I think we can change it to fishing in the lake. You can fish with either hand, right?"

Mustafa nodded vigorously. "Larissa is excellent fisher. Left hand, right hand, bare teeth. Catches large, fat salmon. Enough to feel whole sloth."

Larissa looked almost smug, completely confident in her fishing skills.

"I don't know if they have salmon here. I don't know what kind of fish are in the lake. But I'll find out for you," he added. He tried to remember more about the course, but since they hadn't made it all the way through, his knowledge was limited. He hoped he wasn't lying about anything.

Mustafa slapped the arm of his chair, causing the floor to shake. "I would see this lake. I hear of it, but have not seen it. You will take me there. Now."

"Um—" Could they leave? He didn't know. "I think you'll be safer here until we know that the rogue has been captured."

Mustafa rolled his eyes and scoffed, his scent amused. "Samit is baby bear. How much rogue could he be? I am *Alpha*. If I cannot bring down baby bear, I will turn pack over to Suljo."

Iva and Larissa started laughing and Mustafa joined in. Dalvin guessed that nobody expected Suljo would be taking over the pack anytime soon.

The Alpha walked the few steps across the room and clapped him on the shoulder. "Come. Show me the lake."

"Sure. Okay. But you'll probably want to change your shoes." Dalvin gestured to the man's elegant dress boots, which were covered with colorful embroidery.

"True. I will meet you at car in moment."

The Wolven agent raced out of the house and shut himself in the car, which was pretty well soundproofed. Hurrying, he called Scott.

"Hey, Dalvin," came the other man's voice on the line.

"Quick. How do I get to the lake from the Williams house? I'm supposed to already know."

"No problem, but you'll have to tell me why later. Go to the diner and take a right. Stay on the road until you get to the crossroads with the paved road, then turn left. You'll run right into it."

Thank goodness the windows were tinted, so though Mustafa was already reaching for the door handle, he couldn't see Dalvin.

"Thanks," he whispered and hung up, stowing the phone just as the Alpha got into the front passenger seat.

Sniffing the air, the bear said, "You smell nervous. Is there problem?"

Dalvin shook his head. "I'm always cautious when there are *potential* problems."

Mustafa clapped Dalvin on his sore shoulder, making a shudder run all the way through the younger man's body. The alpha laughed. "Nervous and cautious. They are sisters in the nose, yes?"

Nodding was the only correct answer. "So, let's go to the lake." He prayed that he could follow Scott's hasty instructions.

The sun had finally broken through the clouds so the roads that Scott described were easy to find. There were no other vehicles in the small dockside parking area. A low, narrow wooden plank dock stretched perhaps a dozen feet into the water. The lake, shaped like a crescent moon, probably covered ten acres. A few ducks that should have already traveled south paddled lazily along while shorebirds stepped carefully at the water's edge, looking for food. It was a tranquil little lake. Nice.

Mustafa let out a snort. "*This* is lake? Bah. Not enough fish here to feed sloth for a month, and no river!"

"Will it be okay for the competition?"

The big bear shrugged and looked around more carefully. "Eh. Muddy edges will make them work to get to water. Anica is smaller, so she will have advantage there. But Larissa might jump across whole mud and is strong swimmer, so she will get to big fish faster. Is contest for speed or weight of catch?"

Actually, that was a good question. "I don't know. I'll ask Councilman Kuric."

Mustafa started strolling across the field. "Where is course they will run? I would like to see."

"The Alphas will see the course later today . . . at the same time," Dalvin said, heading back to the SUV.

"It will not matter," the elder Kasun said with a snort. "Larissa will win and our fence will stand."

Dalvin held open the passenger door. "I'm sure that's true. She has a lot of skill." Lying, cheating, sabotage. All skills, just not ones he valued.

CHAPTER 13

Rachel sat in one of the black SUVs with Amber, parked upwind and well out of sight of the start of the Ascension course. The three-quarter-carat diamond brooch Rabi was wearing on the collar of his white-and-gold tunic was actually a video and audio transmitter that he explained he routinely carried on assignments. This way they could stay hidden but still listen in until it was time to drive up for the big reveal. He'd really dressed up for the event. Rachel could believe without hesitating that he was a Council member in the clothes he was wearing. Unfortunately, the SUV didn't have a video screen, so they had to watch the goings-on through binoculars. They had to continually shift around to see through the blowing branches of the trees and bushes that concealed the car, but the audio came in clearly through their radio.

"I decided to bring both families together here, away from the townspeople," he said, then paused, studying all of them, including Dalvin and Tamir. All the delegates were present except Samit Petrovic, who was in the rogue cage in the Williams house, being guarded by the Williamses and Alek. "This way you will not be publicly humiliated by what I am about to do."

"Where is mediator?" the Kasun Alpha asked. He was like-

wise dressed to the nines, in a suit that would look best on
Rodeo Drive and a black cloth hat resplendent with silver and
gold thread. "Why is she not intervening in councilman giving
orders to us?"

Anica's father shook his head and barked out a laugh.
"Because mediation is *over.* We chose to battle through omegas. She has no place." His clothes were clean and pressed but
neither new nor fancy. Either he had no fancy or formal wear,
or he didn't feel this meeting was worth the effort. Same with
his wife, Draga. Where Iva Kasun was painted and posed,
Draga Petrovic was simple and wholesome. Rachel thought they
probably didn't own any formal outfits—they'd dressed the
same way at the welcoming dinner too.

Zara Kasun, the little minx, was dressed in fur and jewels.
She was perched on the edge of the fence beside her brother,
who looked more like a member of the other family in his jeans
and pullover sweater.

"Then who will judge contest?" Zara said. "A judge must be
chosen. I will judge."

"You?" Draga Petrovic barked out a laugh. "A dog guarding
a bone would be more fair."

Iva Kasun took a step forward, her jaw jutting defiantly. "Says
the woman who cannot even keep a fence from being built
under her nose, not—"

"Be silent!" Rabi raised his hands dramatically, and a wave
of magic swept across the field so fast that it blew the grass flat
like a giant crop circle. The Wolven agents and the junior members of both sloths screamed in pain and dropped to their
knees. Even the Alphas struggled to stay on their feet.

"Do you think I'm an *idiot?*!" came Rabi's tinny snarl over
the radio.

Rachel looked over at Amber. "How is he doing that? He
didn't feel this powerful at the town meeting."

Amber gave a small smile. "His sister has a rare talent. She can store magic from multiple sources and feed it to whoever she wants, as long as it's someone she's connected to. I imagine Antoine donated some magic for this little show." She put a finger to her lips. "But you didn't hear that."

From one person to the next, right down the row, Rabi confronted every delegate, plus Dalvin, revealing exactly what each one had been doing to sabotage the competition.

Since Rachel already knew everything he was telling them, her thoughts turned to a question she had had for a while.

"Amber, I'm just a lowly omega. A nobody. You should all be patting me on the head and pushing me out the door. But everyone is talking to me, listening to me, taking me seriously. It seems sort of . . . off."

The redheaded cat sighed. "I really *can't* tell you. But there is a reason. Besides . . . don't you want to know all the secrets?" She grinned.

"Well, sure. But it's weird. Sort of scary. I keep waiting for the other boot to drop."

Amber tapped a finger on the steering wheel, her scent such a mixture of emotions that Rachel figured she was undecided about what to say. Finally, she let out a breath and gave a little shrug. "There is a boot about to drop, and it won't fit you very well. But it's nothing you can't handle and it's necessary."

Well, that sucked! Still . . . "Thank you, I guess, for telling me that. My gramma always used to say it was better to know you'd get beat up before you left. Then at least you'd be carrying bandages."

Amber covered her mouth to try to hold in her laughter. Rachel turned her attention back to the feed.

"Let me explain what is going to happen now." Rabi's words were forceful, and there was a weight of . . . maybe *majesty* was the right word, in his tone. That must be the "channeling Ahmad" part. "I have grown weary of your petty squabbling and would rather simply remove you all from our species.

But the Council has stayed my hand. Instead, by majority decision, the Council has selected an omega shifter to race against your omegas. You met her at the dinner last night—the singer, Rachel Washington."

The bears' shouting was cut off by another wave of magic that shook the ground. "A grave insult was given her by the Kasun Omega and she rightfully demanded an apology. We have decided that if insults can form the basis for a blood feud, then Rachel deserves to be included in this competition."

The Kasun Alpha turned on Larissa and grabbed her by the throat. "What do you say to this singer? You will apologize immediately!"

Rabi shook his head, sending a horrible scratching sound over the radio. Amber winced. "You were there, Mustafa. You heard it just as I did. Not only did you not discipline her at the time, you *laughed*. The only reason I did not discipline her myself was that I was hoping you were enlightened enough to notice there are no Sazi *monkeys*, and discussing blues singing in the same sentence with *chains* is unconscionable. My ruling stands. Rachel Washington will compete for her honor."

Anica's father stepped forward. "What could she possibly win? The dispute isn't about her, or even this town."

The corner of Rabi's mouth turned up in a sly smile. "If the Council's choice wins the race, the *Council* decides the dividing line between your lands, and your dispute is over."

Both Alphas shouted at once.

"*Ne!*"

"No! This is not acceptable!"

Rabi reached out a clawlike hand, looking for all the world like Darth Vader, and clenched his fist. It was almost funny to Rachel until the Alphas began to grab at their necks and gasp for breath. "*I* decide what is acceptable for this dispute. Not you. Be grateful I don't simply kill you all." He sat down in midair, one leg crossed over the other knee, casual. His fingers were steepled, and he peered down at them as if he was seated on a high throne. That was a hell of a trick to pull off; it must have used a ton of magic.

He released the men with a flicking gesture of dismissal, seemingly effortlessly, and they dropped to the ground, coughing.

"That's our signal," Amber said. "Don't hold against me what I'm about to do. It's for show."

"Wha—" The rest of the words in her intended sentence never reached the air. Amber had put her in a hold so tight she could barely expand her lungs.

She heard a ripping sound, and then Amber put a wide strip of duct tape over her mouth, being careful not to get it too close to her nose. "Can't have the feisty little omega running away or screeching, can we?" Then she taped Rachel's hands behind her back and gently laid her down on the front seat.

Ohhh! It was making sense. She was going to be brought into the competition bound and gagged—to show that this wasn't her idea of a good time either. Amber started the SUV and drove up to the other group.

"Ah," Rabi said over the transmitter. "I see our physician has brought the last party guest."

When Amber shut off the ignition, she also turned off the transmitter and hid it in the ashtray. Then she got out, walked around the car, and opened Rachel's door.

Had Amber not given her a warning, Rachel knew, she would feel pissed, terrified, and humiliated, so that's what she had to smell like. As the short, delicate cat hauled her out of the front seat like a sack of animal feed, a memory flashed in her mind.

Bound and gagged, she'd been pulled out of the flower shop van and tossed to the dirt, right at the feet of a leering fat man who had pulled her head up by her braids and slapped the colored beads against her skull until she screamed against her gag.

He'd laughed while one of the other men had kicked her in the stomach. She'd been terrified and furious, both with them and with herself for not watching her back.

By the time she hit the ground, all those feelings were back. "Our third competitor." Amber's voice was as cold as the predator she turned into. "She wasn't as excited about competing as the others."

Dalvin looked like he was ready to tear someone's head off, but she shook her head as though she was trying to get the tape off, hoping he would understand that she was cooperating. She didn't know if he got the message, but he calmed down and set his jaw.

When Amber reached for the corner of the tape, Rachel steeled herself. Nothing worse than duct tape coming off skin. Even worse than a bandage or cast. It felt like Amber was taking the flesh right off. Rachel let out a cry of pain that wasn't faked.

"Motherfucking son of a bitch! What the hell is *wrong* with you?" Her genuine anger sold the whole performance. Larissa and Anica both looked at her with expressions of sympathy.

Perfect.

Rabi looked down on her, one eyebrow raised with an expression of disdain. "Rachel Washington, you are the Council's champion. If you win the competition, you will be rewarded."

She struggled against the bindings. Ruse or not, she *hated* being tied up. "Tie me up and drag me out here . . . yeah, I have a lot of confidence in the Council's word! You promised to let me leave town a week ago. Then you said I had to stay. You promised you'd pay for college and then you yanked it back. Why the hell should I believe you now?

"What if I lose? Why should it be my fault if they're simply better? Plus, they're fighting for their family honor and land. They're going to fight *hard*. Oh, and don't bother to threaten me. Death is a damned sight better than my life now."

All of that was true, so it wasn't hard to get outrage into her voice and scent. Rabi regarded her for a moment the way a cat looks at a bug: interesting and possibly edible. Then he leapt down from the invisible throne in cat form. And what a cat he was! Jesus! He was like a cross between a tiger and a lion, with a massive yellow-and-white mane and golden orange fur.

He lifted one paw and she rose into the air. It felt freaky—not like flying at all—and she flopped around, trying to get her balance. He set her on her feet while she tried not to hyperventilate.

His voice deepened, became a growl. "Those who made past promises to you had no power to fulfill them. I do. Yes, these families fight for their existence, but they also fight for their freedom to live as they will. I offer the same to you. You will be *free*. To live where you choose, as you choose. No restrictions except protection of the secret of the Sazi."

She took a breath, and the scent that wafted to her said he wasn't kidding. This wasn't part of the plan. "Wait. *Seriously?*" She looked to Amber for confirmation.

Amber seemed a little surprised too, but she shrugged. "What he says, goes. He speaks for the Council." She gave him a short curtsy, bowing her head. "As you desire, Sahip."

Rabi stared at Rachel, his eyes blazing with a yellow fire that began to spread to the rest of him. Even his black stripes began to glow with black fire. Damn! That was impressive.

"Omega? What say you? You would not be missed in this town, and your family of origin already believes you dead. You could go anywhere, do anything. The Council will pay for your relocation and education. Is a chance at freedom worth fighting for?"

Hell, yes!

"Okay, yeah. Sure." She tried to keep some annoyance in her response, so it didn't sound like he'd completely sold her. Rabi growled, low in his chest, and his chin dipped enough for her to see his freaking huge teeth. "I mean, um, as you wish, Sahip."

The big cat's head turned sharply; he fixed his gaze on Anica's father. His long tail began to lash back and forth. "And you? Speak for your family, Alpha. Freedom or death?"

Zarko Petrovic straightened his shoulders. "I wish to be clear, Councilman, or Sahip, or whatever you wish to call yourself. I also do not fear death." The growl from deep in Rabi's chest started again and his tail moved even faster, cracking like a whip in the air. "For *myself*. But," the Alpha conceded, "I am here for one reason. To give my family hope and freedom. Death will not give that, so I, and my sloth, will obey."

The Kasun Alpha glowered and smelled so angry he could spit. "It seems I have little choice. Very well . . . Sahip."

The councilman shifted again, regaining human form, though instead of the suit he had been wearing before, he now was dressed in long white robes and a head cloth, like Ahmad had been when Rachel first saw him. "Tomorrow each of you will train on the course. Tamir will train Anica. Larissa will be trained by Nathan Burrows, the schoolmaster of Luna Lake. And our new omega, the owl, will be trained by the Wolven agent, Dalvin Adway."

Dalvin muttered a string of obscenities under his breath. Rabi regarded him calmly, one eyebrow raised. "We have already discussed this, Agent. Do you wish to lose *another* strip of hide? I'm happy to claw off as many feathers as it takes for you to remember your place. You are an owl. She is an owl."

The dark-skinned young man let out a snort. "She already knows the course. She grew up here. What could I possibly train her to do?"

Rabi blinked. "Win, of course. She has lost every previous challenge. If she is to win, it is your job to ensure she can. If she fails, her mentor fails as well. I would suggest you read the original rules of the competition to see what happens then."

Oh, holy Jesus! Rachel's breath stilled when he said that. Not the present rules, but the *original* rules: the loser of the competition and the mentor were beaten bloody for failing. The rule had been intended to ensure that mentors made every effort to help the competitors.

Dalvin clamped his mouth shut and glowered silently. It was a good act. At least, she *hoped* it was an act.

Every muscle in his body was screaming from Councilman Kuric's blast of magic. Where the hell had Kuric gotten that kind of power? It was just as well—Dalvin had to be pissed and worried and frustrated if the Kasuns were going to believe he was being forced into this. The magic helped with that.

"Please return to your residences. Omegas and trainers will have this evening to review maps of the course. They will report here tomorrow morning, promptly at eight o'clock, for training."

Anica held up her hand. "Please, sir . . . am I to still room with Rachel? Or must I move now that she is rival?"

Rabi tipped his head, thinking, then raised his brows at Amber. "Your thoughts, Doctor?"

There was a pause before the healer spoke. Dalvin hoped that the bears would think she was taking time to think, not that she was *acting* as if she was thinking. "Let them room together. I don't want to have to find new places to put people. In fact, since I bunked in the back of the Community Center last night, I'll move in with Rachel too, to keep the peace."

"I will stay with the Kasun family," Rabi said. "Miss Sutton is already at the Petrovic residence. We will all be watching *closely* for additional attempts at sabotage."

Dalvin looked at the sky. There were probably two hours until sunset. He bowed his head and spoke, looking at the ground. "Councilman . . . Sahip Kuric. First, I apologize for however I have failed the Council. It was never my intent to do anything but my best job."

There was a long pause. Dalvin risked a glance up. Kuric was expressionless. He had no emotional scent at all—either he wasn't feeling anything in particular, or he was wearing the Wolven cologne.

"Go on," the councilman said.

"You have mentioned that the competitors would all have a day to train, and that seems fair. But shouldn't the entire group walk the course now, together, so we can agree on what it's supposed to look like? Unless guards are posted the entire length of the course, there's no way to ensure it won't be altered to-night in a way that benefits a single competitor."

Mustafa clapped him on the shoulder and smiled broadly. "This, I like. We were promised to see the course today, *before* training."

The councilman looked at the doctor, who shrugged. "It seems fair. If we all go, there will be no question about whether something is different. It would take too many people col-luding."

"Guys," Rachel said from her awkward position, hands still bound behind her back. Dalvin's temper flared again. What the hell were they thinking, treating her like a prisoner? "I'm the only Luna Lake resident here and I've never run the cat course. I might not recognize changes, if it's *already* been altered. Maybe you ought to bring in one of the cat omegas to take a look." She paused and let out a frustrated breath. "Damn, the cat who ran it most recently is a recovering rogue."

"Rogues do not recover," Iva Kasun said, her face full of disbelief. "They go insane, they die. Or are put down." Draga Petrovic let out a sharp gasp and put her hand to her mouth while her husband growled, but Iva didn't take it back. She just shrugged. "Is true."

Amber crossed her arms over her chest. "Actually, this one *is* recovering. Her imbalance was caused by a third party. Now that he's dead, she's getting better. But she's not completely well yet, and I don't want her to be around as many negative emotions as there are in this group. Is there no one else?"

Rachel didn't seem very confident. "Maybe Ray Vasquez, but I'm not sure. Originally, everyone in town competed every month, and he's older than me, so he might have run the course. That was years ago, but I don't think the route has changed much since then."

Kuric nodded with curt precision and pointed at Dalvin. "You've met him. Find him. Bring him here. We will wait."

Judging from Kuric's expression, he wouldn't take any excuses well . . . and realistically, Vasquez should be somewhere near the police station. Kuric waved one hand, adding, "You may take the vehicle if you choose not to shift and fly."

"It'll be easier to bring him back here if I drive."

Kuric tipped his head in acknowledgment. "We will wait, but our patience is thin."

In other words, don't take the scenic route. Fortunately, it wasn't a long drive back to town, and the police station was centrally located.

Inside the station, he found the Latino man alone, sitting behind a desk, typing on a desktop computer.

"Excuse me? Chief Vasquez?"

He kept typing and dipped his head. "Yeah. What can I do for you?"

"Rachel Washington suggested you might know the cats' Ascension course well enough to give a tour to the delegates."

Ray snorted and looked at Dalvin out of the corner of his eye. "You seem to be on everyone's shit list this week, Agent. That why they sent you to ask?"

Dalvin let out a slow breath and shook his head. That wasn't exactly how he wanted people to know him. "Seems like it this week."

Ray shrugged and stood up, reaching forward to shake his hand. "Don't worry. I've been there. Sometimes the shit list isn't such a bad place to be. Keeps you out of the spotlight, where people notice you."

"Is there a reason why not being noticed would be good right now?" the owl shifter asked carefully.

The older man pursed his lips, leaning against the edge of his desk. "Word around town is someone doesn't want peace."

Dalvin jerked his thumb sideways in the direction of the Williams house. "Yeah, we found that one. Got him locked up."

The cat shifter made a small movement of his tan face that Dalvin recognized as *maybe yes, maybe no.* "Seems kind of obvious, doesn't it? Attacking hikers right out in the open for no reason, with a Wolven agent conveniently nearby to see? I've sort of learned not to trust the obvious."

That had occurred to Dalvin too, but there had been too much going on for him to really think about it. "Have you told anyone about your suspicion?"

Ray smiled, but there was no warmth in it. "I was told my duties when that Russian bear arrived." He held up his fingers and made air quotes. "*'Stay out of our way, keep the citizens out of our way, and keep your mouth shut.'*" He snorted. "That was fine with me. Figure it out on your own if you're all so damned smart."

Dalvin put a hand over his face. *Tamir, you idiot!* "Look, Chief, I apologize for my boss. He can be a . . . well"—this was no time for tact—"a dick sometimes."

"Yes, he can. So, why should I help *you*?"

"I guess my best answer is you'd really be helping three young women who are between a rock and a hard place, and one of them is Rachel Washington."

That got him a sigh. "That poor kid. She can never catch a break. Her, I'll help." He reached for his hat. "Let's get going. You can tell me what they want on the way."

Once they were in the car and on the move, Dalvin said, "Short version: Three omegas are going to run on Luna Lake's obstacle course, to settle all their disputes. The omegas from the visiting sloths, and Rachel. They're going to use the cat course."

"Well, the Ascension course has solved a lot of disputes. But how did Rachel get involved? She kin to someone?"

"No. Another long story that doesn't matter right now. What matters is that everyone wants to walk the course before we train tomorrow so nothing hinky happens overnight, and we don't know what it's supposed to look like already."

They turned past the diner and Ray had to reach for his hat to keep it from dumping onto the floor. "Cat course, huh? Yeah, I've run it. Hell, I helped set it up. But it won't work. Not for two bears and an owl."

Dalvin twisted his head so fast that he nearly drove off the road. "But that was the course Rachel recommended. She said there wasn't a bear course."

The other man nodded. "She's right about that. Never had many bears in town, and all of them were alphic. Only Nathan's left now. No bear course because there wasn't anyone to run it. We talked about a bear course early on but never could settle on a route. What would challenge a bear isn't the same as other species. They're unique."

Huh. "How so?"

"Well, they can climb, but they don't hunt that way. They tend to crawl over obstacles instead of jumping over them. They can dig for grubs and such, but they'd rather eat things that are already out in the open and easy to get, like berries and bugs. They'd fish all day if given the option, and they're sort of casual in how they hunt.

"Plus, we're talking about *omegas*. Their animal instincts will be greater than their human ones on the full moon. You can get them to race, all right, but you sort of have to goad them along and play to their instincts to keep them on track. Alphas have their minds, so it's easy. Omegas . . . not so much."

Crap. Everything Ray was saying made absolute sense. "So why not use the cat course, then?"

"It's nowhere near water, for one. Tigers like water and I'm okay with swimming in animal form, but cougars and lions don't do as well. Unless they're thirsty, if they even smell water, they go the other way. So for the bears, you'd have to drastically change the route to get to the lake.

"Plus you have to find some way to keep them on course. Omegas will frankly get bored and will just wander off unless you shock them or something. It's sort of mean to do the challenge that way. No, you need to keep them interested or you'll be sitting there a long damned time waiting for someone to finish." He shook his head. "Lucky Rachel. She'll win without even trying."

"Really? That would be great!" The Council really wanted her to win. "But it seemed like there were a lot of trees to fly through."

"At first, sure. The route starts in the trees and then goes to flatland, to make the cats run over rocks and such. The main part of the course is at the edge of the mountain, so there's a lot of jumping involved. We use deer urine to keep the cats running. Rachel won't face any serious obstacles. It should be straight sailing to the finish line after the first quarter mile."

"Would there be a reason why she'd suggest that course?"

Ray nodded. "It really is the closest fit, if it was just bears. The bird element is what throws it off."

"So what would you suggest? I remember seeing a multi-species course. Would that be better?" Dalvin pulled over and stopped the car. He wanted to get a better handle on things before delivering Ray to the Council, so he'd know what questions to ask the older cat once they were there.

Ray actually laughed at that. "For *bears*? Lord, no. We race wolves against cats on that. Sometimes birds too. Works fine because they all sort of hunt the same prey animals. Small deer, rabbits, squirrels—we vary them depending on who's running.

"Bears don't. I mean they will if it's convenient or if the prey is newborn, but that creeps out the human side once they remember the night." He shook his head again. "They're *omegas*. Animal brains with the occasional flash of humanity, unless their alphas are going to be in their heads. And if so, then what's the point of the race?"

Dalvin leaned back in his seat and rubbed his eyes with his palms. "Damn it. So, how do we race them?"

His passenger drummed his fingers on the armrest. "For hunting, go with something they can't resist. With Rachel, we used chipmunks and white mice. She couldn't get enough of store-bought mice. For the bears, we could put some live salmon in the lake or some honey up in a tree if there's time to set up the course. The trick is balancing the amounts so they don't just sit and gorge and forget they're in a race."

The details were starting to sink in. "Fish are smelly and I noticed all the bears liked the smell of roadkill on the way here. They'd open the windows wide every time they saw something dead on the side of the road. Once we had to stop just so they could sit there and breathe in the smell, the way other people stand in front of a bakery when bread is just out of the oven." He began to drive again. "Could you help the Council members set up a course by tomorrow morning?"

"Phew! Not asking much, are you?" He shook his head. "That would take all night. Maybe if I had all day tomorrow to work on it—"

The lake was in sight. No doubt he was going to be chewed out, or lose another strip of hide, for taking so long. "No good. People are supposed to train on it tomorrow."

"That's not a problem. It's the same land and, really, they're not supposed to know the configuration until they get there.

Doesn't make much sense for them to memorize it. Mostly they just need to be in shape for it. Climbing, flying, dodging, and searching. The details are up to the race masters. Always have been."

When Dalvin pulled up, he was glad to see that Rachel was no longer bound. She was sitting on the dock, swinging her feet under her, chatting with Anica, Bojan, and Suljo. Larissa and Zara were huddled together near a tree, talking, with their hands close to their mouths. He looked for the alphas, then decided they were probably in the other SUV. Knowing them, the Bosnians would be in one set of seats and the Serbians in the other, with the privacy pane raised between them. Tamir stood guard, staring at nothing and everything

The Council members were watching the others, standing near the edge of the parking area. As soon as Dalvin came to a stop, Councilman Kuric walked up to the car; Dalvin rolled down the window before turning off the engine.

"I presume he was difficult to find?" It was a casual way of asking, *What took you so damned long?*

"Not very, no. But there are things that you two need to discuss. Do you drive?"

That actually made the councilman smile. "Yes, I drive. I enjoy it. I'm a mechanic too. I've built a few hotrods from scratch." He reached a hand past Dalvin's chest. "Rabi Kuric, liaison to the Council. You're Officer Vasquez?"

"*Chief* Vasquez," Dalvin corrected. "Field promotion of sorts."

"Oops, my bad." He dipped his head, instantly transforming into an entirely different persona—closer to the person he'd been in the police station on the first day. "Chief, of course." He opened the door. "Okay, Dalvin, you hop out and make sure everyone plays nice, and I'll drive around with the chief, so we can talk."

Ray was looking at Kuric with interest, like he was trying to get a handle on the man. Good luck with that. Dalvin sure hadn't yet. He unbuckled the seat belt and got out of the driver's seat; Kuric slid in, buckled up, and started the engine. Once they were gone, Dalvin took a moment to study the scene around him. He wanted to talk to Rachel but knew he shouldn't. It was better not to even make eye contact. *God only knows what emotions would fill the air if I looked at her too close.*

If he even thought about her too much, he'd remember the feeling of her hands on him, her lips. She'd driven him insane without even trying.

Steeling himself, he walked over to Larissa and Zara and touched Larissa on her uninjured shoulder. "Are you okay?" Kuric had been pretty heavy-handed earlier, and both she and Anica had been screaming in real pain.

Her eyes were angry, but there was fear in her scent. "I have never experience something like him. It is no wonder people fear the Council."

He rubbed her shoulder. Should he try to explain why that had been necessary? Growing up, his father had explained that people only respected the rules for two reasons: an internal moral compass that pointed to good, or a fear of retribution by someone bigger and tougher. Too many Sazi felt they were above the law and, being stronger than humans, preyed on them. Not always physically . . . moon magic could have a powerful influence on the human mind. But Larissa wouldn't understand that Kuric was trying to impress the Alphas. She just knew it hurt. "Yeah, sometimes they can be real asses."

Out of the corner of his eye, he saw Amber raise an eyebrow at his comment. He'd probably be hearing about that later. He hoped she'd understood why he said it. None of this mess was the girls' fault. They deserved a little sympathy. His concern must have been evident in his scent because Larissa leaned into his arm—not enough for anyone to notice unless someone was watching very closely, but enough that he could definitely feel the pressure.

"Thank you for caring," she said softly.

Did he? *A little . . . yeah.* How could he not feel *something* for her? She'd shared his bed, laughed at his jokes. He supposed she could have faked everything. Part of him wanted to believe she was faking so he didn't feel guilty about what he'd done with Rachel. But the other part wanted to think she cared. It was probably time to change the subject. "When you shift on the moon, do you know it? I mean, are you conscious of your human self after your Alpha helps you shift?" The more he thought about what Ray Vasquez said, the more it made him question the whole Ascension concept.

Larissa looked at him a little oddly, but Zara seemed interested too. "Yes, I am curious like Dalvin. We speak of it little, I know. But I have wondered how you will run in this race when you shift. When we hunt together, you talk very little. Sometimes, when I tell you of berry bush I see, or salmon, you seem . . . as if you don't hear me. But you follow me when I go there."

Larissa made little movements of her shoulders and hands, her scent an odd mix of smells—fear, anger, frustration, but comforted somehow. "I do not think of it much. I remember hunting with you. Seeing and smelling fine berries and my claws sinking into salmon. I enjoy our hunts."

Zara shook her head, her scent growing more frustrated. "But *while* we hunt? Do you hear me when I call your name?"

Larissa nodded but was confused. "Of course. I hear you speak. I have ears."

Zara looked over at Dalvin. "You understand what I ask . . . yes?"

He nodded and touched Larissa's arm. "When Zara talks to you during hunts, says your name, do you understand that Larissa *is* your name?"

Zara nodded enthusiastically, her face finally showing something other than annoyance to Dalvin. "Yes, this. Do you know the *word* 'salmon' means the fish to look for? Because sometimes you bring up trout when I talk of salmon."

The dark-skinned woman furrowed her brow, really thinking. "When I am bear . . . I think light sweet or dark sweet. Dark sweet taste better. Fish are fish. Some are big, some are little." She thought a second more, then shook her head. "They aren't raspberries or blackberries. I mean, I *know* they are when I remember. But they are just light sweet or dark sweet during hunt, and trout are just littler fish. Salmon are bigger fish. I like taste of big fish, but smaller fish are easier to catch. But whole family shares, so I always get some big fish."

Zara looked at Dalvin, realization animating her face. Worry replaced curiosity in her scent. "How she run race? Papa speak of colored markers and clock for speed and weights of fish." She turned and ran toward the SUV. He and Larissa followed. Amber noticed the procession and motioned Tamir over. Zara knocked on the window, hard and fast. When her father lowered the glass, she began to speak quickly in her native tongue, pointing at Dalvin and then at Larissa. Tamir had his hand next to Amber's ear, likely translating.

The longer Zara talked, the more concerned the Kasun Alpha looked. At one point he said something that she apparently disagreed with, because she shook her head strongly. Larissa jumped into the conversation, and moments later Mustafa was out of the car and knocking on the back window. Draga Petrovic rolled down the window.

Perhaps because of the audience, Mustafa Kasun spoke to her in English. "Which of you turns Anica?"

She shrugged and looked at her husband. "Sometimes Zarko. Sometimes me. Why?"

"I have not thought of this until Zara ask me, but does Anica think as human after shift?"

"Think as human?" Zarko leaned past his wife to join the discussion. "How do you mean this?"

Mustafa paused for a moment to think, perhaps deciding how best to phrase his question. "After I shift Larissa, I direct her, keep her with sloth. I pull her . . . use magic to keep her close, like horse pulling cart. Is same for you?"

Zarko nodded. "Yes, of course. I make sure Anica stays close to one of us, or her brothers. She wanders off if we do not tie her to us."

Mustafa raised his hands; his frustration made his magic spike and spill out over Dalvin's skin. "Then how they race?" He pointed to himself and then to Zarko. "It will be you racing me, through them. You see? How this solve our problem? Is not *our* blood feud. They must race *each other*."

Zarko's face went slack. He sat back heavily into the seat, blinking as he tried to process what he'd just heard. He leaned over his wife again, who was sitting calmly, perhaps not fully understanding what was being said, and called out, "Anica!"

The dark-haired woman turned her head and trotted over from the dock. Rachel and the others followed.

Amber stepped into the mix, her eyes watching the Alphas intently. "I think Tamir has brought me up to speed on the issue here." She turned to Anica and Rachel. "How human are your thoughts when you are in your animal form?"

The bear shifter stopped to think. Rachel said, "In the past, I didn't remember anything. The whole night was a blur. I'd wake up and not even remember shifting. But since I joined a parliament, I have more conscious thoughts. Not every month, but some nights I can fly over the forest and see a deer and think, 'Oh, pretty deer,' instead of thinking of it as food or not food."

Dalvin remembered what she'd said when she was yelling at him—now that made a lot more sense. What would it be like not to remember shifting? Not to remember the sensation of flying, of the wind through your feathers? There were things he'd like not to remember, of course—his talons sinking into flesh, ending a life because his animal demanded it. Biting the heads off mice because it was fun. That part might be a blessing not to remember.

Now Anica nodded, her dark eyes filled with understanding. "Yes, I am like this too. Some moons I can look at sky and think stars are pretty. Some months, they are little lights, not stars." She turned to Larissa. "Do you see *stars* or just lights?"

"Stars," came the confident reply. "They are always stars. And the moon is always the moon. It has a word for it. But not everything does. It's . . . I know the words, but I don't know if I could always think of the word if I was asked. Just as speaking English is hard to remember what word goes with a thing sometimes."

"Okay," Amber said, her eyes wide with surprise. "This is a real issue." Everyone heard a vehicle bouncing down the road and turned to see the missing SUV heading back. Kuric was alone in the front seat. "Tell you what . . . let's call it a day and let me talk with the Council. I know everyone agreed to do this Ascension thing, but that was before this came up. I will let you all know what we decide. In the meantime, think of some other options. What else would be acceptable that included all three participants? Or, what would make the current contest fair and not just a battle of wills between the Alphas?"

Dalvin shuddered, remembering other disputes that had turned into emotional battles. *If that happens, the lives of the Omegas might be considered nothing more than collateral damage.*

CHAPTER 14

*W*hat would you like for dinner, Anica? I don't have much in the house." Rachel held open the refrigerator door, peering at what little remained. She'd almost emptied the fridge and pantry in preparation for leaving for Spokane.

Anica came out of the bathroom, rubbing a towel against her wet hair. She smelled of soap and herbal shampoo. "Do you have fish? Any kind is fine. I haven't eaten since some grapes this morning."

Rachel tried the freezer. "Um, a half box of frozen fish sticks." A quick look in the cupboard yielded a thin can. "Or sardines. Sorry. I was about to leave town when all this happened."

Anica sat down and adjusted the jeans that Rachel had loaned her to wear after her shower. She was shorter than the owl, so the pants dragged on the ground. The bear shifter turned up the legs in narrow bands that soon reached midcalf, like capris. She looked cute, like a '50s throwback, wearing blue jeans and a long-tailed man's white dress shirt—one of Rachel's favorites— with the sleeves rolled up to the elbows. She crinkled her nose. "No, freezer and canning ruins fish. Not to worry. I am not very hungry after the day's events."

"Yeah," the owl shifter replied with a snort, leaving the

kitchen to sit across from her guest on the recliner. "I get that. It probably wouldn't hurt me to miss a meal either."

There was a knock on the door. A quick sniff was all it took for her to recognize the visitors. "C'mon in. We're decent." She looked over at Anica. "Friends of mine. You'll like them."

Her reassurance made the girl's expression shift from nervous to relaxed. The door opened, and a heavenly scent wafted in, followed closely by Scott, Alek, and Claire.

Scott raised the boxes like a trophy. "Pizza boy! Anyone hungry in here?"

He was carrying three boxes; one of them, Rachel knew, would be sausage and mushroom, her favorite. "You are the *best*! I'm starved." Anica let out a chuckle, making her shrug and grin. "So I lied. I was trying to be a good hostess."

A broad smile lit Anica's face. "My mother, she does this too. She say, 'No, no, *you* eat. I am not hungry,' when no more food in house and guest has not eaten. You are good hostess." She sniffed the air. "What is food? It smells good."

Scott put the boxes on the coffee table between the couch and chairs and plopped down on the floor. "Pepperoni with extra cheese, veggie supreme and, for the lady of the house, sausage and mushroom." Claire passed out paper plates and Alek put a six-pack of cold beer on the table before he joined Scott on the floor. Scott took the first slice of pepperoni. "Since I helped you throw out the food in the fridge, I figured I'd bring some back to put in." He took a bite and then closed his eyes in appreciation as he chewed. "If it survives the night, that is."

Anica looked at the boxes with eager anticipation. "I have never had American pizza! Which should I try?"

Claire reached for a piece of the veggie supreme. "This one has mushrooms, peppers, onions, and olives. Under that there's tomato sauce and melted cheese."

"This one," Rachel said, putting two slices on her own plate, "is pork sausage with mushrooms."

Anica smiled and reached for a slice of that. "I like sausage. My cousin Rudolph makes pig blood sausage. Very spicy. And mushrooms are wonderful when I dig them out from the forest." She took a bite and chewed slowly. Once she swallowed, she smiled. "Oh! This is *very* good. We need pizza in my town!"

"Pizza," Scott said, "bringing about world peace since 1900." He took another bite and sighed.

Claire sat down next to Alek and touched the side of his face, smiling warmly. It was nice to see that they were still happy together. Rachel aimed a floppy slice of pizza Alek's direction.

"Hey, any word on a new motorcycle? Have you heard from the insurance company?" The mayor had destroyed Alek's bike the night Claire had arrived in town.

He shook his head, swallowing before he replied. "Yeah, but they say it isn't covered. Well, it *is* covered, but the deductible and age chewed up the payout. I got about five hundred, which will almost buy me one wheel and a headlight." He made a mock swipe of his fist through the air and smelled of frustration. "Boy, that policy was worth every penny, huh?"

"Oh. Sorry. So I guess the trip to Russia to find Sonya is off too?" Claire had told her a few weeks before that they planned to use the money from the insurance to buy tickets to go find his sister.

Claire responded with a little sigh. "Temporarily. Amber helped us write a letter to the pack leader, telling them we're working at coming over. But it's still not even certain that the girl is Sonya."

Scott reached for his beer from the recliner, causing his hair to nearly fall in the pizza carton. He caught it just in time. "I have faith. As soon as Denis finishes his sentence, the money will happen. It's all about destiny."

Anica looked at him and cocked her head to the side. "You have very long hair for boy. Are your feathers long too?"

Scott was chewing and very nearly spit out the bite of pizza in an abrupt laugh. "That would be *great*, but no. Just regular feathers. But wouldn't it be cool to have long peacock-length feathers?"

Alek chuckled. "Nah. They'd get caught on the tree branches and it would take hours to get the bark out. And can you imagine them in a rainstorm?"

"Feathers actually shed water, unlike wolves' fur," Rachel said. "When you guys get wet, you're soaked for hours. And we laugh, because we're warm and dry."

Claire stuck out her tongue, which made Anica grin again.

"You are right, Rachel," the Serbian said. "I like your friends. I never know Wolven people except as mean. Is nice that birds and wolves can be relaxed, laughing." She sighed. "I wish I could be friends with other bears. Bojan is very nice."

Alek nodded. "He seemed nice at the banquet. Great chef too. Do you like to cook, Anica?"

She leaned back into the couch and curled her bare feet under her. Alek offered her a beer, but she waved her hand. "I do not drink alcohol. I can cook enough not to starve, but I do not *like* cook. Not like my mother. She cooks for hours just to have femily eat in very short time. Then cleaning. Pfft. Not for me. I will eat raw before I cook when I am alone. Even before I am bear."

Oh, shit! Rachel glanced at Claire—one of them had to change the subject before Alek realized Anica was an attack victim who had turned her family.

But before either of the women could speak past the pizza in their mouths, Alek asked, "How old *were* you when you turned?"

Claire swallowed first, nearly choking, then elbowed him. "That's an awfully personal question, Alek."

He blushed and tried to backtrack. "Oh, hey, I'm sorry if I—"

But Anica waved off the objection. "No, no. Is okay. I have . . . how you say, accept my bear side. I was thirteen when

I was attacked, nearly a woman and already betrothed. But that was ended, as you can understand."

Rachel winced. Claire winced. Alek and Scott were both staring at the Serbian woman like she'd grown a second head. Scott reached out and touched her knee. "You were an attack victim? What happened?"

Reaching out one foot, Rachel kicked Scott in the arm. "Dude. Not cool."

Anica looked confused at the mix of scents—the men both smelling embarrassed and curious, the women horrified and afraid. She looked anxious, realizing something was wrong but not sure what. "Am I saying a wrong thing? Is talking of attack a rude thing?"

There was no way this was going to end well. It had gone too far. Rachel took a deep breath. "Okay, look. Anica, it's not bad to talk about being an attack victim. There's nothing to be ashamed of in this happening to you." She looked at Alek—she could tell he wasn't sure what to think. "Alek, can you let go of the law and order thing for a few minutes and think like a person?"

His face and scent both showed his outrage. "What's that supposed to mean?"

Claire touched his arm. "It means that Anica told me and Rachel something that could get her in a lot of trouble, but she doesn't realize it's wrong, so she doesn't know to stay quiet."

Alek let out a small growl. Scott slapped the back of his hand against Alek's arm. "Bro, cool it. Not everything is black and white in life. Let's find out how serious the damage is."

The older wolf took a deep breath and let it out slow, then nodded. Claire put an arm around him and rested her chin on his shoulder. "Okay, let's have it," Alek said.

Rachel took a long drink of beer for courage. "Okay, über-short version: There was another nest of snakes in Europe doing the same thing as in Texas. Anica is like me and Claire. She was turned against her will."

Alek shrugged. "That's not illegal. Well, not on Anica's part, anyway." He stopped when Rachel raised her hand.

"Her family was *human* before that happened, Alek. Not sloth, not Sazi family. Human."

Scott lowered his eyebrows so far they shaded his eyes. "Did the snakes turn her family too?"

Claire shook her head. "Her father insisted Anica do it. To keep the family together."

Overwhelmed, Alek fell back on his heels and sat there as the realization washed over him. Anica was looking more alarmed by the second.

"Is bad thing my femily has done? Will we be punished?"

Alek looked at Claire with accusation clear in his face. "And you were just going to ignore this? Not tell anyone higher up?"

Claire set her jaw. "Yeah. I was. Because nothing can be done, Alek. Scott is right. Wolven isn't black and white. We have to use our judgment. Anica was turned by force. She didn't know about the Sazi . . . wasn't born into it, didn't have the rules drilled into her.

"Like me. Like Rachel. I don't know what I would have done if I'd made it back to my human family instead of staying with the Tedford pack. Maybe I'd have turned them too. The point is that it's done, was done years ago. Her family at least is trying to play by the rules of the Sazi now that they know a Council exists."

"Except Samit," Alek reminded her, a slight growl in his voice.

"Samit is doing wrong thing, but for right reason," Anica said, her scent and voice sad before becoming determined and on the edge of angry. "Kasun family has sold drugs and guns to rebels. They kill, extort. But nobody stops them. Not even Wolven.

People in villages are too afraid of them, because they are terrifying, but people not know why they are scared. *We* did not know either, until we turned. Now we know of magic and bears that speak like people.

"It not scare us anymore. With new fence, we cut off Kasuns from people they frighten. We think maybe Kasun Alpha know more than he says about snake nest, and we plan to find out. Samit planned to blame attacks on Kasuns, reveal to Council they are bad people. Bad bears. He should not have done this. Should have trusted process. But he is rash, always in a hurry." She looked down at the floor, tugging at a loose thread in the armrest of the couch, her emotions and words spent.

Wow. That was a lot to take in. Rachel didn't doubt what Anica was saying because she didn't trust the Kasuns either, not after seeing how they behaved. What the hell was Dalvin doing snuggling up to those people? How could he possibly not know any of this stuff was happening? Or worse, what if he was part of it?

"Do you think the Kasuns knew the snakes were taking humans and turning them into bears?" Claire asked, looking concerned.

Now Anica's jaw set and the fire in her eyes was equal to the bear she was. "No. I say the snakes take, and the Kasuns *turn*."

The way she phrased that—"Wait. You're saying that like it's not just in the past, back when you were taken," Rachel said.

"No," the Serbian replied, then thought. "I mean, *yes*. There are still snakes and new bears. Even today."

"Wilco Tango Foxtrot," Scott said, his voice low and horrified. "There are still attack victims out there, being turned today? Like you guys?"

Anica nodded. "Yes. I tell Tamir of this when first Wolven arrives for talks. He tells Council members. I hear him. But nothing happen. Nobody comes talk to little bear with no magic."

Now Alek was angry, but for a different reason. "So, wait . . . you reported a crime in progress to a Wolven officer and nobody acted? Are you sure?"

The woman on the couch shrugged. "We come to America, so I am not sure. But we *all* come to America. Nobody left to search. And too, I am not sure where camp is. I escape at night and am lost for long time on full moon before I come home. My femily find me wounded and asleep, nude, on stairs. I am first to come back in village from kidnappings. Whole village have hope. But children keep go missing. Just last month, another gone."

Alek ran his fingers through his hair, clenching them and pulling on his hair like he might tear it out. "God, what a mess!"

Rachel took another long draw of beer. "Well, in my humble opinion, Anica should get a free pass. It was ten years ago and she didn't know any better. The stuff going on *now* is the crime, because there are other attack victims out there, possibly doing the same thing as Anica. If they manage to get out at all."

Claire held up her hands before anyone else could speak. "The first thing we need to do is not talk about any of this anymore. Not until we have a chance to think about all the ramifications."

A new voice, Amber's, came from the other side of the apartment door. "Then you should have remembered to keep your voices down in an apartment complex full of shape-shifters."

Everyone froze. Damn it! She should have remembered that Amber was going to stay in her apartment tonight. Claire and Alek winced; the others, including Anica, sighed. "C'mon in. Might as well make it a party."

The knob turned and the door opened to reveal a pissed-off doctor with glowing yellow eyes. She stepped inside and closed the door quietly. Nobody said a word as she stood glaring at them, tapping one foot.

Finally, Anica spoke, her eyes beginning to leak tears down

her cheeks. "Is my fault. But I did not know I do wrong until now."

Rachel held up her hand, feeling like a heel. "No, it's my fault. Anica told me what happened yesterday, before the town hall meeting. I should have said something to someone."

Claire raised one hand as well. "Yeah, but you only knew vaguely that it was an offense. It was my duty to tell someone, and I failed. I shouldn't get emotionally attached to people. But her story got to me."

Amber finally spoke. Her scent was an odd mix of concern, annoyance, and frustration. "Don't. I'll handle this." She looked at Anica, who was crying more heavily, and spoke a bit less brusquely. "You *did* tell someone in Serbia during the peace talks? You're sure?"

The little bear nodded and wiped her nose with the back of her hand, then snuffled. "I did. I swear. I told bear in charge, Tamir. I remember name because is close to cousin's name, Tamil."

"Did you tell the Council representative who was overseeing the talks, Ahmad?"

Now Anica looked at Amber with disbelief in her face. "Tell head snake about nest of bad snakes? Why would he help? He is probably in *charge*. No, I tell bear, for him to help other bears."

Amber grabbed the back of the wooden chair at the desk and sat down, then rubbed her forehead just above her reddish-gold eyebrows with two fingers. "This whole situation is making my head hurt. She moved her hand to run fingers around her lips. "Okay, here's what's going to happen. I'm going to talk to Tamir, and to Ahmad, and then probably to my husband . . . who is also a bear, Anica.

"If there is a remnant of Sargon's operation still active in Serbia, we'll find it. It would help a lot if you could remember where it was, though. If they've been hidden for a decade, while we've had people actively *looking* for nests, then they're well hidden."

Anica just shook her head. "No, I am sorry. Whole escape is fuzzy in my head."

Rachel raised a finger. "I've heard of people who can see through time, forward and backward. Could they help?"

Amber nodded wearily. "We do have seers with hindsight. But they're pretty busy right now. I might be able to get one from Alek's old wolf pack to come here after we get this race done." She slapped her hands against her pale green linen slacks, which were now showing the wrinkles of a long day. "But until then, let's just move along as though we know nothing.

"I'll take any blame from here on. I'm not going to bring this up and complicate the peace talks any more than necessary. Once the blood feud and land issue are settled, we can work on various other illegal activities." She sat on the arm of the couch and reached forward, straight past Scott's head. He froze, eyes wide. But she just grabbed a slice of pepperoni pizza. "For now, I'm starved. And hand me one of those beers, unless you have anything stronger."

Rachel could tell that Scott wasn't sure if Amber was joking or not. But he offered, "I have a half bottle of vodka in my apartment that Rachel donated when she was packing. It's pretty good stuff, with lemon flavoring."

The Council doctor nodded and said through a bite of pizza, "Get it. I need a drink."

"Great," he said with a smile. "Let me use the john real quick and I'll run downstairs. I *really* need to pee."

Rachel stood up with him. "I'll go. I know where you keep it. The door unlocked?"

Scott tossed her his key ring. "Bottom cabinet next to the stove. Same as always."

She gladly left her apartment. What a mess! That certainly wasn't the way she'd expected the Council to find out about

Anica. But in a way, she was glad it had happened. To think there were still people out there chained to the walls, living in filth, and fearing that each day would be their last . . . it made her skin crawl.

In Scott's apartment, Rachel headed straight for the kitchen. The vodka was right where he'd said and nearly three-quarters full. She grabbed it and the nearly full bottle of whiskey beside it, then took a moment to take a juice glass out of the cupboard and pour herself a shot of vodka in case she didn't get any later. Throwing it back, she felt the burn of the alcohol slide down her throat and warm her chest. The lemon was soft on her tongue and tasted good enough that she poured another shot.

"Better slow down with those. You can actually get drunk."

She turned abruptly, nearly dropping the glass on the floor. Dalvin was standing in the living room wearing only a towel around his waist, fresh from the shower. Crap! "Um, we really shouldn't be seen together." Her words had a fast, panicked edge because her heart was beating like a trip-hammer. He was gorgeous—tall and muscled, his dark skin glistening in the lamplight. She held up the bottle. "And Amber's waiting for this."

He padded closer on bare feet, his eyes fixed on her, heavy, weighted. "Then you should leave."

Inches from her now. He didn't touch her—his hands stayed tight on the edges of the towel. He just breathed in her scent and closed his eyes. Her entire body started to tremble from the sensation of his magic enveloping her, caressing her own magic. It was like nothing she'd ever experienced. It made her knees weak. When he leaned forward and kissed her, she had to lean back against the counter to keep from falling. His tongue slid into her mouth, danced and toyed with hers. Every instinct screamed out for her to put her arms around him, pull him against her, wrap herself around him and keep him there. But she was frozen, unable to move while he kissed her, his lips soft and his jaw hard against hers. Her whole body was flushed. The last time he'd kissed her, it had sent her straight into orgasm. Never had that happen before!

He pulled back and she could barely stand. "Mmm . . . you taste good," he whispered next to her ear. "I'll bet the rest of you tastes just as good." Then he turned and padded back into the bathroom. She watched the play of water drops sliding down his muscles. His lean calves and thighs made her bite her lip. Part of her wanted to follow, but he shut the door with a soft click and she heard him set the lock.

Another shot, I definitely need another shot. She swirled the third sip of vodka around slowly, trying to get the taste of his kiss out of her mouth. Now the bottle was down to a half. There was no way the people in her apartment weren't going to know what just happened. The best she could hope for was tactful silence.

She got it. A few raised eyebrows when she set the bottles on the table and escaped into the bathroom to put a cool cloth on her face and use the toilet, but nothing was said. At least, not until Scott and Alek left, an hour later.

Then, as Amber helped clean up the mess while Anica was in the bathroom, getting ready for bed, the healer said, "He gets you worked up, huh?"

Rachel froze, her hand on the trash can lid. "Who?"

The other woman let out a light laugh. "Who do you think? Be careful with that one. He may seem like a player . . . like everything is loosey-goosey and just for fun, but if it gets serious with him, there'll be no turning back. I know. I got one of those myself."

"I already know that," Rachel said, nodding. "He's like his dad. Still waters. He was always thoughtful. I was surprised to hear he was with so many women."

Pausing in her cleaning, Amber took a sip of vodka, swirling the ice around in the glass. "Charles told me once that he knew what he wanted and knew nearly immediately when a woman didn't have it. So he'd go on one date, maybe two, and then he was gone. He said when he met me, there was a *thunk* in his head, like the last number on a big vault lock had finally hit and he didn't need to look anymore."

"For you too?" Rachel dried her hands on a paper towel as she walked to a chair.

Amber shook her head. She set her glass on the table, then sat down on the couch and leaned back, crossing one leg over the other knee. "Not really. It took longer for me. A lot longer, probably fifty years before I really warmed to him. He can be jovial, but I always seemed to see him at his worst. Council meetings are hard on him, make him cranky and snippy."

Rachel leaned back in the recliner and pulled the handle to bring up the footrest. "So what's the other boot? Is it the race?"

Amber shook her head. "No. The race is just a race. What's going to happen has already started. The wheels are in motion. You'll know what it is when you decide to act. I just don't know if that will be soon or weeks from now. I hope I'm around for it. I hear tell I'm likely to be. But the future is strange. So many things can change it. My sister knows about that stuff. I try not to get involved."

Rachel pondered that for a few minutes while staring at the woman who could think of time in leaps of centuries. "It would be strange to know the future. See people living or dying before it happens. I don't think I'd like it."

Amber wiggled her butt in the cushions. "This couch isn't half bad. I could fall asleep right now." She continued. "Most of the seers I know feel the same. They don't like it. They know why it's necessary, but keeping the secrets, hiding the possibilities from people you love . . . not fun. Having lived a few centuries myself, it's hard to know I'll still be around when others are gone."

"People like me. I'll probably just live a normal human life span."

"Possibly. But you never know. Strange things happen when magic is involved." Her hands were behind her head, propping up the pillow. "I think I'm going to sleep now. You can have your bed. Try to get some rest. Morning will be here quick."

"Thanks." She was really grateful to be able to sleep in her own bed before something as nerve-racking as the race was sure to be. Even as she got to her feet, the little cat closed her eyes and started to breathe slower. A glance at the clock showed it was already eleven! Crap!

Rachel locked the front door and padded down the short hallway. Peeking into the spare room, she saw that Anica was already asleep. Safe in her own room at last, Rachel closed the door, changed quickly, and crawled under the covers. Her last thought was of Dalvin—what would have happened if he'd left the bathroom door open and there hadn't been people waiting back in her place.

CHAPTER 15

The sun was just rising when he pulled up to the lake. Rachel was already sitting on the dock, and beside her was . . . Zarko Petrovic? Rachel was singing "Dock of the Bay" again, while Zarko dipped his bare feet in the water and kicked. It was such an odd scene that Dalvin wasn't sure whether to interrupt it. When the final line reverberated in the air, he opened the car door.

Zarko sighed. "You have lovely voice. Like angel. We have no singers in our family, which is shame." Dalvin started to walk toward the dock, the gravel crunching under his feet. "This is pretty place, Luna Lake. Like Drina valley back home. Quiet, no fighting. Listen: you can hear birds sing, hear footsteps. So nice."

Rachel had leaned back, resting her weight on her hands and letting the sun hit her face. She turned golden in the sunlight, the same color as her feathers. He felt a pang inside, but he wasn't sure what it was at first. Then it hit him. He missed her. He hadn't realized how much until now. She didn't look at him, just closed her eyes against the rising sun. "So why don't you just move here? If the Kasuns want the land so bad, let them have it."

Zarko shook his head. "Is not so simple. Bojan, he dreams whole life of growing raspberries. Even before we are bears. Is father's job to help him, you see? If I have the power to, I must help him."

"Like you helped Anica when she came home?"

Now the sigh was weighty and his scent was wet with worry, a bank of fog over the musty lake smells. "Ah, you know of this? Yes. I tell her to not speak of it, but she has no fear, that one. She wishes to fix the ills of the world. That is hard for a father to watch. I will help her too, if I can. But it is so big, what she wants."

Rachel looked at him with a profound sadness in her eyes. "She wants to fix something that needs fixing. I understand. Sometimes people have to fight the good fight, even when it's hard." She touched Zarko's shoulder. "You're a good father."

He reached over and patted her hand. "And you are good girl. Your father is proud, I am sure."

Her lip started trembling, and Dalvin couldn't help but add, "He is. Very proud." Rachel looked up in shock, as though she wasn't sure if he was kidding. He nodded, serious. "He is."

Her answering smile was filled with joy, and heartbreak, shining through tears. "Good. That's good."

Zarko drew his feet back onto the dock and stood, picking up his old, worn leather boots, which were desperately in need of new soles—an interesting contrast from the boots Mustafa always wore, rare ostrich leather and heavily embroidered, like rodeo trophies. "I suppose it is time. I will go watch Anica train, give her what strength I can." He lumbered off down the gravel, picking up speed and purpose as he walked toward the beginning of the course.

Rachel also stood. Her emotional chaos beat at him. "So."

He nodded. "So. Get in." He walked toward the SUV and she followed, her scent settling into curiosity. He held open the passenger door and she got in.

Once he was around and in the driver's seat, she asked, "Where are we going? We can walk to the course from here."

Starting the engine, he pointed back toward town. "We're not going to train on the course. The course isn't even complete. You need to learn to fly."

Out of the corner of his eye, he could see her skeptical look. "I *know* how to fly."

He shook his head. "No, you don't. Nobody ever taught you how to do precision flying. That changes today."

He turned back onto the town road before taking a right at a narrow drive that barely let the SUV pass. The trees closed in around them like an embrace. He stopped in front of a mail-box where two people were waiting. Rachel's eyes widened as they opened the back door and climbed into the vehicle. "Bitty? Claude? What are you doing?"

The old woman smiled. "Dalvin came to see us this morn-ing, dear. He explained why he thinks you've been failing all the Ascension challenges, and I believe he's right."

"For a fledgling, he's got some brains," agreed the old bird that was the woman's brother. "You need muscle memory, little owl. You simply haven't flown enough to have the memory built up."

"Muscle memory?" Rachel shook her head. "I don't under-stand."

Dalvin drove down an old wagon path into the deep woods, keeping their speed low so the transmission and oil pan didn't bottom out. The ruts were deep, and it took constant attention to keep the tires on the edges of the wide holes. A deer darted out of the way, the tail hairs barely missing the left headlight. "You've been turning for ten years, Chelle. As a three-day owl, that means you've turned about three hundred and ninety times. That's nothing compared to alphas, who can shift at will, multiple times a day if they want."

"And you don't have your human mind," Claude added. "So how can you expect to know what feather to twitch when, other than to keep yourself from falling out of the sky? The problem is that we haven't treated you like an owlet. The second you joined the parliament, we should have trained you as if you were a new child with her first wings. I apologize. That is supposed to be my job."

Bitty smiled and patted Rachel's shoulder over the seat. Her Cajun accent was thick and homespun. "It's not your fault, dear. Van Monk and Lenny Gabriel should have given you over to us to train. But he . . . well, they had their demons. We'll leave it there."

Rachel's voice took on a defensive edge. "So you're telling me I suck. Thanks lots."

Snorting, Dalvin used the same tough love he'd used on her in Detroit when they were children. "Get over the weepy crap, Chelle. How did you learn to sing? Drills. Remember drills in church choir? Scales, octave shifts, do re mi? All muscle memory. Your body has to know it without thinking."

She turned in her seat, fixed each one of them with a wide-eyed stare and a scent of sudden fear. "Drills? That could take months! We only have a day."

"That's why we're all here, Rachel," Bitty said. "We're going to share our power so you stay fully in your human mind all day long. Dalvin is a powerful alpha, but keeping you in your animal form with a human mind is taxing. You saw that the other day. He and Claude will fly with you to keep your mind, and I'll hold your form."

Rachel settled back in the seat and looked at Dalvin with a sort of awe. "Wow."

He smiled but kept his eyes on the narrow trail. "I was told to make you win. But even if I hadn't been instructed to, I would have done this. You felt such *joy* flying the last time. Watching you fly was like listening to you sing. It never occurred to me that you didn't feel that way every time you flew."

They reached their destination—a small flat spot where they could park right near the mountain edge. Dalvin and

Claude got out of the car. "We'll shift over here and leave you ladies to yourselves."

Bitty raised one finger to delay them. "For today, you should be part of our parliament, Dalvin. It'll be much easier to coach Rachel mentally. It can be hard to hear when the wind is gusting. I'll disconnect you at the end of the day. You're not part of a group now, are you?"

He shook his head. "Not officially. My family is my parliament, but we only connect when I'm home. Too dangerous when I'm on missions." He tried to say it in such a way that they understood he couldn't be part of their group.

Claude clapped him on the shoulder with a surprising amount of strength. "Bitty and I are both former Wolven, youngster. No fear we'll spill your secrets. Hellfire, we probably already know! And Amber's approved our plan for today."

Oh. He remembered that Amber knew people here personally. "Then I suppose it's okay." He figured he was powerful enough to cut the tie if he had to; if he couldn't, he'd get his family to do it later.

Bitty held out her hands. "Come touch me and we'll do a simple binding. Nothing fancy, just a mental link."

Rachel didn't hesitate, seeming to take comfort in the woman's touch. Dalvin touched Bitty's hand and felt . . . *old* magic, ancient and strong. When Bitty's eyes began to glow, he felt a wave of power sweep through him that was as light as air and yet was grounded deep in the earth. He had trouble breathing through the magic that pressed against his own, until it eased inside, like water sopping through cotton cloth.

The elderly owl winked one clouded blue eye. "Still a few tricks left in these old bones." Eyes shut and mouth closed, she asked, *Can you hear me?*

He nodded but wasn't sure she saw the gesture. "I can hear you."

With your minds, children. Can you hear me?

I'm here. Rachel's mental voice sounded like her singing voice, like chimes that made his heart beat faster. *I love this part.*

I can hear you. Your voice sounds like bells. He looked at her, seeing her eyes shining bright.

"I've never heard myself," she said. "Your voice is a lot deeper than usual, like notes on a bass electric guitar. It resonates even after you stop talking."

"Your mental voice reflects your soul," Bitty said. "It's your truest self." She removed her hands and clapped them together. "Chop, chop, people. Let's get this training started."

Even though Bitty had said he would just be linked mentally, Dalvin *felt* when Rachel shifted. For him, shifting was easy—a simple thought, and he was an owl. Rachel's body didn't want to change. Bitty had to push magic into her, grab the owl from deep inside Rachel and pull it to the surface. Bitty moved fast, which was good—it would have hurt Rachel a lot otherwise. Dalvin let some of his own magic flow into the link to speed the shift. It probably wasn't necessary, as strong as the leader of their parliament was, but it made him feel better to help.

Bitty gave him a strange look then but didn't say anything. She stayed in human form, on the ground, while the other three took off. As he flapped his wings, he felt like he was somehow still attached to the ground, like he was a kite on a long string. *I've never felt a tie like this before, Bitty. Are you sure this is just a mental binding?*

Something in her mental voice had deeper meaning than the words alone. *It's mental only with* me. She clapped her hands again. *Now show me some strong flying, everyone.*

Dalvin and Claude flanked Rachel, one on each side.

Just do exactly what we do, Chelle.

Claude agreed. *Let's start easy, with some simple turns around trees.*

The mental tie made group flying amazing, like flying with the Thunderbirds. Their wings were inches apart, but he knew

exactly when Claude was going to shift by the *And . . . now!*
that the older owl thought just before he swooped past one tree
and around the next, like slaloming while skiing. The cold wind
was perfect for this kind of flying. It was clean, with hardly any
humidity and no hot spots that created odd air currents.

Rachel was trying to follow, but she was struggling; flying
wasn't instinctive for her. After several tumbles where she
nearly hit a tree, Dalvin had an idea. *Let's treat this like singing.
Do will mean a dip of your left wing. Re will be the right wing. Mi
will be to lift your tail feathers. Fa is tuck your wings. Sol is to raise
your head. La is lower your head. Ti is roll, ti-do is roll to the left,
and ti-re is roll to the right. Let's try it. Scoot back behind me so you
can see.*

Slowing her wing beats, she moved behind him and watched
as he sang and flew. After two tries, Claude got into the spirit.
This could work, youngster. Our little owl thinks in song.

Five times with each note was enough for her to get the cho-
reography. *Okay, ti-re.* He sang the notes and shifted his wings,
and she followed along as though she'd been flying her whole
life. *Okay, I'm going to land. You stay up here with Claude and
try to follow him without me singing. You sing to him.*

She dipped her head. *Okay. I think I'm getting this.*

Claude was an excellent flyer. Dalvin fluttered to a delicate
landing on the hood of the SUV, being careful not to scratch
the paint. Bitty was leaning against the vehicle. They watched
Rachel and Claude go through the same course as before, but
faster and with more precision. It was working.

He smiled, enjoying the sound of her voice singing in his
head. Every wing beat felt like it was his arms moving. He could
feel her heart race as she got faster and faster. He looked up at
the sky and realized it was nearly noon.

"We should give her a break."

Bitty looked at the sky and nodded. *Come back in, you two.
Let's have some lunch.*

Lunch? He hadn't packed food.

Bitty smiled at him. *Didn't you see the basket I was carrying?* Actually, he hadn't.

Claude and Rachel landed on the ground beside the truck. Bitty sent out a wave of magic and changed Rachel back to her human form. Naked and smooth skinned and oh, my, she looked good to Dalvin. The old woman let out a chuckle to say she knew exactly what he was thinking, and with what part of his body. Luckily, Rachel didn't seem to notice his reaction.

Rachel walked over to her clothes, and Claude—still an owl—hopped up on the SUV to stand next to Dalvin. "A-yup. If I were a hundred years younger—"

His sister swatted his wing with the back of a hand. "If you were a hundred years younger, Claude Kragan, you'd still be a hundred years too old for that child." She patted Dalvin's head, saying, "But this one . . . he's just the right age."

Dalvin shook his head. "We're in two different places."

She turned her head and blinked. Her words were innocent, but he could feel the weight of truth through the mental link. "Looks like you're in the same place to me. But my eyes, they aren't as good as they used to be. Maybe you're not really standing here just a few feet away from her after all these long years. Maybe it's *not* exactly where you want to be standing."

Claude let out a few hoots of laughter and flew-hopped over to his own clothes. Bitty got into the back of the SUV. "I'll get lunch ready. Why don't you go tell Rachel what you thought of her flying this morning? A little encouragement goes a long way."

Sneaky old bird. She tapped on the window and pointed a finger at him through the dark glass. *Sneaky is another word for clever. One coin with two sides. Now go be clever, fledgling. Leap out of the nest.*

He took a deep breath and shifted, adding an illusion of clothes, as he usually did when changing in public. He didn't know why he did it, but he always did. Just a quirk. Then he put on his real clothes, and the images blended seamlessly with reality. Rachel was sitting on the ground, tying her shoelaces, when he walked over to her.

"That was some good flying. You're really getting the hang of it," he said.

She looked up, beaming with joy. Unable to help himself, he reached out to touch her hair. The curls were soft, not coarse, like feathers under his fingers. She leaned into his hand, closing her eyes.

I missed you. He hadn't meant to transmit that through the mental link, but could tell she had heard him when she looked startled and her scent was almost afraid.

"We should eat." He nodded and backed away so she could stand. On her feet, Rachel nearly ran to the SUV and the safety of those she considered family. He waited a moment, granting her privacy while she boosted herself into the open hatchback to sit beside Bitty.

He'd seen his parents look at each other that way when they were talking mentally, but he couldn't hear anything through the pack link. It took a lot of power to separate the members of a parliament and talk to them individually. Bitty was much stronger than he'd thought.

He and Claude—now also human and fully dressed—reached the SUV at nearly the same time. Claude handed Dalvin a wrapped sandwich that turned out to be old-fashioned thick-cut ham on fresh-baked bread with white goat cheese and butter. His grandmother had made sandwiches just like them.

"How did you know to make these?"

"Memories are the strangest things," Bitty said cryptically. "Sometimes you don't even remember which are yours and which are someone else's."

What the heck did that mean? He eased into the mental link to see if he could find a clue in her mind and ran into a wall, stone with metal grates. She'd been expecting his intrusion. *Clever and sneaky.* She smiled brilliantly, revealing a missing eyetooth.

It was a good sandwich. Great, in fact. Best food he'd had since he arrived in Luna Lake. To wash it down, there was iced tea so sweet his jaw hurt—but delicious. Bitty clapped her hands again when the meal was done. "Back to work, everyone. We have hours to go and many things to teach. Let's get you back in the air, little owl."

She was *flying.* Really flying, like the birds she'd spent hours watching, trying to figure out how they spun and danced on the air. To have her human mind while she was flapping her wings was something she never thought she'd experience. And to be flying next to Dalvin—

There were no words. She couldn't put a coherent sentence together when he was around. When she'd landed for lunch, she'd thought, *He can't miss me. I'm a different person. He's missing the old person, and I'm not her anymore.*

Bitty had pooh-poohed that right away. *Chère, there are some things inside us that make us who we are. We can never shed them. They are part of our soul. He misses that. I can feel it. He misses something you once had together, once were together.*

She was attracted to him, all right, she thought. But he wasn't the geeky, plump boy she had once known.

Just appearance, Rachel, Bitty said into her mind. *That geeky, plump boy is down deep inside there somewhere . . .*

When she'd seen him with Larissa, she'd felt a sharp pain, though she knew she had no right to feel that way. Still, she wasn't sure she wanted anything more than his friendship.

Not true, Chère, came her Alpha's voice. *What possessed you in that meadow with him was beyond lust. I've felt lust from others before and can block it out. I couldn't block out what you were feeling, because it was part of what a parliament is made from—trust, concern, a sense of belonging. You belong together. I remembered these sandwiches of his grandmother's through you, Chère. You already have a link that I just tapped into.*

Already have a link? She tried to reach out, to feel him like she could feel the other members of their group, but there was nothing there. Yet when he sang a note on the scale, she felt her body move like it was dancing to his music. They'd started to fly faster. She was flapping her wings almost constantly, and the commands were happening quicker. Left dip, then right, then stall with her feathers alone.

The sun was getting low in the sky when Dalvin came up with one final idea. *Remember crack the whip?* She did.

But they had no hands. *How do we play?*

Claude apparently knew. He took the lead and beat his wings hard and fast, gaining speed and creating a vortex for the others to fly in. Dalvin took the second spot and matched his wing beats. Rachel suddenly found herself flying faster and faster, pulled along as though tethered to them. Claude suddenly said *Now!* He and Dalvin veered off so sharply that she couldn't keep up. She was hurtled across the landscape while Dalvin made tones in her head. Her body obeyed without question, and she was darting in and around trees that she could barely see. It was a blur of motion, and she felt more alive than any other time in her life!

Then she went around the last tree, at a lower elevation than before. A massive boulder loomed, and she knew she was going to hit it at top speed!

CHAPTER 16

*I*t happened in the blink of an eye. She was hurtling through the trees, her body shifting position in response to the notes he sang. Her motion was seamless, flawless. He was frankly amazed at how fast she was picking it up, but music had always been part of her being. All Dalvin was doing was tying her movements to the music, like dancing. He was flying above and Claude below, watching as she streaked through the trees from the whip.

He saw the boulder nearly a second too late. But that second was all it took. There was no way Rachel had the wing power to twist around without hitting the rock. At her current speed, the impact would kill her. No question.

Dalvin threw out a net of magic as Bitty screamed a warning. She was seeing through Rachel's eyes. Like the cowboys of the Old West, Dalvin looped his magic around Rachel's body and pulled back hard. The strain was incredible, like grabbing the railing of a speeding train. His magic soaked into her, blended with hers, and gave her the power to turn away from the rock. The turn set off a sonic boom that echoed across the trees and sent rocks scattering down off the mountain.

Damn good thing it didn't start a landslide.

She was panting heavily when he brought her to safely to the ground. Claude landed a second later and shifted forms; his magic-generated clothing had the appearance of medical scrubs. He knelt beside Rachel as Dalvin fluttered to a landing.

"Are you well, little owl?" Claude asked, peering into her eyes. He ran his hands down her wings and checked her legs. "Does anything hurt?"

Her voice was frustrated and her scent was angry, apparently with herself. "Just my pride. I should have been able to make that turn by myself." She looked at Dalvin as he hopped over to stand by her. "Thank you, Dalvin. That must have taken a lot out of you."

He wasn't going to lie. "It was touch-and-go. I'm glad I saw the rock before you did." The next sentence just slipped out, unplanned. "I'd never let anything hurt you, Chelle. I couldn't stand to lose you again. I'd die."

"Thank you," she said quietly, a wealth of emotion in those two words. To give her a little privacy with her alphas, he flew over to his clothes and changed. He seemed to feel the press of her discomfort against his back, like a damp, cool towel, but maybe that was just his own embarrassment at having said something that he wasn't sure was true. He would probably survive Rachel dying . . . again.

Probably.

Everyone was silent as they drove back to town. When the alphas arrived at their homes, Bitty reached back into the car and laid a gentle hand on Dalvin's arm, through the open driver's window.

"Take care of our girl tonight. Y'hear me, fledgling?"

He nodded and smiled. Nobody had dared to call him a fledgling since he was probably ten. But to these alphas, he was barely out of first molt.

Then they were alone. They drove for a time in silence

back toward town. He could feel her heartbeat and had to endure the wash of emotions that left him emotionally spent. Finally, she took a deep breath. "Thank you."

"You said that already. It's okay. My fault anyway."

She looked at him with surprise. "*Your* fault? How do you figure?"

He shrugged, feeling angry at himself. "You were doing well enough that I forgot I was supposed to be looking out for you. I should have been aware of your possible path. If you'd gotten hurt—" He tightened his fingers on the steering wheel.

"Dalvin, stop the car. Right here." He could hear taut anger in her voice.

He hit the brakes. The SUV was still deep in the trees. She unbuckled her seat belt and swung her knees onto the seat so she could sit facing him.

"You saved my life. Got that? How it was endangered doesn't matter. You saved me. *Thank you.*" She leaned forward and kissed him, easing herself onto his lap so that she was tucked tightly between him and the steering wheel.

The kiss took his breath away. Her mouth ate at his; her arms were wrapped around him so tight that he could barely breathe. But he didn't want to. He put one arm around her, then shifted her position until her head was nearly resting on the window-sill. His other hand went around her waist and slid up, under her shirt, to touch her warm skin. The kiss seemed to last an hour yet wasn't long enough. When they came up for air, both of them were breathing hard. He touched her face, sliding the back of his hand down her skin, reverent, hungry.

"I want you, Chelle."

Her scent and her words said the same thing. "I'm scared, Dalvin. What I'm feeling . . . it's almost too much. There's too much history, too much magic right now."

He understood what she meant. He and Bitty had both for-gotten to remove the tether binding him to her flock. Dalvin could feel Rachel's heart beating from both outside and inside his own chest.

"I don't want you to be scared. I want your first time to be like flying. Joyous. No reservations. So," he said, gently disentangling her and easing her back into the passenger seat, "we'll wait. Maybe the time will be right soon. Or maybe it won't. But I don't want regret to be part of how you remember me."

"You're definitely leaving after the peace talks are over?" She looked sad when he nodded.

Staying hadn't occurred to him. Being in Wolven was all he'd ever wanted, from the time he'd been toddling around the big old family house, watching his dad get ready for a mission. After the snake attack, when his father couldn't fly anymore, Dalvin had sworn to himself that he'd keep the skies safe in his dad's name. What would his father think if he quit the service? Even if it was to be with Rachel?

She looked at him with an odd expression on her face. "I just saw that. Your dad, as an owl, soaring off the roof. You were watching him fly away, holding a suitcase in his talons."

She'd seen that?! He looked at her so suddenly he nearly went off the road. "Do memories come through a pack link?"

"Sometimes," she acknowledged. "Bitty has used my mom's words against me more than once when I tried to pretend I didn't know any better about some rule or another. But I've never seen someone else's memories before. That was really strange. But cool. Your dad . . . an owl. How did I never know that?"

He let himself smile a little. "People ignore little inconsistencies all the time. It's easier than trying to understand something that doesn't make sense if you don't know what's really going on. How did my mom get cupcakes to school in the third grade when all the highways were closed because of a blizzard?

"Remember that? It was my turn to bring snack and I'd

forgotten. The teacher said I'd get held back from recess if I didn't have cupcakes for everyone. I ran to the office and called Mom, and she made it to school before the bell and everyone got a cupcake as they were walking out the door."

"Oh, yeah. Mrs. Zycrizick," Rachel said, nodding. "How could I forget? She was a pill. Your mom rocked." She chuckled quietly, eyes shining. "Now that I know the truth, I'm trying to imagine your mom flying over Detroit with a container of cupcakes in her claws. Why was there no YouTube of that somewhere?"

Dalvin smiled as the citrus scent of humor filled the car. "Magic. She's really good at illusion. She probably looked to the people on the ground like a sparrow carrying string to a nest."

Rachel laughed . . . finally, the laugh he remembered from a decade ago: light, free of the weight that he'd heard in her voice since he arrived.

They reached Luna Lake just as the sun disappeared behind the mountain. He let her out at the apartment building. "Go eat some protein and see if you can get a couple hours of sleep. You're supposed to be back at the course at midnight, when the moon is fullest."

"You'll be there?" Her eyes and voice were hopeful. It made him happy to hear that note in her voice.

He nodded. "I'll be working. Don't forget I can't help you tonight."

"I know. But knowing you'll be there makes me feel better." She moved away, her walk close to dancing, singing "Do-Re-Mi" from *The Sound of Music*.

In Scott's apartment, Dalvin wandered into the kitchen, looking for something to eat. The time on the clock on the wall brought him up short and he pulled out his cell phone to confirm that it was only five o'clock. But it was pitch-black outside . . . and they were in a valley, with winter settling in. There was still enough time to eat and maybe even catch a few hours of sleep. He set his alarm for eleven o'clock and turned the volume to high.

There was leftover pizza in the fridge, so he grabbed the box. He texted Tamir to make sure there was nothing new on the schedule. He didn't have phone numbers for any of the others, which was stupid. Exchanging contact information should have been the first thing he'd done when he'd met Claire and Alek and, frankly, Amber and Councilman Kuric.

Stupid, stupid!

He grabbed a couple of slices and ran down the stairs, still chewing, to knock on Rachel's door. She opened it and immediately picked up on his concern. "Are Amber and Anica here?"

She shook her head. "No, and I'm wondering if we're missing something."

"Grab your coat. We should have gone back to the lake instead of returning to town. Now that I think of it, I didn't see any of the SUVs when we drove along Main Street."

"I didn't either," Rachel said, shaking her head. "Crap! Ascension normally doesn't start until midnight, but maybe they changed the time? Let's go to the Community Center. That's where people normally get dressed."

"Dressed? In what?" He handed her the second slice of pizza he was holding and she took a bite.

"Yuck. Pepperoni. Oh, well." She took another bite. "We dress in robes and have chants and such, but also games and sometimes rides. It's like Druid cult meets county fair. No doubt the neighboring towns think we're weird. But it keeps people from wandering this way to ask a bunch of questions."

They piled into the car. A stop at the Community Center confirmed that it was empty, as were the town hall and the diner, which was closed, lights off and door locked.

"We'd better go to the lake. That must be where everything is happening," Dalvin said.

"It's weird that nobody called you, isn't it?" Rachel said. She was getting edgy, and he couldn't blame her. The moon was rising. The weight of it pressed on him, pulled at the bird inside him.

"Very." He pushed down on the gas, speeding, and grateful that there weren't too many turns or curves between the town and the lake. *Late, late, late!* kept echoing in his mind.

They rounded the last corner so quickly the back wheels skidded, spinning the SUV nearly completely around as they entered the parking lot, which was packed with cars and lit by torches that smelled like natural gas. Claude and Bitty ran to meet them.

"Oh, I was so afraid you weren't going to make it, *chère*," Bitty said, looking anxious. "Hurry and get over there to have your robe put on." Rachel raced into the darkness at the edge of the parking lot.

"What the hell happened?" Dalvin asked tersely.

Bitty let out a hiss that rivaled some of his mother's best. "I was afraid of that. That bear agent . . . he is ready to sacrifice himself to make you look bad. Watch him closely."

"Why didn't you just tell me through the mental link that the time had changed? All I got was a foreboding, a sensation of being late, but I didn't know where to go."

Her brows raised. "A pack link can't compete with a mating link, child. When you saved Rachel's life, you blew open that last door."

Mating link? "What are you talking about?"

"Adway! Where the hell have you been?" Councilman Kuric was stalking his way. "We have been looking everywhere for you."

Bitty stepped between them. "Now just you hold on there. I have been with this boy all day. He did not receive a single call, text, or smoke signal that plans had changed. When my brother picked me up to bring me here, I was able to get a vague message to him through my temporary pack binding. You'd better look elsewhere for your problem, because it's not this agent."

"Alpha Kragan," Dalvin said, "I appreciate your support, but I can defend myself." He looked Kuric square in the eye. "I spent the day doing what I had been ordered to do—training Rachel Washington. Since the bears were using the course, we went elsewhere for flying lessons."

Kuric held out his hand. "May I see your phone?" Dalvin pulled it from the holster and handed it over. Using his thumbs, the councilman quickly sent a message. A moment later there was an answering ping from somewhere near the man's hip. Kuric reached into a pocket and produced an identical phone. "Huh. Interesting." He slid both phones back in his pocket and held up one finger. "Wait here a moment."

Taking long strides across the crowded parking area, the councilman pointed at Alek and then at Claire. "You and you. Follow me." They looked surprised but fell in step behind him. The little group approach the benches near the dais, where the Bosnian Alphas were sitting, guarded by Tamir.

Without pausing, Kuric executed an impressive tae kwon do leg sweep that pulled Tamir's legs from under him. The councilman then hit the bear shifter squarely in the chest with an elbow, so hard that Tamir doubled up, stunned, before he hit the ground. The entire assembly went quiet.

"Sometimes it's simply more satisfying to use brute force," Kuric said smoothly. He got to his feet, yanked his tunic back into position, then said to Claire and Alek, "Take this man into custody."

He waved Dalvin over. "You spent the most time with him. Find out who he's working for, who wants to sabotage these peace talks."

Dalvin was taken aback. "I haven't noticed him taking one side or the other."

"Really?" the councilman asked. "Then explain this." Reaching into his pocket, he pulled out the two phones. Returning Dalvin's to him, Kuric held the other so Dalvin could see the screen. "Text Tamir," he told him.

It took almost no time for Dalvin to send a simple message, the letter "K." The other phone pinged immediately, then made a whooshing sound, as if a message was being sent.

The councilman handed Dalvin the second phone and dropped his own into its holder. The most recently received message—the single letter "K"—was identified as having come from "Incoming Wolven."

The same message had been forwarded an instant later, sent to a phone number Dalvin didn't recognize; it was identified as "Outgoing Wolven." It had a country code as a prefix, but not one Dalvin recognized. He checked the contacts list. There were also entries for "Incoming Council" and Outgoing Council." It was the same number. But on Dalvin's phone, Tamir's contact information said his name.

With an undercurrent of anger in his voice, Kuric said, "I have a race to officiate. Find out what this man knows and who his contacts are. Have Amber put an outgoing block on his head, in case he's tied to a pack somewhere, so they can't listen in. I'm tired of bullshit games. We're going to finish this tonight if I have to put down every member of both families myself."

Tamir was beginning to come to. Alek and Claire had put his wrists in handcuffs that had been wrapped completely with pure silver. This would not only block his magic, it was also intensely painful, which meant Kuric was really ticked. The big bear was starting to squirm.

"Where to, boss?" Alek asked, looking square at Dalvin.

"Boss?" Claire nodded. Her blue eyes were glowing with the power she was using to hold Tamir nearly motionless despite his struggles.

"Rabi found the phone you were holding under the dais

while we were doing our security sweep, before anyone arrived," Alek explained to Dalvin. "There was an explosive charge under the bleachers, strong enough to have taken out one of the families. Tamir claimed you'd lost your phone and had borrowed his. It looks like he copied your whole camera roll and e-mail box to the second phone.

"The councilman spoke to me and Claire privately, told us that if you turned out to be the mole, Claire would take over from Tamir because Rabi still didn't trust him . . . but if *Tamir* was the saboteur, you'd be the new senior agent."

Dalvin realized the whole conversation at the start of the mission, about downloading the encryption app for his phone, had had a purpose.

"Damn it! Tamir insisted I download a program to securely lock my phone. I bet that's how he got in. He probably hoped I'd show up at midnight, after everything was done, and he'd waylay me and switch phones. I might not have noticed right away, if everything was in the same place on the home screen." He looked at Tamir, whose face was filled with fury and frustration. "Okay, let's go *chat*, shall we? I'd like my strip of hide back. Maybe I'll replace it with one of yours."

CHAPTER·17

The embroidered white Ascension gown slipped easily over Rachel's head and down along her body. It took only a moment to shed her clothes underneath the wide tent of cloth. The gowns were one of the few dignities of the competition, from a time when people actually cared about those who ran the race. It prevented the whole town from witnessing an omega failing to shift, shifting incompletely, or mutating. Dani, Rachel's attendant, carefully gathered up and folded her clothes and put them in a protective plastic bag.

"Where's Dalvin?" Rachel asked, looking around. "He was here a second ago."

Dani pursed her lips and shrugged. "Dunno. I don't see Alek or Claire either." She put a hand over her eyes and squinted through the bright lights that had been set up at the start line. "Hell, I don't see the Council members either. Oh, wait! There's that cute cat councilman. He's coming this way."

Larissa was fighting with the cloth tent, trying to wear it like a dress.

"What is wrong with this robe? There are sticks that poke me." She kept hitting the poles with her arms, making them swing wildly and probably scrape against her chest.

"Larissa!" Rachel called out, hoping the bear shifter could hear her over the crowd of people surrounding the competitors. "It's so you can get undressed and shift in private. Grab the poles with your hands, underneath the cloth, and pull them down. It creates a tent."

Anica suddenly got it, saying, "Oh! Is clever. It holds itself up. You see, Larissa?" She reached through one of the holes and tapped on a pole through the fabric of the other woman's robe. "Hold this pole inside and pull down. Makes tiny cabana, like at beach."

Larissa ducked her head inside and pulled the poles. "Is sort of stupid. I do not mind undressing in public. I am not ashamed of my body."

Rachel rolled her eyes. "It's just part of the ceremony. Deal with it." She was sorry Dalvin hadn't gotten to see the torch procession. Several hundred people walking through the forest with the torches was a wonderful sight. From the number of cars in the lot, it looked like most people had driven, which meant fewer torches anyway. She could understand why. Clouds were gathering at the mountain edge. It might snow.

Rabi stepped onto the dais, joined by the bear alphas and some of the town members. He cleared his throat, then tapped on the microphone to get the attention of the audience. Most all of the town was here, which wasn't a big surprise. This was a unique event, like having the Olympics come to town.

The townspeople were all dressed in their formal Ascension robes. Most had been embroidered or otherwise embellished over the years to become works of art. Rachel spotted the Williams family; little Kristy was waving at her, dressed in a long buttercup-yellow robe with a circle of teddy bears stitched around the hem.

Kuric raised his hands and a wave of magic swept over everyone, stretching like a thin plastic sheet far above. The

breeze that had been blowing was cut off so suddenly that hair
flew up all over the audience, as though a charged balloon was
pulling their hair toward the sky.

"Your attention, please."

Everyone looked at the stage, because, well, he was worth
looking at. His robes were shining white, glowing with power. If
anything said *Council*, it was shining eyes and skin and the ability to shield the entire racecourse with an aversion spell while
simultaneously holding off the push of the moon to keep the
whole audience from turning.

"Thank you. For those who do not already know, I am Rabi
Umar Kuric, liaison to the Sazi Council from the Hayalet
Kabile tiger tribe."

That caused a few whispers. Rachel heard, "Wait, he's *not* a
councilman?" and "What is the Haylet Kibble?"

"I am here, representing the Council, to settle a dispute
between two bear sloths, one from Bosnia and one from Serbia.
To my right is Larissa Grebo, omega of the Kasun family; to my
right is Anica Petrovic, omega of the Petrovic family. They race
tonight for both their family honor and the right to determine
the fate of their homelands."

Someone yelled from the middle of the crowd, "Why's Rachel running? Hasn't she run this damned course enough?"
Rachel smiled as she recognized the voice of Fred Birch, the
postmaster.

Rabi dipped his head in acknowledgment. "Tonight, Rachel
Washington is an honored guest . . . the Council's own champion!"

Paula, the waitress at the diner, raised her hand from the
front row. "Why does the Council need a champion? Isn't
the Council going to decide who wins anyway?"

That caused more muttering in the crowd. Rabi raised his
hand to silence the critics.

"If the Kasun omega wins, the Petrovics will lose their

homeland. If the Petrovics win, the Kasuns will likewise have
to leave. The Council proposes sharing the land, which both
sides have refused. If Rachel wins, the Council's solution will
be imposed, and each sloth will have territory of its own."

Someone at the back called out, "So because they're being
petty and unreasonable, Rachel has to be humiliated one more
time?"

Both of the Alphas behind her growled. Rabi opened his
mouth, but Rachel stepped forward, gesturing to the microphone, and he gave it to her, with a smile that crooked only
one corner of his mouth—the side away from the audience.

"Look, you guys. I appreciate your concern, but I'm okay
with this now. I wasn't thrilled at the beginning, but there's no
downside for me. Even if I lose, I'm still going to go to college,
like I planned. And if I *win*, the Council is footing the bill. Full
ride, tuition *and* expenses."

"Well, hell!" Jim Jakes, the fifth-grade teacher, said. "*I'll*
run the race for that! I'd love to get my doctorate." There was
a smattering of applause and laughter. Jim started to cheer,
"Ra-chel, Ra-chel, Ra-chel."

Others picked up the chant until the whole audience was
calling her name. That had never happened before. Maybe
Scott was right. Maybe it had just been Monk mind-controlling
the town.

Rabi raised his hand again. "You all know Ray Vasquez, the
new police chief." There was some shouts and applause. "Ray
will officially start the race while I head to the finish line. Could
we please have the competitors' Alphas to the start line?"

Ray hopped up on the stage and took the microphone,
while Rabi got into one of the SUVs.

"Okay, folks, you all know how this usually works, but for
our visitors, we've set up a course like none before. We have
two bears racing an owl! Rather than try to modify an existing
course, the Council members, with help from our own Nathan

Burrows and Agent Dalvin Adway from Wolven, created a brand-new one!"

Say what? Rachel stopped meditating and started to listen closely. When had Dalvin had time to help design the course?

"Here's what's going to happen. The omegas will start on the cat course, which will test the bears' climbing and jumping abilities. The reward at the end of the agility test will be an energy-packed snack that will fuel them for the rest of the race and settle their animals. Then, just like you all enjoy, the competitors will go over logs, under bridges, and across the rocks to the top of the mountain.

"Rachel will test her flying skills, moving through thick branches and along sheer rock faces. In addition, each racer must touch a series of markers that match the color of the collars they will wear. The more marks they miss, the more time will be added to their final score.

"The markers are scented with carrion as well, to make them easier to find. Nathan Burrows and Jim Jakes made the collars, which also hold tiny live-action cameras and trackers so we can chart the competitors' courses and get them back on track if they go too far astray."

Anica looked at her parents. "Jumping over rocks? I am not a jumper, Mama." The female alpha patted her daughter's hand, glowering at Ray.

"After that, there's a hunting test, where the racers will track the scent of their favorite prey. The bears will search for fresh salmon that have been dropped into the lake . . . and don't worry, we stocked the lake with plenty of live salmon, which will be available for the residents once this test is over!" A few cheers went up—the locals enjoyed ice fishing. "Rachel will search for a passel of wild mice that one of our residents donated."

The bird that was fluttering inside her was excited to hunt. Local mice were easy to see, fat, and slow. *Rachel* hated hunting, especially mice and rats, but her owl demanded the squeals and burst of blood. Her limbs started to hurt; her arms wanted to twist into wings thanks to the press of the moon. Only the bubble of magic that Rabi had put up kept her from turning in an agony of breaking bones and shrinking skin.

"After the hunt comes the traditional final leg, the speed race. If the competitors are too tired, Marilyn Bearbird and Councilman Kuric have offered to chase them in their animal forms. Who wouldn't run from an alpha Caspian tiger and golden eagle, folks? I know I sure would!"

He waited for laughter and got it. That got her anger up. *Yeah, laugh away, asshole. You've never had it done to you.* It was humiliating to be chased. She remembered a few races where she was just too exhausted to fly anymore, ready for whatever was chasing her to catch her and be done with it.

"Attendants, please help your champions to the starting line."

Dani picked up Rachel's robe and shortened the stakes. Music started to play over the loudspeakers. The first few notes made Rachel laugh. Really? "Eye of the Tiger"? She tried to catch Rabi Kuric's reaction. Since he was American, she thought he'd get the joke.

Yep. He was struggling to maintain his somber, tough-as-nails councilman visage, but she saw him roll his eyes.

The three women made their way toward the start. Zara Kasun was holding the train of Larissa's robe, and Draga Petrovic was doing the same for Anica. The scent that drifted to Rachel's nose from her competitors was determination, mixed with a healthy dose of fear.

The moon pressed on her. Her chest felt tight and painful from the wings that struggled to break out of her skin. The others seemed to be feeling the same as the moon rose above the horizon.

"Now it is time for the instruction from tonight's judge to

the competitors. Please keep quiet for the benefit of those who wish to listen." Ray turned off the microphone and made a slashing motion across his throat. The blaring music fell silent.

An owl hooted in the distance, *Whoo-hoo, hoo, hoo*, and Rachel responded instinctively.

Her head turned sharply, suddenly intensely aware of the forest around her. No breeze. The food would be easy to hear tonight. She blinked and tried to focus on the shining man who had parted the crowd in front of her, but the night was coming alive and pulling her attention away.

She felt the call of her Alpha. The big owl must be obeyed, even when she was just a tiny human. The old woman smelled of owl, and that was good. A voice echoed through her head. *Focus, Rachel. Listen to the shining man now.*

"Alphas, there have been a few changes to the competition in response to objections by each of you. After you turn your omegas, you may use some of your power to help your omega retain her human mind. Our Council physician will be monitoring you all closely to be sure you are not influencing your champion's decisions. All decisions must be made by your omega."

Two large men, who stank of not-food animal, nodded in agreement.

Rachel felt her mind clearing as Rabi continued. "There will be two hunting challenges instead of one. The first will involve climbing for food. The bears will be looking for a honeycomb inside the top of a hollow tree. Rachel's prey will be near the top of the cliff behind me, inside a crevice where space is tight and she will need to use her talons to keep her position on the rock face."

Great. She hadn't trained in rock climbing, couldn't even remember a time when she'd had to do that.

"For the bears, the second hunting challenge will be fishing. Only whole fish will count toward the total. The goal is five fish, caught by paw or mouth. For Rachel, a box of native mice will be released near the water's edge. She must try to catch five whole mice and return them to a holding basket. A single white mouse will also be released. Returning the white mouse will count as all five mice.

"Two salmon in the lake have been marked with a temporary nontoxic yellow color on their tails. Catching a yellow-tailed salmon is the equivalent of catching five salmon, and the competitor may then move on. The water closest to the edge of the lake has been seeded with food to keep the fish near shore."

The councilman paused to take a drink from a plastic bottle of water.

"We estimate that it will take approximately three hours to complete the course. The woods are still the woods, of course. The racers may encounter native animals that live in this area. It will be up to each of them to engage or retreat from a threat.

"Does anyone have any questions?"

The Petrovic alpha female raised her hand. "What if the girls begin to fight each other?"

Rabi shrugged. "We must start the competitors together. Fighting is a possibility with their animals at the forefront."

There was angry murmuring among the alphas.

"I'll monitor the race from inside the forest," Liz said, stepping forward to stand beside Rabi. "If there is an actual fight, I will separate the parties and get them back onto the course."

Zarko Petrovic nodded. "This is acceptable." He cupped his daughter's face in his hands. "Run fast, my daughter. For all our sakes." He kissed each of her cheeks and she clutched his hands, tears rolling.

"I will do my best, Papa. For you, and for Bojan." Anica didn't mention Samit, causing Rachel to lean toward Bitty.

"What happened to her other brother, Samit?"

Bitty cupped her hands to Rachel's ear. "Deported. Sent home on a plane his morning, with a rather large bandage on his leg."

Mustafa Kasun was giving a similar pep talk to Larissa, if you could call it that. "Do not fail me, Larissa. You know what will happen." She nodded, her eyes filled with fear. Only Zara touched her, gave her a quick pat on the back.

"I'll do my best, Bitty," Rachel promised.

The woman smiled calmly. "I know you will, *chère*. Just fly hard and try not to focus too much on what Dalvin is doing."

"What do you mean?" Rachel asked. She had no idea what Dalvin was doing, or where he was.

Before Bitty could answer, the shield Rabi had erected earlier disappeared.

"Alphas! Shift your champions." The moon crashed down on Rachel so fast and hard it was like a brick wall had fallen on her. She screamed.

Bitty's magic surrounded her, filled her. Her wings spread inside and pushed out of her suddenly liquid skin. As her feathers began to flow, she saw Dalvin in her mind.

He was inside a building, standing in front of a chained Tamir.

"Who are you working for?"

The alpha bear spit at him. "Go to hell, stupid bird! I should have put you down in Serbia."

"*Chère!* Rachel! Go, go!" Bitty was yelling.

Shaking her head, banishing the intrusive image, Rachel realized she was the only one still on the starting line. What the hell had just happened?

"Bitty?" she said uncertainly.

"You're mated, Rachel. Dalvin is your mate. But you must not focus on that. Pull yourself out of his head and stay in yours. I can't help you with that. Now go!"

She took off, the cold wind pulling her into the night sky. *Mated? To Dalvin?* Her eyes adjusted quickly to the moonlight.

Flapping hard, she pressed into the forest to make up for lost time. She could see the blinking red lights of the tracking collars on the bears ahead.

They were colliding with one another, each trying to push the other off course. They seemed well matched, neither giving ground.

Her own first obstacle—a thick branch right across her flight path—was coming up, but it was one they'd practiced. *Re.* The note echoed in her head and her wing dropped. She sailed under the branch without a single additional wing flap.

Chelle? She heard Dalvin's voice in her head and it made her miss a wing beat.

Can't talk now. Racing. Focus. She had to focus. Flapping harder, she caught a tailwind for a moment, shooting ahead enough to once again catch sight of the blinking lights below.

The tailwind tried to turn her, so she fought her way out of it, back to still air. She was catching up! Movement caught her eye, and her head turned toward it before she could think.

Squirrel. Food.

She swooped toward the meat, talons open.

Dalvin dropped to his knees, suddenly flying. The press of the moon felt like a clutching hand, reaching inside him, trying to pull out his wings. But his wings were already out. He felt the air rushing past his face, the beat of his wings. But he still had arms—he held them up and stared at them, trying to sort out the sensation.

Chelle?

She responded, but it didn't sound like a mental response, more like she was right there in the room, whispering in his ear. *Can't talk now. Racing.*

He felt dizzy as he tried to sort out the sensation of his shoulders moving when his arms were at his sides.

Alek touched his arm. "Hey, you okay?" He led Dalvin away from the table where Tamir was bound. Claire continued questioning him.

"We already know a great deal. Enough to convict you before the full Council."

"Do you?" Tamir said with a sneer. "Then tell me."

Dalvin shook his head. "I need some air." Wind pressed against his face as he dove through the cold air. Food. The twitching tail of the squirrel was his whole focus, his whole world. He could nearly taste the warm, sweet meat.

They stepped out of the building and he took in great gulps of air. He put his hands on his head. "What the hell is happening to me?"

Alek was staring at him with an odd look on his face. "Tell me what you see."

"I'm flying. Right this second. I can see a squirrel on the branch. My talons are open. But I'm here too."

Alek laughed. "This is not funny," Dalvin said, furious. "Something weird is going on."

"They've started the race. Didn't you say you had a mental link with Rachel's pack?"

"Parliament, not pack. But yeah. I just contacted her through the link. She said not to bother her. She's racing. But right now I'm watching a squirrel get closer. Like it's right in my vision, overlaid on your face."

Alek nodded. "I'll bet it's Rachel and I bet I know why. Tell her to knock it off and get back to the race."

Hell, it couldn't hurt. *Rachel! Quit hunting. Get back to flying.*

A voice in her head caused her to her falter and make a noise. The food looked up, saw her, and raced into a hole in the tree. Her talons caught thin air.

Shaking her head, she looked down and around. Had she really just heard Dalvin telling her to quit hunting? He wasn't supposed to interfere, but she was glad he had. Fortunately, a quick correction was all she needed to get back on course. The hard dive had actually helped her catch up with the others.

Just ahead was the first hunting challenge. Two dead trees right at the cliff face were marked with dye, one pink, one blue. She looked up and spotted the yellow dye mark that matched the color on her collar, far up on the cliff.

The bears reached the trees and started to climb. Anica was stronger than she looked—she was making her way quickly up the tree. But Larissa had a longer reach and made up the difference in moments.

Crap! I can't keep watching them. I need to get my own prey.

The air currents next to the cliff were all downdrafts. Fighting the press of the wind and flapping hard to gain altitude was exhausting, which she expected was part of the challenge. She reached the yellow dot at just about the same time as the bears reached the hollows in their trees. She tried to reach into the crack in the rock, but her wings kept hitting the cliff face. She backed off, trying to figure out her next step, feeling the clock ticking. Anica had already grabbed her target honey and was devouring it.

Rachel tried to approach the cliffside again, but the wind kept trying to push her down and away. Wait! That was the answer. She flapped hard, rising to the top of the cliff, then swooped down. Air currents pushed her right into the wall, upside down. She grabbed the crack with one claw and opened her wings wide, letting the wind help her hold in place while she used her free foot to reach into the cleft and grope around blindly.

Her claws closed around something soft and meaty. A white mouse, already dead.

Her bird insisted on meat. Closing her eyes, she let the bird take over, still pressed against the rock. The mouse tasted so good! Sweet, soft, with a little crunch. So long as she didn't watch herself eat, she could enjoy the taste.

Finished, she let go of the rock, pulled in her wings, and shot down toward the trees. Seconds before she was going to hit the treetops, she felt the release of the downdraft and snapped her wing open, soaring higher into the sky. The first challenge was done!

CHAPTER 18

Alpha Kragan sat across from Dalvin in a tent set up next to the challenge assembly. To Bitty's right was Rabi Kuric and to her left was Amber Wingate.

"I'm telling you, I didn't know until just moments ago," Dalvin said, putting as much truth and honesty into his voice as he could. "And I didn't understand what it meant."

"There wasn't time to explain what I sensed, Councilman," Bitty said to Kuric. Shifting her gaze to the healer, she added, "You know, Amber, that I wouldn't intentionally interfere with this competition."

Kuric looked and smelled furious. Frowning, he studied the video monitors set up nearby on a large table. One showed the view from a drone flying overhead, tracking the blinking collars around the competitors' necks The other three were each dedicated to one of the racers, displaying images from the cameras mounted on the collars.

Sighing, Kuric said, "Someone explain to me one more time what we're dealing with?"

Bitty sighed. "This morning, when we were training, Agent Adway prevented my omega, Rachel Washington, from flying into a boulder. I believe using his magic to save her life opened a latent mating bond."

"That's what I sensed as well," Amber said, facing the cat councilman. "Rabi, it's not uncommon for a mating bond to take effect when the people involved are under stress. New bonds are tenuous and unpredictable, can go either way. A stress mating can bind the couple fully and permanently, or it can be a one-time shot and might fall apart the next day.

"A stress-driven binding is often paired with sexual contact or intense emotions. I've seen rare instances where that alone can activate the bond. In this particular case, I think there's been physical contact."

How did she know that? Then he remembered that she'd stayed with Rachel last night. She must have smelled that they'd kissed. Or maybe she sensed what they'd done after rescuing the base jumpers.

Kuric raised his eyebrows. "Have you had sex with Ms. Washington? After I specifically told you to stay away from the delegates?"

"No. We haven't had sex." It was the truth. Sort of.

The councilman snarled, his jaw moving sideways as he bared his teeth. "You're lying. I can smell it."

He looked at the wall and the table, unwilling to meet the councilman's eyes. "It's the truth. We haven't had sex. She's a virgin. I don't take that lightly. But we . . . well, we kissed and we sort of got each other off accidentally."

Amber nodded. "That can absolutely happen, and your sexual desire for her will get more intense as the bond grows. If you don't intend to permanently mate with Rachel, you have to let the binding fail, starting right now. Without continued contact, it will gradually fade and you'll be able to go on with your separate lives without pining much."

Kuric gave a curt nod. "Well and fine. But that doesn't address the issue of interference with the competition."

Bitty Kragan shook her head. "Unintentional at best, and likely had no effect on the outcome of the race. The contact was brief, and early enough in the race that even if she had gotten the squirrel, she would have still made up the time."

Amber shrugged, her scent neutral. "I agree it was unintentional. And it will likely happen again because even if they're aware of it, it will be difficult for them to control. I suggest a time penalty or an extra challenge against the racer and nothing more."

Rabi rubbed his eyes. The scent of his frustration was strong, like burning cat fur. He got up and walked out of the tent and the others followed. The bear alphas were waiting outside.

"I've heard the evidence and made my decision. Rachel Washington will be assessed a penalty for unintentional interference. Instead of five mice *or* a white mouse at the second hunting leg, she must catch all six mice in the allotted time."

The news made its way to the announcer. "We have a penalty flag on the play, everyone!"

Adults turned away from games of horseshoes and children stopped playing egg-toss to listen.

"Rachel Washington has received a penalty for unintentional interference!" Boos and angry comments rose from the crowd. "But it's not all bad news! She's *mated* to someone. We'll let you know more as we know it." Shouts of excitement replaced the booing, and people broke into groups to discuss the events.

Dalvin wanted to go hide in a tree somewhere. This was not the way he wanted Rachel to find out—from strangers at the finish line. And he didn't even know who was mated to whom, or whether it was a real mating. Everyone was just guessing so far.

"Can I please get back to doing my job?" he asked generally, not sure who was making which decisions at this point.

Amber shrugged. "I don't see why not. Mating isn't a disability. People work with it every day—including your fellow Wolven agent, Alek. Go back to whatever you were doing."

Kuric didn't object, so Dalvin sprinted back to the small steel storage shed that was doubling as a jail. Claire was sitting across from Tamir, just staring at him. The traitor was squirming in his seat, fidgeting more with each passing second. Alek stood behind Claire, with a hand on her shoulder. Power radiated out of Claire in a wave that lapped at the edge of Dalvin's consciousness. He felt pressure to do the right thing. To not harm anyone.

He almost smiled, remembering Claire's unique gift—empathy. She was trying to project emotions at Tamir, to make him want to cooperate.

It wasn't working. Or at least not as intended. Tamir let out a bark of a laugh. "I am doing the right thing already. I have no guilt to feel, witch."

No, too obvious. Look deeper. Those were Rachel's thoughts. Abruptly Dalvin could see her searching for a path through thick branches. She was right. The upper fly-through would hang her up on the other side, where the space between the branches was filled with needles.

Look deeper. Something grabbed at his memory, or maybe it was a memory of Rachel's. He pulled Tamir to his feet by his shirt, then shoved him against the cold metal shed wall. Tamir sneered at him, but Dalvin spoke firmly, without emotion.

"You made a critical mistake, Tamir. You spoke French to the serving girl at the restaurant in Loznica. We've already picked her up. What do you suppose she'll tell us when a king cobra wraps her in his coils and starts questioning her? Such a pretty little thing. Will she bleed before the venom stops her heart?"

The bear shifter's eyes widened, and he showed fear for the first time. "She is a *child*! You wouldn't dare harm her!"

Dalvin shrugged and released him to land in a heap on the floor, turning his back dismissively. "Eh. You know how Ahmad is. He can be somewhat . . . heavy-handed."

Tamir pushed himself to his feet, using the wall as a brace.

His scent was angry, with the tang of fear laced through it. He spat out his words as though he had venom himself: "Very well. You win. Just keep that viper away from my daughter."

Claire and Alek looked at Dalvin in surprise. His daughter? Wow, nailed that one! He reached out to Bitty through the group mind. *Find one of the Council members. Have them tell whoever is left at the Serbian camp to pick up a waitress named Dejana at the Macak café in Loznica. Hold her for questioning.*

At Dalvin's nod, Claire vacated her chair and Dalvin sat down. Alek hauled Tamir back into his seat. Dalvin stared across the table at the man who had been his superior until just an hour or so earlier, who had taken a strip of his hide. "So, talk."

Rachel was flying harder than she ever had, but also flying faster. Energy surged through her, and she flapped and dove for all she was worth, threading the needle of the narrow canyon, twisting and turning to avoid outcroppings hidden in shadows. She didn't realize at first that she had to touch each of the markers. There were little packets taped on them that sent a fine mist of yellow powder into the air.

Figures they forgot to mention this. Wait, hadn't they? Hadn't she heard something like that? Below her, the bears did the same, racing over rocks that shifted underfoot, shooting pink or blue powder into the air. In some cases, the powder dispensers were mounted so the bears had to reach down to them from a ledge; other times, they were high and the racers had to stretch or jump up.

Who the hell placed these things? Spider-Man? Whoever it was had been an amazingly skillful flyer, taping markers on the walls under ledges, behind tree trunks jutting out from sheer rock, and inside cracks like the one that had held the mouse. She hadn't found and triggered as many dispensers as the bears had, and they were both ahead of her. She had to make up time, and fast.

She flapped hard when she hit the last marker, planning to overtake the bears as they reached the flat ground leading to Luna Lake. She heard a roar of pain and her bird insisted she find the source. There hadn't been enough meat on this flight and she was getting hungry. Pain might mean food.

Kiting over, Rachel saw Larissa slamming her whole body into Anica, trying to push the smaller bear off the narrow path out of the canyon. The ledge led to a bridge onto the flat ground. The canyon floor was hundreds of feet below. Another hard shove and the Serbian bear's back feet slid into open air. She scrambled for footing.

If she fell, Rachel knew Anica might not survive. *Screw the competition!* Rachel narrowed her wings into a dive, heading straight for Larissa, who was edging in for a final push beneath a row of pine trees jutting out from the rock face. Rachel beat her wings against the bear, causing her to back away, bawling. Anica got her feet under her and started to run for the canyon exit. But Larissa wasn't done. She leaped forward, reaching for Anica's back leg. Rachel went for her again. *She thinks someone should explore the canyon? Maybe it should be her.*

She'd just lowered her talons to grab the bear's back when a sharp crack filled the air.

She screamed. A dime-size hole had been torn through the feathers of one wing. What the hell? She'd been *shot*! Looking around frantically, she spotted movement at the top of the cliff. Rachel heard more firing, saw dust kicking up around both bears. They scrambled for cover, forgetting their fight.

Maybe the attack wasn't related to the competition, since the person was shooting at all of them? But why would anyone be shooting at *any* of them? Rachel flew high, then swooped down, trying to get a look at the person with the gun. There wasn't much light in the canyon, so Rachel opened her eyes wide, letting the moonlight turn the night into day. The world came alive with bright gray that offset the darkest shadows. Mice, snakes, and insects became glowing beacons to hunt. But she was looking for bigger prey, and found it. Hidden among the bushes at the top of the canyon was a man, wearing something on his head—probably night-vision goggles—and carrying a rifle.

Keeping her wings tight and silent, Rachel swooped toward him. As she passed directly overhead, she reached out and grabbed not the man, but the weapon—ripping it out of his hands and sending it over the edge, into the canyon.

That the man was fast enough to stand up and grab at her leg was startling. More startling still was that she recognized him: Samit! How was he back in town? She fluttered up, out of reach, spinning around him like a feathered helicopter. "What are you doing, Samit? That's your *sister* down there!"

He growled, pointing at the bears, who had taken shelter behind a rock. "She's no sister of mine! She is a *thing* who turned me into demon!" Samit was throwing off waves of chaotic energy. He really was a rogue. It wasn't an act. Or, at least, it wasn't one *now*.

This was big trouble. She couldn't leave—what if Samit shifted and went after Anica? But she couldn't stop him either. None of the three competitors could, not even if they all worked together. An alpha would barely be strong enough to contain a rogue.

At least, a *local* alpha. But there were alphas in Luna Lake right now who probably were strong enough. And didn't Liz say she was following their trail?

Rachel reached out through the group link, searching for one particular person. *Dalvin! Whatever you're doing, I'm sorry, but this is important. Samit's gone rogue. I mean, really rogue.*

Dalvin and Bitty responded nearly simultaneously. *Samit's on a plane, on the way back to Serbia.*

She looked down again, to be sure. He was still jumping up

at her, trying to grab her leg. *No, he's not. He's in the canyon, in Leg 2 of the race. He shot me.*

White sparkles bloomed in her vision, making her dizzy. *What?!* Dalvin's voice in her head was panicked. *Are you okay?*

Fine. Well, sort of. I lost a few feathers. He shot at Anica and Larissa too, and I don't know if he hit either of them. Is Liz out here somewhere? I took his rifle, but we can't just leave him.

Bitty's voice filled her mind. *Leave him. Liz is just behind you.*

She couldn't. Liz would never find Samit in the dark. Unless—

"There ain't nothing that I can do or nothing I can say, that folks don't criticize me. But I'm going to do just as I want to anyway." Rachel opened her beak and let the words flow out, let the moonlight fill her and add to the song.

"What the hell you doing? Shut up, stupid bird! Owls are not sing!" Samit clutched his ears, ran in a circle, then sat down and began to rock back and forth, hands clutched to his head. *"Stop singing!"*

She switched to a version of "The Lord's Prayer" that she'd heard sung by a bunch of choirs. Maybe a little prayer was needed right now. Too many rogues in this place. It couldn't be the will of any higher power to want this.

"Our Father . . . which art in heeaaaven." A pair of voices from below picked up the song. Apparently, it had crossed international boundaries.

"Shut up, shut up, *shut up!*" Samit was rocking faster and faster, chaotic energy coming off him in waves. Rachel was getting tired of flying but had to stay in the air. Pulling on reserves she didn't know she had, she flew even higher, letting her song be a beacon for Liz.

Okay, Chelle, Dalvin said in her head. *We got you on video. Liz is on it.*

Samit had buried his head under his arms. He was curled in a fetal position and, oddly, his energy was calming down. From her song? She spotted Liz, in badger form, making her way through the brush.

"On earth . . . as it is . . . in heeeaaven."

Liz disappeared from view, and Rachel saw a plume of what looked like dirt fly into the air.

Moments later, Samit plummeted, screaming, into a hole that opened under him. An instant later, Samit fell silent, and Liz, still a badger, emerged from the ground, dragging Samit behind her. Rachel saw that the young man was wrapped top to bottom in what looked like netting; she could feel the press of intense magic that was holding him firmly in place. Liz rose up on her back legs.

"All clear. I'll get him back to town."

Rachel sank into the canyon, toward the rock where the bears were hiding. "All clear," she called. "Liz has the shooter."

The brown bear, Larissa, streaked out from behind the rock and raced for the bridge. Thinking that Anica was scared, Rachel called, "It's okay, Anica. Come on out. Liz caught the gunman."

The little bear didn't even poke her head out. Worried, Rachel landed on the boulder and immediately saw Anica lying on her side on the ground, barely breathing. Crap! Had she been hit? She smelled blood, but it wasn't prey blood, so her bird had no interest. She fluttered down to the narrow ledge and carefully walked over.

"Anica?"

The bear rolled her head over. "Rachel. Knife. Can you reach?"

Knife? Rachel hopped up to the top of the boulder again, trying to see where the blood was coming from. There, in Anica's side, the hilt nearly hidden by her thick fur. It was going to be tricky to remove it without hands. She studied the cliff face, looking for any cracks she could use to hold on. She spotted one, but it was narrow, barely big enough for a single claw.

She stretched across Anica's body as the little bear's breathing grew more shallow. Resting her injured wing on the boulder and bracing her weight on the opposite leg, Rachel was able to reach down and pluck out the knife, an ornate black blade with a bone handle. Blood began to gush from the wound. All she could think to do was throw her whole body weight on top of the bear to keep pressure on the injury.

Anica let out a soft woofing sound at the impact. Rocks were stabbing Rachel in the sides and her wing was bleeding too, though the damage wasn't life-threatening. "Hang in there, Anica. We'll get someone here fast."

Dalvin! Anica's hurt. She's been stabbed. We need Amber up here, right away.

Instead of Dalvin, the leader of her parliament spoke sadly in her mind. *There's not enough time. I've been watching the monitor. It's deep. Too deep.*

We healed Alek, all of us together. Can't we do that again?

But that was different—or was it? Bitty disappeared in her head.

Dalvin's voice replaced the old woman's. *They're discussing something strange. Something you helped with before—blending packs. Are you okay with that?*

She nodded before realizing he couldn't see her. *Yes, go ahead. Whatever it takes.*

Warmth filled her, like a slow, lazy sunbeam. She felt herself drifting along, like an inner tube on a river, inside her own head. She saw Dalvin's face, his dark eyes concerned. Then the sunbeam turned into a fireplace and she was snuggled on a bearskin rug with Dalvin, luxuriating in the warmth. *Hold on, Chelle. Your alphas tell me it's about to get rough.*

Pain. Fire shot out of the hearth and enveloped her. It poured through her and into Anica. The bear screamed, reached back with claws the size of kitchen knives and tried to tear her away from the wound. Rachel would have been happy to leave, except she was glued to the bear by the magic.

She felt herself sink down inside the bear, drip into the hole like she was liquid. The pain was so much like the cave. The snake venom was like this. It *was*.

It *is*.

Abruptly, Rachel was with Anica—really *with* her—in a cave, but not the Texas cave. No birds here, but the chains were the same. Anica, just a little girl, yanked at the shackles until her arms were bloody. Then they came for her. Rachel felt the bear's panic.

"Turn her or be done with it," said the man with the black hair, the one who smelled of viper. When they pulled her out of the cage and turned to shut it, she ran. Ran so hard and so fast. They nearly caught up with her. She screamed as claws raked down the back of her leg, from thigh to ankle. But she was little, and fast, and she ran.

It was night, like this night. A full moon, like this one. And the cave was . . . was near the water. Yes. A bit of the river ran through the cavern. It was hidden, behind the waterfall. Nobody could find it, and the rushing water covered the screams. She'd run in the river. Rachel felt every agonizing footstep. The rocks in the river slashed at her feet, but she had to stay in the water so they didn't track her. How many times had she slipped, gone under, only to come up gasping and spitting, hundreds of feet farther downstream?

The moon made the claw wounds ache, as though acid was cutting deeper into her skin. Ever deeper. Rachel remembered the acid of the moon on the claw marks down her back. Like these, but different. No, not different. The same.

She saw the lights of a town ahead. A little town, just a few houses. A train. She heard the train coming and knew the train was faster than walking. But to reach it, she had to leave the river. She climbed up the bank, her arms shaking with exhaustion, her leg twitching and aching, not working properly. She tried to walk but could barely drag her wounded leg forward. Soon she was crawling down the road, trying desperately to get to the train.

The world split apart and she roared. The pain was so bad, as if every bone in her body was breaking, joining, splitting. Then it was over—even the pain in her leg was gone. She heard the train whistle again.

The train. She started to run toward it in a lopsided, clumsy gait. She saw a man and ran up to him to ask for help. Called out to him. Shouted. Roared.

He yelled in fear and ran away. Why? Couldn't he see she needed help!

People ran toward her and threw rocks at her, chasing her down the road to where the train tracks crossed the land. Confused and frightened, all she could think was that she had to get back home to her family. They would help her. She walked all night, following the tracks, following a faint breeze that smelled of home. There, at last! Just over the fence, the berry bushes of home! The sun was nearly up and she was glad. So tired. She saw the house and then . . . then—

Rachel took a great gasp of air, her heart pounding like a triphammer. *Chelle! Come back! You're too far in, get ou–!*

The voice cut off abruptly. She was back in the canyon, a bird once more.

"Rachel?" came a soft, tired voice beneath her. She scrambled to get off the bear, then fluttered up and over to land near Anica's nose. "What happened?"

The bleeding had stopped. The little bear's fur was matted with blood, but the wound was closed. "I think our packs healed you." She held out her own wing. The feathers had grown back, the hole in her wing just a rubbery scar. "And me," she added, surprised.

"How long have we been here?"

Rachel looked up. The moon had barely moved. "Not long, I don't think. Can you stand?"

Anica's legs were a little shaky, but she managed to get back on her feet. Rachel walked behind her on the path to the flat land.

"What do we do?" Anica asked, "Race is over? We lose?" She paused. "How are we think . . . talk?

Rachel flapped her wings, frustrated. "I don't know. I can't feel my parliament, or your sloth, in my head. But we can, so let's use it. There's still the fishing challenge. Can you make it to the water? At least eat something. And our families are there."

"I will try." The bear nodded and started to walk. Rachel took to the air, flying slowly, keeping pace with her new sorority sister. Like Claire. Survivors all.

CHAPTER 19

"Where did she go? She disappeared from my head!" Dalvin grabbed Bitty's hands, trying to reconnect, but she pulled away.

"We had to let her go, Dalvin. We were causing her to go too far into Anica's memories. The shock of cutting off the magic should have brought her back to this place and time."

Amber was shaking her head, and Zarko Petrovic was holding his head in his hands, as if he had a splitting headache.

"*Should have?* Not good enough." Before anyone could stop him, Dalvin ran toward the canyon, letting the moon pull his bird form out so that he took off from a running start. He tried to reach Rachel in his head, but something had gone wrong. He was alone inside his mind.

Why did that bug him? He flew hard, following the course from the lake backward. It wasn't long before he saw Larissa.

"Larissa! How far behind you are the others?" She ignored him and kept running. Maybe she couldn't hear him?

He could chase her down for an answer, but it was probably better to keep going. Larissa was probably going for help anyway. She could lead Amber back in case Anica was . . . well, he didn't want to think about that. He liked Anica. They shared a love of R & B music. She listened to newer singers whose work he didn't know, like Amy Winehouse. He'd heard the name but never in connection with Motown. But man, could that woman belt out the blues!

Music! That was the key. He thought of Rachel, thought of flying, and began to sing in his head, *do, re, mi, fa . . .*

. . . sol, la, ti, do. Rachel's voice joined his, and white lights appeared in his vision, making him light-headed. *Rachel, where are you?*

Near the canyon. Look for . . . the radio tower on top of the mountain. We're just west of it.

He looked across the sky. The pale red blinking lights of the tower were easy to spot. *Just west.* He swooped down until he was just above the treetops, looking both ways and above him. He opened his pupils fully, let the moonlight in, and didn't care at all that his head pounded from the effort.

There!

Dipping his right wing, he turned and flapped hard to reach the slow-moving bear and the owl who was walking and hopping alongside her. He fluttered down and immediately ran over to Rachel, nuzzling her neck feathers with his beak. "Are you okay? I was worried sick!"

She signed tiredly. "I am now. Anica is still pretty weak, though. I can't leave her."

Dalvin sighed. "Then Larissa is going to win. I passed her on the way here."

Rachel hooted with angry excitement. "She damned well better *not* win! She stabbed Anica."

"Wait," he said, confused. "I thought you said there was a shooter."

Anica shook her head, her eyes barely open. "Yes, but I am not shot. Larissa had knife. Stabbed me in side."

"In human form? But she's an omega."

Again Anica shook her head. "No, in bear form. Blade was is attached to her collar. I did not notice it when we began race.

It was very thin and carefully placed, not to be noticed. We took shelter from Samit and when we are in tiny area, hidden, she strike! Stab me two, three times. Knife comes off collar and she runs away when Samit captured."

Snow began to fall; he blinked to keep the flakes from clouding his vision. "If it was in her collar, then it had to have been placed there by her Alpha."

Anica smelled very confused. She scratched at the snow with her claws. "Is not right. Larissa work for us. She is femily too. Why she try to kill me?"

"Wait, what?"

Rachel smelled and sounded surprised and a little indignant. "So Dani really did hear that right? Larissa was talking to Draga in French? She was going to throw the match?"

The bear's head dipped repeatedly.

"Yes. Is not my idea, is Mama's. Papa not know. I am not supposed to know. Mama is Jancic before marrying Papa. Larissa is also Jancic, but she became brown bear instead of black. Kasuns do same thing to Jancics as they do to us. A blood feud was demanded but never held. They just laugh. There are no Sazi to help Jancics."

It all made sense now. "That's why the original peace talks were supposed to be in the village near Loznica. Half of the phone book is Jancics." Such as the waitress at the café, who took her mother's surname instead of her Russian father's. *Look deeper.* Chelle had no idea just how right she'd been. But why would Larissa turn on Anica? Why would she risk stabbing her when there were so many Wolven agents nearby?

Anica was breathing harder. "I am very tired. Very hungry. I would like to rest now."

She needed to rest. She'd lost a lot of blood. But he couldn't afford to let her stay here. Tamir, Samit, Larissa—who knew if there were more people out there with their own reasons for wanting the Petrovics dead? "Wait here. I'll find food."

Rachel sat down next to her new friend while Dalvin put his wings in high gear to the lake. As he expected, Larissa was busily fishing. And oh, look, how handy! She'd already caught four big salmon and put them in the basket. He swooped down just as the announcer was calling out, "And there's the fifth, folks! And it has a yellow tail."

Dalvin reached out with his talons and grabbed the bucket of fish. He called out to the announcer, "Penalty on the play. Intentional interference. The fish are forfeited. Begin again."

Larissa was just about to start running the final leg. He had to stop that. There wasn't time to explain everything he'd learned. He saw Rabi Kuric look up and then shift forms, the tiger following Dalvin across the ground as they raced back to Anica.

She was very weak when he landed. He shifted forms and petted her nose. She opened her eyes, just barely. He shoved a salmon under her nose.

"Eat something. You'll feel stronger." It was almost too much effort for her to open her jaw, but she did. He hoped that the protein would give her back some strength.

Councilman Kuric sprinted up just as she was finishing the first fish and reaching into the bucket for the second. "Is good fish. Big fish are good."

"What the hell happened out here?" Kuric asked. "We stopped getting images from the drone."

"Plans within plans. We need to arrest Larissa for attempted murder and Draga Petrovic for conspiracy to commit murder. For a start. And we might pick up Alpha Kasun for conspiracy too. I'm not sure which one is guilty, but one of them sure is."

He'd been so focused on Anica that hadn't realized Rachel had disappeared until she dropped out of the sky, carrying something in her teeth. She dropped the object in the snow at Rabi's paws.

"That's the knife that stabbed Anica," she said. "I went back for it. I'll bet someone's prints are on it."

By the time the four of them reached the lake, Larissa had completed the fishing challenge a second time and crossed the finish line. The whole town was congratulating her, and she was roaring in victory.

When Larissa saw Anica walk up, limping but alive, she panicked and tried to run, but Rabi caught her in a net of magic and hauled her back.

Rachel stood beside Dalvin in the falling snow, leaning into him. He could feel her heartbeat under the feathers, and it made him happy. "I'm so glad this is all over."

She turned her head and blinked. "Oh, it's not. Not by a long shot. Does the Council own a private jet?"

CHAPTER 20

Rachel plumped the pillows behind her back and picked up the remote control. Bedrooms. Who knew there were planes that had multiple bedrooms? Sure, the bed was only an oversize twin, but it *was* a bed . . . on a plane! Freaking cool!

Was that a knock on the door? A door . . . inside a plane! She'd never flown in a private plane before and had spent the first few hours glued to the window, watching the landscape sail by. Once they got out over the water, there wasn't much to see except gray. Even the little bumps of turbulence didn't bother her, or the thought of where they were going. She popped out one of her earbuds—she was listening to a singer she hadn't heard of until Anica played a song for her. Instant die-hard Winehouse fan. Pity she'd had such a short career. The best ones always seemed to die young.

"Hello?"

"Chelle? Want some company?"

"Sure. C'mon in." Dalvin entered, wearing a simple pullover sweater and jeans. Man, did he look good. So not the boy she remembered. "Hey."

"Hey, yourself," he said softly. He shut the door with careful effort, trying to make as little noise as possible. Most everyone was asleep by the sound of the gentle snoring she could hear in the hall, droning like white noise. Rachel was too wired to sleep.

She patted the bed, inviting him to sit. The room was small and there weren't many options.

"Take a load off." She tossed him a pillow—there had to be a dozen of them stacked on the bed—and he sat next to her. When he swung his feet up, she pushed them off, saying, "Take your shoes off. These are white sheets. Didn't your mama teach you manners?"

He let out a little chuckle. Deep and wicked, it pulled at things inside her.

"My bad." He twisted to the side and she heard the *thunk* as each shoe hit the floor. He settled beside her again, putting his bare feet on the covers. She hadn't noticed before, but the boy had *big* feet. "So."

"So," she repeated. "You got some pretty quick action on this. Thank you."

He inhaled deeply and let it out slow. His breath smelled of spearmint gum and lime juice.

"You really sure you want to be part of this? This isn't your fight."

She snorted, spewing spit all over the white coverlet.

"The hell it's not!" He hurriedly put a finger to his lips and she winced a little, then lowered her voice to an angry whisper. "The minute they snatched me off the street in Detroit, it became my fight. They're going to wish they never messed with Mama Washington's baby girl."

A corner of his mouth turned up in that same teasing smile she used to love . . . and hate. "I thought you weren't anyone's baby."

"No," she said, getting onto her hands and knees and crawling out from under the covers. "I said I wasn't *your* baby. Not yet."

"Ah." He didn't move a muscle, just stared at her with those golden-brown eyes. His magic was like a second skin against hers, as though he was already caressing her body. It made her shiver all the way down to her toes.

Oh, to hell with it. She crawled on top of him, straddled his legs. She'd intended to seduce him during the flight, provided they could get a second alone. The rough denim of his jeans was delicious against her bare legs, and she could feel the beginning of a bulge against her thin panties. She planted a kiss on his warm, soft lips. Her magic sort of melted into his, mixed like sugar and butter—sweet, thick, and rich enough to stop your heart.

He didn't waste any time. He tugged her shirt over her head and let her do the same to him. He pulled her to him, rubbed all that skin across hers and turned her insides to hot, liquid fire. Her hands couldn't get enough of him. She wanted more, and then even more. He seemed to know just what she needed. He unhooked her bra. Pulling the straps from her shoulders, he pushed her back to look at her, naked.

"My God, you're beautiful." She didn't know how to respond to that. Nobody had ever said it to her. "I never thought I'd see you again. And to see what you've become? I am the luckiest man alive."

He leaned forward before she could speak and started to kiss her breasts. The feeling was beyond pleasure, somewhere near pain as he sucked a nipple into his mouth and pulled until she cried out softly. He let out a little hiss and then made a popping noise with his tongue that made the bird inside her flutter with excitement. He rolled her back and over so suddenly it took her breath away.

Slowly, deliciously, he pulled off her panties. This was becoming what she always imagined her first time would be like.

"I want you, Dalvin."

"No reservations?"

Shaking her head, he would smell only truth in her word. "None."

"I've wanted you since the day you wore that caramel dress. I wanted to pull it off you and do . . . something." He smiled. "I didn't really know what to do with a girl then." The smile in his eyes turned dark and hungry and his voice lowered to match. "But I do now."

A shiver went all the way through her, so hard he could see her body tremble. He let out another of those chuckles that made her crazy and slid his hands under her thighs, raising the whole lower half of her body.

"What the hell?" she said, then gasped as she realized what he was about to do. He gave her a kiss, like on her mouth, but on a whole different part of her body. She had to grab the nearest pillow to scream into as sensations she'd never imagined flowed through her. It was too much, too fast. Her whole body clenched as an orgasm screamed through her. She couldn't think, couldn't breathe.

He didn't relent, tonguing, kissing, nibbling. Soon she was clenching her hands in the sheets, her mind complete putty. He finally laid her back down on the bed, his face shiny before he used another pillow to wipe himself dry. "I've waited ten long years to see you look like that. I don't think I want it to end yet."

She shook her head, looking at all that muscle. It was hers for the asking. "I don't either." She saw that his jeans were about ready to burst. She reached forward and popped open the top button. Dalvin closed his eyes and groaned. The second button was harder to undo, and the third, even harder. He stood up in a rush, letting his pants slide to the floor. His underwear went next, and then she got to finally see his whole naked self. She'd touched him in the meadow but hadn't actually *looked*. It seemed too personal. Now there wasn't any *too personal* left.

Rachel's hands explored his body while he tried to keep his balance. He was glorious, every inch of his dark skin was muscled perfection. "I figured you'd be chubby forever and I was fine with that. But . . . *damn*."

He leaned forward, crawled up on the bed on top of her. "Yeah, well, I didn't expect a skinny, long-legged tomboy to turn out like *you*. Oh, Chelle. My beautiful Rachel. Are you ready for this?"

She looked up into his face, saw the boy who bumped her in the playground and sang next to her on the fountain. Saw the man who stood proud and defiant with her mother and fetched food for a wounded bear. She touched his cheek, his lips, and nearly started crying. "Yeah. I am."

He bent and kissed her, soft and slow. Then, like building up steam in an engine, his breath started to come faster, his hands stopped caressing and grew hungry and demanding. Her hands were demanding too. She kissed him with fervor, pulled his head tight against her neck when he moved his lips and teeth there. When he finally leaned back, both of them breathless, his eyes were so wide she could see the whites. "Crap! I don't have any protection."

She smiled and pointed at the tiny little nightstand with a drawer that wouldn't even fit a Gideon Bible if they tried to stock one. But it held a box of condoms from the airport gift shop just fine. She grinned. "First time on a private plane and I get to join the Mile High Club."

He hooted out a laugh that was more owl than human. "I love you, Rachel Washington."

He meant it. He wasn't lying. She could smell it, feel it like honey against her skin. The thought of it, of him, and the possibility of being mated to him . . . took her breath away.

"I think . . . I love you too."

Those golden owl eyes went from laughing to serious again. He reached into the drawer, showed her how to use what was inside the foil pouch.

She expected it to hurt, had been told it would hurt . . . but it didn't. He sank inside her body as though he was meant to be there. The magic that surrounded him was inside her, blossoming, expanding, filling her. When he began to move, sliding in and out, she was delirious, not even able to put together a sentence. But her body knew what to do. She began to thrust back against him. She needed more.

"Dalvin, please!"

He obeyed. He kissed her again, deeper than ever, tightened his fingers on her hips, and pressed himself into her so hard and fast that when her orgasm hit, the whole bed moved. Maybe the whole plane moved. She felt the moment when their heartbeats synced, knew the moment he was inside her mind like he was inside her body.

When he came, his whole body tensed, and a blinding light flashed across her vision. She saw his memories, his pain, the women . . . so many women, who could never be what he wanted. Because he wanted something he didn't believe existed anymore. He wanted a memory. He wanted *her*.

When they were both spent and trying to catch their breath, she stroked his soft hair and reveled in the sensation of him wrapped around her. "I could come home to this every day," she whispered, staring at the ceiling of a room that wasn't theirs and wondered if there was a place in the world that they could call home.

CHAPTER 21

*A*re you sure this is the place? It's been ten years and she was in animal form," Dalvin whispered in Rachel's ear. They'd been searching for a week now, on the ground in Serbia, looking for the things Rachel had seen in Anica's mind.

"Yeah, I think so." The trick had been finding all the elements within a night's run from the Petrovic family farm.

Zarko was talking to one of the locals while the others waited in the jeeps. Finished, he came over and put an arm around Anica's shoulders.

"I think you are right, Rachel." He still pronounced her name *Raquel,* but she was fine with that. "There was a village just down the road. It is gone now, destroyed in new fighting. But ten years ago, it stood. I do not believe Anica should come any farther. Already she has bad dreams at night."

Anica shook her head and said, "No, Papa. I have bad dreams because I left people behind. And you heard farmer. Just a week ago another boy went missing. We must look. We have a duty."

Her father gave a long-suffering sigh, then smiled. "You have helped Bojan and me with our dream, and now we will help you." He swung one arm in a circle over his head. A clanking, roaring sound came from within the tree line.

Rachel's jaw dropped when she saw the source of the noise as it cleared the trees. "A tank?! You're bringing a *tank*?"

She didn't know much about tanks, but the squareish machine was tall and green, with massive treads. It had an actual gun turret, with a huge cannon that had an opening bigger than her head.

Zarko shrugged. "If Sazi magic is not enough, we have other options." Behind his back, Dalvin grinned.

Rachel wasn't worried about having enough "Sazi magic," since half the Council had joined their expedition. Amber, Liz, and Rabi had come with them from the States, and Angelique, Ahmad, and his wife, Tuli, had met them in Serbia. The tank rolled up to the group of jeeps and ancient pickup trucks; the lid opened and Anica's brother poked his head up.

"Is nice tank?"

Rachel smiled widely. "I thought you were a chef."

He gave her a look of mock insult. "I am chef. Very good chef. And I have appreciation for nice cars." He slapped a hand down on the steel. "Well made, dependable. Not so good on mileage. But very nice car."

She couldn't help but laugh. At least the tank matched their clothes. She, Anica, Liz, Amber, and Tuli were dressed in matching khaki outfits that Zarko had provided. There were tons of pockets in the sleeves and pant legs, which let them carry everything and keep their hands free. Angelique had declined and was dressed all in black wool.

To keep her hair out of her eyes, Anica had created a pair of buns on top of her head and looked surprisingly cute. Dalvin, Zarko, and Rabi wore green camo uniforms supplied by Ahmad.

Dalvin gave Rachel a hand up onto the gunning platform, where she could see in all directions.

"Let's go nuke a nest of snakes!" she said as Anica climbed up to join her. The women held hands as the tank rumbled forward.

This part of the Serbian countryside closely resembled the area around Luna Lake. The pines were a little different and things smelled different, but it was lush and green. She could imagine living here, except for the war raging in other parts of the country. Passing through the checkpoints had been scary stuff, even traveling in the company of people who can snap necks like pretzels and freeze folks in their tracks.

The tank lumbered through the village. The destroyed homes, some still with tattered laundry hanging limply from clotheslines, tore at her. People had lived here once. They had been frightened, had chased off a little black bear to protect themselves. But they hadn't been able to protect themselves from whoever had bombed them out of existence.

After they had passed through the village, Anica gave a little gasp, and Rachel held up a hand to stop the convoy near a railway trestle. The two omegas scrambled off the tank. Rachel thought she heard something.

"Everyone! Shut off your engines."

The tank's motor grumbled into stillness. Once the rest of the engines were off, they could hear the world around them. The grass crunching underfoot sounded right, the sky looked right, the place smelled right.

Anica dropped to her knees at the sound of a train whistle, far in the distance. She looked out, focusing on a tree that was a little wider and a little taller than those around it. Rachel's mind flashed to the same moment, and she knew Dalvin could see the memory too.

"This really is it." His voice was quiet. He touched Anica's shoulder, and she started sobbing.

Her father came over and took her in his arms. "Are you certain you can do this? We can save the children without you."

She snuffled and wiped her nose on the back of her hand. Then she straightened up and took a deep breath. "No. I can do this. I *must* do this."

To prove the point, she sprinted off over the bomb-shattered landscape, where deep holes pockmarked what was formerly farmland. Bojan started up the tank and followed slowly, but the land was too rough for the jeeps. The others followed on foot.

When they came to a river, wide and fast, Anica jumped in without hesitation, standing in the swift-flowing water. Then she shook her head and stepped back onto the bank, where she put a hand on Rachel's shoulder. "You see? You know why I must do this?"

"You have to prove that it wasn't a fluke," Rachel said, completely understanding Anica's position

"Fluke?" The little bear shook her head. "I not know this word."

Dalvin said, "A fluke is an accident, a mistake."

Anica nodded, her sopping shirt and pants dripping on the grass. "Yes, it was not mistake. I am strong. I escaped."

Amber came up behind them, followed by Rabi and Ahmad. "So we're here?"

Rachel nodded. "Close, very close. We have to go upstream a bit. I don't know that we should take the tank any farther. We don't need to advertise. They might slip away."

Ahmad nodded. "Agreed. I'll scout forward, smell for snakes. I am very much looking forward to meeting more *friends* of my father's." He shifted to snake form and slid out of his clothes. His wife, Tuli, gathered them into a stack for him to put back on later. She was an odd one, sort of distant and scary. Amber had told her that Tuli had been an assassin for Sargon; Ahmad had helped her turn good.

Scary.

A chime sounded from Amber's pocket. She pulled out her phone and set it to Silent, looking sheepish. "Sorry."

Other people, including Rachel, followed Amber's example, checking and, if necessary, silencing their phones. Getting sim cards for the phones had been hard, but when it was time to call for help from the human authorities, they would have them.

Amber looked at her phone's screen and said, "Good news. Our seer used hindsight to get Larissa to tell us why she attacked Anica. Mustafa bought her off. She wanted to live in a big city, have servants of her own. Mustafa promised her enough cash to make that possible. He'd already paid her enough to buy a condo, with more coming after Anica was dead."

Zarko spat on the ground derisively. "And to think I once called her family. At least Draga was also horrified. I would have hated to lose my wife and my son in one day. But I will not stand for thieves and cheats. Draga already has apologies to make."

Samit had not survived going rogue; he hadn't even lasted through that first night. Rachel knew he wasn't the first attack victim to fall to insanity, and she prayed every day that she wouldn't be the next.

Dalvin put his arms around her. "I'll never let that happen. I promise."

Ahmad appeared beside her so suddenly she jumped. She couldn't help it, Ahmad still looked like his father out of the corner of her eye. She'd probably jump forever. His tongue flicked out repeatedly, adding to the creepy factor. "I found it. This way."

Tuli joined her husband in snake form, and they led the way, moving quietly through the tall grass. It was sort of nice following a big snake, because all the smaller, dangerous-to-birds snakes near the water scampered out of their big brother's way.

There it was. The waterfall.

Next to Rachel, Anica shivered. The owl shifter put a comforting arm around the little bear. "You can do this." Her whisper was nearly drowned by the rushing water, but Anica heard. She smiled a little and put her arm around Rachel in return.

"You too."

Yeah, it wasn't just Anica who needed this. Claire had

exorcised *her* demons by dismantling the cages and properly burying the dead from the Texas caves. Rachel hadn't had that chance. Even though she didn't want to see what she was likely about to, she desperately needed to.

Rabi and Amber both removed their clothes without any sort of embarrassment and shifted. In animal form, the healer had longer legs than Rachel would have imagined, considering her height as a human. She was lean and muscled under spotted fur. The little tufts of fur at the top of her ears were really cute and Rachel itched to touch them, but now was not the time to ask. Rabi was a weird sort of tiger, with a mane like a lion. He was more yellow than orange and his muscled legs were massive. It was one thing seeing him through binoculars, another entirely from just a foot away.

Both cats checked to be sure they could jump the river. After they jumped back, Ahmad wrapped himself around Rabi's body and gave him a stern look. "Do not miss."

Rabi's jaw dropped and he looked as surprised as a tiger could. "You don't want to swim? I *love* to swim. Here, watch." He put a foot in the water, and Ahmad unwrapped himself and slithered a fair distance from the shore before Rachel could blink twice. The cobra's hood extended and he looked ticked. She didn't ever want that face to look like that at her.

Liz got on Rabi's back instead. "Fine. If you don't want a ride, I do." Rabi leaped across the river and she got off, perfectly dry. Amber carried Tuli over, at which point Ahmad consented to let Rabi bring him across.

Zarko declined. "I will wait here to see if they exit some other way."

Dalvin stood beside him. "I'll watch his back.

On the other shore, Tuli cocked her head, considering, then called, "Come to think of it, I believe I'll wait here too. Snakes for snakes. I might know some of them. I could get them

to surrender, believing I am a friend." Zarko growled his disapproval, causing her to shrug. "Unless you *want* to fight. I am
fine with that too."

Rabi carried Tuli back across the water, then offered Rachel
a lift. She swallowed hard. She'd never ridden a tiger. Hell,
she'd never ridden a *horse*.

Her legs touched the ground, so she bent her knees . . . and
started to slide sideways.

"Just hold on to my mane," Rabi said. "It's only for a second."

She closed her eyes and dug her fingers into the thick soft fur
around his neck, clinging to it for dear life. He padded forward,
then began to move more quickly. For a moment it felt like she
was taking off in bird form, then they were touching down again.

"Oh. That was sort of anticlimactic."

He gave her a look. "I was a little surprised that you were
nervous."

Angelique Calibria brought up the rear, already in bird
form. They'd asked her not to say a word once they got to Serbia. Her voice was too recognizable. She wasn't happy about
it, but fortunately she was good at texting.

Rachel found Angelique to be a thousand shades of annoying, but she was an amazing vocal teacher. Rachel figured it
was sort of like having an Olympic coach: they didn't take on
everyone and they were hard-asses, but the training you got was
unparalleled.

In just a week, she'd learned how to change the tone of her
screech so it had more impact or could be heard over a longer
distance. It was all in the tongue. And the breathing. Rachel
was learning how to breathe all over again. It was nothing like
the way she breathed while singing.

Rabi zipped a finger across his throat, and they all went silent.
The closer they got to the caves, the easier it was to hear the
sound of bears inside the mountain. Easier to smell them too.

Rachel choked back a cough. She wasn't sure if it the stink was better or worse than the bird caves. Less ammonia. More feces.

Ahmad slithered over for a quiet conversation with Rabi and Amber. Rachel could barely hear what he said.

"I have a plan. I will pretend to be my father. In this form, we look identical. I only have to drop my voice a few notes"— and he did—"and they will not question me." The voice, that voice—it sent chills down Rachel's spine, and by the look on her face, Anica had also heard Sargon's voice, or something like it, before. "But I will need Anica."

The young woman nodded and joined Ahmad next to the stairs. He whispered something that made her flinch, but she stayed still while he threw out magic like Rachel had never felt before. It was like hot pokers, or grabbing a lit sparkler—flashes of pain all over her skin. Anica's form shifted effortlessly. Then she rose up on hind legs, climbed up the rocks, and disappeared behind the curtain of water, followed closely by Ahmad.

Amber touched her. "Time for you." The cat's magic felt like an extension of Bitty's, which sort of made sense, since they were part of the same pack, although Amber was only occasionally attached. Rachel felt her feathers flow so smoothly into place that she imagined it was like what being an alpha must feel like. They slipped beneath the waterfall and into a dark, open cave.

I can do this. I can do this. She had to remember that she wasn't alone. There were others, powerful others, who would support her.

Ahmad's booming, Sargon-like voice echoed down the stone walkway. Her feet tried to freeze and time seemed to stop. She knew it was an act. But he really had that voice down. A shudder coursed through her and her heart fluttered frantically.

"Who is the careless fool letting new turns wander the countryside?"

"My lord!" came an astonished and delighted male voice. "We had heard you were killed."

The snake's laugh was rich and self-satisfied. "By my feckless son? Yes, I had Nasil let that be known. My first attack was a failure, unfortunately. But the next one will not be."

Rachel heard Anica make a bawling sound, like she was in pain. "Put this one to work. She seems healthy. Let her make more."

"Of course, my lord. Immediately."

"You. Show me to my chambers." That was the signal. They crept forward on their claws, taking care not to make any clicking sounds, Rachel and Angelique at the front, with Amber just behind to keep her shifted.

"Your . . . chambers, lord? We have no particular chambers set up."

Ahmad's voice went low and menacing. "Then where will I and my consort discuss . . . matters?"

They were close enough now that to see shadows of the speakers, cast on the walls by flickering gas lamps. There were three men, all large but made bigger in shadow.

"I . . I mean—"

The big cobra moved so fast that Rachel wasn't sure what happened, but the other man fell, clutching his chest. He screamed once and then was still. "You were useless. Now you are at least food for the bears. Who is second in command?"

Another person spoke, voice tremulous. "I am. We are few in number, sire, after so many years. But—"

Amber said quietly, "Three, two, one. Now!"

Angelique flew down the passageway like a bullet. Rachel struggled to keep up. When Angelique opened her beak, Rachel did too, and they let out a simultaneous screech that stopped all movement in the caves, except for the good guys.

"Did you have to kill him, Ahmad?" Rabi was touching his

paw to the side of the first man's neck, his scent angry even over the smell of animal waste.

The snake barely turned his head. "Of course. My father was known for killing the first person he encountered at every base. Besides, I doubt that man was in charge of anything other than the list of those who would be turned."

"Watch out," Rachel called. "Incoming!" She was glad she could fly and sorry she couldn't fly higher. The cave was about thirty feet wide but only ten feet high.

One of the bad guys had gotten away and had freed their captives. The problem with attack victims was that even if they successfully shifted, they were often just mindless rogues who would kill anything in their path.

The bears who flooded into the chamber were both brown and black. They could reach all the way to the ceiling, but they weren't very fast. Rachel ducked, dived, and swooped, screeching with every breath. She wasn't as good as Angelique, who could drop enemies unconscious with a single sound.

Pained wash over her, but she hadn't been injured. Rachel looked around and saw that the others were doing fine with their opponents. That could only mean—"Outside! Quick!"

Amber followed her down the passage. The rest stayed to finish the fight in the cave. On the far side of the stream, Dalvin was under attack from a trio of falcons who were slicing at him from all directions. Rachel grabbed one in her talons and tossed it into the roiling waters of the waterfall. When it surfaced, Amber snapped its neck.

One of the remaining attackers was a powerful little bird, fast as a whip, with deadly, sharp nails. Already Dalvin was bleeding from a dozen cuts and punctures. Rachel let out a screech that dropped the two remaining, including Dalvin, to the ground. She pounced on one of the birds while Tuli, fast as lightning, grabbed the other, slamming her fangs straight into its heart. Like the guard inside, the bird screamed once and died.

It happened so fast that she knew she never wanted to get on the wrong side of a snake.

"Rachel, look out!" Dalvin screamed in her ears and her mind. She turned to see a massive bear paw slashing at her. She dodged, but the blow connected with one wing, nearly severing it at the shoulder. She screeched, but her throat was getting dry, so the sound wasn't as effective as it could have been. The bear paused barely long enough for Rachel to get out of its way.

Dalvin attacked the bear like a bird possessed, slashing and tearing. But the bear was giving as well as it got. Dalvin was taking damage—a lot of it—and everyone else was too busy to help.

With her wing damaged, her only real weapon was her voice. And that was gone, her throat parched beyond speech. Rachel had no choice. She half hopped, half fluttered to the water and threw herself in.

"Rachel!" Dalvin shouted.

I'm fine. Keep fighting. He didn't believe her—she could nearly taste his worry—but he struck at the bear anew, pushing it ever closer to the water. Rachel was holding on to a boulder as water swept over her, filling her mouth to overflowing. The pain in her arm was tremendous but was also just the tip of the iceberg. As she clung to the rock, she recalled every pain she'd endured, every humiliation. It was all about this—some maniac's attempt at world domination. Ruining other people's lives for No. Good. Fucking. Reason!

She pulled herself out of the water, feeling like a phoenix rising from the ashes. There were now a half dozen bears and a similar-size flock of falcons attacking her friends. Rachel assumed the others had encountered more trouble in the caves, since they had not followed her out. Relying mostly on her one good wing, she flapped hard to get some altitude.

"Dalvin, Zarko, Tuli! Take cover!"

Dalvin broke away from the bear he was fighting, picked up

Tuli like she was going to be a midmorning snack and, along with Zarko, dove into the river. All three of them ducked under the surface.

Rachel screamed, filling her voice with every good thing that had ever happened in her life. She'd used up all her pain. She was no longer small or helpless or weak. She was powerful and proud. She thought about the persistence and unwavering hope of her parents and family; Dalvin's fierce determination to find her; Scott, Bitty, Asylin, and everyone else who had ever been kind to her, had loved her, had faith in her . . .

She pulled on the memory of everyone she knew and cared about for the magic she needed. She could feel the shock wave spread out, clean as fire, cool as water. Spent, she collapsed into the river.

The ground was littered with bodies. Not unconscious. Dead.

Zarko Petrovic plucked Rachel out of the river as easily as if he were rescuing a drowning kitten, while she gasped and retched up water she had swallowed. "Poor little owl." He repeated the insult Larissa had uttered on the stairs, but in a completely different tone of voice. Had that been just a week ago? "Come to Serbia. *You* will teach *us* to be tough."

Dripping wet, the quartet gathered on the grass. Rachel was still trying to catch her breath, and Dalvin, in human form, was holding her injured wing in place, when the others came out of the caves. They were dirty and bleeding and smelled to high heaven.

Surveying the scene—their little group and the mass of bodies on the grass—Rabi growled. "What the hell happened out here?"

Dalvin patted Rachel's feathers and looked down at her, smiling. "Rachel happened."

CHAPTER 22

The big old Episcopal church on the corner of Seventh Street had seen better days. The neighborhoods surrounding it, which had once filled the pews, were empty now, or nearly so. But it was still home to Dalvin and his family. He heard the pure, clear sounds of choir practice as he walked through the doors. His mom spotted him right away.

"Dalvin, honey! When did you sneak into town?"

He gave her a quick hug. "Just flew in. I wanted to stop by here as soon as I got in." He nodded hello to the choir members and embraced Florence Washington. "How are you, Mrs. W?"

Rachel's mama held him at arm's length and looked him over. "Well, Dalvin Adway, you look like you've been through a war! Where in the world have you been?"

His mother clucked her tongue and waved a finger at the other woman. "Now, you know Dalvin can't talk about his work. Can you, Mister big-time special agent?"

"Actually," he said with a big smile, "this time, I sort of *can*." His mother looked surprised and quickly began to smell anticipatory. She'd always loved to hear the stories of what he did. "Why don't we all run downstairs real quick? I'll bet it's still on one of the news stations."

"Ooo! You got my curiosity flowing now, Son!" In moments, the entire choir was traipsing down the carpeted stairs like a herd of buffalo, heading for the meeting room in the church's basement—the only room in the building with a television. It was mostly used to play religious animated shows for the children during day care. But today? Today would be long remembered.

He found the remote and turned on the set, then had to get help from the head of the day care to switch the input from the DVD player to regular television. He checked his watch: 9 p.m. Perfect.

The station played the special music that signified breaking news, as the anchors, a man and a woman, appeared. "And now back to our lead story, from central Europe." A photo flashed on the screen, showing Dalvin, with his arm around Rachel, who was sporting a sling. Beside them were Anica, with a blanket around her shoulders, being guided by Liz, and finally, Ahmad, bringing up the rear. A real credit hog, that one.

"Oh, my goodness!" Mrs. Jenkins was first to spot him. "Why, that's *you*, Dalvin Adway! Right there on the news!"

"The State Department today has confirmed that operatives of the federal government, in conjunction with members of a UN Special Task Force on Human Trafficking, raided what appears to be a slave camp in Serbia last night. Jill, can you tell us more about how this came about?"

The blonde reporter likely had flown to the site fairly recently. She sounded rushed and breathless, accenting the urgency of her report.

"Sarah, this quiet village in Serbia was apparently the scene of a horrific slave camp that contained children from all over the world." Behind her, viewers could see a steady stream of children getting into vans. The team had found them in side caves off the main cavern. Some had shifted; Amber and Ahmad had changed them back to human form. They all were in shock, both from the sudden shifting and the bright lights in their eyes.

"This is amazing news, Jill. It looks like there are dozens of children there."

Jill put a finger to her earpiece for a moment, then nodded. "There are, and it's hoped that even more will be found. Authorities are crediting two escaped captives with bringing down this ring." The image changed to the photo Dalvin had so carefully staged. Going back to the caves after the bodies had been cleared away and the team had had a chance to shower was a masterstroke, Dalvin thought. His mother was staring at the screen and clutching his hand so tight he was afraid she would break one of his fingers. Rachel's mama was standing stock-still, her whole body trembling.

"We've learned that these two women are Anica Petrovic, a native of this area, and Rachel Washington, from Detroit, Michigan. They have just been appointed as the newest members of the UN task force. Quite a pair."

The studio cut in. "Wait. Jill, are you saying that the same Rachel Washington who disappeared a decade ago from right here in Detroit was being held in a camp in *Serbia*?"

Another pause and another nod. "That's right, Sarah. We have no idea what she had to endure before she managed to escape with her friend Anica, but authorities say it was their tireless work tracking down the constantly moving camp that led authorities to this raid."

The last sentences were drowned out by the screams and shouts praising God, Jesus, and every saint, whether from their church or not.

The live feed cut off and the anchors returned. "Wow. That is *amazing*, isn't it, Bob?"

"It sure is, Sarah. The two women are being held in a secure location, awaiting debriefing by the UN and the American government."

Florence Washington collapsed into Dalvin's arms, sobbing.

His mother rubbed the side of his head like she'd done since he was a kid. "You done good, boy. You done *real* good." She shook her head. "Oh, my. When your father hears—"

Dalvin smiled and whispered to her, "Oh, he's heard. Who do you think picked me up at the airport?" His mother looked at him oddly . . . not a surprise, since he normally didn't use a plane to get home. But one of his fellow passengers couldn't fly so well at the moment. "I'll bet he's upstairs by now. He was parking the car. Let's go up and see."

He led the way back to the sanctuary. His mother, just behind him, stopped cold at the top of the steps. She burst into tears, then moved to let Florence through the doorway.

Rachel stood there, battered and bruised, her arm in a sling.

Dalvin said, "I couldn't think of a more secure location for her to stay."

Florence screamed and raced forward to envelop her daughter. Rachel started crying as she kissed her mama repeatedly, all the while trying to keep her wounded arm away from the rest of the choir, who were all trying to hug her at once. The place was pandemonium.

His dad grinned broadly as he put an arm around Dalvin. "Our boy, huh, Mags?"

"This was a *Wolven* job?" She spoke quietly, but she could have yelled and nobody would have heard.

"Yep," he replied. "Hope you don't mind a new member of the flock. She's an attack victim and a three-day. She'll need some extra help every month keeping the secret. That wing of hers will probably be healed by the next moon or so, and she could use someone to help give her an aerial tour of the parts of the city that have changed."

He paused to let the moment build before he said with a

straight face, "Maybe have a nice meal in the park, or find a bridal shop for her to wander around in?"

"Oh," his mother said, and her eyes widened. "Oh my!"

Then she smiled and hugged him.

Rachel smiled too and hugged her own mama.

It was an ending and a beginning all at once.